SOMETIMES A ROGUE

Center Point
Large Print

Also by Mary Jo Putney and available from Center Point Large Print:

The Lost Lords series
    Loving a Lost Lord
    Never Less Than a Lady
    Nowhere Near Respectable
    No Longer a Gentleman

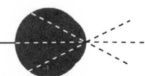

**This Large Print Book carries the
Seal of Approval of N.A.V.H.**

SOMETIMES A ROGUE

MARY JO PUTNEY

CENTER POINT LARGE PRINT
THORNDIKE, MAINE

This Center Point Large Print edition is published
in the year 2013 by arrangement with
Kensington Publishing Corp.

The text of this Large Print edition is unabridged.
In other aspects, this book may vary
from the original edition.
Printed in the United States of America
on permanent paper.
Set in 16-point Times New Roman type.

ISBN: 978-1-61173-875-9 *BP*

Library of Congress Cataloging-in-Publication Data

Putney, Mary Jo.
  Sometimes a Rogue / Mary Jo Putney. — Center Point Large Print
edition.
    pages cm
  ISBN 978-1-61173-875-9 (Library binding : alk. paper)
  1. Kidnapping—Fiction. 2. Twins—Fiction. 3. Sisters—Fiction.
    4. Rescue work—Fiction. 5. Man-woman relationships—Fiction.
    6. Ireland—Fiction. 7. Large type books. I. Title.
PS3566.U83S64 2013
813′.54—dc23
                                                    2013029142

To the Word Wenches:

Blogging buddies,
rockin' writers,
and fine friends.

Acknowledgments

My thanks to Eric Hare for his
information about sailing and yawls,
without which I would really have been at sea!
Any errors are my own.

Chapter 1

"What do you do with a pregnant duchess,
What do you do with a pregnant duchess,
What do you do with a pregnant duchess?
Ear-lye in the moooor-ning!"

Sarah Clarke-Townsend caroled the song to the heavens as she guided the curricle into a green lane leading away from Ralston Abbey. As she drew her breath to start another verse, her very pregnant twin sister, Mariah, Duchess of Ashton, burst into laughter, pressing one hand to her abdomen. "Did you compose that song, Sarah?"

Sarah grinned. The sun was just rising over the horizon, and she was wearing a daffodil-colored dress in honor of a glorious spring day. "I altered the words of a sailors' song I heard once. The original asks what to do with a drunken sailor."

"A drunken sailor would be more graceful than I am at the moment," Mariah said ruefully as she brushed back the golden hair that was the exact same shade as Sarah's. "Don't make me laugh so, or I might have this baby right now!"

"Don't do that!" Sarah said with alarm. "It's bad enough that I let you talk me into taking you for a dawn drive. Everyone in Ralston Abbey will

9

have strong hysterics when they find out even though Murphy is following us at a discreet distance."

"That's why I wanted to get out," Mariah said with exasperation. "I feel so restless! My back aches and my temper is on edge because everyone fusses over me as if I'm made of porcelain. It's driving me *mad!*" Which is why the Duchess of Ashton had dressed herself and tiptoed through dark corridors to tap on Sarah's door and beg for an early morning drive on the estate.

"That's the price you pay for having a husband who adores you," Sarah said, her tone light to disguise her envy. She didn't begrudge her sister having a wonderful husband; Mariah had endured a rather irregular childhood and deserved her happiness. But Sarah regretted having lost her own chance for such happiness.

"True, and I count my blessings!" Mariah winced. "Ow, the little devil is kicking! Adam has been a saint about my moods. I was never this volatile before."

"Soon the baby will be here and you will once more be the serene and laughing Golden Duchess." With one hand, Sarah pulled her soft wool carriage rug close. She and her sister were both warmly dressed and the curricle's hood was pulled up to block the wind, but the morning air was still cool.

"I hope you're right." Mariah hesitated. "I've

been feeling a . . . a cloud hanging over me. As if something dreadful is going to happen."

Sarah frowned, then quickly smoothed her expression. "That's natural, especially with a first baby. But women have been doing this since time immemorial, and you'll manage with your usual efficiency. Mama isn't much taller than we are, and she had twins with no trouble."

"So she claims now, but she may just be trying to cheer me." In a swift change of mood, Mariah grinned. "I look forward to being all calm and sensible when you're wildly moody with your first child. And don't give me any of that nonsense of how you're doomed to spinsterhood. Half of Adam's friends would marry you on the instant if you smiled at them."

Sarah rolled her eyes. "You are absurd. I have no desire to be an imitation Golden Duchess." She slowed the pair of matched chestnuts as they approached a junction. "I don't know the estate well. Which way should we go?"

"Take the right fork," her sister said. "The lane leads up to an abandoned church on the highest hill of the estate. It's very, very old and not conveniently located, so eventually it was abandoned as Ralston village grew down in the valley." Mariah looked wistful. "Adam and I enjoyed riding up there when I wasn't the size and shape of an overfed cow. I look at you to remind myself what I used to look like."

"And will again. Mother said that even though she had twins, she regained her figure very quickly, so it's in our blood to be beautiful."

"I hope she's right." Mariah squeezed one of Sarah's hands. "I'm so glad you're here! I resent all those years we were apart."

"We have years ahead in which to become gossipy crones," Sarah assured her.

The lane had been climbing. As the curricle approached the crest of the hill, they rounded a bend and a plain stone church came into view. "Marvelous!" Sarah exclaimed as they approached the structure. "It looks Saxon. That would make it over a thousand years old. It's in very good shape."

"Adam maintains the church. During the winter when there isn't much field work, this is a project to keep laborers employed." Mariah frowned as she rubbed the great curve of her abdomen. "They even cleaned out the crypt and built oak pews. When the church is all repaired, he'll have to find them something else to restore."

The wind was sharp on the exposed hilltop. Reminding herself that it was spring, not summer, Sarah said, "Shall we head back now? We can't have you catch a chill. With luck we'll be back at the abbey before people wake up and realize you've escaped."

Mariah started to answer, then gasped and bent over, wrapping her arms around her belly. "Oh, Lord, I think this baby wants to come right now!"

Sarah's heart congealed as she pulled the carriage to a halt. "Oh, please, no! Wait until we get back to the abbey! Less than half an hour."

"I . . . I can't!" Mariah clung to the edge of the curricle, her brown eyes wide with panic. "Julia explained to me all the stages and said sometimes birth is quick and sometimes it's slow, and I'd probably be slow since this is my first."

"But being impatient, you decided to produce this baby quickly." Sarah tried to keep her voice light, but she was terrified. She tied off the reins and leaped down to ease Mariah out of the curricle. Blood and fluid were staining the back of her sister's skirts. What to do? *What to do?*

The groom. Murphy had rounded the bend and could see them, so Sarah waved her free hand frantically.

Murphy kicked the horse to a gallop and was with them in seconds. "What's wrong, miss?"

"The baby is coming!" Sarah said tersely.

Murphy's face showed a flash of the horror most men felt when confronted with female reproduction, but he'd been a soldier. It took only an instant for him to collect himself and ask tersely, "Shall I carry the duchess back to the house on my horse? That would be the quickest way to get her home."

"No!" Mariah straightened, her face strained. "I need a . . . slower way. And—oh, God, I need Adam!"

It would be dangerous for a pregnant woman to be carried across a saddlebow, and the curricle was too small for Mariah to stretch out in. What would be better? Mind racing, Sarah said, "I'll take her into the church and make her comfortable. Bring Ashton and a large wagon with a lot of padding—straw and feather beds or some such. And bring Lady Julia, since she's the duchess's midwife."

"Yes, miss." Murphy wheeled his mount and set off at top speed.

"Can you walk?" Sarah asked her sister, trying to sound calm.

"I . . . I think so." Mariah closed her eyes for a moment as she composed herself. "The contractions have passed for now. Help me inside so I can lie down."

With her free hand, Sarah grabbed the carriage rugs from the curricle before guiding her sister into the old stone building. The door, like the roof, looked new and it swung open easily.

Inside a dozen pews faced the chancel, which was a step above the nave and held a simple stone altar. An arched opening on the far side of the nave led to a small room, probably the Lady Chapel. Narrow arched windows made the interior dim, and since there was no glass, the church was cold. But at least they were out of the wind.

Sarah said, "I'll use the carriage robes to make a pallet for you on the dais."

Mariah nodded with mute agreement. Sarah folded one rug in half to soften the cold stone floor, then helped her sister lie down. As Sarah covered Mariah with the other carriage rug, her sister cried out as more contractions wracked her small frame.

Hiding her fear, Sarah held her sister's clenching hand. "Impatient little fellow," she said as calmly as she could manage. "But labor takes time. Adam and Julia will be here before you know it."

"It will take close to an hour for them to get here." Mariah closed her eyes. Her face was white and damp with sweat. "I should never have persuaded you to take me for a drive! If I don't . . . make it, please look out for Adam and the baby."

"You're being morbid," Sarah said, doing her best to sound calm. "There is nothing wrong apart from the baby choosing an inconvenient time and place to make his appearance. Just think, you may give birth to the next Duke of Ashton in a hay wagon! That will give him something to flaunt before the other schoolboys."

Mariah made a face. "More proof that I'm not a proper duchess. If I were, I'd have stayed home in my own bed to have this child."

"Since a proper duke insisted on marrying you, I think you're fully qualified." Sarah brushed the damp golden hair from her sister's forehead. She always thought it strange that she and Mariah looked so much alike, yet were different in so many ways. "Steady on, my dear. Adam and Julia and a nice soft wagon will be here soon, and you'll be back in your own bed by midmorning. This will all be just a bad dream."

"I hope you're right." Mariah's hand tightened on Sarah's with bruising force. "Damnation, another contraction!"

Sarah held her sister's hand, wishing she could do more. The contractions were so close together that the baby really might be born at any moment. Now that it was too late, she recalled that Lady Julia, an experienced midwife as well as Mariah's best friend, had said once that women were often restless and full of energy just before their time. Exactly as Mariah had been.

The sounds of wheels and hoofbeats came through the empty window. "They're here!" Sarah exclaimed with enormous relief. "They made good time. I'll go out and meet them. Adam must be frantic."

She rose and headed to the door, then froze in her tracks when she heard strange voices outside. Not Adam or Murphy or Major Alex Randall, husband of Lady Julia, but a hoarse, uneducated voice. "A bloody good stroke of luck that groom left," the fellow said gloatingly. "He looked like trouble. Now he's gone, we can kidnap the bloody pregnant duchess without having to kill anyone."

16

Chapter 2

Horrified, Sarah wondered if she was hallucinating. But the voices continued. Another man grumbled, "I don't fancy kidnapping a woman who's increasing, Flannery. We'll need to travel fast to escape and if she bounces around too much, it might kill her."

"If she dies, she dies, Curran. We'll go plenty fast with me driving," a third man said. "Mebbe we can take the duchess's curricle and her two fine horses with us."

Dear heaven, why would they want to kidnap Mariah?

The answer was immediately obvious: Mariah was married to one of the richest men in Britain. Adam would pay any price for the safe return of his wife and newborn child—and then he'd kill the kidnappers with his bare hands.

As the men continued to admire Adam's horses, icy fear swept through Sarah. Dragging Mariah off when she was in labor would surely kill her, but what could the two of them do against three or more men? This hilltop was open and grassy, so even if they escaped, they'd be easily spotted.

An idea struck. It was outrageous, but Sarah could think of no other solution. She spun about and raced back to her sister. "Several rough men are outside and they're plotting to kidnap you! You must hide while I convince them I'm you."

"Dear God, kidnappers?" Mariah's shocked eyes flew open. As she absorbed Sarah's words, she exclaimed, "If you impersonate me, you'll be kidnapped instead!"

"If they find us both, they'll either take me with you, or kill me because I'm a witness," Sarah said grimly. "The trick is to convince them that I'm alone here, and I'm the duchess. They might not know you have an identical twin, and with the hood raised on the curricle, they probably didn't see that two of us drove up here. So you must hide while we pray they think I'm you. Hurry, there's no time to waste!" She seized her sister's hand and helped her struggle to her feet.

"You should be the one to hide," Mariah said unsteadily. "If it's me they want, they won't look for you."

"Don't be an idiot!" Sarah snapped as her gaze swept the small, plain church. The altar wasn't much of a hiding place, and neither were the pews. "If you won't consider your safety, consider the baby's. You can't risk him!"

Mariah's face turned gray as she ran a shaking hand over her bulging abdomen. "You . . . you're right. But please, if they take you, be careful! Adam will send men to rescue you, but don't wait for that if you have a chance to escape."

"Don't worry about me." Knowing they were running out of time, Sarah said, "You mentioned a crypt. Where is it?"

"In the Lady Chapel."

Sarah scooped up the carriage robes and they headed into the chapel. When they stepped inside the small room, she glanced around and saw nothing.

Mariah pointed. "There. Behind the altar."

The entrance to the crypt was a plain wooden trapdoor that wasn't visible unless one circled the altar. Sarah lifted the trap to reveal a flight of stone steps leading down into damp darkness. She cringed, thinking it looked like a gateway to hell. "Can you bear going down there?"

"I don't have much choice, do I?" Mariah started down the steps, leaning heavily on the wooden railing. "I've been down here with Adam. At least the bones have been removed and buried outside."

Sarah shuddered at the thought of hiding in the crypt if it hadn't been cleaned. Thank heaven the bones were gone!

"Wait!" Mariah halted halfway down the stairs and sank onto a step, pressing her hand to her belly as a new contraction convulsed her. Fighting the pain, she yanked off her glove and painfully wrenched off her wedding ring. "You'll need this."

Their hands caught and held for a moment as

the ring changed hands. As Sarah gazed into her sister's brown eyes, so like her own, she faced the agonizing knowledge that they might never see each other again.

She couldn't afford such thoughts. Releasing Mariah's grip, she slid the ring onto the third finger of her left hand. She wore no rings herself, so it was a good thing Mariah had thought of this.

The door of the church opened and the men entered. Pulse spiking, Sarah threw the carriage robes after her sister. "Keep silent!" she said under her breath.

As she lowered the trap soundlessly, she heard Mariah whisper, "I love you, Sarah. Take care."

Sarah straightened and closed her eyes for a moment to summon calm and aristocratic arrogance. If her impersonation of a duchess failed, she, Mariah, and the unborn baby were doomed.

A voice in the nave said indignantly, "Where the devil is she?"

Sarah was small, blond, and would have trouble intimidating a basket of kittens, but she'd observed her share of commanding countesses and domineering duchesses. Telling herself that she wasn't Sarah Clarke-Townsend but Mariah, Duchess of Ashton, she raised her chin and sailed into the nave. "Have you gentlemen lost your way?" she asked coolly. "This chapel is private."

Three tough-looking men stared at her as if

she wasn't what they expected. The darkest man asked, "Are you the Duchess of Ashton?"

"She is, Flannery, I seen her once from a distance," a heavyset man said.

Sarah heard a barely audible groan from the Lady Chapel. Raising her voice so they wouldn't notice, she said, "My identity is none of your business. I belong here and you don't." She raised her brows. "Who are you? Apart from being trespassers."

The man with the hoarse voice said, "We was told the duchess is pregnant."

"Babies get born," she said frostily. "My darling son came early."

The dark man gave a raucous laugh. "So her high and mighty ladyship was spreading her legs for the duke before they wed! So much for being a lady."

"You forget yourself," she said in a tone so icy that the man unconsciously retreated a step. "Please leave."

"Where's the baby?" the hoarse one asked, his eyes cunning. "I'd like to wish the little fellow luck. Did you bring him up here for a bit of fresh air?"

"Of course not. He's with his wet nurse." Sarah's tone delicately implied that only peasants would nurse their own infants.

One of the men swore. "We're too damned late, Flannery."

"She'll have to do, then." Flannery stared at Sarah with narrowed eyes. "Come along, your ladyship. We're taking you for a ride."

Refusing to flinch, she said, "The correct title is 'your grace,' and I have no desire to go with you. I suggest you leave quickly. I sent my groom to summon my husband and our guests to join me for an impromptu breakfast. Several of them are military men. It would not be wise to challenge them."

"I expect not," Flannery said with some regret. "We'll be long gone by the time they arrive. We'll have to leave the curricle and horses so they'll waste time searching around here." He reached out to take Sarah's arm. "Move your pretty arse, your bloody grace."

"Don't touch me!" she said with such ferocity that his hand dropped.

The hoarse man swore and pulled out a long, vicious-looking knife. "Then get a move on, or I'll carry you. In pieces if that's what you want!"

Terrified by the blade, Sarah pulled her cloak around her, raised her head, and stalked toward the door. The sooner she got these brutes away from Mariah, the better.

After that—God help her.

Chapter 3

Ralston Abbey was hardly the shortest route from Glasgow to London, but Rob Carmichael decided to avail himself of Ashton's open invitation to stay at his family seat for a few days. The duke was always easy company when he was in residence, and if he wasn't, the Ralston Abbey servants knew that Rob was to be treated as an honored guest. Since Rob was feeling unsociable, he rather hoped Ashton was in London.

That hope was shattered as he approached the impressive entrance to the abbey, where a small riot was taking place. As he spurred his horse to investigate, the movement and noise resolved into a flat hay wagon surrounded by worried people, some of them on horseback.

As Rob reached the group, a harrowing cry shattered the morning air. The cry came from the woman writhing on the thickly padded bed of the wagon.

Good God, the Duchess of Ashton! Her husband knelt beside her and held her small, white-knuckled hand as she writhed in agony. She was in labor, Rob realized, and from the blood saturating the feather bed, it wasn't going well.

Kneeling on her other side was a petite, dark-haired woman who was also very pregnant. She spoke calming words to the duchess while servants and others churned around the wagon.

The head Ashton groom, Murphy, was the wagon's driver. He and Rob were old friends, so Rob moved close enough to the driver's seat to say quietly, "She was taken suddenly while driving on the estate?"

Murphy looked ill, and it took him several moments to identify Rob. "Carmichael. 'Tis much worse than that. The duchess and her twin sister were taking a quiet morning drive when several villains caught up with them. The sister hid the duchess and pretended to be her grace, so the bastards took her." He nodded to the wagon behind him. "On top of being in labor, the duchess is frantic about her sister."

Brave sister to protect the duchess like that. Rob switched his gaze to the wagon. Rob had briefly met Mariah, Duchess of Ashton, in better times, when she was a laughing, golden-haired charmer who lit up a room when she entered and who had a smile for everyone.

Now her face was red and tearstained as she gasped, "You must rescue Sarah, Adam! Every minute those brutes are farther away, and if they discover Sarah isn't me . . . ." Her voice broke as she bit her lip through another shuddering contraction.

Ashton said soothingly, "I'll send men after her

as soon as possible, but now I must get you inside so Julia can take care of you properly." Though his voice was calm, his eyes showed a man in hell.

Two strapping servants approached the wagon carrying a litter. They were directed by a lean blond man who looked as tense as Ashton. Major Alex Randall. Randall and Ashton had been classmates at the Westerfield Academy while Rob was a year behind. The school had been small, so students all knew each other.

Lips tight, Randall said to his friend, "Hand her to me."

Ashton slid his arms under his wife and gently lifted her over the edge of the wagon into Randall's arms. As Randall turned and laid her on the litter, Ashton leaped to the ground and took his wife's hand again.

Randall reached up to the dark-haired woman. "You have your day's work cut out for you, my love."

So this was Lady Julia Randall, duke's daughter and experienced midwife. She went into her husband's arms and clung to him, her face white, after he set her on the ground. As she pressed a hand to her belly, he said with horror, "Dear God, are you going into labor, too?"

"False labor," she assured him, though her face was strained. "But send for the local midwife who visited here. She's very good and she can help me with Mariah."

Randall nodded, but he looked worried.

Rob called, "Ashton! I gather you're in need of my services?"

Ashton looked up, startled, then relieved. "Divine intervention! I can't think of a man I'd rather see, Rob. Mariah's sister Sarah has been kidnapped, and someone needs to rescue her as soon as humanly possible."

The servants were about to carry the duchess away, but she exclaimed, "Rob Carmichael? The Bow Street Runner? God be thanked! Please, find Sarah for me!"

"I will, your grace," he said, his gaze holding hers. "What does she look like?"

"Exactly like me." The duchess managed a wry smile as she waved her free hand at her swollen body. "At least, when I don't look like this. We're identical twins."

"Can you tell me about the men who took her?"

"I didn't see them." The duchess closed her eyes as another contraction wracked her. "She said they were rough looking, but that's no help."

"Don't worry, I'll find her. They can't have gone far." And finding people was Rob's specialty. "I'll need to see where the kidnapping took place."

Ashton flinched as Mariah gave a low cry. "Murphy knows more than I do," he said swiftly. "Take him along if you need help on the hunt."

Rob hesitated a moment. Murphy had been a

soldier and was a tough, capable man. Then he shook his head. "I'm used to working alone, and it will be safer to extract the young lady quietly rather than in a pitched battle. I'll keep you posted as I can."

Ashton gave Rob's shoulder a quick, hard clasp. "Bring Sarah home safely, Rob." Then he turned and headed into the house, holding his wife's hand as the litter bearers kept her as steady as possible. Behind them walked the Randalls, the major's arm around his wife.

Rob spared a swift prayer for a safe delivery, then turned to the head groom, who was still on the driver's seat of the wagon. "Do you hear that?"

Murphy nodded, casting an expert eye over Rob's mount. "Your horse has been working hard. Bring him around to the stables and I'll get you fixed up with Strider. He's the best we have for stamina."

Rob nodded, knowing his own mount, Sultan, deserved a rest in the lavish Ashton stables. He followed Murphy's wagon around the sprawling abbey to the stable yard. In a matter of minutes, Rob's saddlebags were transferred to Strider, a large, relaxed chestnut.

Murphy swung onto a sleek dark bay and the two men headed out into the sweeping Wiltshire Downs at a fast trot. Rob asked, "How long since the kidnapping?"

Murphy glanced at the sun. "Going on three hours. The duchess woke feeling very restless and persuaded her sister to take her for a drive. I followed, of course. When they reached that old church on the other side of the estate, her grace went into labor. I came back to get help. When we returned, the duchess was hiding in the crypt and her sister had been taken." He swore viciously. "I never should have left them!"

"It sounds like you didn't have much choice," Rob said. "Any idea how the kidnappers had such good timing?"

Apparently Murphy hadn't thought of that. He frowned as he turned his horse into a lane leading up a long hill. "The duchess doesn't like being shut in, so she went out whenever the weather was fair. Ashton generally drove her and a groom would ride behind. There are several public paths through the property, so someone watching the stables would see that she went out almost every day."

"That suggests several men and a lot of patient waiting," Rob said, thoughtful. "Well disciplined, not common criminals."

Murphy's face tightened. "The ransom for a duchess could pay for a small army of watchers."

"Was a ransom note left in the church?"

The groom looked chagrined. "Didn't think to look, not with all that was going on—the duchess begging for help for her sister and the duke trying to get her safely into the wagon so we could drive her home."

"With luck, we'll find a note," Rob said. "If it's ransom they want, they probably won't take her too far and they'll have prepared a safe place to go to ground."

Noticing his wording, Murphy asked, "You think it might be something other than ransom?"

Rob shrugged. "A duke makes enemies. Ashton has had trouble with those who disapprove of his Hindu blood."

Murphy frowned. "Aye, but this was aimed at the duchess."

"True. Tell me about the sister. What's her name?"

"Miss Sarah Clarke-Townsend. She and the duchess are nieces of Lord Torrington on the father's side and Lord Babcock on their mother's."

"What's she like?"

Murphy hesitated. "I've not seen much of her. She's a pleasant little thing. Not so outgoing as the duchess, but she's always polite and cheerful. The sisters were like as peas in a pod before the duchess began increasing." After a pause, he added, "Miss Sarah is a good rider and driver."

And brave enough to put herself into danger for the sake of her sister and the unborn child. He wondered if she was regretting that now.

• • •

Rob would have called the old stone building a chapel rather than a church. It stood on a high point of the downs. Nearer to God, but closer to the winds.

After tethering their horses, he and Murphy searched the chapel. Even with the newly built pews, the stony interior offered few places of concealment. Rob didn't envy the duchess her time in the crypt, but the dank hole had saved her.

There was no ransom note. They headed outside so Rob could search the area around the church. Rain during the night had left the ground soft. He pointed to a deep set of wheel tracks. "This would be the wagon you brought up for the duchess?"

Murphy nodded. "The lighter tracks over there were made by the curricle Miss Sarah drove."

"A curricle, not a pony cart? As you said, she's a good driver."

"I doubt she's strong enough to manage a coach and four, but she handles the curricle as well as I do," Murphy said.

Rob's brows arched. "Surely you exaggerate."

A hint of amusement showed in the other man's eyes. "Yes, but only a little."

Rob began pacing around the chapel, studying the grassy soil. On the western side, he found what he was looking for. "A carriage with a team of four stood here for a while. Not too long." He pointed down the hill, where a subtle trail of crushed vegetation could be seen. "They headed west. Did they follow one of the public pathways you mentioned?"

Murphy shaded his eyes with one hand. "Aye, the tracks join up with a public way at the foot of this hill. The path continues west to the back of the estate and crosses the Bristol road."

Rob swung onto his horse. "Any chance a field hand or tenant might have seen the coach?"

"Possible," Murphy agreed as he mounted.

The coach tracks were easy to follow in the damp earth since no other vehicle had come this way recently. Rob scanned the quiet green landscape, looking for any signs of the kidnappers. Nothing. The estate was vast and empty.

They were nearing the Bristol road when Rob spotted a flock of sheep grazing the fresh spring grass on a hill to their right. "Shall we see if there's a shepherd?"

"There should be one."

The sheep were grazing peacefully under the watchful gaze of an efficient herd dog, and the less watchful care of a carrot-haired boy drowsing under a tree nearby. Hearing horses approach, he scrambled to his feet and tried to look alert.

Reining in his mount, Rob asked, "Did you see a carriage traveling along the public pathway earlier this morning?"

"Aye," the boy said. "Noticed it, I did, because I never seen a carriage along there before. Traveled like a bat from hell. Figgered it must be a guest of the duke's taking the short way across the estate to the Bristol road."

Rob leaned forward intently. "Can you describe the carriage?"

"Oh, aye!" the shepherd said, coming alive. " 'Twas a neat traveling coach, not flash, but solid. A tan body and black trim. As fine a team of Cleveland bays pulling as I've ever seen. The off leader had a white sock, and both the wheelers had blazes."

"Can you describe the driver? Was there a guard? Were there passengers inside?"

The boy's face screwed up with thought. "The driver was dark. Beefy. Not sure if there was a guard. Might have been passengers, but I didn't notice."

"You didn't see a pretty young woman inside?"

"No, sir," was the apologetic answer. "Didn't notice aught but the horses."

"Were you able to see which direction the carriage turned into the Bristol road?"

The boy shook his head. "Can't see the road from here."

At least they had a good description of the carriage. "Thanks for the information." Rob pulled a half crown from his pocket and tossed it to the boy. "Maybe you should see if they need help in the Ashton stables since you seem to like horses."

The young shepherd gaped. "Could I do that?"

"Never hurts to ask," Murphy said laconically. "I know the head groom. If you come in to ask for a job, Murphy will hear you out." He turned his horse toward the road.

When they were out of hearing, Rob asked, "Do you need a stable hand?"

"Aye." Murphy gave a glimmer of a smile. "I like a lad who notices horses more than people."

"As long as that red hair of his doesn't scare the horses." Rob thought about the boy's description. The carriage sounded expensive and Cleveland bays were good quality, specially bred carriage horses. A fashionable gentleman would prefer his team to be free of white markings, but men interested in speed and reliability wouldn't care. The kidnappers had money as well as intelligence and patience. Formidable.

The tracks led to the Bristol road and didn't continue on the other side, so as expected, the coach had turned onto the main road. Rob dismounted to study the tracks, but it was impossible to judge which direction the coach had turned.

"What now?" Murphy asked.

Rob stood, brushing grass from his knees and stepping back as a wagon loaded with barrels rumbled by. The road was heavily traveled and a dozen or more carriages and wagons were in sight. "My instincts say they went left. West."

"From what I hear, those instincts are pretty reliable," Murphy remarked.

"Generally." In fact, Rob's hunter instincts were close to infallible, which was why he was so good at his job. He had enough Scots in his ancestry that he suspected his talent might be a form of the second sight. "Time we split up. Since we have a good description of the carriage, it shouldn't take too long to find which way it went. If it's toward Bristol, I'll keep after it. If I don't find any trace of it, I'll return to Ralston."

Murphy gazed to the west, his expression hard. "Sure you don't want any help on this hunt?"

"If I did, it would be you. But at this point, speed is more important than numbers."

Murphy nodded agreement. "I hope you have the lass home before dark."

"So do I." Rob swung onto his horse. But he doubted that would happen.

Chapter 4

During her calm, well-ordered life, Sarah had often longed for excitement. She hadn't expected an adventure to be *boring*. Racing along a rutted road with two large kidnappers inside and two more outside proved to be a regrettable combination of fear and tedium.

As she clutched a handhold to keep from being thrown around the carriage, she tried to engage the men in conversation in hopes of learning something useful. But the leader, Flannery, ignored her, and the other, O'Dwyer, studied her with a disturbing leer, as if mentally stripping her naked.

She tried to block such thoughts by imagining her rescue. As soon as Murphy returned to the church with Adam and a wagon, the alarm would be raised. There were probably already men coming for her. Who would she like to be rescued by?

Adam wouldn't leave Mariah when she was in labor, but his friend Major Randall was staying at the abbey. Randall was tough and immensely capable, so perhaps he'd lead the rescuers. Sarah had fancied him a bit until it transpired that Randall had fallen in love with Lady Julia at first sight, and they were such a devoted couple she couldn't wish it otherwise.

Murphy would come with Randall. Another capable former soldier, he was quite attractive, but she couldn't really daydream about a romantic rescue by a groom, be he ever so dashing.

A pity Adam's friend Rob Carmichael wasn't available. Sarah hadn't been introduced to the man, but she'd seen him at the wedding of Adam's sister. Carmichael was a Bow Street Runner, which was a shockingly intriguing occupation for a graduate of the Westerfield Academy, a school for boys of good birth and bad behavior. She knew nothing about his family, but he'd been listed in a magazine article later as the Honorable Robert Carmichael, so he was the son of a lord. A suitable object for daydreaming.

She hadn't noticed him at first. He'd lurked in the back of the church and he had a talent for going unnoticed. But once he caught her eye, she saw that he was tautly handsome and radiated a quiet sense of danger. Danger in a good way—just what a girl wanted in a rescuer. He looked like a man who could take on four kidnappers and sweep Sarah away to safety. She wouldn't even insist that he ride a white horse.

A particularly deep rut jolted the carriage so badly that Sarah lost her grip and pitched into O'Dwyer, the leering man. He caught hold of her knee as if steadying her, but his fingers dug into her thigh before she jerked away. If she had a sword, she would cut his hand off.

Pulling as far away as she could in the tight space, she stared out the window, fighting back tears. It was all very well to daydream about rescuers, but if she was saved by a short fat ancient with three wives, she'd fall at his feet in gratitude.

She clung to her handhold and gazed blindly out the window as the sun rose in the sky, then began to dip toward the horizon. The wide grassy hills of the downs gave way to woods and fields and villages.

How long would it take for pursuers to catch up with the kidnappers? They were traveling almost as fast as a mail coach. They'd made a brief stop at a coaching inn to change horses. The carriage stayed on the side of the yard and she wasn't allowed out. Flannery and O'Dwyer remained with her, O'Dwyer pointing a razor sharp dagger while the driver and guard watched over the changing of the team.

Remarkable how much more frightening a dagger was than a pistol. A pistol could kill her quickly, while O'Dwyer's vicious smile said that he'd enjoy carving her into bloody pieces. She tried not to look at him. "I need to go to the necessary," she said coolly. "And I'll require food and drink unless you plan to starve me to death."

"We'll find you a nice little bush once we get going again," Flannery said, enjoying her discomfort. "We'll get food the next time we change horses."

They did indeed stop a mile or so beyond the coaching inn. Flannery escorted Sarah into a copse and watched while she relieved herself. It was the most humiliating moment of her life.

Back to the carriage and the pounding pace. They were headed west into the setting sun. When they changed horses again, Curran, the guard, handed a basket of food and drink into the carriage before they raced off again.

Flannery investigated the basket. "Eat this." He handed Sarah a cold and disgustingly greasy mutton pie. She was so hungry she ate it in small, wary bites, though it settled badly in her stomach. The saltiness of the pie made her even thirstier than she'd been already. Hoping to wash the greasy taste from her mouth, she asked, "Do you have any small beer in there?"

O'Dwyer pulled a jug from the basket and took a deliberate swig, then handed it to her. Restraining a desire to kick him, she ostentatiously wiped the mouth of the jug before drinking. Instead of small beer, the vessel contained harsh, cheap whiskey. She began to cough, feeling as if her throat was on fire. O'Dwyer laughed uproariously and even Flannery smiled.

Furious, Sarah upended the jug and let the spirits pour out on the floor. "If this is what you drink, no wonder your brain has rotted!"

"Damned bitch!" O'Dwyer grabbed the jug before all the whiskey was gone. He looked ready to strike her, but a hard glance from Flannery caused him to drop his hand. Muttering under his breath, he finished off the whiskey.

Sarah resumed watching the passing countryside. At least the kidnappers didn't want to kill her, or they would have done so already. That and the knowledge that her family would come after her at full speed were her only sources of comfort.

Though she'd never been sick in a carriage before, the jarring ride, greasy mutton pie, and whiskey roiled in her stomach nauseatingly. She felt so wretched that at first she didn't notice that the carriage had stopped again.

Flannery opened the door and ordered, "Get down and don't say a word or you will deeply regret it."

She clambered from the coach and found that they were by a pier with a yawl moored in the water beyond. There was land visible on the other side of the water, but the distance was so great that she guessed that they were on the bank of the Severn River where it had broadened unto the Bristol Channel on its way to the sea.

A hard hand grasped her elbow. "Come along,

your prissy grace," O'Dwyer said. "We're going for a little sail."

Her heart sank. They could be heading anywhere, and this would make rescue much more difficult. As O'Dwyer marched her along the pier to a dinghy, she looked around for help, but she saw no one. This was a mere village with a single pier and half a dozen fishing boats settled for the night. A small livery stable stood on the opposite side of the street, but there were no people about.

"Into the dinghy," Flannery ordered.

Reluctantly she took his hand as he helped her down. She tried unsuccessfully to keep her feet away from the dirty water sloshing in the bottom. As she sat, she asked, trying to sound calm, "Where are you taking me?"

Flannery climbed down behind her while O'Dwyer took the oars. As the dinghy wallowed toward the yawl, O'Dwyer said nastily, "To Ireland, where no one will ever find you."

Ireland? She stared at him, aghast. The Irish were rebellious and angry with English rule, so it wasn't a good place for an unprotected English-woman. She pressed her hand to her belly as fear churned her already uneasy stomach.

As O'Dwyer gloated, she decided to stop fighting her distressed stomach. She leaned forward with dizzy satisfaction and vomited on the horrible man.

His furious roar was the best moment she'd experienced all day.

It took less than half an hour for Rob's instincts to be confirmed. A small tavern on the road west had half a dozen old men sitting in front, puffing clay pipes and watching the world pass by. They'd noticed the tan carriage because it was traveling unusually fast for a vehicle that was neither a mail coach nor the crested traveling coach of an aristocrat.

Rob summoned the landlord of the tavern and sent a message to Ralston Abbey. Then he set off again, blocking out his fatigue and giving thanks for a fresh, strong horse.

Throughout a long day of riding, he gradually gained on the kidnappers. He tracked the carriage to the waterside village of Burnham, where he found the mud-spattered vehicle parked in front of a livery stable facing the small harbor. An ostler and a boy who looked like his son stood outside grooming a pair of carriage horses. Two already groomed beasts were munching on hay inside the building.

Steeled for bad news, Rob dismounted. "Good day to you. Did the fellows who came in this carriage set sail from here?"

"Aye, about two hours ago. They just caught the tide."

"Did they hire the carriage from you?"

"Nay, we only hire out horse and carriages for local use, not long distance." The ostler patted the horse he was brushing. "This carriage was hired in Bristol and the team works on the Bristol to London road. We'll be sending carriage and team back to Bristol in the morning after the horses have a bit of a rest. They were used hard today."

Rob gazed out to sea, his expression bleak. By this time, the kidnappers were well away and could be headed anywhere. "How many men were in the coach?"

The ostler thought. "Four. A driver, a guard, and two men inside."

The stable boy piped up, "And a girl! A right pretty blonde."

Glad for the confirmation, Rob asked, "Did she seem injured?"

The ostler frowned. "You seem powerful curious."

"I'm a Bow Street Runner." Rob summoned his authority as an officer of the law. "The young lady was kidnapped and I've been sent to rescue her."

"A Runner!" the boy breathed, his eyes widening. "The girl was kidnapped? One of the men was marching her along with a hand on her elbow and she was drooping."

A drooping blonde? Miss Sarah must lack her sister's bubbling energy. All the more reason to rescue her. "Do you know where the ship was heading?"

The ostler shook his head regretfully, but the boy piped up, "Ireland. Cork."

"You're sure?" Rob tensed, his mind spinning. Inspired by the American and French Revolution, many Irishmen yearned to throw off English rule and become a republic—and Cork was a hotbed of republican sentiment. Was there a political dimension to the kidnapping? Given Ashton's rank, that was quite possible.

The boy nodded vigorously. "I heard the guard and coachman talking about how long it would take to reach Cork in these winds."

"Excellent! Can you describe the boat?"

"A two-masted yawl," the ostler said. "With the name *St. Brigid* on her stern and a figurehead of the saint on the bow."

Rob's gaze swept the harbor as he examined the fishing boats moored there. "I need to hire the fastest boat available. Who would be the owner?"

The ostler blinked. "You don't waste time."

"There is no damned time to waste," Rob said tersely.

Chapter 5

Three days as a kidnap victim had crushed Sarah's ability to view her situation as a romantic adventure. Her captors continued uncommunicative, but a day's sail brought the ship to a port that was obviously in Ireland, though Sarah wasn't sure where. It seemed too small to be Dublin.

She'd immediately been hustled into another carriage, this one shabbier than the English vehicle. They didn't travel with the same urgency as in England, but they made as good speed as possible on the rough roads.

When it became too dark to travel, they stopped at a substantial house. Sarah was locked into a closet under the staircase, along with a rough blanket for warmth. The next morning the party continued west into the countryside. She refused to relinquish the blanket and used it as a cloak.

The second night, they stopped at a similar house and she was locked in a revolting root cellar. The space was dark and damp and cold, with *things* crawling in the darkness and a disgusting stench of rotting potatoes.

Sarah warily felt around the pitch black

space hoping to find some way to escape. Unsurprisingly, she found nothing. The kidnappers were nothing if not careful. She wrapped herself tightly in the blanket and sat up all night. It was a struggle not to have strong hysterics. Only the knowledge that weeping and wailing wouldn't help and would leave her in even worse shape helped her maintain her control.

She tried to think of happy things: her sister and the new baby, her parents, the knowledge that her family would never stop searching for her. But it was hard to be optimistic in the cold, reeking blackness. She almost wept with relief after they released her in the morning.

During the long days of rattling along in the carriage, she maintained the cool reserve of a dignified duchess while listening carefully for something that might help her. Some of the conversations were in Irish and completely unintelligible to Sarah, but the rest were in English. Apparently Flannery and his men were members of some secret organization, and they stayed at the homes of other members.

The air of secrecy made her wonder if she'd been taken by political rebels. Perhaps her captors wanted to imprison a duchess to make some bizarre political point. Would she be better off revealing that she was plain Miss Sarah Clarke-Townsend? Probably not. If they wanted a duchess and found that she wasn't one, they might kill her out of hand.

At least she wasn't dead yet.

By the time Rob reached Cork, he was more than a day behind the kidnappers. Even so, he took the time to visit a few taverns and take the measure of the city's mood. He learned that Cork still nourished a rebellious spirit, and that a new group called Free Eire had formed here in southeast Ireland. They were said to be more radical than the United Irishmen, a liberal group that included Protestants, Catholics, and Dissenters. He had no proof that Free Eire was behind the kidnapping, but his instincts were twitching.

He bought two strong riding horses and followed the trail of the kidnappers west into the heart of southern Ireland.

With the coach jolting too violently for Sarah to rest, she spent her time hanging on to a strap and observing the very green and usually wet countryside. Riding horses would be more sensible than this old and rather battered vehicle, but she guessed her captors didn't want to give her a chance to escape.

Wise of them—if they gave her a horse and even a slim chance, she'd be off like a cannon ball. Not that she'd get far. She didn't speak Irish and she'd stand out like a goose in a flock of pigeons. But that certainly wouldn't stop her from trying.

As night approached, they turned into a lane that eventually led them to a substantial stone house about the size of a vicarage. After her captors escorted her inside, Flannery and the elderly homeowner talked over her head in Irish until the owner said doubtfully in strongly accented English, "You're a duchess, child?"

Not surprising that he was doubtful. Sarah had been rained on until her sunny gown was a mess, and her hair was surely a disaster. "Duchesses come in all sizes, shapes, and ages," she said crisply. "Including hungry."

The homeowner clucked. "You haven't fed her properly? I've nought fit for a duchess, but I'll have my kitchen maid heat up the mutton stew before she goes home."

Flannery snorted. "No need, McCarthy. I've been feeding her precious grace boiled potatoes and milk so she'll know what Irish peasants live on."

"But she's a duchess!" McCarthy exclaimed, shocked.

"All the more reason she learn how the Irish live," Flannery retorted.

More and more, Sarah thought her kidnapping must be political. She wondered what her ultimate destination was. From things she'd overheard, she was being taken to the leader of some mysterious organization. And then—ransom? Imprisonment? A spectacular and public execution of the "duchess" to make their political point?

Sometimes Sarah wished she didn't have so much imagination.

"Come this way, your grace," Mr. McCarthy said politely.

"Don't you go bending your knee to her!" Flannery snarled. "We're after getting rid of bleeding aristocrats like her!"

McCarthy scowled. "Aye, but there's no call to be rude to a lady."

Flannery made a disgusted sound, but had enough sense of what was proper to stop arguing with his host. "Serve her some potatoes while I check to see if your pantry is tight enough to lock her up tonight."

McCarthy gave Sarah an apologetic glance before leading the group to the long kitchen at the back of the house. While Flannery opened the door to the pantry to study it, McCarthy gave orders in Irish to Bridget, his pretty red-haired kitchen maid.

The girl hung a pot of mutton stew on the hob to heat for the men, then fried up potatoes and onions for Sarah. With butter and parsley, the potatoes were delicious. So was the rich whole milk; most of the time, Sarah was given plain boiled potatoes and thin milk with the fat removed for butter or cheese.

When Sarah thanked the girl, the girl said in

halting English, "I wish I could help you, my lady, but there's naught I can do." She cast a disgusted glance at Flannery.

"I understand," Sarah said softly. "I appreciate your making so fine a meal of what they ordered for me."

Bridget bobbed her head, then moved to the hearth to stir the mutton stew. It smelled very good after three days of milk and potatoes, and scant amounts at that.

Before Sarah broke down and started salivating, O'Dwyer grabbed her left arm and yanked her to her feet. "Time to lock you up for the night, yer bloody grace."

Sarah jerked her arm free, then scooped up her blanket. It was coarse and ragged around the edges, but it was all that stood between her and shivering through the night.

"If you won't let me take your arm, yer grace," O'Dwyer said mockingly, "I'll lead you there by your titty." He latched on to her left breast with bruising force.

After an instant of shock, Sarah exploded with fury. Knotting her right fingers, she swung her fist up from her side and smashed it into O'Dwyer's crotch.

O'Dwyer shrieked and let go of Sarah's breast as he stumbled backward, clutching his hands over his damaged private parts. "Ye vicious little bitch!" he gasped. "I'll *kill* you for that!"

"No, you won't," Flannery said with a grin as he guided O'Dwyer into a chair, then put a glass of spirits in the man's hand. "Can't blame the girl for fighting back. More like an Irish colleen than a duchess, and I like her the better for it."

His face becoming stern, he told Sarah, "Now into the pantry with you, and right smart if you don't want to be tossed in bodily."

Knowing better than to push her luck any further, Sarah wrapped the blanket around her and walked into the pantry with as much dignity as she could manage. The small room was lined with shelves loaded with sacks of vegetables and flour. Nothing that would supplement her supper. Hams and bacon and cheeses were stored elsewhere.

Before the door closed behind her, she had enough light to see something scuttle across the floor at the back of the pantry. She shuddered and shrank back against the door. Mice, or worse, *rats*.

Biting her lip, she told herself not to be foolish. Of course vermin would be drawn to the pantry. They wouldn't bother her as long as she didn't lie on the floor so the creatures could nibble on her.

She shuddered again at the image. She was too tired to stand all night, but the pantry shelves were wide enough for a small person. Giving thanks for her lack of size, Sarah felt down the shelves on the left till she found one that was about hip high and a foot under the next highest shelf. Enough space for her.

She yanked everything off the shelf, shoving each item toward the back wall. A cloud of flour fluffed into the air, followed by the smash of pottery and the sharp tang of vinegar as a small crock of something pickled went flying. It didn't smell very appetizing, so she didn't investigate further.

When the surface was clear, she wrapped the blanket around her like a cocoon and crawled onto the shelf. There was just enough space if she didn't try to roll over.

As her eyes adjusted to the darkness, she realized that there was a bit of light from a high, narrow window, enough to reveal the shapes of the shelves and the door. Though the window was far too small for her to escape through even if she could scramble up that high, she liked not being in total darkness.

Resting her head on her arm, she closed her eyes with a sigh. At least she was off the floor if there were rats.

After an eternity in dark nothingness, Mariah slowly floated up to awareness. She was in her own bed, she realized. At Ralston Abbey. In the dim candlelight, she recognized the richly woven canopy over her head.

And she wasn't alone in the bed. With enormous

effort, she turned her head to the left and saw Adam. He lay on top of the covers dressed only in buckskin breeches and a rumpled shirt, his dark hair tangled on the pillow, one hand resting on hers.

He was dozing, but when she turned her head, his eyes shot open. He caught his breath as he gazed at her, then pushed himself up on his elbow, his green eyes blazing. "Mariah! You've returned, haven't you?"

"Adam." Her voice was so faint she barely heard herself, but she managed a smile. "The baby? Well?"

"Wonderfully so." He touched Mariah's cheek tenderly. "He's a fine and healthy lad." Sliding off the wide mattress, he continued, "Our young Richard is sleeping in his cradle on your side of the bed. Do you want to hold him?"

"Please!" Coming more awake, she watched as her husband rolled from the bed, circled around, and carefully lifted the wrapped infant from his cradle. With equal care, Adam tucked the baby into the crook of Mariah's arm.

Though she had no memory of seeing her child earlier, he felt utterly right and natural as he gave a small yawn, then settled against her. He was a bonny, wee boy with masses of dark hair like Adam. They'd decided to name him Richard Charles Lawford after their fathers. She studied his tiny face, entranced. Her baby, Richard. Her *son!* She and Adam had made this small miracle together.

She found the strength to tighten her arm around him protectively. "He's beautiful," she whispered as she tried to order her thoughts. "I was very ill, wasn't I? How long?"

"About five days." Adam perched on the edge of the bed. He looked exhausted and he hadn't shaved in days. "We . . . I . . . I almost lost you, Mariah. You were bleeding so badly." He shook his head, as if to rid himself of the memory. "If Julia hadn't been here, I don't know what would have happened."

"How has Richard been fed since I'm useless?" she asked with sudden concern.

"We have an excellent wet nurse from the village," he said soothingly. "Julia has been looking out for both you and Richard."

Mariah closed her eyes, blinking back sudden tears. She felt so weak. Thank heaven for Julia, who had to be one of the best midwives, and best friends, anywhere.

She tried to remember what had happened. She'd persuaded Sarah to take them for an early morning drive. Then . . .

Her blood froze as memories rushed in. The pains that struck at the abandoned church. The villains bent on kidnapping her. The horrible dark crypt where she hid while her sister had placed herself into the hands of violent strangers.

"Sarah! She was kidnapped! Have you found her and brought her home? She was so brave!"

Adam's expression turned grave. "Not yet. By the sheerest of good luck, Rob Carmichael arrived for a visit when we were bringing you back to the house after the kidnapping. He went in pursuit immediately."

Mariah had been aided by Carmichael in the past and knew that he was an alarmingly capable man. "But he hasn't found her yet?"

Adam shook his head. "She was taken to Ireland. Rob sent a message just before crossing after the kidnappers. We haven't heard from him since. But he'll find her if anyone can." He hesitated before continuing, "The situation is grave, Mariah. The abduction might have been political."

Mariah saw in his eyes that he feared Sarah might be murdered by the scoundrels and Mariah should prepare for the worst. "She's all right!" Mariah said stubbornly. "I'd know if something had happened to her. Even when I didn't know I had a twin, I sensed her presence. Surely Rob will find her soon."

"I hope you're right," Adam said softly as he rested his hand on her shoulder.

So did Mariah. She wasn't sure how she could live with herself if her sister died in her place.

Chapter 6

Rob had overtaken his quarry at dusk. As the kidnappers' carriage stopped for the night at a sizable stone home, he watched with his spyglass from the road on a hill above. Though he couldn't make out details, he saw a small figure in the middle of the group of men as they descended from the carriage and entered the house. He was glad to see that the girl didn't move as if she'd been injured, both for her sake and because it would make escape easier.

As the sky darkened, he worked his way down the hill close to the house. An empty shed near the stables provided a place to conceal and tend his two horses. They were sturdy beasts with good stamina, but he'd not had time to locate a sidesaddle. He hoped Miss Sarah wasn't too much of a lady to ride astride.

As he waited for the lights in the house to be extinguished, he made a scant meal of soda bread and cheese. He spent some time in the stables with a sharp knife to ensure that the harness and tack for the carriage and horses would fail quickly if he and the lady were pursued.

Then he scouted around the house, looking for ways to break in. Getting inside would be simple. Locating the girl within the building without waking anyone would be more difficult. He'd have to rely on a combination of logic and his mysterious finder's intuition.

There were still a fair number of lights on inside the house when someone exited from the back of the house. After studying the figure, he identified a strapping female wearing a plain dark cloak and carrying a small lantern. She headed briskly down the lane. Rob guessed she was a servant heading to her home in the nearby village.

Giving thanks for this stroke of luck, Rob followed her silently until she was well away from the house. Then he moved up behind her and caught her in a hard grip, trapping her arms and covering her mouth with one hand.

As she tried to struggle free, he said softly in Irish, "I'll not be hurting you, lass, but I need information about that young lady who was brought to the house this evening. Will you promise not to scream if I take my hand from your mouth?"

Relaxing slightly, the woman nodded. When Rob removed his hand, she said warily, "Who are you and why are you asking? All I know is that she's a sweet little thing and they say she's a duchess."

"I'm Rob. And you are . . . ?"

"Bridget, cook and kitchen maid to Mr. McCarthy." She nodded toward the house.

"I want to know where they locked her up," Rob said tersely, releasing his grip on Bridget's torso. "Her family sent me to steal her away and return her safely home."

"That's good then. I wouldn't leave a dog with those bloody sods." She turned to face him, but the darkness obscured them from each other. "The kitchen and storerooms run across the back of the house on the ground floor. They locked her in one of the pantries, the one to the left at the far end of the kitchen. The side door on the west end of the house will put you into the kitchen."

That was useful information. "Is she guarded?"

"I don't know. I left while they were still eating Mr. McCarthy's food and drinking his whiskey." Her voice turned sour. "A fair mess they're making, I'm sure."

"Do you know who the kidnappers are?"

"Members of a rebel group called Free Eire." Bridget snorted. "Freedom for Ireland would be a fine thing, but I wouldn't trust that lot of villains. My master is none too happy to have them descend on the house with a kidnapped duchess." A worried note entered her voice. "Will there be British troops coming for her?"

Rob understood her concern. Any kind of skirmish would be bad for the house, its master, the neighborhood, and this young woman's employment. "No one but me, and my aim is to free the lady with no one getting hurt." And if anyone was hurt, he would do his best to ensure it wasn't Sarah Clarke-Townsend.

"That's all right then," she said with a decisive nod. "I don't like seeing any woman being bullied, even an English duchess."

Rob guessed that any man who tried to bully Bridget quickly learned better. "Will you swear not to raise the alarm? If you won't swear, I'll have to tie you up and leave you in a shed."

"I swear. The sooner you get the lady away, the better." Bridget chuckled. "I'll go home to my bed and be proper shocked in the morning to hear she's gone."

"Good lass. Here, for your help." He pressed a folded banknote into her hand.

Her fingers closed over it. " 'Tis not necessary, but my thanks to you."

"It comes with the gratitude of the young lady's family. She is dearly loved."

"Then take her safe away, boyo." A husky note entered Bridget's voice. "And if ever you return by daylight, pay me a call. Bridget Malone, and it's been a pleasure."

"For me as well, Bridget Malone." Rob sketched a bow, then watched as she continued on her way home with a sway to her hips. He was damned lucky to find a servant with no loyalty to her master's rebel friends, and sympathy for a girl in trouble.

He turned and headed back to the house to plot

how he'd enter the building—and how he'd get them out again.

It was hours before the lights in the house were extinguished, but Rob had years of practice in patience. The light rain stopped and the sky cleared, revealing a waxing moon that would provide light for another few hours to aid an escape.

Eventually the house became dark, except for a small light on the ground floor level that appeared to be in the kitchen. Since that might mean the captive was guarded, he'd enter through the front door rather than the one Bridget had suggested.

He was good with locks, so the massive front door presented no great challenge. He eased inside, scarcely breathing, then pulled the door almost shut so it would be ready for a quick escape. As he studied his surroundings, he pulled his fighting stick from an inside pocket. He'd acquired it in India, and it was shaped and knobbed to be held in one hand to add extra striking power in a fight.

The house appeared to have a standard layout with stairs coming down the center and rooms on each side. A sitting room was on the right, the dining room on the left. Since Bridget had said the kitchen was behind the dining room, he moved between the table and sideboard to the door that should lead to the kitchen.

Fighting stick in his left hand, he slowly

opened the door—and froze when he was greeted by a raucous snore from inside.

Not moving, he studied as much of the room as he could see. The snoring man was seated on a bench by a long worktable on the right, his head resting on his crossed arms. Next to him was an empty whiskey bottle and the lantern that lit the room. The man seemed to be in a drunken sleep, so Rob decided not to retreat. Not when he was so close to the abducted lady.

Silently he crossed the kitchen along the left side. The snoring man didn't stir when Rob passed less than six feet away.

He reached the pantry door. The key was in the lock, which saved him having to pick it. The key made a slight scraping sound when he turned it.

He held still, not even breathing, but the drunk snored on. Praying the hinges wouldn't squeal, he inched the door open and entered, closing it softly behind him.

A shaft of moonlight from the pantry's high window illuminated most of the tiny room. His first reaction was disappointment that the floor held only a clutter of sacks and boxes and broken crockery, not a sleeping captive.

Something moved on a shelf to the left and a delicate face surrounded by a fluffy cloud of blond hair peered up at him. Miss Sarah Clarke-Townsend looked like an adorable little golden chick. Harmless and helpless and prey to the first fox or hawk that came along.

Hoping she wouldn't squeal or otherwise draw attention to them, he said in a barely audible voice, "Ashton sent me. Shall we be on our way?"

Her eyes widened like a startled kitten and she swung her feet to the floor. "Yes!" Wrapping her ragged blanket firmly around her shoulders, she continued, "Lead on, sir!"

Though her voice was low, he held a finger to his lips to emphasize silence. "There is a man sleeping in the kitchen. We must leave very, very quietly."

She nodded and pulled her ragged blanket close around her. When they got to the horses, he'd find her something warmer.

He opened the door again and moved into the kitchen, beckoning for her to follow since the drunk was still snoring. Silently she wafted behind him.

They were halfway across the kitchen when disaster struck. Something clattered to the floor and Miss Sarah gave a squeak of dismay. As the drunk came awake with a growl, Rob saw that her trailing blanket had snagged a broom leaning against the wall and knocked it to the floor.

The drunk's eyes widened as he focused on them. "The bitch is trying to escape!" he roared as he hauled himself from the table.

Two more heads appeared on the other side of

the table. Rob swore as he realized the men had been sleeping there out of sight. Outnumbered three to one, Rob had only the advantage of being awake and alert. As the two other men scrambled to their feet, Rob lunged for the drunk, who was closest. "Run!" he barked at Miss Sarah.

Before the drunk could react, Rob slammed him in the temple with his fighting stick. The man collapsed backward from the bench, sending his whiskey bottle flying to crash on the flagstone floor.

Not pausing, Rob leaped over the table and attacked the closer of the two men, a wiry fellow who was pulling a knife from the sheath at his waist. Rob slugged him in the belly, then bashed the man's head as he folded up, gasping.

As the wiry man collapsed, Rob swung to face the last opponent—and stopped cold when he saw the barrel of a pistol pointing at him. As the third man cocked the weapon, he snarled in Irish, "I don't know who you are, boyo, but say your prayers!"

Rob was preparing to hurl himself back over the table in hopes of evading the shot when the air resonated with a deep, gong-like sound. The armed man crumpled to the floor. Behind him, smiling gleefully and holding a massive cast iron frying pan in both hands, was his helpless chick, looking absurdly pleased with herself.

Backlit by a lantern, Miss Sarah's hair was a

golden cloud shining like a halo around her exquisite face. A crippling emotion he couldn't name twisted inside him. Yearning, perhaps, because in her beauty, joy, and innocence, she represented everything he'd ever loved and lost.

The feeling passed in an instant because his job was to save her life, not wallow in his personal sorrows. "Well done, princess. Now it's time we are on our way."

He would have preferred to bind and gag the three men, but reinforcements would arrive at any moment and he had no desire for a pitched battle. He scooped up the dropped pistol and gestured toward the kitchen's door to the outside.

"I couldn't agree more!" she exclaimed as she darted toward their exit.

A dozen steps brought him to the door. He unlatched it and ushered her outside. Once they were in the damp, chilly night air, he clasped her small hand. "Now, princess, we *run!*"

Chapter 7

Giving thanks for her tomboy childhood, Sarah raced full tilt across the yard, steadied by her rescuer's strong hand. She couldn't believe that her fantasy had come true and Rob Carmichael had appeared out of nowhere to save her from her captivity. She'd laugh out loud with delight if she didn't need all her breath for running.

Lights were on in the house and she was gasping by the time they reached a shed beyond the main stables. Carmichael said, "Wait," and released her hand. He opened the wide double doors to reveal two saddled and bridled horses. "How good a rider are you? If you're inexperienced, I can carry you on my horse, but that will slow us down."

"I can ride," she said as she panted for breath.

"Then I hope you can ride astride since I didn't have time to find a sidesaddle."

"I'd love to ride astride!" she exclaimed. "I was never allowed to."

"Then into the saddle you go." He linked his hands to help her mount.

She hiked up her skirts, then set her left foot in his hand and swung onto the horse. It felt odd to stretch her right leg over her mount, and this one had a broad back. But once she settled into the saddle, the position felt natural even though her skirts were rucked up to her knees. As Carmichael adjusted her stirrups, she tucked her skirts around her legs, covering as much bare skin as possible, and crisscrossed her blanket around her.

"Are you warm enough?" he asked. "You can have my coat."

"No need. Let's be off before they come after us."

Carmichael nodded and mounted his own horse. He led the way out to the road at a fast walk, increasing his speed when he saw that Sarah kept up easily.

There was enough moonlight to show the way and when they reached the main road, they moved into a swift canter. This time Sarah did laugh out loud from sheer pleasure. *This* was the sort of adventure she'd dreamed of—flying through the night with a dashing hero who had saved her from durance vile. It was so much more enjoyable than being pawed by smelly drunkards and fed a starvation diet.

At this hour, they had the road to themselves. They put a good distance behind them before a mass of clouds obscured the moon and reduced the visibility to near zero. As a light rain began to fall, Carmichael slowed his mount to a walk and fell back beside Sarah. "Well done, Miss Clarke-Townsend. You're a game one."

"Call me Sarah," she said. "It's simpler. You're Adam's friend Rob Carmichael, aren't you?"

He gave her a curious glance. "How did you know? We've never met."

"Not formally, but you attended Lady Kiri's wedding. My sister pointed you out as one of Adam's old schoolmates." Sarah smiled a little, remembering how Carmichael had intrigued her. "One of the society columns in a woman's magazine listed you as the Honorable Robert Carmichael."

"The magazine was wrong," he said tersely. "I no longer have a right to be styled that way. Call me Rob or Carmichael as you prefer. Honorable, never."

He was no longer an Honorable? Restraining her desire to ask what he meant, Sarah said, "Rob then, since we'll surely be well acquainted by the time we return home." Having a quantity of questions, she started with, "How did you manage to find me so quickly? You're based in London, aren't you?"

"Yes, but Bow Street Runners take commissions all over Britain. Ashton gave me an open invitation to stay at Ralston Abbey whenever I'm in the area. By sheer chance, I was taking him up on his hospitality the day you were abducted."

Sarah's friend Lady Kiri would call that fate, not chance. Hands tightening on her reins, Sarah asked, "Is my sister all right? I left her going into labor while hidden in the crypt of an abandoned church."

After a hesitation, he replied, "She was safe back at the abbey and still in labor when I left in pursuit of you. Ashton and her friend Lady Julia were with her."

Though that was some comfort, Sarah had a nagging feeling that the birth had been very difficult. But not fatal. Surely she'd know if it had been fatal.

She was sending a silent prayer for Mariah's health when her horse lurched, scrambled desperately for footing, then pitched over. Sarah went flying and landed with a splash in water that covered her head. As she thrashed frantically for air, strong arms lifted her head above the surface.

"Are you all right?" Rob asked sharply. "Any bones broken?"

"I . . . I don't think so," she gasped as Rob lifted her to a sitting position. She'd landed in a water-filled ditch, not deep but capable of drowning her if she'd been alone and unconscious. "Water and mud are softer than solid ground."

He lifted her the rest of the way out of the water and set her on her feet, one arm around her waist for support. "Your horse lost his footing on the edge of the ditch."

She leaned against Rob, every muscle in her body aching. "Is he hurt?"

"A lame ankle, but I think no worse. Time for

us to go to ground in a nice quiet barn near here."

Sarah nodded, shivering. A bitter wind sliced right through her saturated garments and she'd lost hold of her blanket when she fell. This time she didn't object when Rob peeled off his coat and draped it around her shoulders. It fell almost to her knees and helped some, but she still felt like a block of ice.

"I'll put you on my horse and lead yours to the barn," he said as he helped her back onto the road. "It's not far, perhaps a quarter of a mile."

Rain was beginning to fall again. Sarah squinted into the darkness. "You can see in this?"

"I noted places that might be useful when I rode through this afternoon," he explained. "Habit."

The habit of a good Bow Street Runner, she guessed. When he helped her onto his horse, she could barely lift her right leg over its back and her fingers were so numb she couldn't feel the reins.

By the time they reached the barn, which was at the end of a muddy lane, Sarah was shivering so hard she could barely stay on horseback. Rob unlatched the door and led the horses inside.

It was dark as the inside of a barrel, but getting out of the pouring rain and cutting wind was heaven. Sarah tried to control her chattering teeth and wondered wearily if she'd ever feel warm again.

"Time for some light." Rob produced a tinder-box and struck a spark, which he used to light a candle.

At this season supplies of fodder were low, but there was a large pile of hay in one corner. Other than that, the barn was mostly empty except for some farm tools leaning against one wall.

A lantern hung from a hook in one of the overhead beams. Rob lifted the lantern and set his candle inside. The reflective tin behind the candle increased the light, though it wasn't much for the size of the barn.

Sarah was half unconscious when Rob lifted her from the saddle as easily as if she was a child. "I'm going to do something that would embarrass you if you thought about it, so close your eyes and don't think about it," he said mildly as he set her on her feet.

She gasped, shocked awake when he moved behind her and started unlacing the back of her sodden, daffodil-colored gown. "Mr. Carmichael . . . ?"

"You need to get out of these wet clothes before you freeze to death," he explained as he deftly peeled off her gown, leaving her standing in her saturated shift and stays and stockings. "Because I thought the journey out of Ireland would be simpler if you were dressed as a boy, I bought some used boy's clothing in Cork."

"As . . . as long as the garments are clean,"

Sarah said through chattering teeth. "No, never mind clean. I'll settle for *warm!*"

"You will be soon." Still behind her so she didn't have to look him in the eye, he stripped off her under-things and began rubbing her naked body with a coarse blanket.

It was the strangest experience of Sarah's life. Someday she might think of this as wonderfully wicked. Now it was just . . . strange to be standing rigid and stark naked in a barn with a good-looking man and mostly thinking of how cold she was.

The friction of the blanket warmed her skin a little. He started with her back and arms, then her front, hips, and legs. She closed her eyes as he'd suggested. *Think of the blanket, not the large, strong male hands moving the deliciously rough fabric over your tender bare skin. . . .*

The rubbing ended. Rob raised her arms and dropped a boy's shirt over her head. Made of well worn and often washed linen, the fabric fell smoothly over her torso and well past her bottom. Grateful to be covered and a little warmer, she turned to face him. "I trust you have more than a shirt?"

"Drawers, trousers, stockings, boots, and a coat," Rob said, as unruffled as if he'd just rubbed down a horse. "Can you manage, or do you need help?"

"I can manage." She accepted the stack of

folded garments and scrambled clumsily into the drawers and trousers.

As she rolled up the trouser legs and tugged on the stockings, Rob unsaddled the horses and pulled a paper-wrapped parcel from his saddlebags. "Have some cheese and bread. Food is warming."

Sarah pounced on the packet and tore it open greedily. The bread and cheese had been sliced into small pieces so she didn't have to waste time tearing it up. "This is the best cheese I've ever eaten," she said reverently as she put a second chunk of cheese on a slab of bread. "The bread is really good, too."

"Hunger, the best of sauces." Rob accepted a piece of cheese on bread that Sarah handed him. "But Irish cheddar is fine, no question, and so is the soda bread." He polished off the food in two bites, then turned back to the horses.

After putting hay within reach of both beasts, he examined the lame rear foot of her mount. "No permanent damage, but this fellow won't be taking you anywhere tomorrow. We'll have to trade him for another horse."

Sarah bit her lip as she began to think beyond being free and freezing. "Will the abductors pursue us?"

"Very likely." Rob began brushing down her horse with handfuls of hay. "I suspect the kidnapping is at least partly political. Did you hear anything to support that?"

"Yes, the men are part of some radical independence group. They wanted to get me to their leader without any damage, which spared me from being ravished." She tried to keep her voice level and was embarrassed to hear a quaver. "I'm not sure whether they planned to ransom me to raise money for their group, or execute me as a symbol of the evil English aristocrats."

"Would you have told them that you aren't the Duchess of Ashton?"

She shrugged. "I doubt they'd believe me. I didn't want to tell them that too soon because that might remove what protection I had. And if I'd told them as they were raising the headsman's ax, they would just think I was desperate and cowardly. Feeble."

The corner of Rob's mouth quirked up. "You're right, it would be hard to convince them you weren't the duchess but her identical twin sister. Too much like a gothic romance."

She wrinkled her nose. "So it is. Vulgar and implausible."

"Life is often both." He reached for a fresh handful of hay and resumed grooming. "Dressing as a boy to avoid being caught is also gothic, but practical. In that outfit, you'll be much less noticeable than traveling as an elegant young lady."

"Elegant young lady?" she scoffed. "I look like I've been dragged through a bush backward."

"Which makes it particularly impressive that you still look elegant," he said as he continued to groom the horse with the same brisk efficiency he'd used on her.

She frowned, not sure if he was serious, or had a really dry sense of humor. She was inclined to think it was humor, because she certainly wasn't elegant.

After wringing excess water from her hair, she began finger combing the knots out, which gave her a chance to study her rescuer. Tall and lean and muscular, he moved beautifully, never wasting a motion. Though he had a dangerous edge, she felt no fear. She realized with a shock that as long as he considered her his charge, he'd protect her with his life. It was a humbling thought.

Yet he was a mystery to her. She wondered about his personal life. Did he have one? Did he have a wife or a mistress? Any family? He gave the impression that he needed nothing and no one.

Not realizing she spoke aloud, she mused, "What do you care most about?"

He looked up over the back of his horse and stared at her with cool blue eyes, his hands becoming still. His brown hair was wet and tangled and his face was lean and strong, like the rest of him. Despite his ability to fade into the background when he wished, he was a remarkably handsome man.

"I'm sorry," she said, blushing. "That was an impertinent question."

"True, but an interesting one." His brows drew together as he thought. "I suppose I care most about justice." He resumed his grooming. "Life and society are often unfair. Sometimes I can balance the scales of justice a little."

It was an intriguing answer. But then, he was an intriguing man. "That's why you became a Bow Street Runner? So you could uphold the law?"

"That's part of the reason." His voice turned dry. "Equally important is that a man must eat."

Rarely did the sons of lords admit they must work for a living. She liked his matter-of-fact attitude even as she wondered why he was no longer the Honorable Robert Carmichael. But she didn't want to ask another impertinent question so soon. "What is your plan for returning to England? If you have a plan."

He tossed away the handfuls of hay he'd been using to wipe down the horse. "Make our way to the coast without getting caught and hire a boat to take us back to England. We don't want to head straight back along the roads to Cork or Dublin. A smaller port might be better. Beyond that, we'll just have to see how things go. Much depends on whether we're pursued, and how much time we lose because of this fellow's laming." He patted the rump of her horse.

"At least the rain will wipe out any tracks we might have left." She smothered a yawn, unsure whether fatigue or cold were stronger. "I'd best lie down before I collapse."

He frowned as he studied her. "You're still shivering. We need to use the oldest form of heating. Animal warmth."

Confused, she asked, "Sleep with the horses?"

He grinned and looked far less intimidating. "With each other, in a very chaste way. We'll burrow into the hay and I'll hold you and we'll both be warmer for it."

Sarah blinked at him. In other words, she'd sleep with a man for the first time in her life, and a relative stranger at that. Oh, well. She was long past the stage of being shocked, so she just nodded and crossed to the piled hay in the corner.

She settled gingerly into the pile. The dry stems and leaves prickled a bit, but the hay was soft and sweet scented. With a sigh of relief, she curled up in a compact ball to generate what warmth she could.

Rob blew out the candle, then moved across the barn to join her in the hay. Even though Sarah trusted him to behave, she tensed as he stretched out beside her.

"Relax," he murmured as he pulled hay over them both like a light, gently fragrant blanket. Then he tucked her against him, her back against his front. He was large and warm and comforting.

Sarah sighed with pleasure as she stopped shivering and began to unwind. There was nothing passionate about his embrace, only warmth and protection.

For the first time since Sarah's abduction, she slept well.

Chapter 8

Mr. McCarthy's kitchen looked like a war zone, with overturned furniture and smashed crockery. Flannery paced the length of the room, roaring at his battered and bloody troops. "The three of you let one man break in and carry off the duchess? You're a bunch of bloody bog dwellers!"

Curran said feebly, "Me and Donovan was sleeping. He took us by surprise."

"There were still three of you! And him not even carrying a gun." He glared at Donovan. "Not until he took that fine pistol I bought you!"

"How was I to know the duchess would smash a cast iron skillet over my head?" the driver asked defensively. "I thought she was a lady."

"She's more of a man than any of you!" Flannery bellowed. "Her rescuer must be someone who works for Ashton to come after us so quickly. Wherever the two of them are now, they'll be laughing their heads off."

"The damned fellow wasn't one of Ashton's men," O'Dwyer said sullenly as he washed blood from his face. "I recognized him. The name's Carmichael and he's a bloody Bow Street Runner. One of their best."

"A Scot?"

"Worse. An Englishman. Has quite a reputation for retrieving runaway heiresses and other delicate problems." O'Dwyer grimaced as he explored the massive bruise on his temple. "Does a lot of special commissions for rich blokes."

"Describe him," Flannery ordered. "I'll send word to Free Eire members along every road and turnpike from here to the coast. Carmichael may be a Runner, but traveling with little Miss Duchess will slow him down. Get yourselves cleaned up and fed. As soon as it's light, we're going after them. Remember, no duchess, no reward."

"It was all going so well," Curran muttered.

"That's when you need to be most careful," Flannery growled. "Remember, all we need is the duchess. The Runner you can kill."

Reminding himself that Miss Sarah Clarke-Townsend was a client and a damsel in distress, not a sweet little armful, Rob concentrated on mutual warmth instead of her femaleness. Except for the small part of his mind that was always alert, he fell into exhausted sleep, grateful that she wasn't the sort to have vapors. In that, she resembled her sister. From what Rob had seen, the duchess was admirably levelheaded and down to earth, traits Sarah shared, even if they both did resemble fluffy golden chicks. . . .

He awoke with a burning erection and a soft

female body locked in a heated embrace, only clothing preventing them from joining. His "Good God!" sounded at the same time as her "Merciful heaven!"

Shocked into wakefulness, they scrambled apart. Rob lay on his back and knotted his hands as he cursed himself. He was a grown man, not a hot-blooded youth!

Once more giving thanks that Miss Sarah wasn't given to vapors, he managed to say in a level voice, "I'm sorry. I don't generally seduce the females I rescue."

Sarah made a breathy sound as if she was also clenching her fists. "I don't think that was a seduction. Just . . . animal warmth in action. Because I'm very warm now!"

"So am I." He forced himself to consider how Ashton would react if he learned that Rob had bedded the duchess's sister. That helped his pulse go down quickly.

"You said you don't usually seduce the females you rescue," Sarah said, her voice curious. "Does that mean you do sometimes?"

"Of course not! When I'm hired to save girls from being ruined, I certainly can't ruin them myself."

"Saving runaway heiresses from their own folly, I presume." Sarah chuckled. "That doesn't apply to me. I'm no heiress."

Rob smiled a little into the darkness. "But the

principle remains. My job is to return you uninjured and unruined to your family."

"I know, and believe me, I'm grateful." She sighed. "But sometimes I fear that I'm destined to die a virgin."

Rob choked. "This is not a discussion we should be having!" He drew a deep breath as he tried not to imagine educating this lovely and willing young woman. "Even if you're not a great heiress, any girl as beautiful as you can't lack for suitors."

The light note that had been in her voice vanished. "I don't. But I loved and lost, and I . . . don't think that will happen again."

"I'm sorry." The pain in her voice made him find her hand and hold it comfortingly. "But a man fool enough to leave you doesn't deserve endless mourning."

"He left me by dying, not by an inconstant heart. With him, I felt like the most beautiful, fascinating woman alive. The betrothal ball was to be on my eighteenth birthday. He . . . he was killed in the hunting field a fortnight before." Her voice broke. "I'd been choosing my bride clothes."

"Oh, Sarah." He rolled onto his side and gathered her to his chest. "I'm so sorry. But if he truly loved you, he wouldn't want you to mourn forever."

"I'm sure he wouldn't. Gerald believed in enjoying life to the fullest." She sighed. "After mourning for a year, I told myself it was time to start looking. But when I did, I couldn't find anyone I wanted to marry a fraction as much as I'd wanted to marry Gerald. I've been looking for over seven years without success. Solid, worthy men don't interest me, and I realized that the dashing sorts would break my heart sooner or later."

"As Gerald did," Rob said softly.

"Exactly." Her voice was rueful. "We were both young, and I think we could have grown up well together. But I'll never know. Because I never had time to fall out of love with him, he still . . . holds my heart. Being a maiden aunt will suit me very well, though. In many ways, I prefer being an independent woman."

He wondered if that was really true, or if she was just good at making the best of her lot. "Independence has many advantages," he agreed. "But don't dismiss the possibility of finding a man who will be a good and honorable companion even if you don't love him as you did Gerald."

"Would you marry a woman who is merely a good companion?" she asked skeptically. "I suppose if one hasn't been madly in love, a congenial companion would seem quite suitable."

Usually he didn't talk about his private life, but in the darkness and with Sarah's honesty as inspiration, he found himself saying, "I've known both. I was madly in love when I was about the same age as when you loved Gerald. And I was equally devastated when it ended. Much later, I found . . . the best of companions. At least, for a while."

Sarah's voice softened. "What happened to the woman you loved madly? What was she like?"

Rob seldom thought of Bryony anymore. She belonged to the time in his life when he'd still had hope and optimism.

"She was a wild, beautiful shepherd's daughter on my father's estate. I've never met a girl like her. Black haired and fearless and free." Rob had a swift, searing mental image of Bryony racing across a meadow ahead of him, her long dark hair flying behind as she laughingly teased him to catch her. He swallowed hard. "I asked her to marry me, despite the difference in rank."

"And she died?"

His mouth twisted. "My father bought her off. I don't know how much he gave her. Enough so that she left the area without a word to me."

Sarah's hand tightened. "I'm not sure which way of losing a lover is worse."

Rob hadn't thought about that, but he didn't hesitate to say, "Death is worse. I'd like to think Bryony took the money and built herself a good life somewhere. Her parents were dreadful, and perhaps she didn't believe I was serious about marrying her. The money gave her the chance to be independent. I hope she's happy."

"But you were serious about marrying her." Sarah's words were soft in the night.

As serious as a man could be. "She would have made a splendid officer's wife."

"You've served in the army?"

"No. I'd planned to buy a commission in Alex Randall's regiment since we'd become friends at school. But—circumstances changed."

"You would have made a good officer," Sarah said warmly.

"I'd like to think so." He smiled wryly. "It's a far more honorable calling than being a Bow Street Runner."

"But surely a Runner gets to work more justice," she said.

He was startled by her perception. She was right; a Runner's work could be sordid, but Rob did manage to bring a little more justice into the world.

"What about the companion? She can't have been the best if she left you."

The loss of Cassie was very recent and the ache was deep. "She was brave and dangerous and kind. She traveled a great deal and we were seldom together, but those times were the brightest spots in my life. I thought that someday we might settle down together, but in her eyes, we were bound by friendship, not anything deeper."

"Was she right?"

He opened his mouth, then closed it as he

thought. He'd disagreed with Cassie when she'd told him their true bond was friendship because they were both too self-sufficient to ever need anyone else. "She said we were friends who sometimes shared a bed. I didn't agree with her then, but perhaps she was right." After a long silence, he added wistfully, "Friendship might have been enough if she hadn't found a man who touched her more deeply. But . . . she did."

"So finding romantic love is possible even after one has lost hope. I find that a comforting thought." After a pause, Sarah added, "Though it's none of my business, I'm perishing of curiosity about why you are no longer the Honorable Robert Carmichael."

He shrugged. "My father disowned me some years ago. Legally, he couldn't prevent me from styling myself as Honorable, but I've no desire to do so. Being a flash cove is not an advantage in my work."

"I suppose not." She made a small sound like a suppressed yawn. "I'm ready to fall back asleep, but it's cold in this barn. Do you think it's possible for us to cuddle up without something . . . inappropriate happening?"

He considered. "I'm not sure."

"What if you lie on your side and I apply myself to your backbone?" she suggested.

He smiled. "You won't be able to keep much of me warm, but it would be safer."

"Well, then," she said brightly.

He rolled over so that his back was toward her. There was a rustling of hay as she inched closer. Then he felt delightful female warmth settle along his back and thighs. A small hand slid between his arm and side and came to rest on his chest. She gave a happy little sigh and relaxed.

He did the same. Who would have guessed that he and a fluffy little golden chick could so quickly become friends?

Chapter 9

To Sarah's regret, Rob was gone when she woke. She understood now why sharing a bed was so popular—she couldn't remember when she'd slept so well.

She wistfully contemplated what it would have been like if Rob had been the sort to seduce the females he rescued, but she was grateful for his good sense. Though she didn't want to die a virgin, a casual romp in the hay was not the solution.

Rob was her knight in shining armor and seriously attractive, but she understood why the "best of companions" had left him. He'd probably make a fine bedmate for a brief encounter, but he was so self-contained that it was hard to imagine him wanting or needing anything more.

She stretched lazily, then climbed out of the hay. It was early morning and the rain had stopped. Enough light entered the barn to outline the horses. No, one horse. Rob must have taken the lame one away, leaving his own mount placidly chewing hay.

She stood and brushed straw off her clothing. She was finding trousers odd but very liberating.

She was heading to the door when Rob swung it open and entered, leading a different horse and carrying a basket. "We're in luck." He tethered his new acquisition. "I walked to the farmhouse up the road and told the farmer, Mr. Connolly, a version of the truth—that my young cousin and I are being pursued by villains and we needed transportation. He liked the looks of the lame horse and traded me this one."

Sarah surveyed her new mount. "So he gave you an elderly hack in exchange for a younger, stronger horse that's much more valuable and will be healed in a week or two."

"Exactly. But this old girl isn't lame, which is what matters for now." Rob patted the new horse on her bony rump. "Connolly felt guilty enough to invite us to the farmhouse for breakfast."

"Hot food?" Sarah asked hopefully. "Maybe even hot tea?"

"Very likely—the farm looks prosperous. But I refused. Better they not see you clearly." He studied her with narrowed eyes. "You'll barely pass as a boy at a distance. Close up will be impossible even if you darken your hair and smudge your face."

Sarah sighed. So much for being clean and well fed any time soon. "Is there any of that good cheese left?"

Rob handed her the basket. "No, but Mrs. Connolly packed some fresh bread and a couple of boiled eggs as well as a jug of tea. I'll drop the basket off as we leave."

Sarah dived into the basket. There were two thick slabs of buttered soda bread and a pair of eggs still warm from the boiling. She'd never been so happy to see an egg in her life.

She handed one piece of bread and an egg to Rob, then carefully cracked her egg and turned it onto the bread. It was mostly cooked with a soft yoke, just as she preferred. She took a bite and made herself chew slowly rather than wolfing it down. After a swallow of hot, milky tea, she said happily, "Ambrosia! I shall never meet a finer egg."

Rob actually laughed out loud, which made him look like a different man. She stared at him, thinking he needed to laugh more often.

"I'm glad you're so easily pleased," he said.

She bit off another piece of bread and egg. "Small pleasures are the best because they're everywhere. Anyone who needs grand spectacles is destined to be disappointed much of the time."

"That's a good philosophy." Rob finished off his bread and egg, took a swig of tea, then handed the jug to Sarah. As he began saddling his horse, he continued, "If all goes well, I'll have you back in Ralston Abbey in five days or so. That is, if you're up to that much riding astride. I'd rather not hire a carriage."

She made a face. "I'm straining muscles I didn't know I had, but I can manage."

"I'm asking a lot of you, so let me know if the strain becomes too great." Rob saddled both horses, then packed his saddlebags. He had the efficiency of a man who spent a lot of time on the road.

Sarah braided her hair while he packed, then tucked the braids under the floppy hat that was part of the outfit Rob had supplied. "Do I look suitably boyish?"

His mouth quirked up. "I'm glad the clothes are too large. That helps disguise the fact that you aren't at all boyish. When we're near people, keep your head down so all they see is hat. Are you ready to leave?"

Sarah nodded, but when Rob approached to help her onto her horse, she impulsively set her hands on his shoulders and said, "Thank you." Then kissed him.

He could have avoided her easily, but he didn't. His mouth was surprisingly warm as he accepted and returned the kiss.

She'd truly meant just to express her gratitude, but the desire that had drawn them together in the night flared back to life. Rob's arms locked around her as he kissed with focused intensity, as if she were the only thing on earth that mattered.

She was shocked by her own reaction. Though she'd always found him attractive, she hadn't expected to feel such . . . such *hunger.* Such a desire to melt into a man and let the fire she'd sparked consume her.

They were pressed full length together and his

warm hands kneaded and caressed, sending waves of sensation rolling through her whole body. Then the horse beside them whickered nervously and sidestepped away.

Abruptly Rob released her and stepped back, breathing hard. His expression was oddly vulnerable. "That was . . . delightful but unwise, Miss Clarke-Townsend."

She pressed her fingers to her lips, which pulsed with wanting. "I . . . I know. I won't do it again." She mustn't add fuel to a fire that should be allowed to burn out.

Rob's face returned to its normal controlled calm. "You'll be home in a few days and this will all just be a bad memory."

She gave him a crooked smile. "Not all bad."

"No. Not all bad," he said quietly. "But I'm sure you'll be glad to have hot tea and a warm bed and clean clothing." He linked his fingers to help her mount.

She stepped into his hand and swung into her saddle. Yes, she'd be glad to return to comfort and civilization. But she'd not forget sleeping rough with a Runner in a barn.

A quarter mile or so along the hedgerow-bound road, they came to the drive that ambled up to the farmhouse. A hundred yards short of the building, Rob said, "Wait here while I return the basket. Try to think boyish thoughts."

"Which would be . . . ?"

"Food and fighting," he said before he dismounted, handed her the reins, and continued on foot to the house.

The door opened quickly after he knocked and a tall, broad fellow accepted the basket with a stream of Irish words. Rob frowned and replied in Irish. Mr. Connolly glanced over at Sarah curiously. She tried to think boyish thoughts.

The conversation continued for several minutes, with hand gestures. After a polite nod and fare-well, Rob rejoined Sarah. As he mounted, he said tersely, "Just a few minutes ago, several men stopped by the house looking for a couple of English thieves known to be in this area. Mr. Connolly told them he'd seen no such persons."

"Do we risk running into those fellows ahead?" Sarah asked, alarmed.

They reached the road and Rob turned left, the way they'd come rather than continuing in the same direction. "We should be all right. Connolly told me of a lane that cuts over to a parallel road and eventually leads to an eastbound turnpike."

"How quickly can Flannery and his men get the word out about us? Surely not much faster than we can travel." Knowing that she and Rob were heading back toward McCarthy's house and might run into her captors made Sarah's skin creep.

Rob's narrowed eyes and alertness showed that

he was equally wary. "I don't know how large or well-organized Free Eire is. If mail coaches are used to spread the word, there could be people watching for us all the way to the coast."

She tried not to think about being recaptured. "So we ride fast and watch carefully. You said they were looking for an English couple. I didn't know you spoke Irish, but you seemed very fluent. Can you pass as an Irishman, or was that Scottish Gaelic and too different from the local accent?"

"Despite my name, I'm not Scottish. My branch of the Carmichaels moved south." Rob's tone was dry. "One of my Scottish ancestors betrayed his king and was rewarded with an English estate and title. The noble origins of my family."

Curious to know more about him, she asked, "How did you learn Irish?"

"My mother was the daughter of a Church of Ireland vicar. My father met her when he was visiting his estate, Kilvarra, and fell head over heels. She returned to visit every summer so I spent a fair amount of time here and learned to speak the language."

"That should certainly help us get away safely," she observed. "Do you know this part of Ireland?"

He shook his head. "Kilvarra is farther north in county Meath. I've never been in this part of the country."

Sarah searched her memory for anything she knew about Ireland. "Was Ballinagh near Kilvarra?"

His brow furrowed. "I think Ballinagh is somewhere in the west, but I'm not sure. Do you have friends there?"

Sarah shuddered. "Quite the contrary. Adam's horrible Aunt Georgiana Lawford lives in Ballinagh, if I'm remembering correctly."

"Ah, the one who tried to get him killed so her son could inherit the title. No, she was no neighbor of ours, fortunately."

"Adam stayed at Ballinagh a couple of times when he was a boy. He has fond memories of his visits and his cousins. Not so much for his aunt." She gazed over the hedgerows at the rolling hills. "I'd like to visit Ireland someday in better circumstances."

"It's much more pleasant when one is not running for one's life." Returning to business, he said, "I've got a good sense of direction, but the minor roads wander, which will slow us down. We'll have to risk some of the larger direct routes even if they're more likely to be watched."

In other words, they weren't clear of danger yet. "How long will it take us to reach the coast?"

"Three to four days if we make good time." He gestured toward a lane on the left. "Here's our turn."

She turned her horse gratefully. The new lane was a green tunnel with high hedges on both sides, which would protect them from the gaze of anyone on the road behind them.

The days ahead would be grueling. But she had faith that Rob would bring her safely home.

Chapter 10

After an hour or so of silent riding between hedges, Sarah and Rob passed a crudely built hut. The sun had come out and a dozen children sat in front listening to an older man. The children waved and called out friendly greetings as they rode by. Since Rob waved back, Sarah did the same, but they didn't stop riding.

When they were out of earshot, Sarah asked, "What were those children doing? I noticed similar groups once or twice when I was captive."

"Hedge schools," Rob replied. "Catholics aren't allowed to be teachers. The authorities want children to attend Protestant schools and become good little Anglicans."

Sarah gasped. "That's . . . rather dreadful. I don't expect parents want their children to be forced into a different religion."

"Of course they don't. That's why men with some education teach reading and writing and mathematics to local children in informal hedge schools like the one we just passed." A wry note entered his voice. "It was a hedge school that got me sent to the Westerfield Academy."

"How on earth did that happen?"

"I was spending the summer in Ireland with

my mother at the family estate, so I knew the local hedge school. I was friends with most of the students. I sometimes attended the Irish grammar classes. Because it was a wet summer, I told the schoolmaster they could use an abandoned hut on the estate. I also gave him money from my allowance to buy chapbooks for his students."

"Chapbooks?"

"Short, cheaply printed readers," Rob explained. "Hedge schools use them to teach reading. They were usually adventure stories and great fun to read."

"This sounds admirable." It was starting to rain again, so Sarah turned up the collar of her coat. "How did helping less fortunate students get you sent to a school for boys of good birth and bad behavior?"

"My father didn't approve of educating peasants. He said it gave them ideas above their stations," Rob said dryly. "But my most grievous sin was attending a Catholic Mass. He yanked me out of Ireland and sent me to Lady Agnes immediately so that I wouldn't be contaminated by Catholicism. My mother was his second wife, married because she was beautiful rather than for fortune and social standing. I was living proof that he never should have married beneath himself."

Sarah swallowed hard to prevent herself from making a very unladylike comment. "Your father sounds—difficult."

"An understatement," Rob said with even greater dryness. "He's the worst kind of arrogant, greedy, intolerant English nobleman. He lives a grand and fashionable life, giving much admired speeches in the House of Lords, running up huge debts and not paying the tailors and cobblers that allow him to live in style."

"It doesn't sound as if you have much in common."

"We don't. I haven't seen him since I was eighteen." Rob shrugged. "It was good riddance on both sides."

Behind the casual words, Sarah heard a deep current of anger and pain. "The Westerfield Academy worked out well, didn't it?"

Rob's expression eased. "The best thing my father ever did for me. We were all misfits. It was a good basis for friendship."

They turned a bend in the lane and found a farmer herding a flock of sheep between the hedgerows. Sarah fell behind Rob and the conversation ended as they worked their horses very slowly through the churning, bleating flock.

She understood now why he was so self-contained. He'd had to be to survive his childhood. His strength and integrity were a tribute to his innate character. Very likely his mother had been a strong influence; his voice had been warm when he referred to her.

She also understood why his highest romantic

goal was to find a comfortable companion. A strong, dangerous woman who would be at ease with the life of a Bow Street Runner. Yet when he'd found such a woman, she'd left him because she wanted more. Sarah hoped he'd find another such woman who would stay. He deserved that.

Rob kept a watchful eye on Sarah, but he didn't set a ladylike pace. Despite her petite size and fragile air, she had impressive stamina.

Her horse didn't do so well. It was a decent beast, but old and not bred for speed. Rob was grateful when they came into a town that was having its market day. Not only would he be able to buy supplies, but there was a small horse fair adjacent to the town livery stable.

He pulled to a halt when they reached the crowded market square. When Sarah did the same, he said quietly, "Time to buy provisions and a better mount for you."

"Shall I stay here and hold the horses while you go to market?" In her oversize garments and floppy hat, Sarah was so adorable that he wanted to smile. The carefully applied smudge on her cheek made her look young and mischievous, though he knew she must be twenty-five or twenty-six since she was twin to Ashton's wife.

He reminded himself sharply that his job was to return her safely to her home, not develop a deeper bond that would do neither of them any good. He still couldn't believe how much he'd told her about his younger life. Maybe being in Ireland made him talkative. Or maybe it was that she listened so well. "Lead the horses to the livery stable. You can take a look at the ones that are for sale while I buy what we need."

She dismounted with a nod. Rob did the same and pulled a folded canvas carrier from his saddlebags before he headed into the jumble of stalls. He noted that Sarah stayed between the two horses she led so that no one would see her clearly. Smart girl.

Smart *lady*.

It didn't take long to buy more cheese, bread, meat pies, the previous autumn's apples, and two coarse but warm blankets. They wouldn't have to sleep in each other's arms again, which would be wiser if less enjoyable.

The livery stable had the weathered name "Holmes" painted above the broad doors. Sarah had tethered their mounts adjacent to the ones for sale and was lurking unnoticed behind them. Since the market was noisy enough to cover conversation, as Rob packed his acquisitions into his saddlebags, he asked quietly, "Any of these hacks you fancy?"

She looked up with swift surprise. "A man is asking my opinion about horses? The heavens may fall!"

This time he did smile. "Any woman who can ride like you must know horseflesh."

Her face lit up with laughter, and he felt an odd lurch in the vicinity of his heart. He'd never met a woman who radiated such joy.

She gestured to the left. "That dark bay over there would probably do, I think, but you might ask the livery owner if he has anything better inside."

Rob scanned the line of horses. None of them rated better than adequate. "You're right. Let's go inside. But keep your head down."

She obeyed and became a sullen boy in an oversize hat. The inside of the livery had the familiar scents of hay and horses. A large orange cat sprawled on a bench and watched them sleepily. There were a number of stalls, all of them occupied.

A burly man ambled toward them. "I'm Holmes. If you be looking for stabling, I'm full up till the market closes. I'll have space then."

"I'm looking for a good, sturdy horse with stamina," Rob replied. "Do you have any in here for sale? My cousin's horse outside is old and slow, and I promised him we'd look for something livelier."

The owner barely glanced at Sarah. "Two good horses at the end of the aisle on the left. On the right is a pony that might suit a small lad like this one."

"We'll take a look then." As Rob turned to go down the aisle of stalls, he added, "I'd like to trade in his old horse. You might take a look. She's tethered outside."

The owner nodded and headed out as Rob and Sarah moved down the aisle between the stalls. When they reached the end, Rob asked, "What do you think of the chestnut?"

"Looks like a nervous beast, but probably fast," she said judiciously.

Rob nodded. Her judgment matched his. "The bay is handsome, but let's look at the pony. Holmes was right that you don't need a large horse. A pony will add to the impression that you're a young boy."

They moved across the aisle to study the pony, a relaxed chestnut with a white star on his forehead. "He reminds me of my first pony," Sarah said warmly. "Only larger, close to the size of a horse. I wonder if he has as good a disposition."

She cooed to the pony, apologizing for not having a bit of carrot ready. He butted her in a friendly way, and he was sturdy and healthy looking. Rob guessed that he'd hold up well through several days of hard riding. He opened the stall and moved inside, watchful but reasonably sure the pony was safe.

Sarah followed and stroked the pony's neck as Rob checked the fetlocks and feet. He was straightening up when he heard a familiar voice speaking in Irish. He looked at the open doors and saw one of Sarah's abductors speaking to Holmes—and he was turning toward the stables.

Rob instantly caught Sarah around the waist and pulled her to him as he dropped to his knees so they were below the shoulder-high wall. They were kneeling in straw with her back to his chest. He felt a surge of protectiveness so intense it left him breathless. He would protect any woman in his charge. But this one more than any other.

When she started to speak, he touched her lips with a finger. "Shhhh . . ."

She stilled and he concentrated on the conversation between the abductor and Holmes. It ended after a couple of minutes. He waited several more before whispering to Sarah, "It was one of your abductors, the drunk who was sleeping on duty."

"O'Dwyer!" Sarah hissed. "He was the worst of them. What was he saying?"

"He asked if Holmes had seen a tall Englishman with a young blond woman."

Sarah turned rigid against him. "What did Holmes say?"

"That he'd seen no such people."

She sighed with relief. "A good thing you can pass as an Irishman. But I didn't expect them to be so close!"

"There are only so many roads to the coast.

We'll have to be extra careful as we continue."
Rob frowned. "Any of the three men who were
in the kitchen when I came for you would recognize me, and those three plus the fourth man
will know you. I hope it doesn't occur to them
that you're traveling as a male."

"They weren't very intelligent," Sarah said
tartly. "Except for Flannery, the leader. But if
one of them sees me with you, they'd figure it
out soon enough."

"So we have to make sure we aren't seen." Rob
peered around the edge of the stall. Holmes was
in the doorway talking with a fellow who looked
like a local farmer. Rob released Sarah and
stood. "All clear. Time we bought the pony and
headed on."

She got to her feet, brushing straw from her
clothing. "Lucky you spotted O'Dwyer before he
saw us."

She was right. But Rob didn't like relying on
luck.

Eventually it ran out.

Chapter 11

Sarah stayed with the pony while Rob went outside to talk to Holmes. She was still shaking at the knowledge of how close O'Dwyer had come. She was also unnerved by her reaction to being held by Rob. She liked, trusted, and respected him—and he stirred a physical attraction she hadn't known since Gerald's death.

Perhaps the fact that they faced danger intensified that attraction. More likely it was Rob himself, who was an alluring balance of menace and kindness. Either way, her reaction was a serious nuisance, to say the least.

Firmly suppressing thoughts of too-attractive Bow Street Runners, she took hold of the pony's halter and led him out into the aisle to check his gait. Smooth and easy. She hoped Rob could buy him for a reasonable price.

She hadn't thought about money till now. She didn't have a penny to bless herself with. Rob obviously had some funds, but the amount would not be unlimited. She prayed he had enough to get them back to England.

Rob returned carrying her saddle and baggage. "The pony is now yours. His name is Boru.

Holmes accepted the old horse and a few extra pounds. He also told me how to find a minor road to the east that should be safe."

Sarah hoped so. But she had an uneasy feeling that the word about them had gone out all over southeast Ireland.

The road Holmes suggested wasn't much more than a winding lane, but it was quiet and blessedly free of kidnappers. As dusk fell, they reached another reasonably prosperous farm. While Sarah waited tiredly on Boru, Rob dismounted and knocked on the farmhouse door to ask permission to sleep in the barn in return for a modest payment.

A man opened the door. After a brief conversation, Rob waved Sarah toward the barn, then entered the building. She hoped that meant he was buying some hot food.

She led both horses into the barn, which was larger and less empty than the previous night's accommodation. Three horses in stalls on the left whickered greetings as she put her two mounts into empty stalls opposite. She gave them water and hay, then lurched to the storage bin and collapsed into the golden straw.

She thought the horses would be all right for a few minutes until Rob arrived to groom them. She should start on Boru, but she ached in every muscle, bone, joint, and a few places she didn't know she had. Riding astride used some new muscles. Though she was a good rider, she'd never ridden as far as she'd done on this endless day. . . .

She jerked awake when Rob announced, "Cabbage and potato soup, along with fresh bread, cheese, and ale." He set a tray on the floor beside her. "Do you have the energy to eat?"

"Have you ever seen me turn down food?" Smothering a yawn, she sat up in the straw and crossed her legs. Rob had rubbed down their horses before waking her, she saw. That meant they could concentrate on their supper.

He settled on the floor with his back against a wall and his long legs stretched out in front of himself before pouring steaming soup from the jug into two pewter bowls. He handed her one along with a spoon, then poured ale into pewter mugs from a similar jug. "The lady of the house was generous to weary travelers."

"God bless her!" Sarah wolfed down her meal, not speaking until she'd sopped up the last of the soup with her bread. As she wiped her hands with a clump of straw, she said ruefully, "I'm sorry for my lack of manners, but I was ravenous."

"You should be after all that riding." Rob sliced the remaining cheese in half and handed a piece to her. "You have the stamina of a cavalryman."

"I love riding, and I did a lot of it trying to keep up with my boy cousins." Her brow furrowed. "I've only just thought to wonder why we haven't gone to the authorities for help. Is it because you don't know who might be a rebel sympathizer?"

"That's part of the reason," Rob replied. "There are many anti-British groups, so we might not find much support. We might even be handed back to Free Eire."

Sarah grimaced. "That's not a happy thought. But now that I've seen some of the country, I understand better why so many of the Irish want independence."

"If I lived here, I'd join the United Irishmen myself. It's a moderate group that draws from all parts of society," Rob said. "But since we're English, I think it wise to steer clear of anything political. There are troops in Dublin and a naval installation at Cobh in Cork Harbor, but if we get that far, we won't need them. If we did find military protectors, all chance of keeping your abduction quiet would vanish. Getting you home safely is the first priority, but keeping your reputation intact is also to be desired."

Sarah blinked. "I hadn't thought of that. At my age, reputation isn't as important as it is for younger girls."

His brows arched. "You're hardly at your last prayers, and you look just out of the schoolroom. Even if you don't care greatly about your reputation, surely you don't want everyone in Britain to know you were kidnapped by a band of louts. The story is lurid enough to begin with. By the time the gossips finished embellishing it, you'd be so notorious that you'd never live it down."

She shuddered. "You're right. I would much prefer to avoid that."

"Where were you raised? I know the general outlines of your background, but not the details." Rob divided the remaining ale between their mugs, then leaned back against the wall, one knee drawn up.

Sarah loved looking at him—all long, lean power, with broad shoulders and deft hands. He hadn't shaved in days. She guessed that was a deliberate choice to make himself look vaguely disreputable.

She sipped at her ale, telling herself not to let her mind wander. "You know how my parents married too young, had Mariah and me, and one day after a huge fight, my father went to the nursery, picked up Mariah, and carried her off as if she were a puppy?"

Rob nodded. "I was told your father lived a peripatetic life as a gambler and charming houseguest until he won an estate at cards and reconciled with your mother."

"He says he had too much pride to go back after

they quarreled, and he didn't want to return unless he could properly support his family. After he won Hartley, he could do that." She shook her head in exasperation. "But it took him over twenty years. Such foolishness!"

"Did he take Mariah because she was his favorite?"

"He claims it was pure chance. When he entered the nursery, she toddled toward him, so he scooped her up and carried her off. He thought that with two identical daughters, he and Mama could each have one and not feel deprived."

"I doubt that reasoning appealed to your mother," Rob said dryly.

"You are so right! She used to tell me about my sister. We'd speculate where Mariah was and what she was doing." Sarah had yearned to meet her missing twin so they could become best friends. She'd never expected such a miracle to actually happen. "But Mama did feel grateful that he didn't take both of us. Legally, he could have."

"If he had, I'm sure she'd never have forgiven him," Rob observed. "But a young father would have had trouble caring for two little girls. Even one would be a strain."

"He handed Mariah to his part-Gypsy grandmother and went off to earn his living at the card table," Sarah explained. "Mariah said he visited often, but he didn't do the serious daily work of raising a child."

Rob placed the empty jugs and utensils on the tray and set it to one side. "You must have wondered about your life if your father had taken you instead of your sister."

"Mariah and I have talked about this," she admitted. "Would I be her and she be me? I don't think so, and neither does she. Though we're very alike, we're individuals and we have our differences."

"If your father had taken you instead of Mariah, you might be a duchess now."

"More likely Adam would have drowned because Mariah wasn't in the right place to fish him out of the water. Even if I'd saved him, I wouldn't have fallen in love with him." Sarah frowned. "Or perhaps I would. If I'd lived Mariah's uncertain life, I might have been drawn to his steadiness the way she is. It's a conundrum."

Rob smiled. "The sort of thing that could keep you awake nights if you thought much about it."

"But I don't," she said firmly. "The situation is as it is. I was the lucky twin. I was raised by my mother and I'm glad for it."

"You never did say where you were raised."

She grinned, feeling a pleasant haze from the ale, which was stronger than she was used to. "My mind is prone to wandering. I had a lovely childhood, apart from not having my father and sister. When my father ran off, my mother's older brother, Lord Babcock, invited her to come live with him so she could be his hostess and run his household. Uncle Peter's wife had died, and with four healthy sons, he felt no need to remarry. So I grew up in Babcock Hall in Hertford. My cousins and I were raised together and I was the cosseted little sister."

"I'm glad it worked out so well for you," Rob said. "Your mother was fortunate that her brother didn't resent having to support a sister and niece."

"He didn't have to." Sarah shook her head ruefully. "Ever fond of the grand gesture, my father signed the income from my mother's inheritance over to her to prove that he hadn't married her for her money. We were quite comfortable."

Rob's brows arched. "That was quixotic and honorable of your father." He hesitated. "Do you resent him for returning and claiming so much of your mother's attention when you'd had it for so many years?"

Sarah sighed and dropped her gaze, thinking that Rob was uncomfortably perceptive. "A little. Mama and I were very close. We still are, but— it's different." *And lonelier.* "Now it's your turn to tell me about your life. Do you have a permanent home in London, or do you travel too much for that?"

"I have rooms above a pawnshop near Covent Garden. My associate, Harvey, lives there and handles London business when I'm away."

In other words, there was no room in his life for a woman like her, though perhaps his tough, dangerous lady companion might have fitted in. She suspected that he was deliberately underlining the vast gulf between them.

Made a little reckless by fatigue and strong ale, Sarah asked softly, "Have you wondered how things might be between us under other circumstances?"

He became very still as she caught his gaze. His eyes were striking—a clear, pale aquamarine blue with a night black edge. Those eyes could be intimidating or threatening or kind. Now they were . . . bleak. "I've considered the question," he said as the air thickened between them. "But we must play the cards life has dealt us."

So he also felt that thrumming attraction and recognized that their paths were too far apart to be bridged. The intimacy that was growing in these few intense days must end. Though she knew it was inevitable, she felt sorrowful to have her knowledge confirmed.

Rob broke the mood by digging into his saddlebags and producing a pistol. "Since you were raised with boys, were you exposed to firearms? Some ladies shrink from such infernal devices."

She took the pistol and expertly broke it down.

It was clean, well maintained, and currently unloaded. "Not just exposed but well taught by my uncle. I was a better shot than any of my cousins. Uncle Peter told me to always carry a pistol when traveling. Unfortunately, I didn't think I needed a weapon when riding on my brother-in-law's estate."

"A pistol might not have helped you against four men, but I'm glad you can shoot." Rob handed her a pouch containing powder and shot. "This pistol is mine and it's a nice little weapon. I'll carry the pistol I acquired from one of your abductors since it's larger and heavier. I suggest you keep this until we're safely back in England."

She bit her lip as she regarded the weapon. "As I said, I'm a good shot, but I don't know if I could kill a man. I wouldn't even hunt game at Babcock Hall."

"I wouldn't ask you to shoot another person. But brandishing a weapon and perhaps shooting it over someone's head makes a very forceful statement."

"Very well." She accepted the pouch and practiced loading her new weapon. "Do you usually keep a pistol close at hand? I didn't notice one when you rescued me."

"I was carrying this, but I prefer not to use fire-arms unless it's absolutely necessary. The chance of seriously injuring someone in close quarters is too high. I use this fighting stick in such situations." He reached under his coat and produced a polished wooden stick with knobs at both ends. When his hand closed over it, the knobs protruded on each side. "This adds a lot of punching power when you want to hurt, not kill."

"Oh, very nice! May I see?"

Smiling, he handed it to her. "You have a surprisingly bloodthirsty look in your eyes for a well brought up young lady."

She locked her hand around the stick and made a few practice swings. The smooth wood felt good on her palm, though the stick was too long. "I was raised with boys, which meant a certain amount of rough and tumble when we were small and out of sight of our parents." She handed the stick back. "I'd need one that was smaller for best effect, I think. Not that I expect to do much fighting, but this little adventure reminds me that sometimes a lady must defend herself."

"I hope you'll never have such an adventure again!" he said fervently. "But it's good to be prepared for whatever might come."

"Which means getting some rest so I can ride all day tomorrow." She covered a yawn as she reached for a blanket. "I'll sleep on the far side of the straw stack."

"I'll sleep by the door so I can fend off dragons if any come for my lady," he said in a courtly tone.

"In other words, at a safe distance from me," she said bluntly.

"Exactly. You have a potent field of attraction, Sarah." Wry amusement showed in his eyes. "It would be easier to fend off dragons."

She laughed, glad they could joke about this inconvenient attraction. Then she rolled up in her blanket, tucked herself into the straw against the wall, and slept.

Chapter 12

Sarah slept like a felled ox—and woke the next morning lying beside Rob, her head on his shoulder and his arm around her waist. They both appeared to have moved and met in the middle of the yielding straw. Though they were still wrapped in their blankets like mummies, she was dizzyingly aware of his warmth and strength.

She snuggled closer without conscious volition. His eyes opened and gazed into hers, mere inches away. First awareness, then sharp desire flickered through the aquamarine depths. Mesmerized, she brushed her fingertips across the lovely masculine prickliness of his unshaven jaw.

If he'd closed those inches for a kiss, she'd have responded with an enthusiasm more dangerous than dragons. Instead, he gave her a rueful smile and rolled away. "Tonight we need to put a wall between us."

She sat up and brushed straw from her hair. "I'm not sure even that would do the job. A good thing we're both sensible adults." At least, Rob was. She wasn't entirely sure about herself.

Another long day of riding along back roads produced chafed skin as well as sore muscles. Sarah had abandoned all thoughts of cleanliness;

it was no longer relevant. Reality was mixed rain and clouds and sunshine and changing gaits to keep the horses fit over long hours of riding.

There was no sign of pursuit. Once more as night fell they found a barn to berth in. Rob bought stewed crubeens for them to share. A week earlier she might have balked at pickled pig trotters, but now she dug in eagerly. They were quite tasty, too.

Rob sent Sarah to sleep in the tack room with the door closed. That proved sufficient to keep them apart. Unfortunately.

As they ate their basic breakfast the next morning, Rob said, "We've made good time because you're such a skilled rider. We're within reach of Cork today if we take the turnpikes. I'm told the one near here is not heavily traveled, but it will certainly be busier than the back roads we've been following. And any turnpike is more likely to have people watching for us."

"But we'd reach Cork quickly," she said thoughtfully. "You're the expert here. Do you think it's worth the risk?"

"I think so. The longer it takes us to reach a port and sail for home, the farther word will spread to be on the lookout for us. We don't know how large Free Eire is, but it's possible there are already men watching for us in every village in the southeast. If all goes well, we could be in Cork by early afternoon and maybe even sailing to England before the day is over."

Sarah's heart lurched. She wanted desperately to be home and safe and clean, and most of all, to see how Mariah was, but she would miss her adventure. Or to be precise, she'd miss Rob. She wouldn't find him so attractive if he was a real villain, but the combination of his rough and ready appearance with birth, education, and protectiveness was quite irresistible.

But this odd idyll must end, and the sooner it did, the safer for both of them. She got to her feet and donned her hat. "Onward to Cork, sir!"

It was only about half an hour's ride to the beginning of the turnpike. Sarah's nerves twitched as they halted at the tollhouse. The keeper lived inside the small building so he would be available day and night to lift the bar for travelers. A painted board on the wall declared that the keeper was a Mr. Diarmid Condon, and listed charges in English and Irish for horses, herds, and conveyances of different sizes. The toll for a rider on a horse was tuppence.

She kept her head down and slouched in her saddle as Rob talked to the elderly gatekeeper in Irish. He and she were just two more muddy Irish travelers.

Rob handed over a couple of coins and Condon moved to swing the long pole off the road. Then two men burst out of the tollhouse brandishing muskets: O'Dwyer and a weaselly man Sarah didn't recognize.

"Carmichael, you bastard!" O'Dwyer bellowed. "You're passing for Irish! And our slut duchess is disgracin' herself in britches! No wonder it's been so bloody hard to track you." He snapped a quick glare at Sarah while keeping his weapon trained on Rob.

"Hands up, Runner! This musket is loaded with shot and I'd love an excuse to blast your heart out!"

Rob raised his hands, his face impassive. Sarah could almost hear his mind racing as he considered how to react. But with two muskets aimed at his chest from point blank range, his choices weren't good.

All three men, including the unhappy-looking gatekeeper, were watching Rob and assuming Sarah was harmless. More fools they. She reached into the saddlebag behind her and found her pistol by touch.

She was carrying it half cocked and loaded, which was risky, but she'd taken the chance because something like this might happen. She eased the gun out, checked that the loading was in place, then aimed it over the heads of the men and pulled the trigger.

KA-BOOM!!!!!

As the blast echoed from the hills, she shouted, "Stand and deliver!" because a shout seemed appropriate and she couldn't think of anything better.

Condon dived behind the gatepost while O'Dwyer and the weasel swore and swung around, looking for the shooter. Rob took advantage of their shock to yank out his fighting stick and dive from his horse.

He crashed down on O'Dwyer and carried them both to the ground, Rob on top. He swung the striking stick at O'Dwyer's temple, but the Irishman was large and thrashing violently so the stick struck his shoulder instead. The men rolled across the yard in a tangle of fists and knees and furious blows.

As they fought, the weasel pulled himself together and aimed his gun at Rob and O'Dwyer. His barrel wavered back and forth as he tried to find a way to shoot Rob, but the men were too entangled.

He was ignoring Sarah again. The fellow wasn't very bright. As soon as she reloaded her pistol, she kicked Boru forward straight at the weasel. He shrieked and tried to dodge when he saw the pony bearing down on him, but he wasn't fast enough. Boru sideswiped the weasel and Sarah wrenched the musket from his hands as he fell.

As the weasel lurched backward, Sarah tucked the musket under her left arm and pointed her pistol into the man's face. "Please don't make me shoot," she said in her most earnest young lady voice. "I don't want to accidentally kill you, but I can't allow you to interfere. Raise your hands, and you won't be hurt." She glanced at the gatekeeper. "The same for you, Mr. Condon. You'll note that it was these brutes who started the trouble. All my friend and I want is to use the turnpike."

The weasel's face paled as he looked down the barrel of her pistol. As he lifted shaking hands, Rob ended the fight with O'Dwyer by slamming the knob of the fighting stick into the man's jaw with a sound of cracking bone. O'Dwyer groaned and went limp, a trickle of blood running down his chin.

Rob vaulted to his feet and clamped a hand on the weasel's neck, his fingers digging deep. The man's eyes widened in horror before he folded to the ground.

As Rob studied O'Dwyer with narrowed eyes, Sarah had the uncanny sense that she could read his mind. He was considering whether to kill the man. Not from anger or bloodlust, but as a cool, rational judgment that they'd be safer if O'Dwyer was dead.

"Don't," she said softly. "He's a horrible person, but I don't want his death on my conscience."

"Very well," Rob said after a pause. "Though we may come to regret it." He turned to the gate-keeper. "How much traffic comes through most days?"

"Not a lot, but steady," Condon said warily. "There's never too long between travelers."

"Shall we ride now?" Sarah asked, feeling anxious at the thought of strangers stumbling onto this untidy scene.

"I want to give us more of a lead. Keep your pistol ready while I stash these fellows in the shed behind the house." Rob moved to his horse and removed two pairs of handcuffs from the saddlebags. As Sarah's brows rose, he explained, "No reason to make it easy to resume pursuit once they wake up."

"Rob, you are a constant source of education," she said sincerely, assuming that he had plans for the toll keeper as well.

He gave her a quick smile. "And you are remarkably useful in a fight."

As Sarah watched Condon, who was looking less wary, Rob dragged away O'Dwyer, then the weasel. When he returned, he said to the keeper, "There are two horses tethered in the shed. Is either yours?"

"Nay, they belong to those two gents." Condon frowned. "They said they were looking for two thieves who'd stolen something valuable. What do you say to that?"

"They're liars," Rob said tersely. "They kidnapped my companion. I was sent to rescue her and bring her safely back to her family in England."

Condon examined Sarah's face before nodding. "I believe ye, but I don't want to get in bad with Free Eire. I'll have to release them as soon as you leave."

"Don't worry, I'll tie you up also so their anger won't fall on you. If you come into the house, I'll try to make you as comfortable as possible."

Sarah uncocked her pistol and returned it to her saddlebag as Rob escorted Condon indoors. He returned a few minutes later. "I fed his dog at his request and tied him up on his bed so he'll be all right. If the next travelers to come through are less than honest, they'll pass on by and just be grateful there's no keeper on duty."

Sarah was about to comment when they heard the sounds of an approaching vehicle. Rob tossed her his reins. "Get behind the house and I'll tend the gate."

"You have many talents!" Sarah led their mounts out of sight just before a well laden wagon came round the bend. She dismounted and peered around the corner of the house, then watched as Rob took the toll and chatted with the driver as if he'd been doing the job for years.

More travelers came through, a westbound man on a horse, and a pony cart heading east. It was a relief when the travelers left and the turnpike was quiet again.

Rob returned, and led two saddled horses out of the shed. "We're taking these horses. Not stealing them—they'll be released down the turnpike. But I don't want O'Dwyer and his minion to pursue us any time soon."

She was consorting with a horse thief. "Did you pay Mr. Condon four pence more for the additional horses?"

Rob smiled. "Of course. Not paying tolls would be wrong." Holding the leads of the horses, he swung onto his own mount and led the way out to the turnpike. He set off at a fast trot, Sarah beside him and the two other horses behind.

A quarter mile down the road, when they were out of sight of the tollhouse, he reined his mount in. "Time to switch to their beasts, ride fast until they're tired, then release them and get back on our own horses."

Seeing the sense of that, Sarah dismounted from Boru. "How long do you think it will be until they resume their pursuit?"

"Hard to say. Anywhere from half an hour to half a day." Rob moved to the smaller of the borrowed horses and shortened the stirrups. "It won't be long until someone goes inside the tollhouse to find Mr. Condon. It will take longer to release O'Dwyer and the other fellow since I handcuffed them to iron rings set in the walls of the shed. But after the cuffs are broken, they'll find new mounts and be after us with their tails on fire."

Sarah swung up onto her temporary horse.

"Can we reach Cork before they catch up with us?"

"We might if we were going to Cork, but we're not. We're going to leave the turnpike and head to Kinsale, a small port south of Cork."

She'd never heard of the town, but Rob hadn't been wrong yet. "I assume you know how to find this place."

"The farmer where we stayed last night told me of a track that intersects this turnpike and leads to Kinsale. It travels over rough high ground, but it's manageable on horseback."

"So even if they come after us quickly, we're safe until they run into westbound travelers and ask if they've seen us."

"Which won't take long." He gave her a reassuring smile. "We'll make it home safely, Sarah. Not much longer now."

He was probably lying through his teeth—but she was grateful for it.

Rob and Sarah crested a sweeping hill and looked down on a grand vista of sea, rugged coast, and a town nestled by a small harbor. "Kinsale," Rob said, trying to keep the relief from his voice.

Though he'd been maintaining a show of confidence for Sarah, he was acutely aware of how many things could go wrong. Another lame horse would have been disastrous. "Half an hour and we'll be at the harbor looking for a boat and captain to take us across to England."

"We'd better find someone willing quickly," she said, her voice tight. "Because we're being followed."

Rob turned, and swore when he saw half a dozen men just starting down the track on the ridge behind. Squinting, he recognized O'Dwyer's burly figure in the lead. "They're too bloody efficient! But they're at least a quarter hour behind. That will give us time enough."

The pursuers spotted them and a shout echoed off the hills as they spurred their horses to go faster. Rob's mouth tightened. "Now we *ride!* Lead the way, my lady!"

Her delicate features set, Sarah plunged down the steep track toward the town, Rob close behind. He'd hoped they'd be able to escape Ireland without this sort of hot pursuit, but he'd husbanded the horses' strength just in case.

He gave thanks for Sarah's fine riding. They wouldn't have made it this far if she weren't a superb horsewoman. He'd told her to go first so she could set the pace, and she and her pony tore down the hill at a speed that he'd have been hard pressed to beat.

They reached the edge of the small town without ruining the horses, but when Rob glanced back, he saw that the pursuers apparently didn't care if their horses survived. They were closing fast and near enough that he could see the vicious anticipation on O'Dwyer's face.

Their mounts' hooves clattering on the steep, narrow streets, Rob and Sarah slowed their pace so they wouldn't run down any of the townspeople who drew back hastily. He swiftly assessed their choices. Trying to hide in such a small town when they were strangers would be difficult if not impossible.

There was a British fort, but it was on the far side of the town. Too far. Though they had two pistols and two muskets, a gun battle in the middle of Kinsale would be insanity.

They'd been pursued till they were up against the sea, which left only one chance of escape. A boat.

Chapter 13

If Sarah hadn't been concentrating on riding as fast as possible through Kinsale's steep streets without injuring anyone, she'd have succumbed to strong hysterics. Her abductors were only a few minutes behind them, and she and Rob would be trapped with their backs to the sea. Even Rob wouldn't be able to find a way out this time.

Rob. They'd kill him out of hand. They wouldn't kill her. They'd probably do worse than that because of the trouble she'd caused them.

But she was by God not giving up yet! And neither was Rob.

They reached the waterfront in a clatter of hooves and sweating horses. Sarah's heart sank when she saw only a handful of boats in the harbor. One was moored at the nearest dock and a man was heaving the last of several baskets of fish up onto the wooden planks. The boat had two sails, looked well kept, and the name *Brianne* was painted on the bow.

Rob reined in his horse at the foot of the dock and vaulted to the ground. "Sir!" he called as he raced onto the dock. "Are you the owner of this yawl?"

The man straightened and stretched his back.

"Aye, I'm Michael Farrell. And where are you going as if the devil is on your tail?"

Rob halted beside the *Brianne*, his body rigid with tension. "We need to sail from here *right now!* Can you take me and my companion? We'll pay handsomely."

Farrell snorted. "Are you trying to get yourself killed, lad?" He gestured toward the sky, where thunderous clouds were gathering to the north. "There's a sharp squall coming and I'll not take my *Brianne* out in it."

"I'm trying to *save* us from being killed," Rob said, his voice grim. "Wicked men abducted my companion. I rescued her, but they're right behind us with guns in their hands and blood in their eyes."

"Her?" Farrell glanced at Sarah, who had dismounted. She obligingly removed her hat so that her unraveling blond braid fell down her back, then did her best to look vulnerable and winsome. Vulnerable was easy since she was terrified. It must have worked, because the captain's eyes widened with surprise.

She tethered their mounts to a railing, untied both sets of saddlebags, and threw one over each shoulder to keep herself balanced. Shaking with fatigue from the hard ride and the heavy bags, she followed Rob out onto the dock, praying that he could persuade the captain to take them out.

Rob pulled a pouch from inside his coat and

tossed it in his hand so the clinking sound of heavy coins was unmistakable. "You don't have to take us far, captain. Just away from here."

Farrell's gaze sharpened as he regarded the pouch. "I'd be happy to oblige after the squall has passed, if we haven't lost the tide by then."

"We haven't the time to waste," Rob said tersely. "Surely a seasoned sailor can manage a passing squall."

"Aye, if I had to, but only a fool would try to sail out of this harbor in heavy winds without a bloody good reason." He glanced at Sarah and touched the brim of his hat. "Sorry for the language, lass."

Language was the least of her problems as pounding hooves signaled a dozen armed men bursting from a side street into the open area that rimmed the waterfront. Shouts rose as they spotted their prey and came thundering toward Rob and Sarah.

As she watched, frozen with terror, one of their lead horses staggered and fell. The two horses immediately behind stumbled over the fallen beast and crashed down in a tangle of screaming horses and swearing men that blocked the road. Though the riders behind were able to halt in time, one of the men who'd gone down had crashed into a stone wall and lay motionless.

Sarah uttered a silent prayer of gratitude for this brief reprieve, but it would be very short.

Flannery and O'Dwyer were already sorting out their men.

Rob snapped his gaze from the pursuers to the boat. "Sorry, Captain Farrell, but I must take the *Brianne*." He held out the pouch. "You can have the horses plus this. More than enough money to buy another yawl. If there's anything you want onboard, take it now, because we're leaving."

The captain sputtered, "You can't just take my boat!"

"I can and I will. I'd prefer your consent, but lack of it won't stop me." Rob jumped down into the boat, easily keeping his balance as it rocked from his weight. "Sarah, give me the saddlebags, then take my hand to board."

She obeyed, at the same time giving Farrell her most wide-eyed, heart-melting gaze, the one that always worked on her uncle and father. "Sir, this truly is life or death. Have mercy on us!"

Uncertain, the captain opened the pouch. His eyes widened. Before he could reply, the bang of a musket echoed around the harbor. Water spouted up in a dozen places and pellets rattled off the hull. Rob ducked as another musket blast shot their way. "You see we weren't exaggerating! I advise you to get out of the line of fire."

Jaw dropping, Farrell looked to the shore and saw two men reloading their muskets. "Holy Mother of God!" He shoved the pouch in a pocket, grabbed a bulging canvas bag, and

131

scrambled onto the dock. "Very well, damn you!" He dived into a dinghy moored on the opposite side. "The *Brianne* is yours, and if you get yourself drowned, don't blame it on me! Watch out for the bar at the harbor mouth!"

As Farrell rowed swiftly away, Rob untied the *Brianne* and shoved at the dock so the boat started to drift into the harbor. Then he moved to the forward mast and started to raise the sail. "Stay low and out of the way, Sarah!"

She moved toward the stern obediently. She could see Boru standing patiently where she'd tethered him and hoped Farrell would see that the pony was treated well.

Led by O'Dwyer and Flannery, her abductors were racing down the dock toward the *Brianne*. Fifty feet, twenty, O'Dwyer was raising a pistol and aiming at Rob. . . .

With a crack of canvas, the *Brianne* caught the wind and slid briskly away from the dock. The lurch when the boat began to move almost tumbled Sarah overboard.

"Stay *down,* dammit!" Rob barked.

"Aye, aye, captain." Shaking, Sarah grabbed hold and stared at her abductors. The *Brianne* was well out of jumping distance now. Several shots were fired after them, along with a lot of curses. The ones in English were filthy and those in Irish were probably worse. None of the shots came close; the boat was moving too quickly and erratically for a good aim, she guessed.

They'd made it! They'd escaped the devils who would have taken Mariah and her unborn child and probably killed both in the process.

With relief came fury. Those horrible men had terrified Sarah and would have gladly killed Rob. Standing up and cupping her hands around her mouth, Sarah shouted, "You ignorant fools! I'm not even the Duchess of Ashton, I'm her sister! You got it wrong from the beginning."

Shock and rage twisted Flannery's face. "Don't laugh too soon, you bitch!" he shouted back. "When my chief finds out, she'll come after both of you!"

Sarah blinked. Did he say his chief was female? With the wind and the distance, his voice was trailing off. No matter. She and Rob were safely away, and Adam would insure that Mariah was very well guarded in the future.

The boat lurched and she almost pitched overboard. A strong hand caught the seat of her trousers and pulled her down. "Sit, princess," Rob said dryly. "I understand your need to vent some temper at your abductors, but it's not worth drowning for."

Which was true, but she had enjoyed letting some of her anger loose. She turned and settled on the bench that ran across the stern. The boat was perhaps thirty-five feet long and sat low in the water, with a couple of benches and lockers across the front end.

Rob sat at the tiller in the rear, steering the *Brianne* away from the docks. They had almost reached the mouth of the harbor now. He frowned, his gaze alternating between the lowering sky and the harbor bar Farrell had warned them of.

A gust of wind tilted the boat sharply to the right. Sarah tightened her grip on the gunwale. "You do know what to do with this thing?"

"I grew up in Somerset, the English side of this channel, and learned to sail from the local fishermen in yawls much like this one," he said reassuringly. "But Farrell was right to worry about that squall. I want to be in open water before it hits. Stow the saddlebags in the port locker if there's space. That's on the left. If not, try the other locker on the right. That's starboard. When you move around the boat, always stay low and hang on to something solid."

Sarah scuttled forward, skimming her hand along the gunwale. By the time they reached England, she'd know what to call the different parts of the boat. The *yawl*. "Are all yawls designed like this one?"

"There are a lot of variations, but the fishing yawls are usually about this size and they generally have two sails."

Sarah opened the port locker. Thinking it would be useful to inventory their resources, she said, "There's rope in the bottom and a sort of small bucket, but there's room for our saddlebags. I don't even mind that everything will smell of fish."

"In a few hours, you won't even notice the smell. The bucket is for bailing water. Make its acquaintance, because the way this yawl is designed, you'll be using it sooner or later." He glanced at the sky. "Sooner. Find a secure spot where you can hold on with both hands, and keep your head below the level of the boom so that if we come about, it won't knock you overboard."

Sarah hadn't known what a boom was, but it was easy enough to figure out Rob's warning. She settled down with her back against the locker, one hand on the gunwale. Not only did she feel safe, but she was facing Rob and could watch him at the tiller.

He'd taken off his hat, and his brown hair blew in the wind while his light blue eyes studied the approaching clouds. With his strong features and effortless competence, he was a sight to stir any girl's romantic dreams as he arrowed the *Brianne* out of the harbor. But he was more than a girl's romantic dream. He was real and strong and utterly reliable. Perhaps that meant he was a woman's romantic dream.

Since such thoughts were unproductive, she studied the approaching squall. She could watch the rain and wind sweeping across the gray waves and heading straight toward them. They'd just cleared the harbor when the squall struck, shoving the *Brianne* over so sharply that Sarah gave an involuntary gasp, sure they would capsize.

"Hold tight, Sarah! We can ride this out!" Rob's words were for her but all his attention was on the sea and the wind. The *Brianne* straightened and carried on through the drenching rain.

Sarah held on grimly. Rob's steering was no longer effortless as he fought to control the yawl. With surprise and then amusement, she realized that he was enjoying this battle with the elements. She doubted he'd have that light in his eyes if they were in danger of drowning, so she began to relax.

The rain stopped with startling suddenness and the wind diminished to brisk rather than threatening. As the sun emerged, touching highlights on the waves, Sarah released a sigh of relief. "I'm seriously impressed, Rob. Is there anything you can't do?"

He laughed, looking more relaxed than at any time since he'd rescued her. "There is much I can't do, but I do know my way around boats. This is a sweet little yawl. She'll carry us safely back home."

"How long will that take?"

"Hard to say. If the winds cooperate, about a

day. If we were farther north, opposite Wales, the crossing would be much shorter. I hope Farrell has a supply of fresh water, or we'll be very thirsty by the time we arrive."

"The rest of me is wet enough to compensate." Wet and *cold*.

Rob must have noticed her shivers, because he said, "You can warm up with a dry blanket from our luggage, but first, you'll need to use that bailing bucket. We took on water during the squall." After a pause, he added, "I can do the bailing if you'd like to try your hand at the tiller."

"No, thank you! Maybe if the sea was calm and the winds light. Under these conditions, we'd probably end up in Spain if I tried to steer." After pulling out the bailing bucket, she dug more deeply into the lockers. "Here are pewter mugs and plates and a small jug of something that might be drinkable." She pulled out the cork and took a sniff, then wrinkled her nose. "Some kind of fierce spirits. Care for a taste?"

Looking regretful, he said, "Later, maybe, if I need warming. Anything else useful?"

She found a small keg and turned the tap a little so she could sample a few drops. "This one is water." She returned the keg to the locker and explored further. "Here's a parcel of smoked fish, and bread that smells like smoked fish. Several eggs, probably hard-cooked since he couldn't do much with raw eggs." She sat back on her heels. "That seems to be it. Time to start bailing."

She bent and began scooping. There was a certain freedom in knowing it didn't matter if she splashed water on herself because she couldn't be any wetter. Plus the labor warmed her up.

When she finished her task and stowed the bucket away, Rob said thoughtfully, "I'm not sure Ashton will approve of my returning a scruffy urchin in place of the elegant young lady he lost."

She laughed. "I shall recommend that he pay you full price even if I do look as if you fished me from a pond."

She was starting to feel cold again, so she dug into the saddlebags for one of the dry blankets. "Do you want the other blanket?"

"Better to save it. There may be more squalls."

That was not a welcome thought. She wrapped the blanket around herself and the warmth helped, but not enough. She pulled the blanket tighter and tried to keep her teeth from chattering.

"Come sit next to me so I can put my free arm around you," Rob said. "I'm sorry. It's the best I can offer."

"An offer I accept with alacrity!" Sarah shifted to the bench in the stern and settled so close to Rob that she was pressed against him from shoulder to knee. She gave a small sigh of pleasure. "Even under these conditions, you radiate warmth. It's a useful talent." As Rob's arm came around her, she added, "I'm rather amazed that we escaped."

"We wouldn't have if you'd been the helpless girl I thought you were when I first saw you," Rob said seriously. "But you've been up to every challenge. You're wasted on a civilized life."

She laughed. "Perhaps, but my taste for adventure has been satisfied for some time to come." She burrowed closer under his arm, warmth returning to her numb body. "Do you ever tire of adventures?"

"I don't think of this as adventure. It's just . . . my life." He smiled wryly. "Usually it's quieter than this, though."

"Have you done any sailing since you were a boy?" she asked. "Or are you relying on memory?"

He became very still, and she wondered what caused that reaction. "You don't have to answer," she said quickly. "It was an idle question, the product of an idle mind."

"Your mind is never that." He sighed. "The answer is a long story."

She rested her head on his shoulder and watched the long afternoon rays of sunshine brighten the sea that led home. "I'd say we have no shortage of time."

Flannery hated having to report failure to his chief. Face like granite, he said, "They bought a yawl in Kinsale and escaped just as we were closing in."

She stared at him with fierce, rather mad eyes. "You let them get away? Why the devil didn't you shoot them?"

"We tried. The range was too great and their boat was moving." He clamped his mouth shut. The less he said, the better.

"The weather has been stormy," she muttered. "With luck, the duchess and the Runner have drowned and no one will know."

Since she'd raised the subject, he had to tell her the rest. "As the boat sailed away, the girl shouted that she wasn't the duchess, but her sister. She may have said that just to mock us. Certainly she fit the duchess's description."

His chief slammed her fist onto the table. "The duchess has a twin sister! Like as two peas in a pod, except that the duchess was increasing and near term. *You abducted the wrong damned woman!*"

Flannery flinched involuntarily. The chief might be a mere female, but she had a frightening intensity. He remembered how deftly the sister had explained that the baby was born and with a wet nurse. The treacherous bitch. "We were unaware that there was a sister." Unspoken was his feeling that the chief should have told him that in advance.

"The sister's name is Sarah and she's a spinster.

Worthless, compared to the duchess." The chief's face turned to granite. "She'll pay. Along with that bloody Bow Street Runner."

And Flannery wanted to be the one to exact revenge.

Chapter 14

Very few of Rob's friends knew his sordid past, and they were not the sort to talk out of turn. But he realized that he wanted to tell his story to this sunny, intrepid young lady who had proved to be such a fine companion. He had no fortune, and his honor was of the battered, personal variety. But he could give her a piece of himself in the form of the experiences that had shaped him. He knew her well enough to believe she'd respect such an odd gift.

"I've told the outlines of the first chapter of my life," he began. "My mother was a second wife, a beautiful Irish vicar's daughter. My father liked displaying her in London. He was a creature of the beau monde, a leader of fashion, and a blazing hypocrite who paid ostentatious lip service to religion while having a philistine's soul."

"He sounds very unlikable," Sarah said.

That was a massive understatement, but there was no need for Rob to belabor the point. "In the interest of fairness, I should add that he had good reason to dislike me equally. I was not an obedient son. After I was expelled from two of the better known schools for the sons of gentle-men, he learned of the Westerfield Academy and packed me off to Lady Agnes, which proved a great relief to both of us."

"You said you intended a military career, but it didn't happen," Sarah remarked. She felt so amazingly good under his arm. "Surely he didn't object to the army? It would be a respectable way to get you out of sight."

"I committed two great crimes that got me disowned and exiled," Rob said. "The first was stealing my father's beloved and very valuable snuffbox collection, and the second was announcing that I was going to marry Bryony, my wild shepherd's daughter." He glanced down into Sarah's wide brown eyes. "I'm a thorough-going rogue, you know. I have that on my father's authority."

Her mouth quirked up on one side. "You may be a perfect rogue, but I doubt that you stole his treasures to pay gambling debts or mistresses."

He felt inordinately pleased at how well she'd come to understand him. "I used the money to settle accounts with tradesmen whom my father had patronized but never paid. Some were on the verge of debtor's prison. The snuffboxes brought almost enough to pay off everyone. The tailor's bill was by far the highest."

"I suspect your mother and vicar grandfather must have shaped your character before your father could ruin it," Sarah observed. "And you're a better man for it."

"But a far worse gentleman," Rob replied dryly. "It's just barely possible that I might have survived selling the snuffboxes, but insisting I would marry Bryony was the final straw. Since I was only eighteen I needed my father's permission, but I thought he'd be glad to give it so I could take Bryony off to follow the drum and he'd be rid of me. With any luck, I'd die honorably in action."

Sarah winced at the bald statement. "He must have been horrified at the idea of his noble Carmichael blood mingling with that of a peasant."

"Exactly. Once Bryony was out of the picture, he probably intended to buy me a commission to get me out of the way, but before that happened, my brother decided to remove the blot on the family escutcheon. Edmund was the heir and he followed in our father's fashionable footsteps. Since he was about to marry an heiress from a famously fertile family, there was no need to keep a spare heir like me around."

Sarah's brow furrowed. "What did he do?"

A sharp gust of wind gave Rob an excuse to concentrate on sailing long enough to control the anger that thoughts of his brother always stirred. "Dear Edmund sold me to a press gang."

"Dear God!" Sarah gasped. "That's *evil*. How

was it even possible? The law governing impressment is quite clear. You were not a professional sailor, and as a gentleman's son, you must have carried a protection."

"The law may be clear, but those who enforce it can be corrupt. Dear Edmund had no trouble arranging for me to be seized and gagged and delivered to a ship in need of crew." Rob's mouth twisted. "So in answer to your question, yes, I had later sailing experience. As a common sailor on an India trading ship." And he had the lash scars on his back to prove it.

Sarah shook her head in disbelief. "How could he do that to his own brother?"

"Very easily. My father and I had a relationship best described as cordial dislike, but Edmund and I truly loathed each other. My last sight of my brother was his smile of satisfaction as I was beaten by four men, then tied, gagged, and hauled away."

Sarah made a small, anguished sound, but knew better than to speak about the unspeakable. "How long did you sail before the mast?"

"About a year. I escaped from the ship in Bombay and found work with a high official of the East India Company. Mr. Fraser hired me on the strength of my Scottish name. He treated me well and gave me opportunities to learn. I became something between his private secretary and his bodyguard." Rob had improved his fighting skills as well. Four men attacking him at once were no longer too many. He'd once saved Mr. Fraser when half a dozen dacoits attacked them.

"I'm glad you found someone who valued you! How long were you in India?"

"Almost five years. I considered staying, for it's a fascinating place." Even now, he would sometimes wake with the scents of the spice bazaars in his nostrils, or the brilliant tropical colors blazing in his memory.

Dusk was falling, but there was still enough light to show her delicate features when she asked, "Why did you leave when you loved India and had a good position?"

He smiled with self-mockery. "A hard, roguish Bow Street Runner shouldn't admit such sentimentality, but . . . I'm British in my bones. I missed my homeland. So I gave half my savings to Fraser to invest and booked passage for London. I'd learned how to conduct discreet and sometimes dangerous investigations, which is how I ended up on Bow Street." He brushed a lock of hair from her face. "Rescuing fair damsels."

"I'd miss England dreadfully, too," Sarah said. "Did you ever confront your horrible brother?"

Rob shook his head. "In a triumph of civilized restraint, when I returned to England I decided to put all that behind me and open the second chapter of my life." He would not have survived if he hadn't forced himself to let go of his fury and sense of betrayal. "I was tempted to let the family know I'd become a Bow Street Runner just to horrify them further, but there was nothing to be gained by seeking apologies or revenge. They wouldn't give the former, and I didn't wish to be hanged for achieving the latter."

"You were wise." There was silence except for the sound of the waves and wind until Sarah said softly, "Are you happy in the life you've built for yourself, Rob?"

"Happy?" he mused. "Certainly I'm content. I'm very good at what I do, and that's satisfying. I help people and provide justice on occasion." He squeezed her shoulders. "I even get to rescue fair damsels. Yes, I like my life."

"I'm glad." After an even longer silence, she said haltingly, "It's going to be hard to say good-bye, Rob. You've become . . . very special to me."

His heart tightened and he wished with sudden ferocity that things could be different. "We've had a chance to become close in a way that's rare between men and women who in the normal course of events would never meet."

"Yes," she sighed, recognizing the distance he was putting between them. "Would it be possible for us to remain friends?"

He thought of his rooms above the pawnshop.

They were neat and comfortable, at least for him, but he couldn't imagine Sarah there. "There would be no point to it. Some things are meant to end."

He bent his head to give her a kiss that he intended to be light and sweet, a wistful tribute to what could never be. But she met his kiss with an ardent yearning that burned the night. Forgetting his good resolutions, he pulled her hard against him, exploring her mouth, the warm curves of her body, the power of passion concealed in her small frame.

She matched his desire, her thighs bracing his left leg, her hips grinding urgently against his. Dear God, she was intoxicating, innocence and fire and generosity that touched forgotten places in his soul. "Sweet Sarah," he whispered. "My golden princess . . ."

The *Brianne* heeled over so hard they were almost swamped. Damnation, he'd released the tiller! He grabbed it with one hand and lunged to catch Sarah around the waist before she could slip overboard. Heart pounding, he corrected their course while he locked her slim body against his side.

"Well, that was interesting!" Sarah said with a slightly mad bubble of laughter. "I've heard of a kiss moving the earth. We managed to move the sea."

He smiled, his tension fading because she could

laugh. "I think the sea moved us. You seem to have a guardian angel intent on protecting your virtue."

She sighed, her breath warm through the damp shoulder of his coat. "Sadly true."

They stayed pressed close, neither of them willing to pull away. The wind was steady and the waves moderate now, but that wouldn't last. Soon they must separate, and this time for good. A small boat at sea was no place for passionate dalliance.

Rob's shoulder was starting to numb from the weight of Sarah's head when she asked, "Have you ever thought of changing your work? My uncle's steward is near retirement age, so my uncle will be seeking a man to take over. I should think you would do such work well."

For a moment he actually considered it. Steward on a lord's estate was a position of responsibility and respect and usually came with a fine salary and house. It was a good position for a family man. A lady like Sarah might marry such a man, if he was of good birth. It wouldn't be considered a good match, but neither was it a complete mésalliance. He and Sarah could be together. . . .

The possibility died almost as quickly as it had appeared. It would never do to live as a dependent of one of Sarah's relatives. *Poor Carmichael, unable to support a wife properly without family charity.* No. They both deserved better.

"It's a generous thought, Sarah, but it wouldn't suit," he replied, choosing his words carefully. "One of the best aspects of being a Runner is that I'm largely independent. I'm not fond of taking orders, and I'm certainly not knowledgeable about estate management. Your uncle needs a proper steward."

"I knew you'd say that," she said bleakly. "But I had to ask."

She'd had to ask. And he'd had to refuse.

For the first time in years, Rob damned his brother for destroying all chance for him to have the life he was born to.

"You must be exhausted," Sarah said into the gathering darkness. "Do you want me to take a turn at the tiller so you can get some rest? We seem to be holding a fairly steady eastward course."

"I can manage. A yawl like this is easy to sail single handed. But if you want to try steering, this is a good time." He stood and moved around the tiller, keeping a hand on it while Sarah slid across the stern bench and took hold of the long wooden bar.

She was intrigued by how the tiller transmitted all the vibrations and subtle shifts of the *Brianne*. The yawl was like a living creature, and she dimly recognized how a good sailor could become attuned to his vessel.

Then Rob released his hold and suddenly

Sarah was fighting to keep the tiller at the correct angle. She breathed a curse and dug in her heels to hold the bar steady, but even so, the yawl was being pushed off course. "This is much harder than it looks!"

Rob set his hand on the tiller from the other side, and Sarah was immediately able to manage. "Steering isn't difficult, but it requires strength," Rob explained. "You're strong for your size, but that size is . . ."

"Unimpressive," she suggested when he seemed stuck for a polite word.

"Exquisitely petite," Rob said firmly.

"Very gallant, but I've long since resigned myself to being a little dab of a thing," Sarah said with a smile. "My friend Lady Kiri Mackenzie has many enviable qualities, but the one I really crave is her height. When she enters a room, she's like a Hindu warrior goddess, attracting all eyes. I'm that little Clarke-Townsend girl."

Rob slid his hand back along the tiller so it rested warmly over hers. "You're exactly the right height. Taller would be too tall. And you'll be an economical wife because you'll need less fabric for your gowns."

She laughed. "I shall be sure to point that out to any future suitors. The Clarke-Townsend twins: there's the glamorous Golden Duchess, and her echo of a sister. Less sparkle and glamour, but agreeable and good at housekeeping."

His hand tightened on hers. "Don't mock what is unique and special about you, Sarah."

She didn't reply for a moment. "I don't, not really. But I'm a moth next to Mariah's butterfly. Her unpredictable life made her quick and charming and adaptable. I'm just . . . less interesting. Mariah didn't really remember that she had a twin, but she created an imaginary friend named Sarah who was always perfectly, boringly correct. That's me, except not perfect."

"So the two of you compare yourselves to each other unfavorably. *'Lord, what fools these mortals be!'*" Rob said with a smile in his voice. "While you doubt yourselves, any male seeing you together will know himself twice blessed. Two lovely young women, equally beautiful, yet deliciously different."

"You say the loveliest things, Rob." Unconvinced, Sarah smothered a yawn. "Since I'm unsuited to guiding the *Brianne*, I'll put together a supper for us. I just realized I'm ravenous."

"We haven't had anything since a bite of breakfast at dawn." Rob took over the tiller as Sarah moved away. "But by tomorrow evening, we should be on land with our choice of food. The day after, you'll be with your family at Ralston Abbey."

"I hope so!" Sarah unlatched the locker that held the food and pulled out parcels of bread, cheese, and smoked fish. "Do you want some of the whiskey?"

"Not straight. Add some water and I'll have that. I'd recommend the same to you since it's warming."

As she located the two pewter mugs, she asked, "Where do you think we'll make landfall?"

"If possible, I'd like to sail into Bristol, though I'm not sure enough of where we started, or how far south the squall drove us. But I know the English coastline along the Somerset and Devonshire coasts rather well. There are a number of small harbors that will suit us if that's where we make landfall."

"How will you manage during the night? You need some rest and we've established I'm no good as a substitute pilot."

"I'll take down the smaller sail and reduce the area of the mainsail," Rob replied. "Then I'll lash the tiller in position and catnap beside it. If the wind or weather changes dramatically, I'll come awake immediately."

She didn't doubt it. She suspected that Rob could do anything. They ate their supper in peaceful silence. She was hungry enough that even the smoked fish tasted good. She doubted she'd develop a fondness for spirits, but the whiskey and water was drinkable and warming, as Rob had said.

After they ate, she wrapped herself in both

blankets at Rob's insistence and wedged herself down beside him. The sounds of wind and sea were very restful.

Someday she'd look back at this sailing adventure with wonder since it was so very different from the rest of her life. Just as Rob was.

At least she'd have the memories.

Chapter 15

The morning dawned red and ominous. *Red sky at night, sailors delight/Red in the morning, sailors take warning.* Rob didn't know how old the saying was, but suspected the idea had been around since Noah turned his hand to ark building.

As he studied the sky, the blanket roll that was Sarah heaved, then unwrapped to reveal its tousled blond contents. She sat up and stretched, looking so delectable that he hastily turned his gaze to the sky again.

"Sleeping on a wooden deck makes me appreciate the comforts of haystacks," Sarah said cheerfully. "Did you manage to rest during the night?"

"Yes, the winds were mostly light. I was able to doze a good bit of the time."

She folded the two blankets neatly and stowed them in a locker. "I won't know what to do with a real bed when I have one again."

Rob wished she hadn't mentioned beds. A drawback of quiet sailing was that it allowed too much time to think about one's distractingly attractive shipmate. "If all goes well, you'll sleep in a proper bed tonight."

"A real bed," she said reverently. "And if I'm truly blessed, a real *bath!*"

"Take care! Too much civilization at once might be overpowering."

He must have failed at sounding casual, because she studied him with a frown. "Is something wrong? We're not being pursued, are we?" She sat up higher and scanned the sea behind them.

"Not that, but a storm is coming. Probably a big one." He gestured toward the red dawn. "I'm not sure when it will hit. I hope not until we're safely ashore, but we've a long sail ahead of us."

"We came through the squall easily," she said. "This will be worse?"

"Squalls are brief. A storm can go on for hours or days." And he'd sailed enough to have a bad feeling about this one.

Sarah gazed at the eastern sky, her face very still. His fluffy golden chick looked calm and determined. A woman, not a girl. "Then we must prepare as best we can. First, breakfast. Then what can I do to make it easier to ride out the storm?"

"Breakfast is a good start. Eat well—we'll need the energy later. After we've eaten, stow away everything loose and bring out the rope you found yesterday. We both need safety lines securing us to the yawl."

She swallowed hard. "So if we get washed overboard, we might survive?"

He nodded. "A lifeline is just a precaution, but I'd rather be safe than sorry. I'll tie the knots. They'll hold well, but they can be released with a single tug if necessary."

From her expression, she was imagining all the possible ways she might drown, but she said only, "Aye, aye, captain."

They ate their breakfast in watery sunshine, sitting side by side on the stern bench in easy silence. He liked that Sarah didn't feel the need to chatter. She was within touching distance, and he felt an odd mixture of peace and desire. Not a bad way to spend what might be his last breakfast on earth.

As Sarah wrapped the leftover food, she asked, "What aren't you telling me? If we're going to die today, I need warning so I can send up some last prayers."

He blinked at her perception and calm acceptance of danger. "I devoutly hope we don't die today, but . . . it could happen. If this storm hits hard from the direction it's coming, we could be blown into the English shore. The southwest coast has a lot of rugged areas where it will be hard to land safely during a tempest."

She absorbed that. "So we could be wrecked and drowned on the shores of home. That would be ironic."

He was glad he didn't have to spell out the danger. "I don't think we can outrun the storm and make landfall before it hits, so I'm sailing parallel to the coast until the storm has passed. But if the winds are strong enough, I won't have much control."

"I'll polish up those prayers then." Sarah moved forward to stow the last of the food. "But first, lifelines."

Sarah found it eerie to live through a day that might be her last on earth. Frightening though her abductors had been, she'd never thought death was imminent and unavoidable. This danger was different—not the threat of dangerous men, but of vast, impersonal nature. They might survive; she had great faith in Rob's competence. But they might not. The fact that Rob was worried spoke volumes.

Sarah didn't want to die. Not *at all!* But death could come to anyone, at any time, and she'd had twenty-six good years. Many had less time than that.

She hated that her family would never know what had happened to her. They'd make inquiries in Ireland, but the trail would end at Kinsale with the realistic assumption that she and Rob were lost at sea.

If Sarah died today, she'd never know whether Mariah had a son or a daughter. They would never have the chance to make up for the years they'd been separated. She'd never really know her charming and sometimes maddening father.

Not to mention the irritating fact that Sarah would die a virgin. She thought, half seriously, that she should have seduced Rob when they were on dry land. She might have succeeded, despite his considerable willpower.

She'd left it too late, though. The wind had been steadily rising and now the *Brianne* was sliding up and down sizable waves. Rob was focused on sailing. After he'd made the lifelines, with Sarah secured to a bench with a rope around her waist and Rob connected to the base of the mizzenmast, enough rope remained for him to create a harness that allowed him to lock down the tiller if he had to move away.

The harness would ease the fierce physical demands of sailing the yawl. He'd furled the mizzen sail and reduced the area of the mainsail as much as possible while still allowing him control. They spoke little because there was nothing to say.

Sarah stationed herself at midship with the bailing bucket in her hands. Waves were splashing into the cockpit already and it was steady work to remove the water. She was glad she could do something to contribute to their possible survival, but if they didn't drown, her back and shoulders would ache for days.

A large wave broke over the bow at an angle that deposited six inches of fresh water into the boat. With a sigh, Sarah resumed bailing, careful to follow Rob's rule that she always have one hand gripping something solid. She wondered what time it was. The sun had vanished behind dark, churning storm clouds, but it must be well into afternoon by now.

She was dumping a bucket of water over the port gunwale when she thought she saw something in the distance. "Land, ho, I think. England. *Home*." She swallowed hard, surprisingly moved. She'd been gone less than a fortnight, but it seemed longer because of all that had happened.

"So it is," Rob said, raising his voice to be heard over the wind.

She studied the coastline somberly. "That's not good news, is it?"

"It's not great," he allowed. "Even with reduced sails, the wind has been pushing us hard toward the shore. The drift will get worse when the full force of the storm hits." He frowned at the distant shore. "Since I know this coast well, I'm trying to steer us toward an area of open beaches where we can reach land safely."

She was about to reply when the full screaming power of the storm struck, and there was no more breath to waste on words.

Bail, bail, bail. The world had been a shrieking cacophony of tearing winds and gigantic waves for so long that Sarah could barely remember silence. Her muscles ached, and surely Rob's ached more because he'd been fighting the tiller through this endless day. She'd been drenched and shivering with cold for so long, she no longer noticed. Life had narrowed to scooping water and prayers for the storm to end without destroying the *Brianne* and her crew.

A hideous grating sound assaulted her ears and a violent shudder rocked the yawl. "We've hit a rock! Sarah, hold tight!" Rob yelled as the boat slewed sideways and a towering wave crashed into the cockpit.

She grabbed for the gunwales, but the avalanche of water swept her overboard and dragged her down into the sea. She struggled against the force of the water, trying to follow the taut safety line back to the boat. But she wasn't strong enough to move against the currents pounding her. She was being dragged helplessly through the water. Couldn't breathe, *couldn't breathe . . .*

So this was death . . .

A strong arm locked around her waist and hauled her back onto the yawl. "Dear God, Sarah, are you all right?" Rob called urgently. "You can't be dead, you weren't under that long, please, *talk to me!*"

She tried to reply, but couldn't speak. Rob carried her to his seat in the stern, then draped her limp body across his lap, face downward. A smart slap on her back with his open hand made

Sarah gag, then cough up water convulsively.

As she drew blessed air into her lungs, Rob pulled her up against him, one arm around her shivering body. "Are you all right?"

She coughed again, then said hoarsely, "Not. Dead. Yet."

He drew her closer and she burrowed against his chest. They were both soaking, rain still hammered down, and even Sarah could tell that the yawl was in dire straits. She was dimly aware that the tiller was held by the steering harness with help from Rob's right arm while his left was locked around her.

She gazed into the chaos of wind and water, seeing some shapes blacker against the black, and occasional white ruffles of breaking waves. Ahead was a heavy, regular roar of waves crashing into the shore.

Feeling unnaturally calm, she said, "We're going to die, aren't we?"

Rob said in her ear, his urgent voice pitched to cut through the storm, "Maybe not. This is an area I know well. Too damned well, but I know the rocks, and there's a shingle beach beyond them. Likely the *Brianne* will break up before we get that far. I'm releasing the knots on the lifelines so we won't be dragged down. I'm also taking my boots off. You do the same. I don't suppose you can swim?"

"I was never allowed to join my male cousins

in the pond," she said with regret. "I was irritated then, and even more so now!"

"Since I was raised on the coast, I'm a strong swimmer. There's a good chance I can get you ashore. If I lose hold of you, or—if I can't continue, keep heading toward land any way you can." His voice broke. "I'm sorry I've failed you, princess."

With a detachment beyond fear, she replied, "Our fate is in God's hands, and He can overrule even Bow Street Runners." She bent forward to wrench off her boots. "You've done your best, Rob. One can ask no more."

"Ah, Sarah, Sarah." He turned her face up and gave her a swift, hard kiss that brought a tingle of warmth to her chilled body. Her fingers curled into his arms and she wished rather desperately that she would never have to let him go.

He yanked at the loose end of her lifeline and it fell free. "Hang on, my dear girl," he said as he reached for his sodden boots. "We're going in!"

Chapter 16

Cursing the ironic fate that had brought the *Brianne* back to the stretch of coast Rob knew best, he squinted into the deluge, looking for the best passage between the rocks. They couldn't be more than a few hundred yards from land since he could hear the surf pounding on the shingle beach. At least the beach gave them a chance to survive. If the yawl had been driven into sheer cliffs, they would have been doomed.

He reluctantly removed his left arm from Sarah so he'd have both hands on the tiller. It was almost impossible to control the *Brianne* in these heavy seas, but even a small amount of steering could make all the difference.

"Will it unbalance you if I put an arm around your waist?" Sarah asked, raising her voice to be heard above the gale. "You're a good solid anchor to hold on to."

"As you wish, princess," he said with an easing of his tension. She'd been generous to forgive him in advance for his likely failure to save her.

In his arrogance, he'd thought he could take her safely home all by himself. Now that it was too late, he realized that a British military camp would have been the wiser choice. Though her abduction would have become common knowledge and her reputation badly damaged, at least she'd be alive. Instead, they were unlikely to see the dawn.

But if they drowned, it wouldn't be for lack of trying to survive. He cut the tiller sharply to starboard to avoid an ominous stone pillar that loomed abruptly out of the darkness and rain. The yawl rocked and the hull scraped along the pillar, but they made it past.

The turbulence increased and whirled them straight into a towering rock. They hit with a hideous crunching sound and a jolt that threw them both forward. Rob clung grimly to the tiller and Sarah hung onto him as the yawl spun sideways, then slammed into another rock. As water rushed in, Rob snapped, "Time to abandon ship, Sarah! Can you hold on to my shoulders while I swim to shore?"

"I . . . I don't know," she gasped. "My fingers are numb from the cold and I might lose my grip."

He'd feared that. He stripped off his sodden coat so he could swim more freely. "I'll keep one arm around you as I swim. It will be slower, but I'll keep you above water." For as long as he could.

Her pale oval face tilted up toward him. "Is there anything I can do to help us reach shore?"

"Stay still and let me pull you along." As he spoke, the *Brianne* smashed into another water-slicked boulder. The yawl was almost completely filled with water and at the mercy of the surging waves. He wrapped his left arm around Sarah's waist and launched them into the maelstrom, pushing away from the rock formation where the yawl was trapped and being pounded to pieces.

Complete immersion in the sea was even colder than being in the boat, if that was possible. He followed the current toward shore, lying on his side and kicking with both legs while he stroked with his right arm. Sarah was obeying his order, floating under his left arm and keeping out of the way of his kicks.

He knew it wasn't far to shore, but the crashing waves made it almost impossible to stay afloat. His strength was draining away as he fought the frigid water, but not much farther now, surely not much farther . . .

A wave shoved them into a rock. He managed to ward them both so they scraped one side of it rather than crashing full force. Sarah's breathing was harsh in his ear, but she didn't interfere as he continued doggedly toward land. He'd reached the numb place beyond fatigue where only blind tenacity kept him swimming.

He was vaguely aware that if he let go of Sarah, he'd be much more likely to survive, but the knowledge was irrelevant. Life would not be worth living if he survived at her expense.

The shore was closer now, the waves rougher. He managed, barely, to avoid a low-lying mass of rock with white spray shooting into the air, but as he pushed them away, they were caught by a fierce current. They were hurtling straight into a jagged pinnacle and it was Sarah who would smash directly into it.

No! He wrapped himself protectively around her, ducking his head to minimize the impact, but it wasn't enough. He crashed into the rock with the full force of the sea behind him, and the world splintered into pain and blackness.

"Rob! *Rob!*" A shuddering impact almost tore Sarah from Rob's embrace. His body slackened for long moments. Then he clumsily resumed paddling toward the shore.

Desperate to help, she kept her arm around him and kicked feebly until a giant wave caught hold of them and hurled them on. They crashed downward onto solid ground in the heart of a drowning wave, and she almost lost consciousness herself.

Then the water reversed and began dragging them back into the sea. Swearing, she dug the fingers of her free hand into the rough pebbles of the beach, keeping her other arm around Rob. She gulped air frantically when the wave retreated, then held tight as another wall of water engulfed them.

They had to get higher. In the calm between waves, she pushed to her knees and looked around. There was just enough light to show that they were on a narrow crescent beach with steep stone walls around them. Rob lay on her right, apparently unconscious and with a dark smear of blood oozing down his forehead.

"Rob, we have to move!" As another wave splashed over her, she shook him hard. "We have to get above the waterline. I'll try to help you, but I can't lift you alone. Another wave is coming. Try!"

As the wave swept in and pushed them higher, she pulled at Rob's shoulder to lift him up. He lurched to his hands and knees and struggled forward, holding her tight as the water pulled back. Again. Again. *Again.*

Finally they were above the crashing waves. They both folded onto the pebbled surface and panted for breath. Rob was dazed and silent, but at least he could move. The rain had finally ended and the sharp wind was clearing clouds from the moon.

Able to see better, Sarah scanned their surroundings, hoping they weren't trapped in this cove like rats in a barrel. Ah, a path angled up the rocky cliff face! If they could make it to the top, they should be able to find shelter. Though they had survived drowning, the cold and wild night could be just as lethal.

"Rob, there's a path up the cliff. If I help, can you climb?"

He didn't speak, but he struggled to his feet. She guided him to the bottom of the path. He still seemed barely aware, a result of being banged on the head when protecting her. She hoped his ability to understand her and move forward meant the damage wasn't too serious.

He began climbing, his right hand skimming the cliff wall for balance. The path was too narrow to walk side by side so Sarah followed, ready to steady him if he lost his balance, though that might mean they'd both fall since he was so much larger.

She was so tired and numb that she was half-way up the cliff before she realized that she was barefoot. The clawing waves had dragged off her socks. Yes, Rob was also barefoot. Her feet would be bruised and bleeding in the morning. She wouldn't mind, as long as she was *warm*.

After an endless interval of exhausted climbing, they reached the top of the cliff. Sarah folded onto the wiry sea grass and gasped for breath. She would never, *never* wish for adventure again.

Rob stayed upright, though he was weaving. She followed the direction of his gaze and saw not a cottage, but a looming Gothic castle straight out of Mrs. Radcliffe's alarming tales. But the building was close and lights were visible inside. Sanctuary. She sent up fervent thanks as she struggled to her feet again.

Moving to Rob's side, she draped his arm over her shoulders while she encircled his waist. "Shelter from the storm, Rob. Just a few steps more."

He mumbled what sounded suspiciously like a curse, but started walking toward the castle. Though perhaps stumbling was a more accurate description. Step, step, step, step. If she stopped moving, she'd never get going again.

They entered the castle grounds through a wide, open gate set in a ragged stone wall. The wall had been mined for stone over the centuries, but it still provided some protection from the wind.

Now that she was closer, she saw that the building wasn't a real castle, though it had turrets and towers. The underlying structure appeared to be a sprawling stone manor house that had been altered to look like a castle during the craze for all things Gothic. No matter, as long as someone was home to let them in.

The path led to the side of the faux castle and ended at a wide stone staircase leading up to a massive double door. Hoping there was a knocker, Sarah dragged herself up the half dozen steps. She wasn't sure who was supporting whom, but at least she and Rob were moving forward together.

There was indeed a knocker, a massive snarling beast so heavy that it took both of her hands to wield it. She bashed the ugly thing into the wooden door as hard as she could, which wasn't all that hard. But she heard its boom echoing inside.

No response. She hammered on the door again, wondering if it would open before she or Rob collapsed. He was still silent, his head bent and black-looking blood trickling down his face and neck.

The door creaked open and an immaculately dressed butler regarded them with disgust. "Beggars are not admitted to Kellington Castle." His gaze flicked to their bare feet. "Continue down the road to the village. There's a workhouse there."

Sarah stared at him. "We're not beggars! We survived a shipwreck and we desperately need shelter."

In answer, the butler started to close the door. Rob stepped through the doorway and pushed the servant out of the way before guiding Sarah inside. He slammed the door shut with a force that threatened to rock the stone walls. The entry hall had been decorated in a grand style several decades earlier with a double staircase sweeping down before them, but the chamber looked faded and worn now.

Rob scanned the hall. "Bloody *hell*."

With a small sigh like a punctured bellows, he slowly folded onto the cold marble floor and curled up on his side, unconscious. Alarmed, Sarah dropped to her knees and felt for a pulse in his neck. Yes, it was there and steady. He was just battered and exhausted.

Looking up at the scowling servant, she said, "For heaven's sake, bring something warm to drink and some blankets! Better yet, have him taken to a room where he can be cared for properly. Do you want a man dying in your hall because you refuse to help?"

Before the servant could reply, Sarah heard a tapping sound. She looked up to see a white-haired woman dressed all in black. With a cane in one hand and ramrod straight posture, she advanced down the left-hand stairs. From the richness of her dress and the arrogance of her expression, she was an aristocrat and part of the family that occupied this great pile of stone and history.

"What is all this clamor?" she snapped as she reached the bottom of the stairs and tapped her way across the room.

She stopped short by Rob, her expression appalled. Lifting her cane, she used the tip to shove Rob's shoulder hard so that he rolled onto his back.

With oozing blood and several days' growth of beard, he was a fearsome sight, but even so, the woman's reaction was extreme. "Robert," she said with acute distaste, "you're supposed to be dead."

What was *wrong* with these people? Invigorated by anger, Sarah scrambled to her feet. "You know him?"

"Oh, yes. This disreputable rogue is Robert Cassidy Carmichael. My grandson." The old woman's thin nostrils flared. "The Earl of Kellington."

Chapter 17

Sarah's jaw dropped. "Rob is the earl? What about his father and brother?"

The old woman, who had to be the Dowager Countess of Kellington, said flatly, "My son, the third earl, died three months ago of a fever. Edmund, his son and the fourth earl, died a fortnight ago in a London riding accident." She poked Rob in the ribs with the cane. "We've assumed Robert was dead, and good riddance."

The deaths explained her mourning gown. What were the odds of being wrecked on Rob's family estate? He'd said he knew the coast here, but this was ridiculous.

Kiri would call it karma. Remembering what Rob had told her, Sarah asked, "Wasn't Edmund married? Or did he leave no sons?"

The countess scowled. "He was betrothed some years ago, but the stupid girl jilted him. He'd recently become betrothed to a splendid and most suitable young woman. Edmund died three days before the wedding. Now the earldom falls to *him*."

She made to poke Rob in the ribs again. Furious, Sarah snatched the cane away and hurled it across the hall, not caring if the countess fell on her noble backside. "If Rob is indeed the new earl, he is now the owner of this moldering pile," she said through gritted teeth. "He is entitled to the respect and obedience of everyone in it." Her gaze snapped over to the butler. "You are all here on his sufferance."

The countess glared at Sarah. "Who are you to make threats here, you disgusting urchin?"

Sarah straightened to her full, if modest, height and returned the glare. "I am Miss Sarah Clarke-Townsend, sister of the Duchess of Ashton and niece to Lord Torrington and Lord Babcock."

As she let her words sink in, she realized that she needed more if she was to have any authority here. She'd have to lie. "Rob and I are betrothed. Since he is injured, I'll give the orders in his name."

The countess sputtered, unable to come up with a rejoinder. Sarah turned to the butler. "If you like being employed, collect some men to carry Lord Kellington to a decent room with clean sheets and a good fire. A similar room for me nearby. If you have a tub large enough for his lordship, draw a warm bath. At the least, heat water so he can be washed up. He was badly chilled saving our lives as we sailed from Ireland through the storm, so bring warm tea and broth."

The butler shot a nervous glance at the countess as he retrieved her cane and handed it over. The old woman growled, "I suppose you must obey the trollop's orders until the *earl*"—she almost spat the title—"recovers sufficiently to take charge. With luck, he'll succumb to lung fever."

She pivoted and marched from the room, heels and cane tapping her anger.

How could that horrible old woman be so hateful to her own grandson? Leaving the question for another day, Sarah turned to the butler. "Your name?"

"Hector," he said warily.

"Well, Hector, if you can have Lord Kellington safe and warm within the next ten minutes, I'll overlook your original treatment." She cocked a brow. "If that's unacceptable, I shall go through Kellington Castle until I find someone willing to do the job he's paid to do. Do I make myself clear?"

Resentful but polite, he said, "Yes, Miss Clarke-Townsend. I'll be right back with help to carry his lordship upstairs." He left the room at a near run.

Exhausted by the scene just enacted, Sarah crumpled down beside Rob and took his hand. His skin was warming up now that he was inside, and his pulse and breathing were strong and regular. She hoped he'd wake up *soon*. Presumably he was better able to deal with these lunatics than she was.

It took more than ten minutes, but Hector returned with two husky men garbed as grooms and carrying a litter. They appeared to have dressed in haste, but they looked strong and willing. The larger man, a redheaded fellow in his thirties, exclaimed, "Master Rob! It really is you!"

Rob didn't stir. The redhead looked worriedly at Sarah. "Is he hurt bad, miss?"

She rose wearily. "He's cold and battered and exhausted, but he managed to climb the path from the beach so I don't think he has serious injuries. You know him?"

"Aye." The redhead and his companion carefully moved Rob to the litter, then lifted the ends. "I'm Jonas, the head groom. When Master Robert was a lad, he spent half his time in the stables. I was starting out as a stable boy and assigned to care for his pony. We spent a good bit of time together, we did."

And they'd become friends, Sarah guessed, though the groom would probably think it presumptuous to claim friendship with the new earl. At least there was one man here who was glad to see Rob.

"Hector, lead the way to the earl's room," Sarah said. "Have you ordered the bath and broth?"

"Not yet, miss."

"Then it's time you did. After you show us the way to the bedroom," she said in a voice that brooked no argument.

Silently Hector led the way up the sweeping

staircase. Sarah held her breath, worried that Rob might fall from the tilted litter, but Jonas and his man were careful.

The hastily prepared bedroom was in the right wing of the house. It was an average guest room, not the master's quarters, but the bed had been made up and a fire was burning on the hearth.

As the grooms eased Rob onto the bed, Hector said, "I'll arrange the bath and hot broth, Miss Clarke-Townsend. It will take time for that much water to heat. Your room is across the corridor when you're ready to retire."

"Thank you." Sarah was reeling with fatigue, but felt that she needed to stand guard over Rob so his grandmother didn't slip poison in his tea.

When Hector was gone, Jonas said, "You're in a fair state yourself, miss. Why not go to your room and rest? I'll see that his lordship is properly taken care of." Seeing her hesitation, he said reassuringly, "I won't let any harm come to him."

He seemed trustworthy, and Sarah was in no condition to keep going. "Thank you, Mr. Jonas. I'll do that."

"Just Jonas, miss. I'll send one of the maids, Francie. She'll take good care of you." He glanced at his assistant. "Barney, find Francie and send her to the lady's room."

Barney nodded and held the door open for Sarah. She crossed the corridor to the similar room on the other side. It had also been made up and had a fire. At least Hector had got that right.

Too tired to do much of anything and too bedraggled to slip between the sheets, she flopped onto the bed, rolled herself in the quilted counterpane, and slept like the dead.

Sarah had a dim sense of being gently wakened, helped to undress, and deposited into a hip bath full of deliciously warm water. A mug of hot beef broth was pressed into her clasp. By the time she finished sipping the broth and the water had cooled, she was warmed to her bones.

The same kind hands helped Sarah from the tub, dried her, dropped an oversized nightgown over her head. Then once more blessed sleep.

Sarah woke abruptly, rested and full of energy. Her adventure didn't seem to have injured her. She slipped from the bed, wincing at the bruises and sore muscles she'd acquired. Her feet were particularly sore from climbing the cliff bare-foot. There were no serious gashes, though.

She opened the curtains to a clear dawn sky and the sight of rolling green hills. The storm had blown over, and it looked like the day would be lovely. They'd arrived at the castle in mid-evening, so she'd had a good long rest.

But what about Rob? He'd taken a much worse beating. Long nightgown dragging, she left her room and crossed to his. He was breathing peacefully under the covers. He'd also been cleaned up and he had a neat bandage around his head.

She pulled the curtains of both windows open to admit light. This room had a fine view of the sea. She moved to the bed and took his hand. "Rob? Are you awake?"

His eyes flickered open. "Sarah?" He touched the bandage on his head warily, but his speech was clear. "So we actually made it to England. Are you all right?"

She felt a rush of relief. "I'm fine. We're not only alive, but at Kellington Castle. The storm blew you home."

"Damnation! I thought I was dreaming. Or having a nightmare. What were the odds?" His eyes squeezed shut. "So I've landed in hell. You deserve better than the infernal regions."

"The odds were infinitesimal, but not impossible," she replied. "The storm was the infernal part. I'm grateful to have food and warmth and comfort."

He pushed himself up in the bed, wincing a little. Jonas hadn't shaved him the night before so he did look rather roguish. But he was a *handsome* rogue.

"I have an almighty number of bruises, but nothing seems broken," he said after taking inventory. "How did I end up wearing this expensive linen nightshirt?"

"I ordered the butler, Hector, to summon help and see you were cared for."

Before she could continue, Rob said thoughtfully, "Hector. He was a footman when I was a boy. A supercilious fool, if I remember correctly."

"That's him," Sarah agreed. "He brought two grooms to take you upstairs. I think he intended calling on them as an insult, but it worked out well. The head groom, Jonas, recognized you and was glad to see you alive."

"Jonas!" Rob's expression eased. "He was my companion in mischief. I'm surprised that he's still here. He used to talk about going for a soldier. Are my appalling father or brother present? With luck, they're in London at this season."

He'd heard nothing of the conversation the night before, she realized. "They're both dead, Rob," she said bluntly. "You're now the Earl of Kellington."

He became utterly still. "You're *joking*."

"Not that I know of. We staggered into this fake castle last night and an alarming old besom who claimed to be your grandmother said that your father died of a fever several months ago, and your brother died in a riding accident about a fortnight ago, leaving no legitimate heirs."

"Edmund never was as good a rider as he thought." Rob looked as if he'd been thrown from a horse himself. "He didn't manage to sire an heir?"

"He didn't even manage to acquire a wife. According to your grandmother, the girl from the famously fertile family jilted him, and he died just before marrying a different, very suitable female."

"I shudder to think what kind of female my grandmother would consider suitable," Rob muttered. "A harpy with a fortune and an excellent pedigree, I imagine."

"I was startled by your grandmother's attitude," Sarah said carefully. "I gather the two of you didn't get along?"

Rob shrugged. "She doted on Edmund, whose mother was another 'very suitable female.'" He caught his grandmother's intonation with wicked accuracy. "I was a reminder of my unsuitable mother. I suspect that marrying her was the only unsuitable thing my father ever did."

"Whatever the dowager might think about your mother's bloodlines, she'll have to adapt." Sarah made a sweeping gesture to encompass their surroundings. "All this is yours now."

Rob slid from the bed and walked to the window, his wide shoulders rigid under the expensive but short nightshirt. Sarah could see bruises on his legs and feet from their stormy passage the night before.

"Bloody hell," he said softly as he opened the casement window. A cool sea breeze entered the room. He locked his hands around the sill so hard that his knuckles whitened. "Bloody, *bloody* hell!"

Frowning, Sarah moved to join him at the window, close but not touching. "Is the prospect that bad?"

"Worse." A pulse beat in his throat. "Not only have I inherited a generation's worth of profligacy, debt, and neglect, but I've become what I despise. A damned *peer.*"

Sarah's brow furrowed. "You have a number of friends who are peers, don't you? I thought you liked and respected Ashton and Kirkland and your other classmates, many of whom have titles."

"Because they were all shipped off to the Westerfield Academy as misfits and eccentrics, like me. They are men who were early humbled by life, and became better for it." His mouth twisted. "They're not like my father and brother. Idle, useless wastrels who are the products of a corrupt system that deserves to be smashed."

She blinked, thinking she shouldn't be surprised that Rob was a radical, given his upbringing. "There are idle, useless wastrels at all levels of society. Peers just have more to waste. But not all are like that. My uncles who are lords are fine gentlemen. Is it the peerage you hate, or the fact you're now the Earl of Kellington?"

Rob thought about that. "I think the peerage is

an idea that has outlived its usefulness, but you're right. It's being Lord Kellington that I really loathe. I have a life that I like. I don't want the life I've just inherited."

"You really don't have a choice, though," Sarah said softly. "The peerage is fixed in your blood. You can walk away from your heritage and all the responsibilities that go with it, but I have trouble imagining you doing that. Think about people like Jonas and the other servants and tenants who are part of Kellington. They need a strong, fair, responsible master, which they haven't had in too long."

"I've no doubt they've been treated abominably for years," he said sourly.

"All the more reason for you to do the job better. Wouldn't that be the best revenge?" Sarah took his hand. "Perhaps the financial situation isn't as bad as you fear."

Rob squeezed her hand. "It's probably worse. But you're right, I can't walk away. I need to find out exactly how things stand. We also need to send word to your family that you're safe. They must be worried sick. I should take you to Ralston Abbey, but we both need a day of rest, and I might be needed more here."

She nodded. It seemed like ages since she'd been abducted, but it was less than a fortnight, and her family would be frantic. Her adventure was over. On the whole, that was a good thing. She glanced askance at Rob. But she'd miss him, she surely would.

He caught her gaze, and they stared at each other for long moments as memories of shared danger and companionship pulsed between them. Rob released her hand and took a step back. "It's time we remembered your reputation, starting with the fact that you should not be in my bedroom wearing a nightgown. If any of this gets out, you might end up having to marry me."

She winced. "I forgot to mention that last night, I told your grandmother and Hector that we were betrothed. I needed authority to give orders, and that seemed the simplest way. But don't worry, you're safe. I'll jilt you. There will be no breach of promise lawsuit. My persistent virginity is proof that you haven't debauched me."

He looked startled, then amused. "I could charge *you* with breach of promise if you've declared we're betrothed in front of witnesses. But if you return to your own room, we're both safe enough."

This was the end of their intimacy, she realized. Rob had just inherited a very public position. What he did would be watched and gossiped about. He'd hate that. Because he'd rescued her, she should make his new position as simple as possible. That meant a swift withdrawal from his presence and his life.

A lump in her throat, she stood on her toes and

put her arms around his neck. "Thank you, Rob, for everything. Beginning but not ending with my life and freedom." Then she kissed him.

She'd intended a quick, sincere good-bye kiss, but the instant their mouths touched, it became much more. Rob made a choked sound and pulled her into his arms, their bodies pressing together. In their nightclothes, only two layers of fabric separated them. She felt the heat and hardening desire of his body, the protective arms that had saved her again and again. The strong hands molding her body. She wanted to sink into him forever.

Suddenly she was cold and alone. Rob retreated several steps and swallowed hard. "Go, princess. Go *now*."

She pressed her fingers to her mouth, still feeling the heat and desire. Forcing herself to be calm, she lowered her hand. "I know you don't want this, Rob. But you will manage the responsibilities of Kellington well because you do everything well. Remember that when you feel overwhelmed."

Then she turned jerkily and left the room.

Rob's world had just become enormously complicated and stressful. She mustn't make the stress and complications even worse. She owed him too much for that.

Chapter 18

After Sarah slipped from the room, her expression masked, Rob closed his eyes and tried to sort out his chaotic thoughts. *Earl of Kellington.* A title and burden he'd never expected and didn't want.

Did it mean anything that after a dozen years avoiding the place like a leper colony, in the tempest he'd blindly headed home, like a pigeon returning to its nest? There were things he'd loved about Kellington when he was a boy.

And now it was his. He couldn't walk away from his duty, but where to start?

By getting dressed. It was hard to look authoritative when wearing a too-short nightshirt. Even dressing would be a challenge since the clothing he'd worn when he stumbled into the castle was in tatters and the rest of his modest wardrobe was in London.

But Jonas had looked after him the night before, and he'd always been the practical sort. Rob opened the wardrobe and found an outfit that looked like it would fit. The garments were for a man his height, though broader in build. Probably the clothing was from Jonas's own wardrobe since they were of similar height.

Before dressing, Rob washed up, then donned the linen shirt and buff breeches. He tried to avoid seeing himself in the mirror over the shaving stand, which showed why his grandmother thought him a rogue. His face was bruised and his hair was storm tossed and far too long. A few more days and he'd have a serious beard.

There was no razor, but he found a comb. He was trying to neaten his hair over the bandage when a knock sounded at the door. "It's Jonas," a familiar voice called.

Rob spun around. "Come in!"

The door opened, and Jonas entered. His red hair had darkened with time, but his round face and good-natured expression were instantly recognizable. "Good morning, my lord. Sorry to disturb you, but I wanted to see how you're faring after your shipwreck."

Rob crossed the room with one hand extended. "If you keep calling me 'my lord,' there's going to be trouble, Jonas!" As they shook hands, he clapped his friend on the shoulder. "Damn, but it's good to see you! The only good thing about Kellington. You look well. Did you marry your sweet Annie?"

"Aye." Jonas smiled. "Two children and a third on the way. There aren't so many horses on the estate as there used to be, but enough to keep me busy."

"Give my regards to Annie." Rob grinned. "I

never did understand what a girl so pretty saw in you."

Jonas laughed. "What she saw in me is none of your business!"

Rob's smile faded. "I still haven't recovered from the shock of learning that I'm the latest Lord Kellington."

"You didn't know?" Jonas asked, surprised. "I thought that if you were alive, you'd hear about it right away. You used to keep track of everything." He scowled. "Of course, there was no reason to think you were alive. You just vanished a dozen years ago. I thought you'd let me know that you were all right."

"You had a right to expect that," Rob said quietly. "But for a long time I was in no position to write and then I was in India for several years. I decided it was best for me to act as if my family didn't exist, so I avoided all news of them. That included death notices." Wanting to change the subject, Rob waved for Jonas to take a seat. "Thanks for finding me clothing. Did you lend me your Sunday best?"

Jonas nodded as he settled in a chair. " 'Twas the best I could find on short notice. I brought a razor. I hope you know how to use it, since I'd not make a good valet." He handed over a wooden box that contained shaving instruments.

"I wouldn't know what to do with a valet." Rob returned to the shaving stand and draped a towel around his neck, then lathered his face. "I owe you a new set of clothes, assuming the Kellington inheritance has enough money for that." He carefully removed a swath of whiskers. "How bad are matters on the estate?"

Jonas's humor vanished. "It's common knowledge that the estate is in a bad way. The outbuildings are falling to pieces and the tenants' properties have been neglected since your grandfather died. 'Twas said your brother wanted to break the entail so he could sell off some of the land, but he died before he could act on that."

Rob's grandfather must have been spinning in his grave over such heresy. "I presume the estate has a steward."

"Aye, a Kentish fellow named Buckley."

"A foreigner then," Rob observed, knowing that anyone from more than a dozen miles away was considered foreign. "What is he like? Honest? Capable?"

Jonas grimaced. "He's a fair hand at squeezing every farthing out of the estate. Whether he's honest I can't say. In the months after your father's death, your brother never once came to Kellington."

"He thought London was the center of the world. What about my grandmother? She had a house in Bath, didn't she?"

"Aye, but in recent years, she's been spending more time here. She's a fearsome old lady, but it was good to have at least one member of the family in residence."

Rob agreed. His grandmother had always despised him, but she had good sense, and wasn't as mad about fashion and gambling as her son and Edmund.

"I'll ride around the estate this morning to see how things look. Then I'll talk to Buckley. I presume the stables still have a couple of decent riding hacks?"

Jonas nodded. "Your father's horse isn't showy, but he's a sound beast with good manners. If your brother had taken Oakleaf to London, he'd probably still be alive. Word is that he had a high-strung, showy chestnut that threw him in traffic."

That was Edmund—choosing style over quality. If he'd been riding a steadier mount, Rob wouldn't be in this trouble now. "Sounds like Oakleaf will suit me. I'd like you to come along since you probably know the estate better than anyone."

"I'll do that. Will your intended be coming with us?" Jonas grinned. "Miss Clarke-Townsend is quite the fierce little lady. When I heard how she threw the dowager's cane across the front hall, I fair fell about laughing."

Rob turned and stared. "Sarah did *what?*"

"You collapsed in the front hall," Jonas explained. "Your gran heard the commotion and came down. When she recognized you, she started

191

poking you with her cane like you were a dead fish. About the third time she did it, your young lady grabbed the cane and threw it away, telling the dowager and Hector that as the new owner, you deserved respect and obedience." He shook his head. "Wish I'd seen it myself. A maid was watching from upstairs, and she made a round tale of it in the kitchen later."

Naturally the return of the long-missing and presumed dead heir would be the main topic of conversation in the servants' hall. Showing up with an apparent fiancée would send everyone below stairs wild. "I wish I'd seen that myself. Miss Clarke-Townsend is . . . quite remarkable."

"And as pretty as my Annie. Is her sister really a duchess?"

Rob nodded. "She has very high connections." But was quite remarkably down to earth when necessary. He finished shaving and wiped the last of the soap from his face. The bruises were even more visible now. "Miss Clarke-Townsend might wish to ride out with us, though she doesn't have a riding habit."

"I'll dust off a sidesaddle then."

Belatedly remembering what should have been his first task, Rob said, "I need to send messages to Sarah's family and to London. I'll write the letters after breakfast."

Which would delay his ride over the estate. Already he could feel the complications of his new life chewing at him. He pulled on the brown coat, then sat and tugged on the boots, which were surprisingly comfortable. "With luck, I'll be at the stables within the hour. Thank you for the information."

His friend nodded as he got to his feet. "I'll help any way I can, my lord."

Rob caught his gaze. "I need old friends who call me Rob. Can you bear it?"

Jonas gave a half smile. "Easier than remembering to call you 'my lord.' Thank God you're back and in charge, Rob. Kellington needs you."

Jonas's words were more weight on an already massive burden. Maybe Rob's unwanted inheritance would look more manageable after he'd eaten. Now that he thought about it, he hadn't had a proper meal in days. He liked bread and cheese, but he was ready for more variety.

He didn't remember entering Kellington Castle the night before, but as he headed down to the breakfast parlor, the house was eerily familiar. Tired and shabby, but otherwise unchanged. His father and brother hadn't cared enough about the house to make changes. They preferred to spend their money in town.

Once he reached the ground floor, he pivoted and headed to the breakfast parlor in the back of the house. Though it had been a dozen years since he'd set foot here, it was still his childhood home. Once he'd known every closet and chimney and servants' staircase. With his excellent memory, he probably still did.

Though the house wasn't wrecked, it was sad. Had it ever been happy? Yes, when his mother was alive. The best times were the summers at Kilvarra, the Kellington family estate in Ireland. Those days had ended when his mother died, a little before his eleventh birthday. She'd a sunny nature, and Rob and his father had adored her. Edmund didn't, but he was usually off at school, so it was easy to ignore him.

Rob wondered if this house would ever be happy again.

Halfway to the breakfast room, he was intercepted by a portly man with an easy smile and cold eyes. "Lord Kellington!" The man bowed. "We're all so glad to learn that you're alive and taking up your responsibilities as the new earl. Permit me to introduce myself."

"No need," Rob said coolly. "You'd be the steward, Mr. Buckley, I think?"

The steward looked momentarily off balance by Rob's knowledge. Recovering, he said, "Indeed I am, my lord. I imagine you'll wish to discuss the estate and its revenues. I'd be happy to meet with you now, if it's convenient."

"It's not convenient," Rob said shortly. "I'll have breakfast, then ride over the estate to get a sense of its condition. I'll see you this afternoon."

"I'll be happy to accompany you."

"Thank you, but I prefer to become reacquainted with Kellington on my own."

Buckley frowned, but bowed again. "As you wish, my lord. I'm at your service."

"Yes, you are." Rob was too hungry to be polite. "If you'll excuse me . . ."

He moved past Buckley and entered the breakfast room. There was no sign of food or place settings. The room looked as if it hadn't been used in years. He gritted his teeth with irritation. Wasn't there anyone in the kitchen who realized that the new owner might like to be fed? He'd have to head down to the kitchen; surely there would be food there, even if he had to cook it himself.

His thoughts were interrupted by the opening of the door on the opposite side of the room. Sarah swept in, wearing a simple gown the shade of Devonshire cream and with her hair tied back to cascade over her shoulders in shining blond waves. She was so beautiful that all he could do was stare.

"Rob!" She gave a smile that lit up the room. "I'm glad to see you looking so well after our shipwreck."

He felt as if the sun had emerged from behind storm clouds. "The feeling is mutual. You look splendid."

"One of the maids, Francie, took me in hand."

Sarah indicated her dress. "She even basted a quick hem in this gown so it wouldn't drag on the floor." She turned to the servants entering the room behind her. "Hector, please put the covered dishes on the sideboard. Mary, the tea tray should go there also. We'll serve ourselves this morning. I'll consult with Lord Kellington about his preferences for the future."

"Yes, Miss Clarke-Townsend." Hector deftly laid out half a dozen covered dishes on the sideboard, set the table for two, then followed the kitchen maid out.

Rob lifted the cover from the nearest dish. Delicious-smelling golden sausages. He lifted two more covers. Eggs scrambled with herbs under one, potatoes cooked with onions under the other. "What magic have you worked?"

Sarah laughed. "No magic. The servants didn't know what was expected of them, so I went down to the kitchen and explained."

His brows arched. "That had to be more complicated than it sounds."

"My mother ran her brother's sizable household, so I learned how it's done. She said one must always be polite and respectful to servants, but make it clear that the only imaginable outcome is for them to do as they're ordered." Sarah took a plate and headed toward the sideboard. "I'm starved, and you must be downright ravenous! This is the first proper meal we've had in ages."

"A fact of which I'm very aware!"

After they'd filled their plates and Sarah had poured them tea, they settled on opposite sides of the table and ate like polite wolves. Rob couldn't remember a meal he'd appreciated more. It didn't hurt that Sarah was opposite him, looking beautiful and eating with refreshing gusto.

As Rob rose to get seconds, Sarah said, "When you entered the breakfast parlor, my first thought was how lordly you looked. Decent clothes and a shave make a remarkable difference, and you've certainly mastered the air of authority."

"Credit for my appearance goes to Jonas, who lent me clothing and a razor." Rob filled his plate again. "As for the authority, just before I reached the breakfast room, I was intercepted by Mr. Buckley, the steward. He was keen to speak to me as soon as possible. I was hungry and snappish, which must be why I arrived looking lordly."

Sarah laughed. "Testiness isn't required. What are your plans for the day?"

"Finish breakfast. Write to Ashton and my man Harvey in London. Do you want to send a message to your sister along with my letter?"

"Oh, yes." Sarah topped up their teacups. "Who is your man Harvey? A valet?"

Rob paused, his fork in the air, as he thought. "His position is hard to define. He's my friend and assistant in my duties as a Bow Street Runner.

He runs my very modest establishment, but he's no valet."

"He sounds useful. Are you going to summon him to Kellington?"

"Yes, but I'm not sure he'll come. He's a Londoner to the bone."

"I hope to get a chance to meet him." Sarah spread pear preserves on her toast. "I wonder what Buckley wants to hide. His pressing desire to get your ear before anyone else sounds a little suspicious."

"That remark is cynical but probably correct," Rob said. "Which is why first I'll ride the estate without his telling me what to think. Jonas is coming. Will you join us?"

"I'd like that. I'll see if Francie can find me a riding habit that comes somewhere close to fitting." Sarah grinned mischievously. "If that's not available, a boy's outfit so I can scandalize Kellington Castle by riding astride."

Her intimate glance made him smile. She'd looked delightful in her breeches when they were haring across Ireland. She was the most intrepid female. . . .

The door opened and his grandmother marched in looking ready to join battle. Rob got to his feet, thinking that being unconscious the night before had at least spared him from having to talk to her. "Good morning, ma'am. I'm glad to see that you're in good health." A cool greeting for a grandmother he hadn't seen in a dozen years, but the best he could manage given that she'd jabbed him with her cane as if he were a dead fish.

The dowager halted, her gaze sharp as she scanned him from head to foot. He stood rigid. She'd terrified him when he was a child; he discovered that age, experience, and a newly inherited peerage didn't entirely eliminate that. A good thing he'd shaved.

"You're less of a disgrace than last night, but you need to dress like a gentleman even if you aren't one," she snapped. "I'll summon a tailor from London since you certainly can't be seen in public without a new wardrobe. Full mourning, of course."

Rob's youthful fear dissipated in a rush of pure rage, but before he could explode, Sarah stood and said brightly, "Good morning, Lady Kellington. I apologize for not being properly turned out, but since we arrived here with only the clothes on our backs, we must be grateful for the kindness of your staff in outfitting us. Being shipwrecked was an interesting experience, but not one I care to repeat."

Tirade interrupted, the dowager glared at her. Sarah smiled with unshakable sweetness. "Would you care for a cup of tea, Lady Kellington?"

After a moment of bafflement because Sarah wasn't cowed, the countess said testily, "Tea would be welcome. Milk and a heaping spoon of sugar."

Since his grandmother intended to stay, Rob pulled out a chair for her, then resumed his own seat. He hadn't finished his breakfast, and he'd be damned if he'd let her ruin his appetite.

Sarah set the cup of prepared tea in front of the dowager, then topped up the other two cups without being asked. The old woman sipped at her tea and seemed disappointed to find nothing to complain about. "You'll need to speak to Buckley, the steward, and send a letter to our solicitors in London. They've been dealing with your cousin George, who assumed that the title had come to him."

"The sooner he knows otherwise, the better," Rob said coolly as he tried to remember his cousin. Another elegant wastrel, if he remembered correctly. A pity he couldn't hand the whole inheritance over to George, but inheritance and entail didn't allow that. "I assume the family solicitors are still Booth and Harlow?"

She looked surprised that he knew. "Old Caleb Booth died several years ago, so his son Nicholas now handles our affairs. He's young, but capable."

By Rob's estimate young Nicholas Booth would never see forty again, but he'd do for now. If the lawyers approved of the way his father and brother had exploited the estate, he'd have to look around for a new firm. "I'll write Booth after breakfast. Then I'll ride out with Jonas and Miss Clarke-Townsend to survey the estate."

His grandmother's mouth pursed. "I assume you'll take Mr. Buckley with you."

"No, I'll meet with him later."

"What have you been doing all these years?" she asked abruptly. "Some low occupation to keep you from starving, I assume. I hope it was nothing criminal."

"My occupation is indeed criminal," Rob said. As his grandmother's jaw dropped, he said, "I'm a Bow Street Runner. A thief taker and solver of problems." He got to his feet. "If you'll excuse me, I need to write Ashton and Booth."

Sarah stood. "I'll join you and write to my sister. Until later, Lady Kellington."

As his grandmother stared in shock, they made their escape. Once they were clear of the breakfast parlor, Rob guided his fictitious fiancée to the left. "My father's study is at the end of this wing. I presume we can find pen and paper and sealing wax there."

Sarah took his arm as they headed down the corridor. "It must be strange to be back here after so many years."

"Very," he agreed. "Not sentimental strange in a way that makes me weep for my lost youth and family. Just . . . strange." After a half dozen more steps, he added, "I know I should be mourning my father and brother, but I feel no grief." His smile was twisted. "Perhaps there really is something fundamentally wrong with me, as I was always told."

"Nonsense," Sarah said briskly. "Would you have mourned if you'd just learned Jonas had died while you were away?"

He frowned. "Of course. We're friends."

"While your father and brother were not your friends. I see no reason to go into mourning for two men who treated you abominably."

Rob blinked as he ushered Sarah into the study. "For a well-brought-up young lady, you have some radical thoughts."

"I just dislike hypocrisy. Your brother sold you to a press gang, for heaven's sake! You're entitled to celebrate his departure from this mortal coil."

"I find that a very soothing thought." He surveyed the small room, which was dark and shabby. There was a double desk, several chairs, and not much else.

"Not a cheerful spot," Sarah observed. "Did your father spend much time here?"

"I'm not sure. My only visits were to be dressed down and told why I wasn't worthy of my noble name."

"Charming." Sarah opened a drawer on one side of the desk. "Pen, paper, and ink, as you said. Plus a small notebook and some pencils. But this study will need work if you want to use it regularly."

"What an appalling prospect," he murmured.

Seeing his expression, Sarah said, "You can

choose a different study. A house this size must surely have more pleasant rooms."

"That's a good idea. I always liked the library. It's sunny and has a fine view of the sea. Perhaps I'll set up an office in one end."

"You're an earl now," Sarah said. "Since there are plenty of disadvantages, you might as well enjoy the pluses, such as working in the library if you like."

His mouth quirked. "It will take time to get used to that idea after being on my own and keeping life simple for so long."

She smiled as she settled on her side of the desk. "I promise you'll adapt, and find much that you like about your new position."

As he sat on the opposite side of the desk, he hoped glumly that she was right.

Chapter 19

"Francie, can you find me a riding habit that more or less fits?" Sarah asked when she tracked the maid down. "If not, a boy's outfit so I can ride with Lord Kellington."

Brown-haired and bright-eyed, Francie was about Sarah's age, and a cousin of Jonas. Looking mildly scandalized, she said, "I can find a habit, though it will be old and oversized. You should not meet the tenants for the first time dressed as a boy!"

The first time would be the last time because in a few days Sarah would be gone, but she didn't argue the point. "I'll be delighted with any habit you can locate, Francie. Will you act as my lady's maid as long as I'm here? I need a miracle worker!"

Francie laughed. "With pleasure, miss. Come up to the attics with me. I know just where to look." She turned and headed toward the attic stairs.

Sarah followed, grateful that Jonas had enlisted her help. Like her cousin, Francie was good natured and capable. And, it appeared, during boring moments in her time as a servant, she had explored the attics and had a good idea of what was stored there.

Once they'd reached the second attic, Francie headed unerringly to a dusty trunk and dragged it over by a small window. "Here, if I recall correctly."

She lifted the lid and pulled out masses of green velvet. As she shook it out and held it up for inspection, she said, "Old but in good shape, and not too far off your size."

"Francie, you're a genius!" Sarah said fervently. "Are there any riding boots down there?"

"Yes, though they're rather battered." Francie handed the habit to Sarah, then dug in the trunk again. "Here's the matching bonnet. Ah, boots. Will these do?"

Sarah judged the size. "A bit large, but they're better than no boots at all. Now to get dressed. Lord Kellington will be impatient to look over the estate."

As they headed for the steps, Sarah decided this was a good time for some questions. "What do the people here think about the new earl?"

"It's a shock, miss, what with everyone assuming he was dead," Francie replied. "Some folk, like my cousin Jonas, knew him when he was a boy and they're glad to see him alive and the succession settled."

When Francie seemed unlikely to say more, Sarah said, "You said that was 'some folk.' What about the others?"

When Francie hesitated, Sarah said, "Please,

Lord Kellington won't punish people for what they're thinking, but he needs to know what he's facing here."

They'd arrived at Sarah's room, so Francie held the door open for her. Once it was closed behind them, she said reluctantly, "The late earls, his father and brother, always spoke badly of him. They said Master Rob was a thief who stole from his family and an incorrigible rogue with no sense of what was proper. Good riddance to him."

Sarah nodded grimly as she kicked her slippers off, then turned so Francie could unfasten the back of her gown. "I rather expected that. If the opportunity presents itself, you might suggest people give him a chance. They'll be pleasantly surprised."

"Jonas said Master Rob was fair and honorable to a fault." Francie lifted off Sarah's gown, then dropped the riding habit over her head. "Cousin George Carmichael, the one they thought was the heir, visited once. Every maid in the house learned to step lively around him if she didn't want to end up with a black and blue backside."

"He sounds dreadful." Since Francie had finished lacing the gown, Sarah sat on the chair and tugged on the riding boots. They were loose but adequate.

"Not only a pincher, but he never showed a lick of interest in the estate, either." Francie smoothed out the green velvet. "The skirt is too long so walk carefully, but that won't matter once you're mounted, and the color is fine on you."

Sarah turned and scanned her image in the mirror. The green was indeed a fine shade for her. Her appearance was fairly decent for an urchin in borrowed clothing. She donned the wide-brimmed bonnet after removing a crushed nosegay of silk flowers and turned to leave the room. "I look forward to seeing the estate."

"It's not in good shape, miss," Francie said with a sigh.

"All the more reason to see it." Sarah caught up the skirt in front and headed for the stairs. She quite liked the sweeping staircases. Any woman would feel lovely and romantic floating down the steps.

Especially if a handsome man was waiting at the bottom and watching with a stunned expression. "Is this really the hard-riding tomboy who crossed Ireland with me?" Rob asked in amazement.

She laughed. "Clothing really makes a difference, doesn't it? Francie, who's a cousin of Jonas, conjured this from the attic."

Rob offered his arm. "She was younger than we were, but I remember she was a pretty little thing. I'm glad she's able to help you so much."

Sarah took his arm, holding up her skirts with the other hand since otherwise she'd trip and ruin the illusion of ladylike elegance. Jonas was waiting for them in the barn with saddled horses.

When a gentleman helped a lady up onto her horse, it was a traditional opportunity to flirt. Today, there were too many serious issues to allow room for playfulness. But as Sarah placed her foot into Rob's linked hands, she was disconcertingly aware of his nearness and his strength.

After she settled into her sidesaddle, she showed him the notebook and pencil she'd brought. "I'm prepared to take notes and make myself useful."

Rob grinned. "Why do I have the feeling that besides learning housekeeping at your mother's knee, you learned estate management at your uncle's side?"

"Because you're perceptive," she said with a laugh. "I was always tagging behind Uncle Peter and often acted as his secretary. I learned to keep the books, too."

"I may need to hire you." Rob mounted and the three of them rode out of the stable yard. "I learned very little about estate management from growing up here because I never expected to inherit. My interests were elsewhere."

"I'm glad one was tracking down abducted females!" Being mounted gave Sarah a good view of the grounds. "Is that a real castle down there on the edge of the cliff?"

"Yes, it's the original Kellington Castle, though

as you see, it's mostly ruins. It dates from Norman times. The present house was built for comfort and the castle was abandoned, but it was a wonderful place to play, full of rooms and tunnels." Switching topics, Rob said, "Which tenant farm will we visit first?"

"Oaklea. The tenant now is Rupert White," Jonas replied. "He took possession after you left."

Sarah's lightheartedness faded as they rode to Oaklea. She'd been raised on an estate that glowed with care and concern. Kellington displayed none of that.

Fields needed better drainage, the stock needed improvement. Putting Kellington to rights would be a huge job. Huge and expensive.

As they approached Oaklea farm, the tenant saw the three of them riding in and he came out to greet them, his expression wary. "Good morning, Mr. White," Jonas said as they halted their horses. "You may have heard the new earl is here, and he's wishful of meeting his tenants."

White scowled. "I heard. Also that he's a thief and a wastrel. Not much point in coming around here, your bloody lordship. Your father and brother already took everything of value."

Sarah gasped at his rudeness. He sounded like a man with nothing left to lose.

Rob said mildly, "I gave up thieving to become a Bow Street Runner. I'm coming around now to get acquainted and ask what needs to be done at Oaklea."

"Everything!" White spat out. "The roof needs repairing. Need a new barn and a well, too. I fix what I can, but I can't handle everything. I thought I was lucky to be given the tenancy of Oaklea, but it's the worst decision I ever made." Seeing Sarah writing, he asked suspiciously, "What's she doing?"

"Miss Clarke-Townsend is acting as my secretary," Rob explained. "There is much to be done. The first step is to find out what's needed."

"You're really going to order repairs?" the tenant scoffed. "I'll believe that when I see it."

Jonas, who had been silent till now, said, "At least you're seeing the earl in person. When's the last time that happened?"

"Never," White allowed. "But maybe he's just come around to count the silver so he can take that."

Rob said, "One last question. Has Mr. Buckley dealt with you as he should?"

"Buckley!" White spat, then spun on his heel and stalked back into his house.

"I think that answers that," Rob said dryly. "Time to head to the next farm."

As they rode away, Jonas remarked, "You've learned to control that temper of yours, I see."

"A Bow Street Runner attracts insults and

verbal abuse," Rob explained. "One becomes accustomed."

That surprised a laugh from Sarah. "Training for your current position! If you like, I can point that out to your grandmother if she criticizes your former occupation."

"Tempting," Rob said with a half smile. "But it would be bad form to cause her to fall into a frothing fit. What's the next farm, Jonas?"

That was the last levity of the estate tour. A few tenants remembered Rob and were glad he was alive, and none were as rude as White. But all were angry and without hope. Sarah didn't blame them. The previous Lords Kellington had not fulfilled their landlordly obligations.

Sarah knew that Rob would if he could. But that was the crucial question. Would there be enough money to do all that needed to be done? Sarah was afraid of the answer.

The estate was vast, and they didn't finish visiting the tenant farms until well after noon. Rob remained patient and thoughtful, and Sarah filled over half the notebook with lists of things to be done, broken down into urgent, less urgent, and useful but not vital.

After they visited each tenant, all three of them discussed what they'd seen, with Rob encouraging Sarah and Jonas to give their opinions. Rob listened intently. Sarah could almost see the gears spinning in his mind as he learned.

They had a hot cheese pie and ale at Jonas's house. Sarah suspected that was because there was no other home on the estate where they could be sure of a warm welcome. His wife, Annie, was pretty and pregnant, the two toddlers were adorable, and it was clearly a happy house.

But Sarah was aware that the foundation of the home was Jonas's position as head groom with a decent, regular salary. If the debts of Rob's father and brother destroyed the estate, Jonas's family and everyone else who lived on the Kellington property would be affected. And that didn't count what other properties might be part of the Kellington inheritance. She silently damned Rob's relations for their selfishness.

By midafternoon, the three of them were tired and subdued. As they left a small farm called Hilltop, Rob asked, "That's the last of the tenant farms, isn't it? Is it my imagination, or are properties increasingly run down as they get farther from the castle?"

" 'Tis not your imagination. My guess is that Buckley knew the former earls weren't likely to ride very far to see how their tenants fared." Jonas nodded toward the rugged hills rising to the east. "Do you want to visit the shepherds in the high country?"

"They'd be hard to locate, and it's not really

212

necessary." Rob gathered his reins. "It's time we headed back."

Jonas nodded and turned toward the castle, but Rob lingered, his gaze on the hills. Sarah drew her horse up beside his. "Are you thinking of Bryony?" she asked quietly.

"You notice too much." He swallowed hard. "She lived in the hills. I met her when I was riding up there one day. Being here reminds me of all the times I'd ride up to meet her. How much we enjoyed being together."

Sarah remembered how Rob had described his first love: black haired and beautiful, wild and free. Such a girl might have made a spirited, resilient army wife if Rob had become an officer. That life had been stolen from them. "You can look for Bryony. She probably lives in this area still."

"No," Rob said softly. "That time is gone."

He wheeled his horse around and rode away.

Aching for those two vanished young people, Sarah cast a last look at the hills, then headed back to the shabby faux castle by the sea.

Chapter 20

The sky was darkening by the time Rob and his companions reached the stables. As Rob dismounted, Jonas said, "I'll take care of the horses if you want to talk to Buckley now."

"Are you hoping I'll wring his neck for not doing his job?"

Jonas considered, then nodded. "Yes."

Rob helped Sarah from her mount. "And people think that *I'm* bloodthirsty. Sarah, may I have your notebook for ammunition?"

"I want to go with you," Sarah said as she handed him the notebook. "Since I've had some experience with estate management, perhaps I'll be useful."

"If you're not too tired, I'd like that." He'd like it a lot. He was over his head in this business, and having a knowledgeable woman at his side was comforting. "I need all the help I can get."

The steward's office was a small building set at right angles to the stables. Sarah caught up her voluminous skirts and took Rob's arm. In the green velvet, she looked deliciously pretty and useless. Like a fluffy golden chick, in fact.

"You're my secret weapon," Rob said as he led

her across the yard. "Don't hesitate to speak up if you feel it's needed."

Sarah grinned. "You know I won't hesitate. While you're talking to Buckley, I'll drift around his office and see if I find anything interesting."

"You have the instincts of a spy or a Runner." He smiled down at her. "I like that in a woman."

She blushed adorably. He was amused to see how her expression changed when they reached the steward's office. All signs of intelligence vanished. She looked cheerful and rather vacant. Not like an expert in anything except perhaps fashion.

Rob knocked and Buckley bade him enter. Before walking inside, Rob schooled his face to his best intimidating Runner expression. He wouldn't have to say a word to make the steward nervous.

As they entered the office, he noted that it was expensively furnished, more like a lord's library than a steward's work area. A handsome Oriental carpet lay in front of the mahogany desk, framed oil paintings and maps adorned the walls, and the wall behind the desk consisted of a built-in bookcase and cabinet, also in mahogany. The furnishings would have cost more than the complete contents of Rob's spacious flat in London.

Buckley rose and bowed as Rob entered with Sarah on his arm. "Welcome, Lord Kellington!

I've been waiting for you. I assume this charming lady is your fiancée?"

Sarah gave a dazzling smile. "Indeed I am. This is all so exciting!"

Buckley cast an admiring glance over her shapely figure, dismissed her as a brainless bit of fluff, and focused on Rob. "Would you like sherry or claret, my lord?"

"No, thank you, but I'll have a seat." He guided Sarah to one of the chairs facing the desk and settled in the chair beside her. "The estate and tenant farms are in a deplorable state. You must know that." Rob held up Sarah's notebook. "I have listings of the most urgent needs. Pray explain why this has been allowed to happen."

Buckley froze like a rabbit confronted by a fox as he struggled for an answer to such a blunt question. He settled on passing the blame. "I was following the orders of your father, and then during his brief ownership, your brother. Both were concerned with generating the maximum possible revenue from the estate, and they had no interest in investing unnecessary capital."

"Repairing roofs so Kellington tenants don't die of lung fever is not what I'd call 'unnecessary,' " Rob said, an edge to his voice. "Not only are the tenant farmhouses falling to pieces, but the fencing has been badly neglected and drains have fallen into disrepair." He slapped the notebook onto the desk. "It's a disgrace!"

"I've done what I could!" Buckley said defensively. "But I couldn't refuse your father's direct orders!"

"A good steward should have been able to convince the old earl of the dangers of grabbing short-term profits while destroying long-term revenues." Based on the comments Jonas and Sarah had made, Rob was able to sound much more knowledgeable than he actually was. Buckley began to sweat.

Sarah rose from her chair and drifted around the office as if bored. But she paid sharp attention to everything she examined, and after a few minutes pulled a ledger from the bookcase behind Buckley.

She leafed through quickly and silently, her brows arching at what she found. When she reached the end, she opened the doors to the ceiling-high cabinet. Inside were record boxes and a strongbox on the bottom shelf.

Hearing her, Buckley turned and asked suspiciously, "Are you looking for something in particular, Miss Clarke-Townsend?"

"I was hoping to find a novel or two, but these books seem to be boring volumes of agriculture and the like," she said, batting her lashes shamelessly.

"This is my place of business," he said tersely. "If you're looking for amusement, you might enjoy the book of English county maps on the top shelf of the bookcase."

"Oh, yes, that would be delightful!" Her expression was vacuous but pleased.

Rob half expected Buckley to see through Sarah's act, but he didn't. Instead, he turned back to Rob and gave an unconvincing explanation about why so much timber had been cut.

Rob continued to ask questions until Sarah turned with a ledger in her hands and gave him a satisfied nod. Clearly she'd found something interesting.

Frowning, Rob cut Buckley off in the middle of a sentence. "Considering how badly you've run the estate, I see no reason why I should retain your services."

Buckley's face paled. "My lord, that's unfair! I'm a very good steward! I've managed Kellington according to your father's orders. After his death your brother told me to continue your father's policies. If you wish to improve the estate, I will do so gladly. After the difficulties of serving the late earls, I would welcome the chance to do my job properly." He leaned forward over the desk, his expression intense. "You owe me a chance to prove myself!"

Rob hesitated. He didn't particularly like Buckley, but it was true that if the steward had been ordered to squeeze the estate, he would have had to obey or resign, and another such position would be hard to come by. Based on the quality of his clothing and the furnishings of his office, Buckley had been paid well, and it was understandable that he wouldn't want to give the position up.

Sarah spoke up for the first time, peering over the heavy ledger. "You don't owe Mr. Buckley anything, Rob. In fact, I'd say he owes you a good deal. He's been skimming off a substantial percentage of the estate income. At least fifteen percent, perhaps more. Discharge him. Better yet, charge him with embezzlement."

The steward gasped and spun around in his chair, his face white. "That's utter nonsense! You can't discharge me based on the word of an inexperienced girl."

Sarah smiled like a petite gold angel. An avenging angel. "The official ledger lists ridiculously high prices for everything from stock to equipment. You record purchases of first-rate breeding bulls and English Leicester rams from Coke of Norfolk himself but I see no signs of their bloodlines in the herds."

"What does an unmarried girl know about breeding?" he sputtered. "Such things take time. The improved stock may not show up for years."

"You've *had* years," she said coolly. "The first alleged purchases were ten years ago. You must have had singularly bad luck with your studs, since you list replacements every year since. *Expensive* replacements."

"We . . . we have had bad luck," he said

defensively. "The tenants are a surly lot, not cooperating with my instructions to improve productivity."

Rob was beginning to enjoy himself. "Really? They all seem to feel that you've ignored their requests and flatly refused to make even the most modest improvements. What else did you find, Sarah?"

She shelved the ledger and lifted a thin, drab volume. "This book's title, *Sermons for a Sinful Soul at the End of Life*, should guarantee that no one will ever pick it up. But it turns out to contain not sermons, but a very interesting set of—let's call them auxiliary figures." She opened the volume and glanced inside. "Mr. Buckley, you appear to have defrauded the Kellington estate of over five thousand pounds."

Rob's brows shot up. It was a very substantial sum. Not enough to fix everything that needed fixing on the estate, but enough for a good start.

And Buckley had been stealing that money while tenants' houses were leaking icy winter rains. "I'll have you charged and thrown in jail, Buckley," he said with cold fury. "If you're lucky, you'll be transported instead of hanged. Sarah, is there any indication of where he's stashed his ill-gotten gains?"

"That's not clear, but I haven't had long to search," she said apologetically. "My guess is that he's keeping it close so he can carry the money off if his crimes are detected. You felt safe, didn't you, Mr. Buckley? The earls you served never looked at your work in detail as long as they received quarterly funds for their vices."

Pure panic in his eyes, the steward bolted for the door. Rob caught him easily. As he twisted Buckley's arm behind his back, he snapped, "Don't try to escape a Bow Street Runner! You won't succeed, and it irritates the Runner."

All the fight went out of his captive. "Please!" the steward said raggedly. "I *am* a good steward, that's why I was hired in the first place. But your father didn't want me to tend the estate. All he wanted was every bloody penny I could squeeze out. He never checked my work, so . . . I couldn't resist the temptation to secure my own future."

Rob shoved Buckley into a chair, then scanned the secret account book Sarah handed him. Page after page of meticulous numbers recorded how much Buckley had siphoned from Kellington each month. He probably was a good steward, or he wouldn't have kept such detailed records of his crimes. "Obviously you were tempted a great deal. Where's the money, Buckley? Produce it and I might not press for you to be hanged."

"Some of it has been spent, but as Miss Clarke-Townsend guessed, the rest is nearby," Buckley said with desperation. "I'll show you where if you let me go free."

Rob's mouth tightened. "These are not small

crimes, Buckley. I've spent years putting lesser criminals in jail. Why should I release a man who has damaged everyone at Kellington?"

"I have a wife and children. What will become of them if I'm hanged?" His shoulders were shaking. "They . . . they won't believe I could behave so badly."

Rob found himself feeling some sympathy. Buckley's concern for his family seemed genuine, and they were apparently innocent of his crimes. But the crimes were indeed considerable.

"He has a point, Rob," Sarah observed. "I don't think Mr. Buckley is an evil man. Just weak and lacking in character. If he'd been properly supervised by your father, he'd probably have done his job capably and not succumbed to temptation."

"No question about the weak character," Rob said tartly. "What do you suggest I do with him?"

"Retrieve the money and let him and his family go with a hundred pounds or so to support them until he finds a position elsewhere." Her smile was satiric. "One in which he will not face temptation."

Rob thought about it. He didn't want Buckley's family on his conscience, and it was true that his father's neglect had created a situation that allowed the steward's weaknesses to flourish. It was also true that the money embezzled from the estate would now be available for improvements.

If Buckley had been honest, that money would have been spent by the late earls.

Coming to a decision, he said, "Very well, Buckley. Produce the money. When I have it, go home and tell your family to start packing. I want you gone tomorrow. I will allow you the use of an estate wagon to take your family and goods to a larger town. You will have a hundred pounds to live on, as Miss Clarke-Townsend suggested. I will watch you in the future. If I discover you embezzling somewhere else, I will be forced to take more severe steps. Do I make myself clear?"

"You do." Buckley's mouth twisted. "I swear I won't steal again. I can't bear the consequences."

Rob studied the man's face, then nodded. Buckley wasn't a confirmed criminal, so fear of consequences should keep him honest in the future. "Where is the money?"

"Right here in this room." The steward turned and knelt in front of the built-in bookcase behind his desk. A six-inch-wide board ran below the bottom shelf. He stretched his arms and pressed a spot at each end. The baseboard fell forward.

Inside the space were four long, narrow wooden boxes. Buckley lifted them onto the desk. The last was noticeably heavier. He opened the boxes. The first three packed with banknotes. The fourth contained solid rows of golden coins.

"Heavens!" Sarah exclaimed. "I've never seen

so many guineas at once in my life. With gold scarce, I believe a gold guinea is worth twenty-six or twenty-seven shillings instead of twenty-one."

Which meant that Buckley's treasury was worth more than the face value. Rob estimated the number of coins in the box. About a thousand. More money than most people would see in a lifetime. "Sarah, will you help me count?"

"With pleasure!"

With the two of them counting, it didn't take long to confirm that there was close to five thousand pounds in cash. Rob counted out a hundred pounds in banknotes and handed them to Buckley. "Give me the keys to this office."

The steward tucked the banknotes in an inside pocket, then opened a desk drawer and removed a key ring with several keys. "Here are the keys to this office, plus a spare set for the steward's house. I have another set of office keys there."

"Give them to Jonas," Rob ordered. "Then tell your family to start packing. Don't try to take any of the furnishings that were in the house when you moved in. I have a good memory of what was there. Is there anything in this office that is really yours, not owned by the estate or bought with stolen money?"

Buckley's gaze scanned the room and halted. "That watercolor. It's my wife's work. She gave it to me as a wedding present."

It was an undistinguished picture, so Buckley was probably telling the truth. "Take it. If your wife wants to know why you've been discharged so abruptly, tell her that the new earl is an ill-mannered boor who doesn't want to keep on his father's steward. It's true, after all."

"But—a kinder reason than the whole truth. Thank you," Buckley said quietly as he lifted the picture from the wall. "You're a better man than your father or brother."

Rob had no idea how to reply to that, but Sarah said briskly, "That's certainly true, Mr. Buckley. Now go forth and sin no more."

Buckley jerked a short nod and left. Sarah exhaled as she folded into a chair. "That was interesting!"

"Indeed. Thank you for giving me the ammunition I needed." Rob felt a pang of guilt when he saw how tired she was. "Do you mind keeping an eye on this office while I take the money to the house? I doubt Buckley will return, but if he does, one look at you and he'll depart in haste."

"He'll not cause any more trouble," she said confidently.

Rob removed the strongbox from the cabinet and emptied the contents, then placed the boxes of embezzled money inside. "Good that it's not all gold, or I might not be able to lift this."

"Five thousand pounds will make a huge

amount of difference to the tenants." Sarah wearily brushed back a strand of bright hair. "Assuming the money goes to farm improvement. There are surely other debts."

Rob grimaced as he buckled the strongbox shut. "Within the week, I imagine the Kellington lawyer will send me a list of them. But I can't think of anything that's more important than improving the tenant farms. They generate the revenue, after all. Because it's spring, the improvements can take effect this year."

"Make sure you buy some of Coke of Norfolk's breeding rams," she said with a glint in her eye. "They really are the best."

"I will," he promised. "After I stash this in the house and ask Jonas to supervise Buckley's departure, I'll be back for you. I hope that the magic you worked in the kitchen means we'll have a good dinner."

"I believe so." Sarah smothered a yawn. "The cook is quite pleased to have the new earl in residence, and she's anxious to prove her skill."

"I'll have Hector find some good wines to go with the meal. If there is anything first-rate at Kellington, it will be the wine cellar," he said dryly.

With Sarah's laughter following, Rob left the office, the strongbox under one arm. His new circumstances were looking a bit less grim. Besides having a small fortune in cash, he looked forward to dining with Sarah at a candle-lit table.

If he was really fortunate, his grandmother would choose to dine in her room.

Jonas was in the stable, and more than happy to see the back of Buckley. He promised to stay as late as necessary to help the family prepare to leave in the morning. Since Jonas knew them all, he'd ensure the process went smoothly.

Years before, Rob's father had installed a safe in the ugly little study. Because Rob had always been a good observer, he knew where it was and how to open it, so it didn't take long to stash the embezzled money safely.

When he returned to the steward's office, Sarah was sitting at the desk and dozing with her head resting on her crossed arms. She straightened and gave him a sleepy smile, her brown eyes as warm and welcoming as hot chocolate.

What would it be like to see such a smile every morning over a pillow? Suppressing the thought, he said, "Everything is in order, and we can relax over a good dinner. My lady?" He offered his arm.

"Thank you, my lord." She laid a small, light hand on his arm and they left the steward's office.

Night had fallen, though the western horizon still glowed orange. Strange to think that just the day before, they'd been fighting for their lives on the voyage from Ireland. And Rob had been a contented Bow Street Runner instead of an unhappy earl.

As they climbed the steps to the main entrance, Sarah asked, "How long do you think it will be before my family learns that I'm safe? Surely no more than a day or two."

"Perhaps as early as tomorrow evening. If not then, the day after. Wiltshire isn't that far from Somerset." He added, amused, "I wouldn't be surprised if your parents and Ashton come swooping in to see for themselves that you're all right."

"I hope you won't feel too overwhelmed if that happens," she said with a chuckle. "Because it probably will. Maybe even Mariah. She might have just had a baby, but she's very determined."

"Having your family descend on Kellington will be a minor disruption compared to everything else that will be happening." He swung open the heavy door and she glided through, as grand as any princess in her borrowed green velvet riding habit.

Rob followed. As he closed the door behind them, he found that they'd walked into a maelstrom. Lady Kellington stood at the foot of the stairs, her expression appalled, while Hector, the butler, was making ineffectual hand gestures as if he could dismiss the unpleasantness.

In the middle of the hall stood a roughly dressed

old man who seemed vaguely familiar. His hand locked on the arm of a scrawny girl child with a ragged too-short dress, he snarled with a thick country accent, "I'm stayin' here until his bloody lordship returns! He'll bloody well take her, because she's his! Damned if I'll keep the little bastard under my roof any longer."

The girl jerked free of his grip and spun around furiously. She was eleven or twelve, with a mass of tangled black hair falling to her waist. And blazing from her smudged face were light, clear blue eyes exactly like Rob's.

"Bryony!" he breathed.

He had a daughter.

Chapter 21

The girl looked so much like a miniature Bryony that Rob could barely breathe. She was like an enraged kitten, gallant and frightened and unutterably brave even in a terrifying new place when the only family she knew was throwing her away.

"He's lying," Lady Kellington snapped. "Don't be a fool, boy, or you'll have every bastard in Somerset landed on you!"

"She's my daughter." Eyes narrowed, Rob studied the old man. "I didn't recognize you at first. You're Owens, the shepherd. Bryony's father. Where is she?"

"Dead," the grizzled old man spat out. "Two years ago, and left me with her brat. She always claimed you were the father, but everyone thought you was dead so I was stuck with the little bastard. Since you're here and alive, she's yours. I wash my hands of her." He stalked out the door and left with a window-rattling slam.

The furious kitten glared at Rob. "You're my bloody father?"

Lady Kellington shuddered at the profanity, but Rob knelt on one knee in front of the girl, his gaze intense and his voice gentle, as if he was soothing a nervous horse.

"I am," he said. "I didn't know you existed. I loved your mother and we planned to marry, but my family interfered."

"If you loved her so much, why didn't you run off to Gretna Green when your bloody family disapproved?" she asked suspiciously.

If anyone deserved the truth, it was his daughter. "My father gave your mother money to leave me. I was about to search for her when my brother sold me to a press gang," Rob said flatly. "I was forced onto a ship bound for India and didn't see England again for six long years."

Lady Kellington gasped. "Your brother would never do such an appalling thing!"

"I was there, Grandmother. You weren't." Rob got to his feet. His daughter looked wary and ready to bolt, so he kept some distance between them. "We haven't been properly introduced. What's your name?"

"Bree." The girl's eyes darted around the room as if seeking escape.

"That's pretty. You're named Bryony for your mother?"

Bree scowled and nodded. "Bryony is a useless weed, a clinging vine. That's why my grandfather named my mother that."

Rob managed to control his surge of fury. Owens had treated Bryony abominably, and it sounded as if he'd been equally bad to Bree.

"If you must acknowledge the brat," Lady Kellington said with exasperation, "at least get her out of here quickly. Put her into service or find an apprenticeship."

It was what he expected of his grandmother. "No. With her mother gone, Bree belongs with me."

The old lady snorted. "You need to marry an heiress, and no decent woman will accept a man with bastards about the house."

Sarah spoke up, voice calm but eyes flashing. "Nonsense. What decent woman would want a man who won't take responsibility for his own child?"

Bree's eyes slid back to Rob. "You want me to stay here?"

"Of course." His gaze held hers. "If I'd known about you, I would have found my way back to Somerset much sooner."

Sarah smiled warmly at the girl, who relaxed visibly. It was impossible to be frightened of Sarah. "You must be tired and hungry. With your father's permission, I'll find you a room and a bath and supper."

"Of course. Make her comfortable," Rob said, relieved that Sarah had stepped forward to look out for the girl.

His *daughter*. He'd had no idea that Bryony was with child when they were separated. She probably hadn't known, either. But now that he knew they'd made a child, he felt fierce and utterly new emotions. Bree was *his,* and he'd protect her. "When Bree is settled for the night, come find me. I'll be in the study, sorting through papers."

"How fortunate that I asked you to have rooms prepared for visitors, Hector. We'll use one for Lord Kellington's daughter," Sarah said. "Order bathwater and send Francie to join us."

Looking relieved to be able to escape, Hector bowed. "Yes, miss. The Rose Room should be suitable for a . . . young lady." He had some trouble referring to the new arrival as a young lady, but at least he was trying.

As Sarah led Bree away, Rob thought how dramatically his life had changed in a day. But this change was one he welcomed. Something of Bryony had survived.

As Sarah and Bree followed the butler up the stairs, the girl's gaze darted around as she tried to absorb her new surroundings. She looked over-whelmed, and determined not to show it. Sarah guessed that Bree had learned to guard her emotions when living with her dreadful grand-father.

The Rose Room was next to Sarah's bed-chamber. Though it was as worn as the rest of Kellington Castle, the room had been cleaned and a fire was laid. Right after they entered, a maid followed with sheets to make up the canopy bed. Rose brocade hangings and a thick, slightly shabby Belgian carpet with more roses created a welcoming warmth. Bree's eyes widened when she entered.

Hector lit the two lamps, then condescended to light the fire laid on the hearth himself rather than waiting for a lower servant to do the menial task. He bowed again. "I'll send Francie and the bathwater up. Is there anything else, Miss Clarke-Townsend?"

"Supper on a tray, please. Bree, is there anything particular you'd like?"

The girl looked startled at having her wishes consulted. "Something hot. Mebbe a mutton stew? Or a meat pie?"

"I'm sure that Mrs. Fulton will have something equally satisfying. Be sure there is also bread and cheese and sweets, Hector. And perhaps a pot of hot tea?" Sarah glanced over at Bree, who nodded numbly.

Hector left and Bree drifted across the room to finger the brocade draperies on the bed. "I can really stay here tonight?"

"Indeed you can, and rather longer than that. I don't speak for Lord Kellington, but it sounds like he plans for you to make your home here."

Bree looked at her, the clear aquamarine eyes

unnerving. "The butler didn't call you Lady Kellington. Are you his lordship's fancy piece?"

Sarah blinked. "No, I'm a friend. I was abducted from my home and taken to Ireland. Lord Kellington rescued me and brought me back to England yesterday." Was it really only yesterday they'd arrived here? It seemed much longer. "I'll be going home in a few days." Home was going to look very boring after a fortnight in Rob's company. "You can call me Sarah."

Bree frowned, looking so much like Rob that Sarah wanted to laugh. "Why was he rescuing you? Lords don't do anything useful."

"Rob wasn't Lord Kellington then. He was a Bow Street Runner in London. His job was to catch criminals and find stolen people and property," Sarah explained. "His family treated him so badly that he turned his back on them. It wasn't until we washed up here that he learned his father and brother died recently, so Rob is the new earl."

"His folks sound almost as bad as bloody Owens." Her face twisted into an expression that was not young at all. "I'm glad the old bugger is gone. Would have done nasty things to me if I'd let him."

Sarah winced. Thank God Bree had been able to defend herself, but it was regrettable that she'd picked up her grandfather's vile language.

"Did you and your mother live with him your whole life?"

Bree shook her head. "Me mum had money from the old lord, and she was a good seamstress, too. We had a cottage in a village just down the coast, Bendan. 'Twasn't till she died and Owens came to get me that I met the old bugger. He took Mum's money and sold the furnishings. Said it was due him for taking care of me."

"Perhaps it was. You and your mother lived comfortably?"

"Oh, aye!" Bree looked wistful. "We had plenty to eat and Mum made me the prettiest dresses. She sent me to a dame school so I could learn reading and writing and numbers. I had friends."

Until she'd been hauled into the lonely hills by her grandfather. At least she'd had a decent life before that. "Did your mother ever talk about your father?"

"Mum said her Rob was a fine handsome fellow who asked her to marry him, but she knew his family would never allow it so she took money to go away. Later she heard that he'd disappeared. She thought his brother had murdered him."

Bryony sounded admirably direct. No wonder Rob had loved her. "Not murdered, but close enough. His family was horrified by the idea that he wanted to marry a shepherd's daughter."

"What's m'father like?" Bree regarded her with that unnerving gaze again.

How best to describe Rob? "He's strong and very brave. He rescued me from the middle of a group of Irish radicals." Sarah thought of how Rob had handled Buckley. "He's intelligent and honest and fair. He believes in justice, but he's also kind." Certainly he'd been kind to her. "He'll make you a very good father, I'm sure."

"Does he really want me?" Bree sounded wistful again. "Or is he going to apprentice me to a milliner like that old bawd wanted?"

Sarah wondered how the countess would react to being called a bawd. "Oh, he wants you," she said softly. "When he realized you were his daughter, he looked like he'd been given a piece of heaven. It will take time for you to get to know each other, of course. Just remember that he's nervous about you, just as you're nervous about him."

Bree stroked the china washbasin. "I didn't know I had a father."

The door opened and Francie entered, a smile on her face. "Such excitement! So his lordship has a daughter?"

"Yes, isn't it splendid?" Sarah made the introductions, then asked, "Can you find some clothing that will fit Bree?"

"A nightgown is easy, and I can find a shift and morning dress. Shall I have the village seamstress come tomorrow to take her measurements for a basic wardrobe?"

"Yes, and a shoemaker. Anything and everything a young lady will need." There might not be much money, but there should be enough to outfit the new earl's daughter.

The door opened again and two servants entered with canisters of steaming water. As Bree stared at the luxury, Francie said in a conspiratorial voice, "I can get you lavender-scented soap if you'd like, Miss Bree."

"Oh, yes. A whole tub of hot water!" Bree looked dazed and very, very tired, but on the whole, she was managing well. By the time Francie returned with the lavender soap and other toiletries, the tub was filled and the footmen had withdrawn.

Francie clucked her tongue. "Miss Sarah, you look almost as tired as Miss Bree. You run along and get some supper while I take care of the new member of the family."

Sarah hesitated. She was exhausted, but she didn't want Rob's daughter to feel abandoned. "Will you be all right, Bree? I can stay if you like."

"No need." The girl smiled wearily. "A bath and a bite of supper and a bed are more than I dreamed of."

"I'll see you in the morning then." On impulse, Sarah gave Bree a quick hug. The girl's arms went around her and Sarah realized she was shaking. How long had it been since Bree had known kindness? Probably not since her mother died.

"You're safe now," she whispered. "Your new life has begun."

A life that would remind Rob every time he saw his daughter of the woman he'd loved and lost.

Chapter 22

Wearily Sarah made her way down to the study. She was still wearing the heavy velvet riding habit since she'd not had time to change.

The dismal study hadn't improved since Sarah saw it earlier, but Rob was always a pleasant sight, even when frowning at a column of figures. In the lamplight, his features were handsome and austere. In Ireland, she'd seen his physical strength and mastery. Here, she saw his intelligence and discipline.

Then he looked up and smiled and she saw his warmth. "How is she?"

"Settling in well, though this is all so strange for her. Bree is intelligent and adaptable, and she very much wants a home." Sarah sat in a chair on the opposite side of the desk. "Have you found anything interesting in your father's papers?"

"It's all routine information relating to the estate. Since he lived mostly in London, the more important papers would be kept there. Not that I expect to find much of anything except debts." Rob sighed. "I suppose I must travel up to town and go through Kellington House before I put it on the market. When I attend Parliament, I can stay in my flat near Covent Garden." He smiled a little. "I'll be the only member of the House of Lords who lives over a pawnshop."

Sarah laughed, glad Rob was beginning to accept his fate with some humor. "I can see you intend to put your own mark on the earldom."

"I haven't spent my life in a pampered cocoon like most lords. They're stuck with me." He rose and moved to a cabinet. "Would you like something to drink? There's a good variety here. Brandy, port, claret, sherry . . ."

"Claret would be lovely. Anything stronger and I'll fall asleep on your desk."

Rob poured a generous amount of wine in two goblets and offered one to Sarah. "Shall we drink to our survival? When I have time to think about it, I'm impressed that we didn't drown."

"To survival." They clinked glasses. After they drank, Sarah added, "And to a future for you that is better than what you're expecting now."

They both drank to that. Rob swallowed half the glass of claret, then topped it up and sat down. "Did you find out anything about Bree's earlier life? About her mother?"

"She said they lived in a cottage down the coast and were happy. Bryony sent her to a dame school so she should have the basics of reading and writing." Sarah smiled ruefully. "But she'll need a tutor to correct the accent and language she learned from her horrid grandfather. She called your grandmother an old bawd."

Rob laughed out loud. "I wish I dared tell the dowager that! I'm glad the money my father paid Bryony to go away was enough to keep them in comfort."

"Bree said her mother knew your family wouldn't permit marriage, which was why she took the money. When you disappeared, Bryony suspected that your brother had murdered you."

Rob closed his eyes for a long moment. "I'm glad Bryony didn't think I'd betrayed her. Knowing she might believe that haunted me."

Sarah could imagine. "Bryony must have been very beautiful to have such a beautiful daughter."

"They look very alike, except for the eyes. To see her is to know what Bryony was like at that age." Rob's expression softened. "Sarah, it's a miracle. I never guessed what it would be like to discover I have a child. It's . . . life changing." He swirled his goblet, studying the ruby red wine. "Bree gives me a reason to look forward to the future with hope, not fatigue."

His words gave Sarah a better understanding of just how deeply he'd loved Bryony. Though she was gone, the child they'd conceived in love meant that Bryony wasn't completely lost. Bree gave him a reason to carry on.

"I'm glad for you both," she said simply. "Though Lady Kellington has a point. You do need to marry an heiress, and you'll have to find one who is tolerant of having an illegitimate stepdaughter in the household. But that's not an insurmountable problem. You're handsome and honorable and there's the title. A sufficiently dowered merchant's daughter will go a long way to repairing the Kellington fortunes."

"No!" Rob's exclamation was explosive.

"Surely you're not a snob!" Sarah said, startled. "Your chances of securing an heiress are far better if you look to the merchant class rather than the beau monde."

His face tightened. "I'm not rejecting merchants' daughters. I'm rejecting the whole idea of becoming a fortune hunter. I'm losing the life I built for myself. I'm not going to give up my right to choose my own bedmates."

Sarah blinked. "Plural? That will not sit well with most potential wives."

His expression eased. "I've never wanted a harem. One woman at a time is more than enough. But I want to choose a wife because I like her."

Like, not love. No woman could ever hold the place in his heart where Bryony lived. "Surely you can find a woman who is like that good companion you lost, only with money."

"It's true that I no longer need a woman who is adept at spying and can take down a man twice her size in a fight," he said dryly. "But I haven't had a chance to think much about a potential countess."

"Maybe it's time," Sarah said briskly. "Because the right wife could save Kellington and make your life much easier."

"I know you're right," he said with a sigh. He poured himself more claret. "I suppose my ideal countess would be a capable woman who can run a large household and move comfortably in society. Someone with a generous heart, but not extravagant tastes. And someone I like, of course."

"It should be possible to find a woman like that who comes with a fortune." Sarah sipped more of her own wine. Useful things, drinks, for covering up emotions. "You have much to offer."

He snorted. "I can't imagine why an heiress would want me apart from the title. I have a shabby imitation castle, an illegitimate daughter, and horrendous and possibly insoluble financial problems. Any sensible female would run screaming."

Sarah considered herself sensible, but she'd be willing to consider an offer from him. She wasn't sure she'd accept, but she'd certainly consider. So would any intelligent female. But after Rob had time to think about his situation, the idea of marrying an heiress would sound more appealing. Of course they should like each other, but having money didn't make a female unlikable.

Not wanting to think about the lucky, likable heiress, she said, "The financial situation might not be as dire as you fear."

"It's more likely to be worse than better," he said pessimistically. "Since I wasn't the heir and was estranged from my family, I'm ignorant of the most basic information. I don't know which properties are entailed and which aren't. Any unentailed property is probably mortgaged to the hilt and ripe for foreclosure. Entailed property can't be foreclosed on, but the income can be seized, which would leave nothing but an empty, meaningless title. I just have no idea."

"I assume there's a London house. They aren't usually entailed, are they?"

"No, but Kellington House is probably mortgaged. It's on the top of my list of things to sell. I've scarcely ever seen the place, though I remember it as rather grand."

"The uncertainty of your financial situation must be driving you mad," she said sympathetically. "Once you know where you stand, you'll start finding solutions. I'd lay money that you wrote the family lawyer this morning."

"You'd win your bet." He ran tense fingers through his hair. "I suppose I need to go up to town to talk with the lawyer in person. If Ashton hasn't arrived or at least sent a carriage, I can deliver you to Ralston Abbey on the way. Maybe two days from now? There is much to be done here before I leave."

Sarah felt as if she'd been thrown from a horse and she couldn't breathe, and not just because she felt like an inconvenient parcel that needed to be delivered. So her adventure was over. She'd no longer be able to talk and laugh with Rob, or admire that long, lean, powerful body. She'd probably meet him again someday, but she wasn't part of his real life. She never had been.

A thought struck her. "Bree will need a woman to care for her and about her. I'd suggest your housemaid, Francie, Jonas's cousin. She's kind and clever, and she's done a good job of looking after me. We already discussed bringing in a seamstress from the village to make a basic wardrobe."

"That's a wonderful idea. Bree is too old for a nursery maid, and a governess will have to wait." He shook his head. "I'll do my best to be a good father, but I can't begin to guess how to be a good mother."

"Still another reason to marry," she said, keeping her tone light. "I'll be glad to get back to my family, but I'll miss you and all the excitement."

His gaze caught hers. "Don't confuse me with the excitement, Sarah. It was a grand adventure that we both miraculously survived. But I'm not particularly interesting myself. I just do some interesting things." He made a face. "At least, I used to. My life is about to become much less interesting."

"Paperwork will be dull after years spent

catching villains and rescuing damsels in distress," she agreed as she struggled to control her sense of hurt. She'd thought there was something special between them. A friendship as well as an attraction. But maybe he was like this with all his rescued damsels.

Her instincts said no, and a touch of deviltry made her want to prove it. She set her glass of claret aside and circled the desk to where he was sitting. "I found this quite interesting." She cupped his face with her hands and bent into a kiss.

They'd kissed before, but with doubt and hesitation. This time she held nothing back. Only her hands and mouth touched him, but her lips were hot and hungry and it triggered an instant response. His arms went around her and he pulled her down so that she was straddling his knee, her breasts pressed into his chest and folds of green velvet cascading around them.

"Sarah, Sarah," he breathed. "A perfect princess."

One hand slid down her back, shaping her curves and leaving trails of fire in its wake as he pulled her even closer. The fingers of his other hand slid into her hair, loosening the pins and cradling her head tenderly.

She'd experienced the intoxicating dawn of desire with Gerald, and she'd known a few sweet kisses in the years since. But they were nothing compared to the deep, powerful passion Rob aroused. The two of them might not love, but they could easily be friends and lovers.

She wanted to devour him, surrender every shred of propriety. They were pressed together so intimately that his heat and hardness burned through the layers of green velvet. She pulsed against him, wanting more. Wanting everything.

She gasped as his hand slid up her leg under the skirt. His touch was leisurely and skilled. When his fingers caressed the inside of her thigh, she thought she'd go mad with desire. Surely they could meld. . . .

He froze when he heard her gasp. Then he abruptly stood, catching her so that she didn't fall and setting her on the edge of the desk as he backed away. "This is a really, really bad idea," he panted.

She pressed a hand to her heaving chest, seriously tempted to pick up the chair and smash it over his stubborn head. But as her blood cooled, she had to admit his point. "You're probably right. But I wonder—is this much attraction rare? I've not experienced it before, but then, I don't have much experience."

"It's not common." He closed his eyes a moment as he mastered himself.

She sighed. "It seems a pity for us to waste it, since passion is considered a good foundation for marriage."

He looked at her uncertainly, as if wondering whether she was making an oblique proposal. Apparently deciding that she wasn't, he said, "Passion is certainly a plus, but not the foundation. Friendship and shared values are the foundation, I think. Along with a willingness to work together." He smiled wryly. "But what would I know? I've never been married. I'm a mere observer."

"But a very good observer, since observation is so important to your work." She slid from the desk to the floor and tried to brush down her hair and riding habit. "It has been a most educational fortnight, but I've had as much education as I can stand for one day. Good night, Rob."

Head high, she strode to the door. Perhaps she'd been foolish to initiate that kiss, because it would make leaving him that much more difficult. Yet she didn't regret it.

But it didn't seem fair that since Gerald's death she hadn't met a man she could imagine being married to. Now she'd met one—and she couldn't have him.

Rob stayed in the study long after Sarah left, staring sightlessly at her half-empty claret goblet. He'd inherited a title and a financial disaster and discovered a miraculous daughter. But at the moment, all he could think about was Sarah, and how much he'd miss her when she was gone. Hard to imagine that he could do better if he was looking for a life's companion.

Earlier, he'd been unable to imagine her living in a flat above a pawnshop, and now he couldn't imagine dragging her into the financial morass that was his inheritance. She deserved a husband who could dote on her and keep her in comfort. What attention he could spare should go to his vulnerable young daughter. He was in no position to take on a wife. If he did look, it should be for an heiress.

The idea made his stomach turn.

Sarah's advice was wise: the first thing he must do was determine how dire his situation was. He was good at solving problems once he knew what they were.

He wouldn't think about a wife. Especially not one who was beautiful and sunny and sensible and made his mind shut down altogether . . .

Swearing to himself, he turned off the lamps and left the study. It was late and he was too tired to continue looking at estate papers.

When he reached his room, he noticed light under a door down the hall. It was his grandmother's suite of rooms. She'd always been a night owl. Since he'd have to talk with her eventually, maybe he should get it over with.

After he tapped at the door, it was opened by his grandmother's maid, the accurately named

Miss Cross. She scowled at him. It was a familiar expression from the past. "I'd like to speak with my grandmother. Is now a good time?"

The maid said no, but her refusal was overridden by his grandmother's sharp, "Send him in!"

Reluctantly the maid stood aside and Rob entered his grandmother's parlor. He wasn't sure he'd ever been in her rooms. The old lady was sitting by the fire, still dressed in her black mourning gown. "Ma'am." He inclined his head. "I'm sorry to have survived against your wishes."

She snorted. "Wishes are so seldom fulfilled. Sit." She indicated the chair on the opposite side of the fire. "But first pour us both some brandy. We'll need it."

Reluctantly amused, he moved to the drinks cabinet and poured their brandies. After handing her a glass, he settled in the opposite chair. "You wish to fight with me?"

She gave him a gimlet gaze. "Are you going to continue to tell lies about your brother?"

He sighed. "I've never lied about him in the past and I'm not lying now. I don't go out of the way to tell people how abominably he treated me. Though if you wish, I could give you a list of his other crimes against brotherhood. Is it so hard to imagine him as a bully to those who were younger and weaker than he?"

Her gaze dropped to her brandy and she didn't

reply. He guessed that meant she recognized Edmund's less saintly qualities.

He sipped his drink. The brandy was smooth and expensive. "Now a question for you. Is Kellington Castle now your primary residence?"

"Trying to get rid of me?" she said acidly.

"The place would be a good deal more pleasant without you snarling like a wolverine and wishing me dead," he retorted. "If you behave decently, I won't ask you to leave, but I won't have you treating Bree or Sarah badly."

She gasped. "You'd forbid me my family home?"

"If necessary." Seeing her expression, he smiled without humor. "If you wanted me to treat you well, you should have tried a little kindness when I was a boy."

"The trouble is that you looked so much like your mother," the countess said unexpectedly. "She was too . . . too emotional. Impulsive. Underbred. Sometimes I thought she was a witch who'd cast a spell on your father to get him to marry her."

"What a novel perspective. Perhaps he thought she was warm and loving and a pleasure to be with." Like Sarah. He continued, "But I didn't come here to argue with you. I didn't want this inheritance, but I intend to do my best to manage it properly. Assuming that the debts aren't insurmountable, that is. Do you know if my father and brother managed to bleed Kellington dry before they died?"

"Have you no respect?" she said furiously.

"Respect must be earned. My father and brother gave me no reason to respect them." He studied his grandmother's lined face, a little surprised. "You I do respect. Though you treated me like a horrible mistake who didn't belong in the family, you were fair with the servants and tenants. You also recognized that responsibilities come with rank. That's probably why you're here now."

"I'm glad you approve," she said tartly. "You're right. I have been spending more time at Kellington because a family member should be here regularly."

"And it wasn't my father or brother. I rest my case in regard to their worthiness of respect. But you didn't answer my previous question. Is the estate sunk in debt beyond redemption?"

She hesitated. "The financial situation is . . . not ideal. Consult with Mr. Booth. He'll know more."

"I've already written Booth. I expect I'll get a reply soon, unless he's been embezzling and disappears."

She scowled. "You have a poor opinion of people's honesty."

"Being a Bow Street Runner can have that effect," he agreed. "Though that's reinforced by the fact that the Kellington steward, Buckley, has been embezzling for years."

"Surely not!" She slammed her brandy glass down on the table beside her. "He's such a fine, courteous man."

"Courtesy has nothing to do with honesty. I made him return most of his ill-gotten gains and discharged him." Weary of the conversation, he stood. "If you're tempted to be rude to my daughter, bear in mind that she would be the legitimate Lady Bryony Carmichael if not for the interference of my father and Edmund."

His grandmother frowned, unable to refute his point. "I'll be civil. But keep her out of my way."

"I'm sure she'll be happy to avoid you." He tilted his glass at his grandmother in a not entirely ironic salute and finished the brandy.

As he took his leave, he reflected that this was the most civilized encounter he'd ever had with the Dowager Countess of Kellington.

Chapter 23

The letters Rob and Sarah sent from Kellington made their way across England by swift mail coach. The first arrived at Ralston Abbey the evening of the day it was sent. Eager for news, Adam had given orders for all letters to be brought to him immediately, but he wasn't expecting a missive with "Kellington" franked across the corner.

He frowned. That title belonged to Rob Carmichael's older brother. Could something dreadful have happened to Rob and his brother was writing to inform Rob's friends? That seemed unlikely from what he knew of Edmund Carmichael.

Adam broke the wax seal and scanned the contents, his brows arching. Then he sought out his wife, who was reading in the nursery with their son in a cradle beside her.

"Good news!" Adam announced. "Rob Carmichael has rescued Sarah and they're back in England."

"Thank God!" Mariah's expression turned incandescent. "Where is she?"

"In Somerset, at Kellington Castle. Rob just inherited the Kellington earldom," Adam said with interest. "I've been so busy down here I missed the news that his older brother died in an accident a couple of weeks ago."

"Just when Sarah was abducted and I was inefficiently delivering your heir." Mariah bent and tenderly touched the tiny clenched fist of her sleeping son. "I think you can be forgiven being behind with the news this time."

Adam consulted the letter. "Rob says the kidnappers wanted to hold Sarah—or rather, you—for ransom. After he retrieved her, they sailed home. When they arrived in England, he learned of his inheritance, so he's taking a bit of time to study the situation."

"Is there a note from Sarah?"

"Yes, addressed to you." Adam removed the smaller paper enclosed in Rob's letter and handed it over.

Mariah broke the seal eagerly, then frowned over the contents. "Her handwriting is too much like mine, which means it's hard to read. Her tale is much more colorful than Rob's. Apparently he extracted her from the middle of a house full of radicals and they were chased across Ireland, sleeping in barns and the like. I trust Rob is discreet? Sarah is the twin with the unblemished reputation, and it would be nice to see that preserved."

"Rob is so discreet that he doesn't even tell himself what happened," Adam assured her.

"What else does Sarah say? She really is all right?" He hesitated, hating to put his fears into words. "She wasn't assaulted by her captors?"

"She assures me she's fine, apart from bruises received when their yawl was wrecked on the Somerset coast during that big storm. Rob said nothing about that?"

"His reports are generally just the facts."

Mariah held the letter next to the light so she could see the words better. "After their yawl was wrecked, they fetched up at his family estate and she told people on the estate that she and Rob were betrothed to make things simpler." She frowned. "She doesn't say they're *not* betrothed. What does that mean?"

She glanced at Adam questioningly. "I know Rob is one of your oldest friends, and he's therefore fearless, honest, utterly reliable, and generally above reproach. But what kind of husband would he make? This seems to have happened very quickly!"

Adam grinned. "I can't say I've ever considered Rob from a romantic point of view, but he's a good fellow. As for quickness—the first time I saw your smiling face, you informed me that I was your husband, and it never occurred to me to doubt you."

"It made sense at the time," Mariah said with a mischievous smile. "How long will Rob be in Somerset?"

"I don't know. He'll have his hands full with Kellington. It's said that the estate has been drained dry, which must be why he's staying there for several days rather than bringing Sarah here right away. Can you bear not seeing her instantly?"

Mariah bit her lip. "I won't really relax until I see Sarah with my own eyes. Can we travel down there? It's not that far. Less than a day's journey."

Adam hesitated. "Are you strong enough? You were knocking at death's door for several days."

"I'm almost recovered now," Mariah assured him. "We'll go in the extremely comfortable Ashton travel coach. It will be easy."

"Can you bear to leave Richard?"

"He'll come with me, of course. Sarah will want to see him."

"Very well," Adam said, quelling his protective instincts. He couldn't shut Mariah in a golden cage. "But if the journey is difficult for you, we'll stop immediately."

"We'll be fine." Mariah picked up the baby and cuddled him. "Order the carriage for first thing in the morning while I write a note to my parents that Sarah is safe. I'm glad they're in Hertford at my uncle Babcock's rather than in Cumberland, so they'll get the good news tomorrow."

Adam suspected that as soon as his in-laws

received Mariah's message, they would also race down to Kellington. Rob would hate being the center of so much attention. But he'd need to get used to it. A peer of the realm might be private by nature, but he must play a public role some of the time. Adam had learned to master the dual roles, and Rob would, too.

He'd still hate it.

Mariah asked, "What kind of fees does Rob charge? I can't even guess."

"For this sort of work, it's a daily fee plus expenses incurred." Adam had a brief, horrific vision of Mariah and Richard dead in a pool of blood. He'd see that in nightmares for a long, long time. "I believe the compensation should suit the service." And in this case, the service of both Sarah and Rob had been immense.

The intriguing story of the new Earl of Kellington took half a day longer to reach London. At the law firm of Booth and Harlow, the family lawyer, Nicholas Booth, stared at the letter, unsure whether it was good or bad news that the family black sheep was alive and in possession of the Kellington estate. Either way, Booth's duty was to start the process for letters of patent and gazetting, and to gather financial records for the new earl.

Their first meeting would not be a happy occasion.

· · ·

Jeremiah Harvey read the note from his friend and employer with mild surprise. Not because Rob was safely back in England after rescuing the young lady—he was very good at that sort of thing. But becoming a bloody earl? Rob damned well wouldn't like that.

Harvey didn't need to pack. He always had a bag of essentials ready to go.

James, Lord Kirkland, co-owner of the most fashionable gambling club in London, Scottish shipping merchant, and British spymaster, frowned over Rob's note. He had information for Rob, and he suspected that Rob would have information for him.

He reached for pen and paper. Before he consulted his files, he'd send a note to Lady Agnes Westerfield. She'd be interested in this news.

The news broke swiftly in society circles. The late Lord Kellington had a younger brother? One who'd never moved in good society? How delicious!

Several men and women among the well off and well born had had occasion to use Rob Carmichael's services, and to be grateful for his discretion. He'd do.

Matchmaking mamas and ambitious young ladies welcomed the news that there was a new young earl who was unmarried and in need of an heiress. One female in particular read the notice with great interest. Why wait for him to come to London when she had a perfect excuse to seek him out?

She began to pack.

The young man about town hadn't quit the card table till dawn, so he slept until dusk. He read of the new earl over coffee as he tried to wake up. He'd better hustle to get his claim in before it was too late.

Politicians speculated about which party the new earl would support. The Tories rather complacently reminded themselves that the earls of Kellington had always been Tories. Whig leaders said hopefully that since nothing was known of the fellow, perhaps he could be recruited for the Whig cause. Those men who actually knew Rob Carmichael guessed he'd be a prickly indepen-dent rather than a follower of either party.

Lady Agnes Westerfield laid Kirkland's note aside as she remembered her first meeting with a young and very angry Rob Carmichael. Yet he hadn't turned out to be one of her more difficult boys. He'd responded well to kindness and fair treatment.

He would not be happy with this inheritance, not at first. But Rob had proved to be remarkably adaptable to life's circumstances. He'd sailed before the mast, thrived in India, become a Runner, and was one of Kirkland's most valuable resources. He'd adapt to being an earl equally well. Perhaps someday he'd even get pleasure from the rank.

Some would say it was pure chance that a newspaper with the story of the new earl ended up in that particular Dublin coffeehouse. Since Patrick Cassidy didn't live in Dublin and seldom bothered reading London newspapers when he did visit the city, it might have been weeks until he learned the news that the Honorable Robert Cassidy Carmichael had become the fifth Earl of Kellington.

But Father Patrick didn't believe in chance. When his gaze fell on the news item, he called it the hand of God.

Chapter 24

Francie had located and hemmed a morning gown for Sarah's use. It was outdated and the faded gray flannel was not flattering, but after a long day in a heavy riding habit that didn't fit, Sarah welcomed the gown. She'd be glad when she had her own wardrobe back, though.

After Francie fastened the gown in the back, the maid said, "I borrowed some clothing from my youngest sister for Miss Bree. I'll take it to her now."

"I'll go with you." Sarah wrapped a warm paisley shawl around her shoulders. "I want to see how she's doing. This must all be so strange to her!"

"Strange," Francie agreed, "but in a good way. Easier to get used to comfort than to being poor and miserable."

"I suggested to his lordship that you take charge of Miss Bree." Sarah checked her appearance in the mirror, glad her voice sounded so calm. "She needs a woman to care for her and help her adapt to a new life. Someone who is more than a maid. You've been so good to me that I know you'll be an excellent choice, if you're willing."

"Of course I am." Francie's face softened. "Would his lordship mind if I brought my youngest sister here to have tea with Miss Bree? They're near the same age."

Sarah thought of the varied circles Rob moved in and almost smiled. "I'm sure he and Bree will both be pleased."

Together they left Sarah's room and moved to Bree's. Sarah tapped on the door. "Bree, it's Sarah and Francie, who is going to look after you. Francie has clothing and I can guide you to the breakfast room."

The door opened to reveal Bree, wearing her nightgown and with a blanket wrapped around her. Her dark hair was even wilder than the day before. "Do you have a comb?" the girl asked. "I look like a bloody bird nested in my hair."

"Right here." Francie dug into her canvas bag and produced a tortoiseshell comb.

As Bree eagerly accepted the comb and began working knots out of her hair, Sarah said, "I'm also going to give you a lesson in language. Words like 'bloody' and 'bugger' and 'old bawd' are considered unsuitable in polite society."

Bree frowned. "Owens always talked like that."

"Would you consider him polite society?"

"He bloody well wasn't!" Bree exclaimed. Then she bit her lip. "How can I say that in ways that won't shock everyone?"

Sarah laughed. "You could say that he was a

vulgar fellow. You're not like him, Bree. You're a young lady and will be raised as one."

"I'm really going to stay in Kellington Castle? His lordship didn't change his mind last night?"

"He was very clear that you are his daughter and belong under his roof." Thinking caution was appropriate, Sarah added, "The estate has many debts and the future is uncertain. But no matter what, your father will want you with him."

Bree stopped combing. "Rich lords can lose their homes?" she asked incredulously.

"Not all are rich. The same men that kept your father from marrying your mother were also notorious spendthrifts. But your father will sort matters out as best he can."

Bree glanced around the room. "This is bigger than my bl—vulgar grandpa's whole cottage."

"And much nicer, I'm sure!" Francie shook out a blue morning dress. "This should fit you. I hope you don't mind that it's from my youngest sister, Molly."

Bree stroked the fabric. "It's better 'n anything I've had since me mum died."

"Molly would like to meet you." Francie glanced at Sarah. "Perhaps I can invite her this afternoon? You can play together in the nursery and take tea."

Bree's face lit up. "Yes, ma'am! I'd like that." She scooped up the garments Francie offered and retreated behind the screen to dress, but her voice carried over. "How can I learn to look like a bloody lady, Miss Sarah?" There was a stricken pause. "Can I say 'like a blasted lady'?"

Sarah grinned. " 'How can I learn to look like a lady?' will do."

Bree sighed. "I don't talk nice like you, I don't know how to dress, I don't know nothin'."

"Which is why you have Miss Francie," Sarah said. "You're a clever girl, and you'll learn quickly. A year from now no one will believe that you didn't grow up in a manor house."

"I hope you're right." Bree emerged from behind the screen, looking striking in the blue dress. She would be a real beauty. She looked in the mirror and involuntarily smiled with pleasure. "Thank Molly for me, and please, I'd really fancy meeting her."

Francie asked, "Miss Sarah, is it all right if I nip home and invite Molly while you're eating breakfast?"

"Please do." Sarah smiled at Bree. "Now we find our way down to the breakfast parlor."

The girl frowned. "I thought you knew the way."

"I guess well." Sarah handed Bree a shawl. "You'll need this."

Francie chuckled. "I'll take you down. This place is a right maze and it's easy to get lost."

It was, too. Sarah was glad for Francie's guidance.

266

She wouldn't be here long enough to learn her way around.

Rob stood when Bree and Sarah entered the breakfast room. Two beautiful females, and almost the same height. Bree would be tall, like both her parents.

Sarah was golden and bright, like sunshine walking. At first he couldn't tear his gaze away.

Her eyes showed grave yearning, but it wasn't evident in her voice when she said, "Good morning, Rob. Bree, would you like tea?"

He wrenched his attention to Bree, who didn't answer Sarah because she was staring so hard at Rob. He stared back just as hard, hungry to learn everything about this unexpected daughter. She was so beautiful, so full of promise. So like her mother. He swallowed hard. "Are you comfortable, Bree? Has everything been satisfactory?"

She nodded vigorously. "Yes, sir! It's been bloody wonderful." Then she shot a stricken look at Sarah. "It's been wonderful. Sir."

Rob suppressed a smile. "I see that you're already learning the ways of society. You'll make mistakes at first, but with practice, you'll know to save swearing for situations when it's called for."

"I can swear sometimes?" she asked, her brows knit.

"Some situations call for nothing less," he said gravely. "Just remember that the fewer times you swear, the more effect it will have when you do."

Bree absorbed his advice, then gave a sharp little nod. "Aye, sir."

When her gaze went to the covered dishes on the sideboard, Rob said, "Have some breakfast. You must be hungry."

Bree didn't have to be asked a second time. She scooped a large spoonful of scrambled eggs onto her plate and was reaching for a second when she suddenly gasped and sent a frightened look to Rob.

Seeing the fear, he said soothingly, "You may have as much as you want."

The girl relaxed. "When I took too much food, the old bugger would beat me."

Rob winced, and not at the language. No wonder she was so thin. "And of course, you didn't know how much was too much until he got angry."

She nodded, looking older than her years. He wondered when her birthday was. "I don't ever want you to be afraid of me, Bree," he said firmly. "Also, when is your birthday? You must be almost twelve now."

"Yes, sir. On April twenty-fifth." Bree took a careful half spoonful of eggs, then added sliced ham and toast. Sarah poured tea for them, then collected her own breakfast.

Bree fell on her food like a starved wolf, using both fork and fingers, while Rob and Sarah watched in fascination and some concern at how hungry she was. Table manners could wait for another day, when she wasn't so hungry. Rob guessed it would be a while before she would be able to relax and eat slowly.

He waited until they'd all finished eating before he said to Bree, "I was educated at the Westerfield Academy, a school for boys of 'good birth and bad behavior.'"

Bree looked startled. "You were bad?"

"Often, but I learned not to be bad without a good reason." Rob regarded his daughter gravely. "I'm going to ask you the two questions the headmistress asked when she was deciding whether or not to accept me as a student. First, she wanted to know what I loved and had to have, and what I hated and refused to have any part of. Will you answer those two questions?"

Bree frowned. "Will you throw me out if you don't like the answers?"

"No, I'm your father, not your headmistress," he replied. "But I would like to know what's important to you."

She chewed on her lip. "I can say anything?"

"You can."

"I want . . . I want a pony," she said in a rush. "A real pony just for me!"

He thought about the massive debts on the

269

estate, but ponies didn't cost much. "Yes, you can have a pony. Do you ride now?"

"A little." Her expression suggested that she was exaggerating.

"You can start riding lessons tomorrow. When you've had time to practice, we'll choose a good pony for you."

She beamed. "A pony!" She turned to Sarah. "Did you hear? My father is going to give me a pony!"

Sarah smiled back. "I spent half my childhood on a pony."

After Bree had had time to absorb some of her bliss, Rob asked, "The second question is what you hate."

This answer came quickly. "I hate being hit. If I were bigger, I'd've killed the old bugger!" Bree said fiercely.

"I will not beat you. I swear it. Is there anything else?"

This answer came almost as quickly. "Don't say nasty things about me mum, and don't lie to me."

"These are easy," Rob said. "Your mother was wonderful and I could think all week and not come up with anything nasty to say about her."

Bree bit her lip. "She was the best mum in the world."

"My mother died when I was about your age," Rob said softly. "I still miss her." She would have loved this granddaughter. Voice normal, he continued, "I don't like lying so I won't lie to you, but I'd like you to promise that you won't lie to me, either. Tell me the truth, no matter how appalling. I won't hit you."

She blinked at him. "I won't lie to you. I swear it."

Then she smiled at him, and his heart twisted in his chest. No matter how great a burden the earldom was, it was worth returning to Kellington to discover his daughter.

Bree bit her lip again, but this time it was thoughtful, not distressed. "Can I have my first riding lesson this morning?"

Rob hesitated. She'd probably love riding astride, but at this point, she needed training in ladylike behavior. "Sarah, might there be a riding habit Bree's size?"

"Bree could wear the one I used yesterday," Sarah replied. "It will be loose and long on her, but there's lots of padding if she falls off the pony."

Bree's eyes were shining. "Sir—Papa—could you teach me?"

Rob felt startled, and absurdly pleased. "I don't know if I'd be a good teacher, but we can try and see how it works." He glanced out the window. "Since the sun is out, we don't want to waste it."

"The lesson would need to be this morning,"

Sarah said. "This afternoon Francie's sister Molly is coming to have tea with Bree."

Still more reason to be grateful to Sarah for all she was doing to make Bree feel welcome. "Then we'll have the lesson as soon as Bree has changed into the habit. Sarah, do you have plans for the day? You could join us for the riding lesson."

She shook her head. "I thought I'd explore the house. There's plenty of it."

"Leave a trail of bread crumbs," Rob advised. "It's easy to get lost."

She laughed and got to her feet. "I'll bear that in mind. Until later."

Then she left, and the room lost most of its sunshine.

Chapter 25

Rob was approaching the house after his riding lesson with Bree when he met Sarah emerging from the side door. The sunlight transformed her hair to gold, and the sight made him smile. "Are you going for a walk? I can show you around the grounds."

She smiled back. "Thank you. I'd like to see more before I go."

He hated knowing that she was going to leave. But all the more reason to enjoy her company while he could. He offered his arm. "Would you like to see the original castle? I'm curious how much has fallen into the sea."

Sarah's warm hand tucked inside his elbow. "I gather the castle was built too close to the cliff."

As they strolled through the formal gardens, he said, "It probably seemed a reasonable distance in the fourteenth century, but for the last hundred years or so, bits have taken to falling off."

"A good thing the present house is well back. Speaking of falling off, how did the riding lesson go? I hope Bree wasn't falling off!"

He grinned. "I'm not sure she was ever on a horse's back before today, but she's a natural. Jonas produced a very gentle old mare and Bree did well. It won't be long before she's ready for a pony of her own."

"Did you enjoy spending time with her?" Sarah's tone was casual, but she watched him closely.

"I really did. I've not had much experience with children, but knowing she's my daughter . . ." He shook his head. "I'm going to be like butter in her hands. All she has to do is call me Papa and I want to give her anything she asks for."

Sarah laughed. "How quickly the steel-hard Bow Street Runner melts! But I'm sure you'll learn to discipline her as needed after you become used to fatherhood."

"I hope so." After another dozen steps, he said intensely, "I want to get this right, Sarah. But I'm amazingly ignorant. What does she need? How do little girls want to be treated?"

Without missing a step, Sarah asked, "What do men need? How do men want to be treated?"

After a surprised moment, he said, "I take your point. Both men and little girls are individuals." He studied Sarah's heart-shaped face. She was distractingly lovely. Reminding himself to stay with the subject, he continued, "You've met her and you were once a little girl. Do you have any suggestions? Should I hire a governess? Send her away to school?" He grimaced. "Assuming I can afford either."

"Don't be too hasty," Sarah warned. "Is there a

village school she could attend? Or perhaps she could have lessons with the local vicar?"

"I don't know," he admitted. "My father wasn't interested in educating the lower orders. He believed that too much learning made them difficult."

Sarah made an unladylike sound of disapproval. "Starting a school is another item for the list."

"The list of things to do around the estate? It's long already."

"I started a new list today," Sarah said apologetically. "When I was exploring the house. It really is a maze, with a mixture of treasures and trash. Overall, the condition of the house is better than the tenant farms, probably because your father and grandmother spent time here. But I thought it would be useful if you knew what would need to be done over time."

He suppressed a sigh at the prospect of still more responsibilities. "Thank you. My knowledge of housekeeping is even less than my knowledge of estate management."

"Good people can be hired to manage both. But a householder needs to know enough to ask the right questions in order to find good managers."

"I should hire you to manage Kellington Castle," Rob said, wishing it wasn't a joke. "You'd do so much better than I. But back to Bree. I shouldn't send her to school?"

Sarah shook her head. "Not now, perhaps never.

Bree needs to feel that she has a real home. That she's wanted and safe here as she was with her mother. Perhaps later a school will make sense, but you'll have to choose one carefully since she's illegitimate. She'd be tormented unmercifully in some schools."

"A pity that Lady Agnes doesn't have a school for girls," he observed. "She has never allowed legitimacy to be an issue among her students."

"The Westerfield Academy for girls of good birth and bad behavior?" Sarah said with amusement. "You should suggest that to Lady Agnes."

"Perhaps I will." They emerged from the gardens onto a grassy swath that ran along the cliff. In front of them the ruins of the original castle stood on a promontory thrusting out into the sea. Stone walls of various heights sketched the shape and size of the buildings that had stood there.

As they walked toward the old castle, a rabbit bolted away from the path and seagulls cried mournfully. The ruins ended abruptly at the cliff edge and pounding waves could be heard below.

He scanned the site, remembering. "When I was last here, the whole of that building was intact. A brew house, I think. Now half of it is gone."

"It's nice to have a legitimate set of ruins," she remarked. "Building false ruins because they look picturesque is expensive."

He chuckled. "These are certainly authentic. I played here often with village boys like Jonas. It's a great place for hide-and-seek. There's a maze of tunnels below. One of them runs well inland and comes out by an old icehouse near the modern house. I'm not sure if the tunnels were used for smuggling or for private comings and goings. I discovered my talent for finding people here. It was very hard to hide from me."

As Sarah laughed, they turned to the left and along the path that paralleled the cliff edge. "I have a few other thoughts concerning Bree," Sarah said. "First, if you are considering an heiress, don't just take her word that she adores children and she loves the idea of being stepmother to your illegitimate daughter. Look at what she does, not what she says. Some women will say anything to acquire a title."

"That's good advice." If he married for cold practical reasons, it would be easier to be objective in his observations. "What are your other thoughts?"

"This is a rather small thing." She glanced up at him. "Bree will turn twelve in a few weeks. Perhaps you could arrange a birthday party for her with the friends she had when living with her mother in that village. Bendan, was it?"

"Yes, it's only about five miles." Cakes and sandwiches for half a dozen girls were well within his budget. "That's a fine idea. She'll be happy to see her friends again, and it will remind her of the good life she had before the old bugger."

Sarah grinned. "Careful. That might slip out when you're talking to others."

"I hope to have no reason to ever discuss the man again." Rob halted them and gestured down the cliff. "This is the path we came up after the yawl was wrecked."

Sarah peered down it. "Good heavens, we really climbed that path in the dark on a stormy night? I'm impressed. It would give mountain goats pause."

"The path is steeper than I remembered," he agreed. "Lucky that I was more or less unconscious when I climbed up so I couldn't see what I was doing."

"Have you ever considered putting a handrail along the cliff?"

"I haven't, but it's a good idea." He scanned the shingle beach below. "There are some scraps of wood that might have come from the *Brianne*."

"Alas, poor *Brianne*," Sarah said mournfully. "She was a good yawl."

"She brought us safely across the sea," he agreed. "It wasn't her fault we didn't have a good place to land."

"Now that I think of it, why are boats always called 'she'?"

He grinned. "Because they're beautiful, capricious, and dangerous?"

"I'm not sure whether to be flattered or insulted," Sarah said thoughtfully.

"I decline to offer an opinion."

Both laughing, they turned back. It felt so easy, so natural, to talk to her. When she returned to her real life of comfort and privilege, he was going to miss her like an amputated limb.

As they approached the house, the rumble of wheels and thunder of hooves could be heard. At least one heavy coach, perhaps more. Rob calculated distances. "Someone's coming. It could be the Ashtons if they made good time."

Sarah's pace quickened. "Oh, I hope so!"

As they emerged from the garden, two large travel carriages swept up the drive and halted in the driveway in front of the house. "Those are the Ashton arms painted on the door!" Sarah exclaimed. "She's here!"

She took off at an impressive speed and reached the lead coach as the door opened and Mariah tumbled out, not waiting for the steps to be lowered. "Sarah!"

"Mariah!" They fell into each other's arms, Mariah weeping. Sarah said, voice shaking, "I have a wedding ring of yours."

Mariah cried even harder.

Rob realized that the incandescent joy of the sisters' reunion was a reflection of the agony Mariah would have suffered if Sarah's sacrifice had proved fatal. Mariah's grief and guilt would never have fully healed if that had happened.

Seeing the sisters together was disorienting since they were so similar, yet not truly identical. The duchess had the gentle roundness of new motherhood, while Sarah . . . was Sarah. Her face was slightly narrower, the personality she projected subtly flavored with her own style of mischief.

Even so, they were as like as two golden peas in a pod.

Ashton emerged from the coach after his wife. Dark haired, quietly elegant, and reserved, he didn't look like one of the most powerful noblemen in Britain. Unless, perhaps, one looked into his unexpected green eyes.

He circled the women and came to Rob's side. Holding out his hand, he said simply, "There are no thanks strong enough, Rob."

"I was just doing my job, Ash." Rob accepted his friend's handshake, which conveyed more than words. "Or what used to be my job. I've acquired a new one."

"From what Sarah wrote, rescuing her was a good deal more exciting than 'just a job,' " Ashton said with amusement.

Rob shrugged. He'd never been good at accepting praise or gratitude. "We wouldn't have made it here safely if she wasn't amazingly intrepid."

"Like her sister." Ashton regarded the two women fondly. "They both look like spun sugar angels. So very misleading."

So very true. As Rob chuckled, another round, comfortable-looking woman climbed from the carriage, a bundled baby in her arms. Mariah said proudly, "Sarah, meet your nephew, Richard Charles, the Marquess of Hawthorne."

Sarah gasped and took the baby, who was dark haired and brightly interested in what was going on around him. "He's so beautiful! He looks like both of you."

"So far, he has a very easy disposition," Mariah said. "I don't expect it will last!"

"Perhaps it will if he takes after his father more than you," Sarah said with a doting smile as she cradled the infant in her arms. The tenderness in her gaze took Rob's breath away. She'd make a wonderful mother.

"We can talk after the ladies are settled," Ashton said to Rob. Lifting his voice, he suggested, "Perhaps we'd best move this reunion indoors? You look tired, Mariah."

"He's right," Sarah said. "Come inside and I'll tuck you and the baby up and we can gossip over tea and cakes."

The duchess smiled. She was beautiful enough to stop men in the streets, but her face was pale and her eyes shadowed. "I must be tired, or I'd resist all this fussing."

281

Sarah laughed and escorted her sister, the nurse, and the baby into the house. "Relax and enjoy it since you have no choice."

Inside, Sarah ordered tea and refreshments, then had Hector escort the female party upstairs to the royal suite, the best rooms in the house. Rob asked Ashton, "Do you prefer to talk over tea or brandy?"

"Tea. If we're to talk business, we'll need our wits about us."

Rob ordered tea to be sent to the library, then took Ashton there by a wandering route. "Under the faux castle trappings it's just a house, and not all that old."

"But a pleasant, spacious house." Ashton halted to gaze out a window toward the sea. "Because I live in a real abbey, I will testify that too much authenticity isn't always comfortable. Ever since I inherited, I've been working to prevent icy winds from whistling down ancient chimneys and menacing stone corridors."

Rob grinned. "You exaggerate."

"A little," Ashton admitted with a spark of amusement in his eyes. "But this house is appealingly eccentric. I hope you don't mind if we stay for several days? There was no holding Mariah back from seeing for herself that Sarah is all right, but I'd rather not tire her with another journey before she's feeling stronger."

"You're welcome for as long as you wish to

stay. I've taken advantage of your hospitality at Ralston Abbey more times than I can count," Rob said. "In fact, that's how I happened to turn up right after Sarah's abduction. A lucky chance created by your generosity in giving me carte blanche to stay when in the area."

Ashton paused, arrested. "Do you know, I hadn't once wondered about that? You appeared, it was a miracle, and it left me free to worry about Mariah. My Hindu ancestors would call it karma, not chance."

As a pragmatist, Rob had no opinion whether his appearance was chance or fate. He was just glad that he'd arrived in time to help. If he hadn't . . . His mouth tightened. He didn't like to think what would have happened to Sarah.

They'd reached the library, where sunshine poured in the west-facing windows that over-looked the sea. He realized with wonder that this was indeed a pleasant house, and the library had always been one of his favorite rooms.

Since arriving in a state of collapse two days earlier, he'd been so weighed down by the burden of Kellington that he'd forgotten the pleasures. This had been a happy house when his mother was alive. It could be again.

If he could afford to keep the damned place.

Chapter 26

As Rob and Ashton entered the library, a footman was just laying out the tea tray between the leather-covered chairs at the far end of the room. After pouring, the man quietly withdrew. Was it Sarah who had the household running so smoothly? Rob told himself to ask her about that.

As they settled into the comfortably worn chairs, Ashton said, "I was so involved at Ralston Abbey that I didn't realize your brother had died until I received your note. I'd met him a few times, but I didn't know him well."

"I hear a note in your voice that suggests you didn't much like him." Rob stirred a small chunk of sugar into his tea. "If you'd known Edmund better, you could have disliked him more."

Ashton nodded. "I suspected as much. Rumor has it that your father and brother were deep in debt. Do you know how bad the situation is?"

"Not yet. I'll have a better idea after I talk to the family lawyer." Rob grimaced. "I don't expect good news. While you're here, can you ride over the estate with me? You're enormously more knowledgeable about such matters than I am."

"For you, anything," Ashton said simply. "I'm

still trying to work out a suitable reward for what you did."

Rob did a swift mental calculation. "It was an expensive mission. Between my time and the acquisition of horses and sailboat, the total is probably near five hundred pounds. I'll draw up an itemized account for you."

"No need, and nowhere near enough." Ashton shook his head. "I'm going to have nightmares forever about how close I came to losing my wife. Mariah would surely have died in the hands of the kidnappers if Sarah hadn't had the courage and quick thinking to take her sister's place. I owe Sarah even more than I owe you."

"Some things are beyond price, so there's no point in trying to figure out what they're worth. I'll settle for my usual fee." Rob smiled. "I imagine Sarah will settle for being your son's godmother."

"Are you sure there's nothing I can give you?"

"I could use a good temporary steward." Rob tried one of the Welsh cakes that accompanied the tea. "The man here was embezzling and I had to discharge him."

"Already? That was quick work on your part."

"Sarah's doing. While I interrogated the steward, she wandered around his office and looked at his books. She'd worked with her uncle, Lord Babcock, on his estate enough that she was able to spot a number of problems."

Ashton laughed. "At which point you terrorized him into confessing and returning his ill-gotten gains?"

"More or less. I didn't have him charged since Sarah pointed out that if he hadn't been so ill supervised, he'd not have succumbed to temptation." Rob took another couple of Welsh cakes. He must meet his cook. "But you can see that I need a steward who is honest as well as capable, and who's willing to take a temporary post."

Ashton thought. "The Ralston Abbey steward has an assistant, Crowell, who is very capable and would love the chance to be in charge of an estate. If things work out at Kellington and you want to offer him a permanent job, you have my blessing. I'll send for him right away if you like."

"I'd be most grateful. I assume he can return to you if I lose the estate?"

Ashton studied him thoughtfully. "It's rare for a situation to be so dire that a peer of the realm loses an entailed estate. I'm not even sure that can happen under our laws. When a new man inherits and shows willing to reduce the debts, it should be possible to work matters out with the banks and other creditors. It wouldn't be easy and it would take quite some time, but it shouldn't be impossible."

Rob refused to accept a stirring of hope. "Possibly, but I'm coming into the estate with no significant property or reputation to make such a thing happen."

"I'll stand surety for you."

Rob stared. Such mild words for a huge act of faith. "Seriously? Kellington is a black abyss of debt and problems."

"Perhaps, but I have faith in you to efficiently settle whatever problems you find," Ashton said imperturbably. "When you talk to your solicitor, remember that you are not without resources." He topped up his tea. "Speaking of Sarah, she told Mariah that when you two arrived here, she claimed to be your fiancée. Is that true?"

Feeling thin ice under his feet, Rob replied, "No, she just wanted authority to give orders while I was unconscious."

Ashton's brows rose. "Your journey sounds more and more interesting. But if word gets out that the two of you traveled together across Ireland, the situation will become complicated."

"An understatement," Rob said dryly. "If you're wondering whether I seduced your sister-in-law, the answer is no."

"If there was any seduction taking place, it would have been with Sarah's enthusiastic participation." Ashton's eyes glinted. "Or even her initiation."

Which raised some interesting questions about Mariah that Rob was not fool enough to ask. "I hoped her abduction wouldn't become common knowledge, but that's looking less likely."

"You've gone from a very private life to a rather public one. People are far more likely to gossip about an earl than a thief taker." Ashton lifted the teapot and topped up their cups. "I'm not a great believer in people marrying just to avoid scandal. But if a scandal does appear—well, the right woman could be very helpful as you establish yourself in your new position."

In other words, a woman like Sarah. At least Ashton wasn't pounding his fist and demanding Rob marry her to save her reputation. But fist pounding wasn't his style, not to mention the fact that Ash must know Sarah deserved a more solvent husband. "If you're asking obliquely whether I have any intentions toward Sarah," Rob said wryly, "I should mention that she's been coaching me on what to look for when hunting an heiress."

Ashton's eyes narrowed. "Would you marry for money? The advantages are obvious. The disadvantages rather less so."

"Until I understand my financial situation, I'm in no position to even think about marriage." Realizing he'd neglected an important piece of news, he continued, "A further complication is that yesterday I learned I have a daughter. She's the child of the girl I wanted to marry when I lived here."

Ashton was one of the few who knew Rob's history. His brows rose. "What an unexpected gift. What about her mother?"

"Bryony died two years ago and our daughter, Bree, had been living with her ghastly grand-father." Rob's jaw set. "Now she's here with me, and here she'll stay. Not all potential wives would be happy about that."

"Any woman you'd want as a wife will accept your daughter. What is she like?"

"Beautiful and fearless and eager to learn." Rob smiled. "Like her mother."

"My congratulations on the new member of your family." Changing the subject, Ashton continued, "Several weeks ago, I attended Wyndham's wedding. You know that he has emerged safely from France? He appears to be in very decent shape for a man who spent ten years in a French dungeon."

"I knew he was back." Rob had met Wyndham the same night he'd discovered that Cassie viewed their relationship very differently from the way he did. He'd wanted to kill Wyndham, the golden charmer to whom everything had come so easily.

Now Rob realized that the pain had faded. Cassie had been right: she and Rob were too much alike. "His wife, Cassie, was one of Kirkland's people. Wyndham is a lucky man."

"He is indeed." Ashton's voice was so neutral

that Rob couldn't decide if he knew about Rob's relationship to Cassie or not. "The new Lady Wyndham is a ravishing redhead with a deep inner serenity. They . . . heal each other, I think."

And both of them had needed healing. Ten years in prison must have matured Wyndham, maybe even made him good enough for Cassie.

For as long as Rob had known her, she'd dyed her hair drab brown. Now, finally, she was free to be herself. *Live long and happily, Cassie. You deserve it.*

Thinking of her made him recognize that Cassie was the past, albeit one of the best parts of his past. What mattered now was the future.

"Much as I love Ralston Abbey, I envy Kellington's sea views." Mariah was perched on a padded window seat in the morning room. In theory, she was writing letters, but she spent more time gazing out to sea. Sarah didn't mind; she enjoyed having her sister in the same room. They still had years of separation to catch up on.

"The sea isn't so pleasant in winter with a gale blowing in from the Atlantic," Lady Kellington said acidly as she set tiny stitches into the canvas stretched over her tambour frame. The frame was set by another window so she'd have strong enough light for her embroidery. "The wind will freeze your bones."

"On a lovely spring day like this, it's hard to

remember winter's fury," Sarah said. Not that she'd ever forget the storm that had driven them into the rocks below Kellington Castle. That seemed like another world, though.

She'd had two blissful days since Mariah and Adam had arrived. Rob and Adam were off doing manly things around the estate while she was enjoying an afternoon of female companionship in the morning room.

"Bugger!" Bree muttered over her embroidery hoop.

"Language, girl!" Lady Kellington barked. "What is the problem?"

"I'm sorry, Lady K.," Bree said meekly. "I don't know how to do this stitch."

"Bring it over and I'll show you," the countess ordered.

Sarah hid a smile as she applied herself to her mending. One of the many similarities she and Mariah shared was a lack of enthusiasm for needlework, though both were competent. However, Lady Kellington turned out to be a master of needlework skills, and in a twist that Sarah could never have predicted, she was now teaching Bree.

The dowager countess had emerged from her lair the day before. Clearly she approved of having a duke and duchess as guests, and the presence of the Ashtons might be raising her opinion of Rob.

She'd had no use for Bree at first, but if she

wanted to sit with the other females, she needed to be civil since Sarah had invited Bree to join her and Mariah. Sarah suspected that Rob had insisted his grandmother be polite to his daughter.

By the end of the afternoon, an odd bond began to form between Lady Kellington and her bastard great-granddaughter. Bree had asked if she could do some embroidery since she'd learned basic needlework skills from her mother and enjoyed doing it. Lady Kellington had pulled a canvas from her basket and ordered Bree to work.

Sketched on the fabric was a floral design for a pillow. The girl stretched the canvas over a wooden hoop and started to embroider. Her swiftness and skill earned Lady Kellington's grudging respect. Soon they were selecting silk thread colors together.

Sarah suspected that Lady Kellington had been lonely as well as grieving for her son and grandson. Having a great-granddaughter who was polite, if occasionally profane, was cheering her up.

"There's a carriage arriving!" Mariah said excitedly. "I think it's the parents come to see that you're all right! And of course Mama wants to hold Richard."

Sarah put her mending aside and joined Mariah at the window while Bree rose and looked out Lady Kellington's window. Only the countess ignored the visitors.

"Yes, that's Uncle Peter's carriage. Mama is getting out, and now our father. Oh, look!" Sarah began to bounce. "It's Uncle Peter himself! I haven't seen him in so long!" She hopped from the window seat and headed for the door of the morning room, closely followed by Mariah.

"Acting like a pack of urchins," Lady Kellington grumbled. "Bree, stay here and get on with your needlework."

Bree hesitated, then obeyed, so only Sarah and Mariah scampered to the front hall to meet the visitors. After hugs and greetings all around, Mariah escorted the guests to the drawing room for refreshments while Sarah lingered to talk to the butler. "Do we have enough rooms made up, Hector?"

"We will by the time your family has finished with their refreshments," he assured her. "I'll tell the cook we're having more guests."

"Thank you. A good thing this house has so many bedrooms!" She discussed the arrangements with Hector in more detail, thinking it was odd how she'd slipped into acting as the lady of the house. When Sarah was gone, would such duties fall to Lady Kellington? She'd suggest to Rob that he hire a housekeeper to work with Hector.

They were about to leave the front hall when the knocker sounded smartly. "The house is becoming quite busy," Hector murmured as he crossed to open the front door.

The door opened to a sturdy man with a weathered face and a wooden peg leg. "I'm here to see Carmichael," he said in a cockney accent. "Him what is the new earl."

Hector said in freezing tones, "What is your business with his lordship?"

Taking an educated guess, Sarah approached the man and said warmly, "Surely you must be Mr. Harvey, whose position defies easy classification?"

He cracked a smile. "Right you are, miss. Jeremiah Harvey. Are you the young lady he chased to Ireland for?"

"I am." She offered her hand. "Sarah Clarke-Townsend, generally known as Sarah. Rob is off looking at fields or something of that nature, but he'll be back by the end of the afternoon. May I offer you refreshment?"

He shook her hand gravely. "Nay, I had a pint and a pie at the local pub. I brought some of Rob's—his lordship's—clothing from London. If you point me toward his room, I'll take his traps up."

Sarah said to the bemused Hector, "Lord Kellington has told me about Mr. Harvey." Turning back to the newcomer, she added, "He'll be very glad you're here. Hector, will you escort Mr. Harvey up to his lordship's rooms?"

"I can use some help with the baggage," Harvey added.

Hector bowed stiffly. "As you wish."

As Harvey headed outside again, Sarah whispered to the butler, "Isn't life more interesting now?"

Hector said dourly, "You say that as if interesting is a good thing."

Laughing, she headed off to join her family. Interesting was indeed a good thing.

Chapter 27

Rob was hiding in his father's dismal little study calculating costs when Sarah ran him down the next afternoon. She sailed into the room with her shining smile. "I thought you might be lurking here. Feeling overwhelmed by my relations?"

The sight of her made Rob's muscles start to unknot. "A bit. Individually they're all pleasant, but collectively"—he shook his head—"I'm starting to feel rather hunted."

"Soon we'll all be gone and you'll be able to relax again." Sarah folded gracefully into a chair on the opposite side of the desk. "If you're going to use this place as a retreat, it could use some redecorating."

"If I make it attractive, more people will come," he said with irrefutable logic as he feasted his eyes on Sarah. She'd always looked lovely, even in scruffy boy's garments. Now that her own wardrobe had arrived from Ralston Abbey so she was wearing clothing that fit, she looked even better.

"You're probably right," she agreed. "The library is thoroughly infested with guests. That's the drawback of turning it into your office.

296

Perhaps you need two libraries, one for you and one for everyone else."

He smiled at Sarah's whimsy. They'd not been alone together since the sky had filled with falling relatives, and he missed talking to her. "I've already been interrogated about my intentions toward you by Ashton, your father, and your uncle."

"Good heavens," she said blankly. "Why would they do that?"

"There is the small matter of you and me traveling across Ireland unchaperoned," he pointed out.

She frowned. "That seems so long ago that I forget how scandalous it could be considered. Did any of my relatives tell you we had to marry to save my reputation?"

"On the contrary, they all seem rather relieved to hear that I had no intentions and was in no position to consider marriage to anyone," he said dryly.

"My mother and sister have been asking indirect questions about you and us. As if there was an *us*. Such foolishness." She dismissed it with a wave of her hand. "One reason I hunted you down was to see if you have more information about the estate's financial status. You and Adam and my uncle have been having such long discussions."

"They've both been very helpful. Your father

has had less experience as a landowner, but he made a couple of good suggestions also." Rob drew a quill pen through his fingers. Steel pens lasted longer but cost more. Lately, he found himself thinking about the cost of everything. He didn't like the idea of living like that forever. "I still don't have firm information, though. It's only been four days since I wrote the Kellington lawyer. I expect I'll hear from him soon."

"I hope so. The uncertainty must be maddening. But it will pass." She looked apologetic. "The main reason I'm here is that your grandmother has ordered me to produce you for predinner drinks in the salon, and when she gives orders, I obey."

Rob frowned. "Is she being rude to you?"

"Only her natural rudeness," she assured him. "I'm growing rather fond of her. Did you know she's teaching Bree advanced embroidery techniques?"

He blinked. Bree? His grandmother? "I'm having trouble envisioning this. Are we talking about Bree, my pony mad daughter? When she and I talk, it's mostly about horses. Or has some other Bree moved into the house while I was busy elsewhere?"

Sarah laughed. "There's only one Bree. She's hungry for all these new experiences. Riding, needlework, new friends, the conversation of older women. She absorbs it all. She rather reminds me of what I was like at that age."

"I'm glad she's settling in well." He sighed. "Apart from the riding lessons, I haven't spent much time with her. I need to do better."

"Bree is well looked after," Sarah said. "Speaking of which, earlier this afternoon I took her to the vicarage to meet the vicar, Mr. Holt, and his family. They're schooling their own three young children, and they're willing to include Bree for a modest fee. They're pleasant people and Bree liked them. Do you want to proceed with that?"

"Yes, and thank you! It sounds like just what she needs." He straightened the papers he'd been working on and got to his feet. "So. Predinner drinks in the salon. Do I look sufficiently respectable?"

"It's your house, you can wear bearskin and feathers if you like," she said with a chuckle. "But yes, you look suitably lordly. Like me, you've benefited by having your own clothing delivered so you needn't wear garments foraged from the attics."

She flattered him; he was dressed like a doctor or lawyer, not a lord. But since he didn't possess a lordly wardrobe, his dark blue coat and buff trousers would have to do.

As he moved around the desk, she said quietly, "This is something of a going away party.

Tomorrow, all your uninvited guests, including me, will be leaving."

He felt as if she'd punched him in the midriff. She was leaving tomorrow? So soon? He'd known she must go, but somehow, he hadn't thought of all his intense consultations about the state of the estate as subtracting time from being with her. It was suddenly hard to breathe. "Which of your homes will you go to? Your sister, your parents, or your uncle?"

"My sister," she said immediately. "The Ashton houses are so large that I don't feel underfoot, and this way I get to spend more time with my adorable little nephew. I intend to be a model aunt." Her tone was light, but a little wistful.

She should be having babies of her own, but he couldn't bear to let his thoughts run in that direction. "I'm sure Mariah will be glad of your company as well. You two are thick as thieves."

"We have years of conversation to catch up on." She shrugged. "Quite apart from the pleasures of gossiping with my sister, there's a gentleman near Ralston Abbey who has shown signs of interest in me. Now that I've had my fill of adventuring, I intend to take a closer look at him. Mariah assures me that he's wealthy, witty, and kind as well as quite passably good looking."

Once more he had breathing problems. Was she tormenting him deliberately? No, they'd both accepted that they had no future together. Having discussed his marital prospects, there was no reason for her not to mention her own. "I'm sure your protective male relatives will make certain that he's a suitable mate."

"They're allowed opinions, but the decision will be mine." She stood. "We'd best get to the salon before your grandmother sends a hunting pack after us."

He opened the door for her. "After you, princess."

She did a brief, elegant curtsy. "Thank you, my lord. By the way, I've wondered. Did you know that Sarah means princess in Hebrew?"

"No. It just seems to suit you." He drew her into his arms for a hug. Not a kiss; that would be too dangerous. But he needed to feel the warmth of her body against him one last time. Soft and female and so very dear. "I'm going to miss you," he said softly.

"I'll miss you, too, Rob. It was a grand adventure, wasn't it?" She pulled away, her usually expressive face unreadable.

A grand adventure that was over. Silently he escorted her out into the hall and they headed across the sprawling house while a drumbeat in his head said, *She's leaving, she's leaving, she's leaving.*

The shortest route to the salon was through the vast front hall. As they entered, he surveyed the walls and wondered if he really needed so many stuffed animal heads.

The knocker sounded. Since there was no servant in sight, Rob opened the door himself. Standing on the front steps was a very fashionable young man about town.

The man stepped inside, his gaze lingering appreciatively on Sarah before returning to Rob. He produced a card with a flourish. "I'm here to see Lord Kellington."

"Why?" Rob looked at the card. The Honorable Frederick Loveton.

Loveton looked offended. "My business is with his lordship, so take him the card, my man."

"I'm Kellington, and not your man," Rob said dryly. "I have no recollection of ever doing business with you."

Loveton gave a quick, startled glance at Rob's unfashionable attire. "So sorry, my lord! I knew your brother, poor fellow. Which is what brings me here." He produced several folded papers from his pocket. "These need to be settled."

"Gambling chits for . . . ye gods, almost ten thousand pounds?" Rob said after a quick scan of the papers.

"Nine thousand seven hundred pounds, to be precise." Studying Rob's expression warily, Loveton said, "I'm willing to offer a discount since you've just inherited and must be still sorting matters out. Perhaps ten percent? Say, a nice round nine thousand quid?"

Rob was not in a good mood, so he didn't bother with subtlety. He ripped the papers in half, then again, and handed the ragged quarters back to Loveton. "You've wasted your trip from London, Loveton. But at least Somerset is pleasant in the spring."

"But, but . . . it's a debt of honor!" Loveton sputtered.

"Nothing to do with my honor," Rob said, feeling more cheerful.

"I shall see that every gentleman in London hears of your churlish behavior," his visitor growled. "There won't be a club in town that will allow you into the card room."

"Feel free to tell the tale. With luck, that will mean that other cardsharps with my brother's vowels won't bother me," Rob replied. "Since you must have horses chilling outside, I suggest you leave."

Loveton's lips thinned as he shoved the torn gambling chits into his pocket. "You, sir, are no gentleman!" he spat out before slamming the door behind him.

Rob turned to find Sarah helpless with laughter. "That was splendid!" she gasped. "His face when you tore them up . . . !"

His brows arched. "You don't mind that I have no honor?"

"You've got honor of the kind that matters," she retorted. "Your brother doesn't seem to have had any of that."

"I'll try to repay tradesmen's debts," Rob said, "but I'll be damned if I waste what money I can scrape up paying Edmund's gambling debts." He offered his arm again. "The predinner drinks had better include brandy."

"Ask for whiskey," she said with an endearing giggle. "It's not a gentleman's drink, as I understand it, and you must be true to your colors."

He was laughing when the knocker boomed again. With a sigh of exasperation, he left Sarah and turned to open the door. "I hope that twit's carriage hasn't broken down. If he needs to stay here for the night, he'll have to settle for the stables."

He threw the door open—and found himself confronting a tall, voluptuous brunette wearing a magnificent black satin mourning gown with a feather-trimmed black cloak. He blinked at her décolletage. If she was a new widow, she appeared to be shopping for a replacement husband.

She studied him with interest before asking in refined accents, "Are you by any chance the new Lord Kellington?"

"I am," he said shortly. "If you want to collect a gambling debt, you're out of luck. I just ripped up a pack of vowels and sent their holder away."

"Is that why Freddie Loveton was just leaving?

No matter. My purpose is very different." She gazed at him with soulful eyes. "I'm Vivien Greene."

He searched his memory. "Sorry, I don't know you and don't believe I've ever heard your name. Unless you wished to engage me for a job? If so, I'll have to decline. I'm about to resign from the Bow Street Runners."

Her gaze intensified. "You were a Runner? How delicious! But my purpose is not to engage you. At least, not in that way. I was betrothed to your brother and I've been mourning since he was tragically taken from us. I've come to mourn with you."

She embraced Rob so fervently that he stumbled backward a step. As her lavish curves flattened against him, he noticed she wore far too much heavy perfume.

He tried to peel her off, but the damned woman was like ivy. "I'm sorry for your loss," he said as he removed her arms from around his neck, "but surely you should seek comfort from your friends and family and vicar."

When he managed to put some distance between them, she looked up reproachfully and batted long, dark lashes. "You were Edmund's brother, I his beloved. Surely we can comfort each other better than anyone else!" Great tears formed in her blue eyes. "He fell from his horse in Hyde Park and was trampled by a coach and four, you know. He spent three days in agony before he mercifully died on . . . on what would have been our wedding day." She produced a lacy handkerchief and dabbed at her eyes.

The last time Rob had seen Edmund, his brother was gloating as he sold Rob into what was damned close to slavery. "Three days of agony are nowhere near enough," Rob snapped. "I hope he burns in hell for eternity. So you see that we have nothing in common, Miss Greene. It's time for you to leave."

She looked shocked, then calculating. "I'm sorry the two of you were so estranged. But that doesn't mean you and I can't be friends. I'm not Miss Greene, but Mrs. I'm a very wealthy widow with complete control over the fortune my dear old Walter left me. Edmund and I suited each other very well. He wanted an heir and a fortune, and I wanted a title and entrée into the highest levels of society."

She laid a suggestive hand on his arm. "There's no reason why you and I can't make a similar bargain. Your estate badly needs an infusion of cash, and I'd like a husband." She ran a frank gaze over him. "And I must say you're a good deal more attractive than Edmund. What do you say, Robert? Shall we further our acquaintance?"

He felt like he'd fallen into a really vulgar dream. Sarah had said that he needed a merchant class heiress, and Vivien's accent had been getting less refined the longer she spoke. There she was, the opulent answer to Kellington's problem, because her fortune had to be real or Edmund wouldn't have proposed to her.

He'd marry her over his dead body.

Where was Sarah? He scanned the hall and saw her standing to his right, looking fascinated and bemused. When their gazes met, her brows rose in a look that clearly said, "Well, what are you going to do now?"

"As interesting as your proposition is, Mrs. Greene, I must decline. I'm already betrothed." He closed the distance between himself and Sarah and wrapped an arm around her waist.

Vivien's brows arched. "Sorry, Kellington, but she's already married to the Duke of Ashton. Unless he just died? Surely not. I'd have heard."

"The Duchess of Ashton is my twin sister," Sarah said brightly. "And Lord Kellington is *mine*. It's time for you to leave."

"She's a pretty little thing," the widow said critically. "But too young for you, and I guarantee she has less money than I do. It's not too late to change your mind."

Rob tightened his grip on Sarah. "Sorry, but you're barking up the wrong earl."

Vivien laughed and fluffed her feathery cloak. In a more natural voice, she said, "You can't blame a woman for trying. There aren't all that many eligible earls around, and even fewer who are young and good looking. I expect I'll have to settle for a baron."

"Good luck finding a lord less poisonous than my brother," he said dryly.

"I'd love to know what drove you two apart," the widow mused. "But I expect you won't tell me."

"Quite right. Good-bye, Mrs. Greene."

With a last flash of her décolletage, she said, "No doubt I'll be seeing you two lovebirds in London."

Sarah smiled sweetly. "If you come near Rob again, I'll scratch your eyes out."

Vivien laughed. "I could like you. Take care of him, pet. Good men are hard to find. Just as a hard man is good to find. . . ." She left in a fluttering of feathers.

"Did that really happen?" Rob said, a little dazed by his recent visitors.

"It did indeed. Really, Rob, you could do a lot worse," Sarah said thoughtfully. "You'd have to confirm the money, of course, but she seems to be rich and eager to be a countess, and she certainly looks fertile."

Her words were the last straw. "No! Bedamned to common sense!" Rob turned and gripped her shoulders with his hands. "Sarah, will you marry me?"

Chapter 28

Sarah's jaw dropped. "You can't mean that! You said you're in no position to marry, and it's not as if we're in love with each other."

"No, but I'm tired of being noble and sensible and doing what's best." His aquamarine eyes were blazing. "There's no good reason for you to marry me. I have a shabby imitation castle, an illegitimate daughter, and my financial situation is still unknown and probably dreadful. I may end up having to lease the estate to a nabob since I won't be able to afford living here. As you say, we're not in love, and I have it on good authority that I'm no gentleman."

Struggling with her instant impulse to accept, she said, "You make a compelling case for declining your offer and running for the hills."

"I want to be very, very clear." He stepped back, his hands clenching into fists. "I don't want you to agree out of gratitude because that would be a terrible foundation for a marriage. Nor do I want pity even if my situation is dire. Though you'd have a title, you'd not have the luxurious, fashionable life that usually goes with being a countess. But I swear that I would do whatever is necessary to provide a decent home for you and Bree even if that means working as an assistant steward for your uncle."

She bit her lip, torn by so many emotions she didn't know what she felt. "Why are you offering? A wife would just be a complication now. Or are you looking for a mother for Bree? A year from now you'll be in a much better position to decide what you want in a wife, or even if you want a wife at all."

"I'm not asking for Bree's sake, though if you recall, you told me to watch how a prospective wife acted toward Bree rather than just listening to her words," he pointed out. "I've given her riding lessons, but it's you who made sure she has a room, a wardrobe, friends, an education, and everything else she needs. You've done it for no reason beyond the fact that she needed to be cared for, and you seem to like her."

"Liking Bree is easy. She's a delightful girl. But if you're not marrying for her—why?" She had to know before she could give an answer. "Do you want a wife to help you with all the burdens that have dropped on you? Or do you want *me?*"

He opened his mouth to reply, then closed it again, frowning as he sorted out his thoughts. "I'm out of my depth, Sarah. A really competent, knowledgeable wife like you would be a great blessing. I need a capable woman who can run a large household and move comfortably in society. Someone with a generous heart, but not extravagant tastes. But I don't mean a woman *like* you. I mean *you*. In the last weeks we've seen each other under difficult conditions and have a good idea of each other's characters."

"What do you see in me?" she asked curiously.

He smiled with a warmth that came from deep inside. "You're beautiful, of course, but you're also resilient and intelligent and good natured. Enjoyable to be with. And—honorable."

She didn't need to be told how much honor meant to him. Or how desperately she'd miss him if she left. Trying to be as sensible as he was, she said, thinking out loud, "Life has been dull since my parents reconciled. They're so happy together that I feel rather like an intruder. And I did not like winter in Cumberland."

"Somerset is one of the warmer parts of England," he pointed out.

"It is that." Her lips curved up. "And life with you would not be dull."

"Since we've both loved and lost, we're well matched," he said quietly. "Without romantic illusions, we're free to be friends."

Something unpleasant twinged in the vicinity of Sarah's heart. "Shouldn't husband and wife be more than friends?"

He stepped forward and drew her into his arms. "There is also *this*."

He kissed her not as a guilty pleasure, but as a lover, with passion and tenderness and promise.

One hand slid into her hair, loosening pins to clatter to the floor.

She opened her mouth under his, savoring his taste and his teasing tongue. They could be friends and lovers and share common goals, she realized. That would be enough, and so very much more than what she'd had.

As her eyes closed, she slid her hands under his coat, feeling the flex and power of his muscles through his linen shirt. His hand was caressing her breast deliciously when the door to the hall opened and a gasp sounded. Sarah tensed, breaking the kiss.

"What is the meaning of this?" boomed from the doorway.

Sarah looked up to see Lady Kellington glowering at them. She looked ready to break her cane over someone's head.

Rob's embrace tightened protectively. "Isn't it obvious?" he said mildly. "I'm kissing Sarah."

Before the countess could explode, Sarah spoke up. "Rob and I have just become betrothed."

"I thought you *were* betrothed!" the old lady snapped.

Sarah could feel the joy blazing through Rob as he heard her words. "The situation having changed, we needed to reconsider," he explained. "Can you blame me for celebrating the fact that she has accepted me again?"

"Hmmph!" his grandmother snorted. "If the chit has a fortune, it's the first I've heard of it."

"Alas, I'm no heiress," Sarah said. "My portion is a mere two thousand pounds."

Lady Kellington snorted again. "You could have done better, boy, but I suppose you could also have done worse. Come to the salon and make your announcement. It's bad enough that I had to come looking for you."

"We'll be there in five minutes," Rob promised. "But we have a few things to discuss before we make the announcement. Could you send a servant to collect Bree and bring her down to the salon?"

"Five minutes then." She cast a scathing glance over Sarah. "Use it to make yourself decent, girl." She pivoted and marched away, cane tapping.

"Are you reconsidering your acceptance?" Rob asked as the door slammed behind his grandmother. "I should have put her on the list of reasons why you wouldn't want to marry me."

Blushing and laughing, Sarah broke away from him and bent to collect her hairpins from the floor. "My grandmother Babcock was a similar old tartar. She lived with us in Hertford, barking orders at Uncle Peter and my mother like they were still in the nursery. We all adored her. She died when I was fifteen and I still miss her."

"My grandmother terrifies me, so I leave you to deal with her." Rob offered his hand as she rose with her recovered hairpins. She didn't need the help, but she liked holding his hand. She was still giddy with the idea that this handsome, dark-edged man wanted to marry her. They would face problems—but together, they could solve them.

"Where and when would you like to be married?" he asked. "Your family church in Hertford? At your parents' home in Cumberland? Ralston Abbey? London?"

"Here," she said decisively as she coiled her hair at her nape and stabbed in a hairpin. "This will be our home, so why not begin as we will go on? The wedding of the local lord will give the people of Kellington something to celebrate. A good symbolic start to the new era of the fifth earl of Kellington."

"I like that idea. When?"

"How long would it take to get a special license from London?"

Rob's brow furrowed. "Perhaps three or four days. I'll admit that I'd like to marry sooner rather than later, but do you want it that soon?"

She finished securing her hair, then shook out her gown. "Most of my favorite people are right here, so we might as well take advantage of that." She gave him a sultry look. "I don't want to wait any longer than necessary, either."

"Ah, princess." He smoothed back a strand of hair that she'd missed, his fingers warm against her throat. "If you don't stop looking at me like that, we might end up consummating our betrothal right here."

"And be caught when your grandmother comes looking for us again? No, thank you!" She took his arm, but didn't start walking. "I just thought of something awkward. Who should give away the bride?"

"Why . . . ah, I see. Your father and uncle are both here. Your father is your father, but your uncle raised you." He regarded her thoughtfully. "Which would you prefer?"

She hesitated, remembering all the years she'd tagged around after her uncle, learning to ride, to shoot, to keep the books for an estate. He'd doted on her, carrying her on his shoulder when she was little and saying she was more fun than all his sons put together. She always giggled and kissed him and called him a silly when he said that. "Uncle Peter."

"Then ask him. Your father might not like it, but he's a fair-minded fellow. He'll understand."

She gave a decisive nod. "Uncle Peter it is. Mariah will be my matron of honor, of course, but I'd like Bree to be my bridesmaid. Do you think she's too young?"

He smiled. "She'll love that. It will be a good start to our becoming a family."

As they headed to the salon, Sarah wondered what to wear. One of the gowns Mariah had brought from Ralston Abbey would have to do. She began making mental lists, grateful that this would be a simple country wedding.

Just outside the salon they intercepted Bree, who was being brought down by Harvey. Bree wore one of her new gowns, a pretty blue linen with dark blue trim. With her hair pinned up, she looked every inch a young lady.

Rob smiled at his daughter and his friend. "I'm glad to be able to break the news early to both of you." He patted Sarah's hand where it rested on his arm. "Sarah and I just became betrothed."

"Surprised it took you this long to ask her," Harvey said with an approving nod.

Bree stopped in her tracks. "Bloody hell!" She frowned at Sarah. "You're not my mother."

"No, I'm not," she said, not raising an eyebrow at the language. "You had a fine mother who will always be part of you. I'm just Sarah. You can think of me as your stepmother, or a sort of aunt, or even a big sister if you like. But we will be part of the same family. That makes me happy."

Bree looked unconvinced. Sarah guessed that since the girl had just discovered she had a father, she wasn't inclined to share him with another female.

Rob caught his daughter's gaze. "You and I will both benefit by having Sarah in the family, Bree. I guarantee she'll be much better at demonstrating how to be a lady than I will ever be." He held out a hand. "Will you celebrate with us?"

She approached warily, then burrowed into Rob's side under his arm, her face hidden. Sarah said, "Bree, I'd like you to be in the wedding as my bridesmaid. You and my sister would be my attendants because you're my family. Will you do that for me?"

Bree raised her head and peered across Rob, looking unnervingly like her father. "You really want me in your wedding?"

"I really do," Sarah said seriously. "Some families are born, others are built. I want the three of us to build a family together."

"I . . . I'd like that," Bree said as she straightened.

"Good girl!" Rob crooked his left arm for his daughter to take. "Now let's go into the salon and break the news to the others."

They entered the salon with Sarah on Rob's right arm and Bree on his left. Conversation paused as the half dozen guests turned their way.

"In case it isn't obvious," Rob said, "Sarah has done me the honor of accepting my proposal. Since you're all here, we plan to be married in three or four days, depending on how long it takes to get a special license from London."

There was an arrested moment and Sarah saw surprise on most faces. Apparently she and Rob had done a good job of convincing everyone there was nothing romantic between them. Then Adam raised his glass. "To Sarah and Rob. Congratulations on finding each other. I'm glad we'll be brothers-in-law." He smiled at Bree. "And what a bargain to acquire a niece at the same time!"

As Bree blushed, everyone else toasted the news and the room exploded with talk. Sarah's parents and uncle approached, beaming. Her mother said, "I'm so glad, darling! I was beginning to think I'd never have the chance to cry at your wedding!"

Sarah hugged her mother, tears in her eyes. Anna was the one who'd held her when Sarah wept inconsolably after Gerald's death. Through Sarah's childhood, Anna had been not only her mother, but her best friend.

The return of Anna's husband had changed that. Sarah had acquired Mariah, but her relationship with her mother had inevitably changed. Still, they'd always be close, and Sarah thanked God she had Anna as her mother.

Uncle Peter gave her a burly bear hug. "So my little girl is getting married!"

Realizing that there would be no better time, Sarah took her father's hand. "I don't want to hurt your feelings, Father, but—Uncle Peter, will you give me away?"

Her uncle glanced warily at Charles. "I'd be

honored, as long as it doesn't cause trouble in the family."

"You earned the right, Babcock," her father said ruefully. "I missed so many years of Sarah growing up. At least I'll be here for your wedding."

"Thank you for being so understanding." Sarah gave her father a hug, feeling very fond of him.

After congratulations and best wishes had been exchanged in all directions, Lady Kellington said in a piercing voice, "I'm ready for my dinner."

"An excellent idea." Rob looked around the salon to find the butler. "Hector, could you add another place setting for my daughter? She should celebrate with us since this is a family occasion."

Bree beamed at him. Sarah was grateful the girl was adjusting so quickly.

Since the evening was informal, there was no parade by precedent into the dining room. Mariah took advantage of that to take Sarah aside. "I'm sorry, but I have to ask," she said softly. "Rob seems like a fine fellow and Adam thinks very highly of him, but are you in love with him? From what you've told me, I worry that you aren't."

Sarah bit her lip, wondering how to explain in a way her twin would understand. "If Adam died, would you ever be able to love and marry again?"

Mariah winced. "I can't bear to think of that." She frowned, looking away before saying haltingly, "Perhaps. But I could never love another man the same way."

"You and Adam are fortunate that you've been able to marry your first great loves. Rob and I lost our first loves," Sarah said quietly. "That makes us well matched. We care about each other. We trust each other." *We desire each other.* "He's the only man I've met since Gerald that I can imagine marrying. I think we'll suit very well."

Mariah's expressive face showed under-standing, but also regret that her sister wouldn't have what Mariah and Adam had. "That's a good beginning, and the bond between you will only grow stronger after you marry." She smiled conspiratorially. "I have a perfect gown for you. It's the duchess dress that I brought."

"Duchess dress?"

"When I travel, I always have one grand gown just in case," Mariah explained. "Because I'm a duchess, I'm often asked to visit schools and open church bazaars and the like. I've found people are disappointed if I don't live up to their image of what a duchess should look like." Mariah grinned. "As a countess, you'll get this, too. The duchess gown I brought on this trip is one I've never worn. I'd love to give it to you. That is, if you like it."

Sarah laughed. "I'm sure I will! You know how we're always choosing the same colors and styles. What does it look like?"

"Ivory silk with long sleeves and crystal beading on the bodice. There's gold lace and a gold underskirt, with a demitrain and a matching shawl. It will look wonderful on you."

"It sounds beautiful! Tomorrow I'll try it on." Seeing that everyone else was already in the dining room, she said, "And now, let's eat!"

Chapter 29

Sarah went to bed exhausted, but found she couldn't sleep. Visions of everything that needed to be done for the wedding danced in her head. She and Rob needed to visit the vicar, Mr. Holt, and talk to him about scheduling the ceremony. Rob's man Harvey would leave first thing in the morning for London to procure a special license at Doctors' Commons so they wouldn't have to post banns and wait three weeks to marry.

She flopped over and kneaded her pillow, trying to get more comfortable. Lady Kellington was making lists of important local people who should be invited to the wedding of the local lord. Sarah had asked Francie if she'd like to become a lady's maid officially, since she'd been doing the job unofficially. Francie accepted with pleasure, and would continue to look after Bree as needed.

One thing Sarah didn't have to worry about was food for the wedding breakfast. Anna had taken on that task and disappeared into the kitchens for a long discussion with the cook. It was a relief to consign such a major responsibility to her mother.

So much had been done in a few hours, but so

much more awaited! Sarah flipped and flopped and knocked her pillow onto the floor twice, but her brain remained obstinately active.

Finally she sighed and got out of bed. Maybe she could find something to read down in the library. After belting on her long wool robe and donning slippers, she headed down, a candle in her hand. Strange to think that she'd be walking these passages for the rest of her life.

Unless they couldn't afford to live here, of course.

The library had two fireplaces, so Rob set a blaze in the eastern one, which was at the end of the long room he'd turned into an office. He stripped off his coat and cravat, tossed them aside, and stretched out in a wing chair with his feet on a chubby little ottoman. There were a thousand things he should be thinking of, but at the moment he didn't give a damn about any of them. He'd save productive thought for the next day. For now, brandy and a fire sufficed.

He heard the library door open and glanced up to see Sarah. Interesting that he immediately knew it was her even though Mariah was sleeping under the same roof. Her long blond hair fell in a braid over one shoulder and she wore a floor-length blue robe belted at the waist. Almost every inch of her was covered, and she still looked ravishing.

She hesitated in the doorway. "Would you rather be alone?"

"You're the one person in this house I'm happy to see." He rose and crossed the room to scoop her up. She made an adorable squeak before settling comfortably in his arms. He returned to the wing chair with her as a warm lapful, her head tucked under his chin. "I gather you couldn't sleep either?"

"My mind was churning like a waterwheel," she agreed. "I came down to find a book of sermons that would put me to sleep."

He chuckled. "I should have thought of that. Would you like some brandy?" He offered her his half-empty glass from the side table. She took a sip before handing it back. A small thing, but so very intimate.

Was marriage made of such small, intimate moments? He'd not really thought much about that in the past. Marriage had never seemed inevitable, much less imminent.

As he stroked her back, he said, "I didn't realize that a betrothal puts one into a strange new world. Over port, I felt that I was being initiated into the fraternity of married men. Men of substance, men of affairs. Men with gravitas. Marrying you will increase my value to society."

She laughed. "It was like that with the women when we adjourned for tea. Mariah and my mother and your grandmother were treating me differently." She gave an exaggerated shudder. "I was terrified that Lady Kellington would insist on explaining the facts of life to me."

Mildly alarmed, he said, "I assume that isn't necessary?"

"I grew up on a farm so I think I'm reasonably well informed. If I have any questions, I'll ask Mariah."

It was a long time since he'd been an eighteen-year-old virgin, but he and Bryony had managed to work things out to their satisfaction. She'd possessed a frank physicality that made everything easy.

Sarah wasn't missish and he was no longer inexperienced, so they should do all right. But he'd better start thinking of something other than his wedding night before he couldn't think of anything else. "Ashton and Mariah's wedding present will be to pay for the celebration for everyone on the Kellington estate."

Sarah's eyes widened. "That's incredibly generous!"

"Tactful, too. With him paying, I don't have to count pennies. The tenants deserve a good time. They haven't had much to feel good about for years."

She glanced up at him, her brow furrowed. "Does it bother you that you can't afford to do it yourself?"

He grimaced. "I've been self-supporting and

debt free my entire adult life, so I resent having to worry about costs and debts that aren't my own. But I won't let stiff-necked pride prevent me from accepting help when it's offered. Particularly since Ash keeps saying that his debt to me is too great to ever be paid."

"He's right," Sarah said seriously. "Rescuing me took enormous courage and skill. You're a hero." She smiled up at him. "*My* hero."

"I was just doing my job." He couldn't resist kissing her, though he kept it quick and light to avoid escalation. "Did you know that he rates your courage even higher than mine? Putting yourself in the hands of a group of unknown villains was—extraordinary."

Sarah looked surprised. "Not really. The villains were already there. Stuffing Mariah into the crypt meant at least one of us might escape."

"It would have been far more ladylike to collapse with strong hysterics." He grinned. "I'll never forget your expression after you bashed one of your abductors over the head with a cast iron skillet. You looked so proud of yourself."

"I *was* proud of myself!" she said indignantly. "I thought I was being quite enterprising."

"Without your joining in, the odds of our both escaping safely would have been much slimmer." He bent his head for another kiss, and this time he didn't try to keep it light. His petite lioness . . .

She made a purring sound as she kissed him

back, her fingers curling deliciously into the nape of his neck. He caressed her breasts, very aware that she wasn't wearing stays or much of anything else under her robe.

She wriggled in his lap to change her position, her round and perfect rump arousing him to the point where his brain quit altogether. "My golden princess . . ." he whispered huskily as he leaned deeper into her embrace.

They slid off the chair to sprawl on the worn Oriental carpet. Rob realized they were falling in time to shift his weight so that he landed on his hands and knees around Sarah instead of squashing her underneath him. "Are you all right?" he asked urgently.

She responded with a fit of giggles. "I think we're meant to behave ourselves until our wedding night!" she said when she caught her breath. "Either that, or it's a lesson that the proper use of chairs is for sitting."

Relieved, he sat back on his heels and helped her sit up. "Interesting things can be done on chairs, but not tonight." He took both her hands in his and just gazed at her. Bright eyed, laughing, indomitable.

Marrying Sarah might be the least sensible thing he'd ever done. But it felt exactly right.

The next morning turned into a giddy, impromptu female planning and fashion event. The ladies of the household gathered in the morning room, along with the lady's maids and Hannah, the baby's nurse. Young Richard was the only male allowed into the room, and he was only interested in sleeping.

Naturally everyone wanted to see the gown first, so Sarah and Francie moved behind the painted screen and Sarah donned Mariah's duchess gown. Francie murmured, "I need to tighten the lacing a bit since the duchess just had a baby, but otherwise, this is perfect. Go show everyone."

When Sarah stepped from behind the screen, there was a collective sigh from the other women. "You look like a fairy princess!" Bree exclaimed.

Sarah crossed to the tall mirror that had been brought in for the occasion, catching her breath when she saw herself. The heavy ivory silk fell in luxurious folds, the pale shade bringing out her delicate blond coloring. The long sleeves and décolletage were modest, in keeping with the gravity of a wedding ceremony, but the crystal beads on the bodice sparkled like falling stars.

"There are matching shoes," Mariah said. "Gold kid with crystal beads sewn on, and a heel so you won't look quite so short beside Rob. Do you like it?"

Sarah touched the gold lace that edged the neckline and echoed the gold of the satin underskirt, then turned sideways and walked a few steps. The demitrain glided behind her with a whisper of silk. "This is the most beautiful thing I've ever worn, Mariah! Are you sure you don't want to have it back?"

Her sister laughed. "It's yours, Sarah. Even if we are twins, I swear it looks better on you than me."

"Sarah has that bridal glow," her mother said. "The color is similar to what I wore when I married your father." She smiled mistily. "What is it about a wedding that brings out the tears?"

"The knowledge that everything to come will be inferior," Lady Kellington said tartly, but even she had a sparkle in her eyes. "It's not a good season for flowers. A pity the conservatory here has been allowed to go to rack and ruin."

"I don't need exotic flowers," Sarah said. "There are miniature daffodils in the garden that will look beautiful with snowdrops and greens. I thought nosegays for me and Mariah and Bree, and perhaps tussie-mussies for you and Mama."

"What musicians are available?" Anna asked. "Does the church have an organ?"

"Yes, and the vicar's wife plays very well. You'll need some fiddlers for the wedding breakfast and the tenant celebration. The head groom, Jonas, is a member of the local group, so he can organize the music."

"Thank you!" On impulse, Sarah kissed the old lady's cheek. "I'm so glad you're here."

The dowager blushed but didn't pull away. "You're the only one who feels that way." She gave a ferocious scowl. "Mind you produce an heir as quickly as your sister did. But not in less than nine months!"

Sarah laughed. "I promise that won't happen. Bree, now it's time for you to try on your dress. The white gauze is pretty, but it needs more trimming for the wedding. Perhaps some gold lace to match my gown?"

"That would be bloody fine!" the girl exclaimed.

Lady Kellington scowled. "No profanity in the church, or there will be consequences!"

"God will strike me dead?" Bree said innocently.

"If He doesn't, *I* will!" the dowager growled. "Sarah, do you have a suitable hat to wear for the ceremony?"

"I thought she could use this one of mine." Anna lifted a hatbox from the floor beside her and produced an elegant deep-crowned straw hat. "It will need new trimming, but the shape and style are good."

Bree said hesitantly, "Sarah, I thought . . . I've been embroidering a hatband. It isn't finished yet, but I can have it done by the wedding. Would you like to see it?"

"I'd love to." Sarah would say it was beautiful no matter what, but in fact, no exaggeration was needed. The band was about two inches wide, and over half was embroidered with exquisite tiny blossoms in gold and ivory. "Bree, this is wonderful! Mariah, Mama, look how fine Bree's needlework is! She was already skilled, and Lady Kellington has been teaching her the more complicated stitches."

"Perfect!" Anna also knew the value of encouraging a young girl who needed to know that her presence mattered. She wrapped Bree's embroidered band around the crown. "This will look beautiful. Are you sure you can finish it in time?"

"Oh, yes!" Bree exclaimed. "Even if I have to stay up all night every night."

"I don't want you too tired to be my bridesmaid!" Sarah said as she hugged Bree.

Lady Kellington gave a rare nod of approval. "The embroidered band will look very fine. Mind you get it finished." She hesitated, then said almost shyly, "I think the hat needs a short veil to fall back over the bride's head and shoulders. It could be tucked under the band."

"That would look lovely, if we had a veil." Seeing the dowager's expression, Sarah asked, "Do you have one?"

Lady Kellington nodded. "I wore it on my own wedding day. It's an ivory shade that will go with the gown and it would lend a bit of history to the day."

Sarah refrained from pointing out the irony of the countess's veil being anchored by the embroidery of the illegitimate great-granddaughter she'd started out despising. "That would be *perfect*. I'm so lucky to have you all here!"

"It's our pleasure," Mariah said. She looked a little wistful. Her wedding to Adam had been quietly magnificent, and they'd both radiated so much happiness that the church, St. George's on Hanover Square, had scarcely needed the masses of candles used to light the interior.

Sarah had been the maid of honor so she was in the heart of all the activities, and the wedding had drawn her and Mariah closer. But that ceremony had not had the sweet intimacy of this small, swiftly cobbled together ceremony.

Sarah was lucky indeed.

Chapter 30

Rob hadn't seen Sarah all day, so he was pleased when they met in the front hall for the short journey to the vicarage. They had several purposes. One was to accompany Bree for her first lessons. His daughter was excited to be returning to school, particularly since one of the Holt daughters was close to her age.

The other reason was for Rob to meet the Holts, since they were vital members of the community and would be teaching his daughter also. And, of course, they had to schedule the wedding.

While Mrs. Holt assessed Bree's academic skills, Sarah introduced Rob to the vicar. Holt was a lean, balding man a few years older than Rob, with humorous eyes and a genuine concern for his parishioners. That boded well for the future of the parish; it was good when the vicar and the largest local landowner could cooperate.

Mr. Holt congratulated them on their upcoming nuptials, and was happy to hear that they wanted the ceremony to take place in the church, even though a special license meant it could be held anywhere. They walked through the church together. Rob had always liked its classic simplicity and Norman tower. Sarah had been right; this was the best place to marry. They picked five days later for the date to make sure that Harvey would be back with the license.

As they drove away, leaving Bree at the vicarage for the rest of the afternoon, Rob asked, "Is my grandmother behaving? I presume she'll be glad to see me making steps to secure the succession, but that doesn't mean she'll stop criticizing everyone in sight."

"She's actually been quite helpful," Sarah replied. "I think she enjoys the activity, as well as the knowledge that she's the local expert on everything."

"I suppose she's been bored," he said thought-fully. "She's been pretty much alone here for most of the last couple of years, keeping an eye on the estate without help from my father or brother." In addition, he suspected that even his curmudgeonly grandmother wasn't proof against Sarah's charm.

"She ordered the servants to clean the master suite for us," Sarah said. "Are you willing, or would you prefer to stay in other rooms with fewer memories?"

Rob frowned, slowing the light carriage as they came up behind a farm wagon. "I wasn't in those rooms often enough to have many memories. I do recall that they're spacious and well laid out, with a bedroom each for the master and the mistress, two dressing areas, and a sitting room. Gloomy, though. Why not take a look and see what you think? Heaven knows the house has no shortage of space."

"I'll see if the suite is livable or whether it will send us both into a melancholy." She chuckled. "I wonder how many years will pass before I learn my way around Kellington Castle."

"Many. Carry a ball of yarn to mark your trail if you go into the farther reaches."

"I presume you are the fearsome Minotaur lurking in the center of the labyrinth?"

"I try," he said gravely.

When she laughed, it occurred to him that there were few traits more endearing than a woman who appreciated one's jokes. His humor was usually so dry that most people didn't know he had any.

He was tempted to take his betrothed on a drive so they could enjoy more of the spring day, but they both had too much to do, so he headed directly back to Kellington. As he drove into the stable yard he saw a strange horse tethered, and a tall man dressed in black was talking to Jonas.

Rob halted the one-horse carriage and secured the reins. Before he could help Sarah down, the man in black turned. He was a Roman Catholic priest—and a man from the past. "Well, I'll be damned," Rob breathed when he saw the familiar face.

"I don't doubt it for a minute," the newcomer said with a richly rolling Irish accent. He held his hand out. "I just learned that fortune decided to kick your arse."

"So it did, Patrick." Rob shook the priest's hand vigorously, enjoying the reunion even though he had a good idea what problems this visit would bring. "But watch your language, please. My fiancée is here." He turned to the carriage and helped Sarah down.

"Sorry, miss!" Patrick studied her, his gaze calculating under his outgoing manner. "Or would that be 'my lady'?"

She smiled. " 'Sarah' will do. And you would be . . . ?"

"Patrick Cassidy," Rob said. "My companion in hell-raising when I visited Ireland as a boy, and my second cousin from the Catholic side of my mother's family. Apparently Father Patrick now."

"In the flesh," his cousin said genially. "Parish priest in your own lands."

Sarah's gaze moved from Rob to Patrick and back. "I see the family resemblance. A pleasure to meet you, Father Patrick. I haven't met much of Rob's family."

But mentioning Rob's lands changed the atmosphere from lighthearted to something darker. Rob said, "You'll not be calling on me just to say hello."

336

"Indeed not. Is there a place where we can talk?"

Rob hesitated. "The house is full of visitors."

"We can go to the much despised study," Sarah suggested. "That's private."

"I'll take care of your horse," Jonas said, moving forward to take hold of its bridle. "You take care of your business."

Patrick frowned at Sarah. "This is no matter for the lady."

"Sarah has been in Ireland. She can hear what you have to say." Rob smiled faintly. "Having a lady present might prevent us from killing each other."

"A fair point, cousin." Patrick's tone was genial but wary.

They reached the study, which was as dismal as ever. Considering how often Rob ended up in the place, perhaps he should do as Sarah suggested and fix the room up. A coat of whitewash would do wonders.

As soon as they were private, Rob asked bluntly, "What do you want, Patrick?"

"I can't be visiting my own kin without an ulterior motive?" Patrick asked, his expressive face all innocence.

"You must have jumped onto a packet ship from Dublin as soon as you heard I'd inherited," Rob said dryly. "And you were just guessing that I'd be here. That suggests a pressing need."

His cousin's blue eyes narrowed. "If you want blunt, boyo, you shall have it. People at your estate of Kilvarra are dying of hunger and neglect. Your father and brother did nothing except wring every damned penny they could from the tenants. I'm praying to God that you spent enough time at Kilvarra to care about the people, and be willing to make improvements." His mouth twisted. "Is that straightforward enough?"

"Impressively concise, especially for someone who was a master of tale-telling." Rob never would have predicted that his cousin would become a priest, but it was said that the wild boys were often the ones who heard the call. "I'm guessing you have some suggestions for improving matters."

"Right you are. First, fire the steward, Mr. Paley. He's a brute and bully and probably a thief." From an inside pocket Patrick pulled a paper covered with small handwriting and tossed it on the desk. "On the packet, I wrote down instances of his bad behavior that I know of. There are many more."

Rob glanced at the list, frowning at still more evidence of what happened when bad men were given power and allowed to run loose. He passed the paper to Sarah, who acquired a matching frown as she read about the incidents.

"If you're telling me the truth about Paley, and

I assume you are, he'll be gone within a fort-night," Rob said. "Is there anyone on the estate you trust to take over and do the job competently?"

"No one there at the moment, but I'd suggest my brother Seamus. He's ten years older than we are so you'll not have seen much of him, but he's working as a steward near Dundalk, and he'd like to come home now that our folks are getting along in years."

Nepotism, but probably of the productive sort. "Seamus sounds like a good choice, but before he gives notice, I should warn you that my inheritance is a disaster, and I'm guessing that all the unentailed property is mortgaged to the hilt. That probably includes Kilvarra. Though I can get rid of Paley, I may lose possession of the estate. I'll probably know within the week just how bad things are."

Patrick, who had been looking optimistic, sighed heavily. "I should have known it was too good to be true. You'd be a better landlord than your father, but you're saying you might not have the chance?"

"I'm afraid not. Plus, some of the problems are going to be much harder to solve than firing a bad steward."

" 'Tis the curse of Ireland that our fine soil can support a whole family with no more than a potato patch and a milk cow," Patrick said gloomily. "That's a larger problem for another day."

"Too many people for the available land," Sarah said thoughtfully. "What about emigration? Would any of the tenants be willing to move to the colonies in hopes of a better life?"

Patrick looked bemused. Apparently he was another man who didn't take her seriously at first. "There have been folk from Kilvarra who've moved to other lands and prospered, but that takes money."

"How much?" Sarah asked curiously.

Patrick considered. "Maybe a hundred pounds a family. Enough to cover the cost of passage with enough left to get established in the new country. Less for single folk, of course. There are some who would do it, but it's far too much money for most to find."

Sarah pursed her mouth. "Father Patrick, would you mind stepping out for a few minutes while I discuss something with Lord Kellington?"

Patrick probably wasn't used to pint-sized blondes asking him to leave the room, and he didn't know if her wanting to talk to Rob was good or bad. But he rose obligingly and headed to the door. "As you wish, Miss Sarah. I won't go far."

When the door closed and left them private, Sarah said, "The Irish property is special to you, isn't it?"

He nodded. "Yes, because it was my mother's home. She was always so happy to return for a visit with me in tow. Patrick and I and other local lads ran around like hellions. I spent enough time there to resent the way England treats the Irish."

His mouth twisted. "The hell of it is, I don't know how much I can do to help the people at Kilvarra. If I have to sell or forfeit unentailed property in England, I know the tenants will probably be all right under new owners. Better than when my father and brother owned the property. But if I lose Kilvarra, the odds are that the new landlords will be no better than my father, and quite possibly worse."

"That's what I suspected." She took a deep breath. "Rob, use my portion to help people emigrate to places where they have a chance to build better lives. The money you retrieved from Buckley is needed here to help the Kellington tenants and just to keep the place running while you get sorted out. My two thousand pounds isn't enough to save Kellington, but it can make a huge difference to the people of Kilvarra."

He stared at her, amazed at her generosity toward people she didn't even know. "It would. But why are you even thinking to suggest this?"

"Because Kilvarra is special to you," she said gravely. "You'll feel much happier if you can do something for them right away."

"You can read my mind of thoughts I haven't

even had yet," he said ruefully. "It's a good thought. I'll start with a thousand pounds for emigration money. If enough people take me up on that, we'll think about another thousand." He raised his voice. "You can come in now, Patrick. Just in case you missed any of the details."

The door opened and his cousin entered, a wide grin on his handsome face. "What a very fine lady you're marrying, Robert."

Sarah blinked. "You knew he'd be listening at the door?"

"For something this important, of course." Rob smiled at Sarah. "I'd do the same, you know, if I thought it needful. Not being a real gentleman has its advantages."

"I like that about you." Sarah got to her feet. "Now that you've sorted out your business, I assume the two of you would like to catch up on the past over a few pints of good country ale?"

"Definitely a mind reader," Rob said. "I'd be most grateful if you could have a pitcher of the best ale brought here."

She nodded and turned to his cousin. "We'll be getting married in five days. I do hope you'll stay for the wedding, Father Patrick."

He hesitated. "I'd be delighted, but mightn't it be a bit awkward to have a Catholic priest here? A blood relative of his lordship, no less?"

"I'm thinking we should all begin as we wish to go on. As Rob's cousin, you are welcome in our house." She inclined her head and withdrew.

His gaze admiring, Patrick watched her leave. "Now there's a lass that could make a priest forget his vows."

"Don't even think about it," Rob said coldly.

"Can't stop a man from thinking, even if he's a priest," Patrick said, his eyes twinkling before his expression turned serious. "You've chosen well, Rob. Especially since it sounds like you'll need a good woman at your side."

"I'm lucky." Rob realized he was beaming like a fool, so he made himself stop and return to business. "Do stay for the wedding, Patrick. The day after, you can head back to Ireland with my associate, Mr. Harvey. He'll have full authority to act on my behalf, and he's as shrewd as they come, so don't be trying to pull any wool over his eyes. If what he finds confirms what you say, he'll get rid of Paley and start talking to people about emigration. You can trust him as you do me."

His cousin studied him thoughtfully. "I don't know what you've been up to these last dozen years, but you're sounding very much like a lord."

Rob winced. "Is that good or bad?"

"That depends on you," Patrick said. "But you were a decent lad, and I think you'll be a decent lord."

Rob hoped his cousin was right. The last thing he wanted was to be a lord in the style of his father and brother.

Chapter 31

After Sarah gave orders for provisions to be sent to the study and for another guest bedroom to be prepared, she went in search of her sister. Finding her in the library, she said, "I'm about to survey the master suite to find out if it's livable. And if it's awful now, whether it's salvageable. Care to join me?"

"I'd love to." Mariah set aside her correspondence. "I often had to improve living quarters during the wandering years with Papa. Adam's households are so well run that I never need to do anything of that nature, and I miss it."

Sarah laughed as she led the way upstairs. "Feel free to make suggestions. And thank you for lending me the Ralston head housemaid to accompany the temporary steward Adam is lending Rob. I'm hoping they'll be here today."

"Since Mr. Crowell and Sally Hunt are keeping company, it made sense to invite them both. I hope that your finances will permit hiring them permanently. They're both very good at their jobs and deserve top positions."

"We certainly need people like them." They reached the master suite, which took up the whole eastern end of the floor. As Sarah unlocked the door, she remarked, "Rob said he remembers these rooms as spacious but gloomy."

"He was right about the gloom," Mariah said as they stepped into the sitting room. "We start by opening those draperies. This room should have a sea view."

So it did, Sarah saw when she stopped coughing from the dust raised by opening the heavy draperies. They were layered velvet of a dismal gray green color. It was hard to imagine anyone choosing that shade voluntarily.

She studied the sitting room. "This was expensively decorated at the height of the Egyptian craze. I've always found it unnerving to sit on sofas with crocodile feet."

"There's the constant fear one will be bitten." Mariah thoughtfully rubbed the sphinx head on a chair arm. "What an enormous amount of ugly, expensive furniture!"

"I wouldn't mind the ugliness so much if it was comfortable." Sarah rapped the spiky excrescence on a chair back. "I hope Kellington Castle is like most great houses and that old furniture never leaves, it just moves to the attics. After we finish the survey here, we can take a look there. Onward to the master bedroom!"

Mariah opened a door on the far end of the sitting room. "The crocodiles invaded here as well. Lord Nelson's victory at the Battle of the Nile has much to apologize for."

"Plus the colors are dreadful. Do you suppose the gray green draperies are supposed to look like the muddy Nile River? Whatever the reason, they're depressing." She swung open a door. "I wonder if this door connects to the mistress's room. No, it's the earl's dressing area. Complete with some very expensive garments that must have belonged to Rob's father since his brother never came here after inheriting."

Mariah joined her. "His father's valet would have inherited most of the earl's wardrobe in London. It's rather sad to see clothing waiting for a man who won't return."

"That's a poetic way of looking at it," Sarah said. "I look and see a lot of things that need to be packed away if Rob is to live in these rooms. I don't think he'd enjoy reminders of his father. Let's see where this door leads."

She opened it and gasped. "A bathing room! It's as splendid as the ones in Ashton House. I'm glad the old earl aimed some of his extravagance in this direction."

"The tub is large enough for two." Mariah opened another door. "And I see they were clever enough to install a water closet at the same time. Convenient!"

"More examples of the old earl wasting money." Sarah continued through the opposite door into the countess's dressing room. She moved to a window and drew back the draperies.

"The furniture looks like it might have been chosen by the earl's first wife during the Gothic craze. Gloomy, but at least no crocodile feet."

Mariah touched the dry, long dead blossoms in a dusty vase. "Do you think this room has been locked and untouched since Rob's mother died?"

"Quite possibly. It's more pleasant than the earl's room. Cleaning and brighter draperies and bed hangings will make a huge difference." Sarah imagined Rob scampering in to see his mother when he was a small boy, perhaps bringing flowers or other treasures. The room might have been gloomy, but love had warmed it. "Rob's mother might have been the only person his father ever loved. After she died, he stopped caring about much of anything, which made him a very bad earl and landlord."

"It's much healthier to have many kinds of love in one's life." Mariah crossed to one of the windows. "Instead of a sea view, this looks over the gardens. The room will be warmer than the other when the winter gales blow through."

Sarah eyed the canopy bed and had a swift, sizzling image of sharing it with Rob. Reining in her thoughts, she said, "Let's see what we can find in the attics. I wouldn't be surprised if there's a matching set of Gothic furniture for the master's room."

There was, but they found something even better in a back attic: two sets of light, elegant

Sheraton bedroom furnishings. Sarah pulled the holland cover from an end table and ran her fingertips over the delicate satinwood inlays. "This furniture is beautiful! It must be what was removed when the old earl's first wife went mad for the Gothic style. I wonder if there are draperies and hangings as well."

Mariah slid behind a wardrobe into the corner. "There are two large trunks here that look promising. Bring the lantern back so we can look."

By the time Sarah reached her sister, Mariah had opened the first trunk. The tang of lavender wafted out from the sachets of herbal preservatives. She raised the lantern as her sister lifted the first fold of fabric. A floral motif in shades of rose and burgundy was set against a background of ivory brocade. "Lovely! They must be the draperies for the countess's room. Let's see what's in the other trunk."

Mariah raised the lid to reveal a similar brocade, only with the pattern in shades of blue. "This must be for the earl's room. You've struck gold here!"

Sarah grinned. "That makes it worth the fact that we both look like rag pickers. The master's rooms will look very different and much better."

Mariah nodded. "Now it's time to put every maid and footman to work refurbishing the suite for your wedding night!"

Sarah blushed, glad the dim lighting concealed her reaction. Despite all the wedding preparations, the idea that she would be married in a few days was somewhat unreal. Reminding herself that women had been marrying from time immemorial, she closed the trunk.

Take it all one step at a time.

Sarah and Mariah were about to return to their respective bedrooms to change into clean clothing when they passed the staircase that swept down to the ground floor. "This place is like a London coaching inn," Sarah said as she looked over the railing into the front hall. "So much coming and going! Some is because of Rob's inheriting the title and some is wedding related. But more is permanent, I fear."

Mariah nodded. "A great house is a buzzing hive of people. When I was plain Mariah Clarke, it was easy to be private, but it's different for a duchess. I learned from Adam how to draw boundaries to protect myself."

"I suppose I must learn how to do that, too," Sarah said without enthusiasm. "Staying a spinster aunt would have been easier than becoming a countess."

"Marriage isn't about becoming a grand lady. It's about being with the one you love," Mariah said quietly.

Her sister's searching gaze made Sarah want to change the subject. She'd already explained how the relationship between her and Rob was different from that of Mariah and Adam. It was not a topic she wanted to return to.

She was about to continue on to her room when the knocker banged on the front door. Who was it this time? She and Mariah paused to see. A footman crossed the hall and opened the door to reveal a couple standing on the front steps.

"It's Mr. Crowell and Sally Hunt here from Ralston Abbey!" Mariah said excitedly. "And none too soon."

She scampered down the steps to greet the new temporary employees. Sarah followed, giving thanks for the extra help. Any steward or housekeeper trained in the Ashton household would surely be well skilled.

Sarah recognized Sally Hunt from Ralston Abbey. She was a neatly put together young woman in her late twenties. Interestingly, she'd donned a subtle air of authority. Instead of a senior housemaid, she now looked like a housekeeper, a woman of high responsibility in a large household.

If Sally could change her demeanor, so could Sarah. Speaking as lady of the house to her housekeeper, she said with a smile, "Miss Hunt, welcome. I'm so very glad you've arrived." Her gaze shifted to the steward. "Mr. Crowell. We've not met, but you come highly recommended."

He bowed. "I look forward to the opportunity to serve Kellington."

Like Sally Hunt, he carried himself like an intelligent, ambitious person who appreciated the opportunity to reach a high position at a relatively young age. Both of them would work hard to prove themselves capable.

"Mariah, could you take charge of Miss Hunt? Show her to her quarters and introduce her to the senior staff members." She smiled wickedly. "And get her started on that project you and I were discussing. I'll take Mr. Crowell to meet Lord Kellington."

The new employees exchanged a glance. Yes, they were a couple. If the positions here worked out, they'd surely be wed within the next year.

Now to put them to work!

Chapter 32

Today is my wedding day. Sarah's fingers were shaking so badly that she couldn't get the wires of her earrings into her ears.

"I'll take care of your earrings, my lady," Francie said in a soothing voice.

"I'm not 'my lady' yet," Sarah pointed out as she gratefully handed the golden hoops to her maid.

"It won't hurt me to practice so I'll be ready when you become the countess." Francie deftly inserted the wires in Sarah's ears. Tiny gold spirals hung from the main hoops and they captured the light whenever Sarah's head moved. The gold emphasized her golden underskirt and lace. Her face might look like a wax work death mask, but at least she glittered.

"Sister Sarah, you look so stunning that Rob will keel over when he sees you coming down the aisle." Mariah, lovely in a pale peach gown, entered the bedroom. She was trying to look understated so as not to draw attention from the bride, but Mariah couldn't help but look beautiful. Sarah didn't mind.

"Give the credit to your duchess gown." She hugged her sister, then Bree, who was following. Rob's daughter looked excited but demure in her white gown with gold lace trim. It was hard to remember the ragged urchin who'd been delivered to the castle.

"You both look marvelous!" Sarah exclaimed. "Are you prepared to fight off any abduction attempts on me? Lady Kellington said that was the original purpose of bridal attendants. To protect the bride from being stolen away."

"I'll fight for you!" Bree said, looking more like the fierce urchin she'd been.

"I'll help defend you, too," Francie offered, eyes twinkling.

"Let's skip that part since you actually were abducted not so very long ago," Mariah said with a shudder. "Are you ready? It's time to leave for the church."

"I'm in a flat panic." Sarah dabbed on the day-time perfume sent by her friend Lady Kiri, who was Adam's sister and a brilliant perfumer. "Otherwise all is well."

"It's normal to feel nervous." Like Francie, Mariah was using the soothing voice designed to keep anxious brides from strong hysterics.

"I don't recall you being this nervous," Sarah said as she stepped into her slippers. The gold kid and crystal beads looked like fairy foot-wear, and she liked the two inches of height she gained.

"I was marrying Adam, so of course I wasn't nervous." A furrow formed between Mariah's eyes. "Are you having doubts about marrying Rob? It's not too late to change your mind."

Sarah made herself think seriously about Mariah's question. Yes, she was panicked, but Rob was the most interesting man she'd ever met as well as the most attractive. Together, God willing, they could rebuild Kellington and have fine, handsome children. She hoped any offspring would get Rob's height, not hers. "Rob is excellent husband material. I'm just . . . nervous. As you say, that's common."

"Here's your hat, Sarah." Bree opened the hatbox she'd brought and reverently lifted out the redesigned hat.

"Oh, Bree, your embroidery is exquisite!" Sarah traced the finely stitched blossoms with one fingertip. "Did you have to work late every night to get this done?"

Bree nodded, but her eyes were shining. Sarah had a brief mental image of the girl someday wearing the hat to her own wedding.

She turned to the mirror and set the hat on her sleek blond hair. The band of embroidery secured the creamy lace of Lady Kellington's veil, which swept over the crown to fall back past Sarah's shoulders. Now she looked like a bride, not a duchess.

Francie tweaked the position of the hat. "Last of all, a bit of color." She wielded a hare's foot to brush a hint of pink onto Sarah's cheeks. "And this lip salve." The salve was also colored pink.

Francie's deft application of cosmetics made Sarah look natural and healthy rather than like death walking. Sarah said in a less than steady voice, "I look as good as I'm going to, so it's time to get married."

Bree led the procession down the stairs and out the front door to the waiting flower-bedecked carriage. Sarah's parents and uncle and the dowager countess had left earlier in another coach. Most of the servants were already at the church as well. Two or three had stayed behind so the house wouldn't be completely empty.

Hector himself helped the four females into the coach, a slight but actual smile on his face. When they were settled and on their way, Sarah said, "When we get there, remind me which one is Rob. We've both been so busy I've hardly seen him in days."

Mariah patted her hand. "That's why you're so nervous. You'd feel better if you'd spent more time together. But you've used these days well. The master suite is splendid, and even that dull little study is much improved."

All true. The new housekeeper was a gem, and the people of Kellington were excited and optimistic about the future. It had been easy to hire extra help from the village to clean and rearrange. The castle was starting to look like a home.

All too soon they arrived at the church. Sarah felt numb when she climbed from the carriage. Francie was carrying the flowers in a basket, so she produced Sarah's nosegay. "Here you are, my lady. Those bright yellow daffs are as pretty as sunshine."

As Francie gave flowers to Mariah and Bree, Mariah said, "Don't hold the flowers so high, Sarah. Keep them at waist level. Now onward, favorite sister!"

"I'm your only sister," Sarah pointed out as she lowered the nosegay to her waist.

"So you have no reason to doubt you're the favorite!"

The footman opened the church door for the bridal party, and rich organ music poured out. Uncle Peter waited in the vestibule. He beamed at Sarah as she entered. "Aren't you the prettiest sight!" He held out his arm. In a lower voice, he said, "I'm so glad I've had you as a daughter even though you weren't."

His words almost started her crying. Taking his arm, Sarah said, "You were all the father I needed."

At that, he looked teary as well. While they talked, Francie lined up Bree and Mariah, then cracked the door to the sanctuary. "All is in order," she whispered. "Miss Bree, you first. Remember to walk slowly so everyone can admire how pretty you look."

Expression determined, Bree clutched her nose-gay at waist level while Francie signaled the organist to start the processional music. Mrs. Holt performed an expert transition that moved into a solemn march.

Francie swung the door all the way open and Bree stepped out into the aisle. Her head was high and she seemed nervous but happy.

Then Mariah, looking serene and lovely, and probably confusing anyone who didn't know Sarah had a twin.

"Your turn, pet," Uncle Peter murmured. "He's a fine man. You've chosen well."

Had Sarah really chosen Rob? Or was this a marriage of convenience and proximity? Frantically reminding herself to carry the nose-gay low, she stepped through the door into the sanctuary, glad she had her uncle to steady her. The church was full to overflowing, and there was an audible gasp of admiration when she appeared. Mariah's duchess gown was doing the job.

Sarah's gaze locked on Rob, who stood in front of the altar with Adam beside him. Her breathing was swift and shallow as her uncle escorted her down, then stepped back to sit beside Sarah's parents.

Rob was all lean, broad-shouldered strength. But as she approached, he looked cold, so cold. His handsome features were still as marble and his clear light eyes were ice. Could he be regretting this marriage?

Even if he did, he was too honorable to walk away. If anyone was to stop this ceremony, it would have to be Sarah.

"Dearly beloved," the vicar intoned, beginning the familiar service in a rich, deep voice, *"we are gathered together here . . ."*

If Sarah didn't marry him, what would her life be like? Living with her parents in the far, cold north? Becoming a permanent spinster aunt in her sister's home? Live at Babcock Hall as a spinster cousin?

While her chaotic thoughts stampeded through her mind, the vicar continued through the service. She was dimly aware when Rob expressed his willingness to have her as his wedded wife with a firm, clear, "I will."

Then Mr. Holt turned to Sarah. The words floated past her until he said, *". . . forsaking all others, keep thee only unto him, so long as you both shall live?"*

As long as you both shall live! Sarah sucked in her breath. The words sounded as final and deadly as a falling guillotine blade. Her gaze flashed up to Rob's face. His expression was intense, unreadable.

She was ready to bolt when he took her right hand, raised it to his lips, and brushed the lightest of kisses across the back of her gloved fingers. His gaze held hers, and with a jolt she recognized that he was nervous, too. Did he know how close she was to leaving him at the altar? Probably; the damned man was entirely too perceptive.

Memories flooded her mind. So many memories for such a few weeks. He'd saved her and protected her, warmed her by night, and laughed with her by day. With his new rank, now he needed her help. They might not love the way Mariah and Adam did, but together they were stronger than they were separately. Surely that would be enough.

Her silence had lasted so long that people were starting to shift in their seats. She squeezed Rob's hand and gave him a tremulous smile. "I will."

He smiled back with a warmth that started to dissipate the chill in her bones. The rest of the service passed in a blur. She became aware when Rob slid a plain gold band on her third finger, left hand.

"What God hath joined, let no man put asunder!" made her flinch again. It sounded so very, very permanent.

Because it was. Divorce was virtually impossible, so these vows they took today would bind them for as long as they both lived.

Too late to worry now. The vicar pronounced them man and wife, and the organ filled the church with a river of joyous music. Holding

Sarah's hand firmly, Rob turned them and led her up the aisle and onto the porch as the organ music was joined by the jubilation of the church bells ringing with a force that saturated all Kellington.

On the porch, she said apologetically, "I'm so glad that's over!"

His smile was full of relief. "So am I."

Within moments, they were surrounded by well-wishers offering congratulations as the whole community celebrated. Their marriage was a pledge to the future.

Her mother's hug came with happy tears while her father beamed with pride. Jonas shook Rob's hand with the approval of a long-married man, and Father Patrick gave both of them exuberant hugs and Catholic blessings. Mr. Crowell and Miss Hunt stood side by side, discreetly holding hands. There were faces she recognized from riding the estate with Rob, though she couldn't put a name to them.

And—Lord Kirkland? One of Rob's close friends and partners in covert missions. He looked travel weary, as if he'd just arrived, but he bowed graciously when her gaze caught his.

Now that she was officially a wife—and Countess of Kellington!—there was no going back. So she might as well enjoy the celebrations!

Chapter 33

Rob felt a rush of relief when the wedding service was over and Sarah was officially his wife. She'd looked shatteringly beautiful when she entered the church in a swirl of ivory and gold like an angel come to earth. But the nearer she drew, the more terrified she looked. Surely he'd given her no reason to be afraid of him?

There had been one truly dreadful moment during the ceremony when he was sure she was going to pivot and bolt up the aisle, flowers flying. Then he realized how natural her nerves were. When he'd proposed to Bryony at eighteen, he had no real understanding of the enormous, life-changing commitment he was making. Neither had Bryony. All they'd known was that they'd wanted to be together.

This time he had a much better understanding of how profound and life changing marriage was. But unlike Sarah, he wasn't terrified. Sobered by the vows he was taking, yes, but he had no doubts. He and Sarah would suit very well.

As they greeted people on the porch of the church, she seemed to have recovered completely from her attack of nerves. After the last person had offered good wishes, he wrapped an arm around Sarah's waist and tucked her close to his side. "Even with the extra inches of those charming slippers, you're just a little bit of a thing," he said fondly.

She looked up at him with a laugh, golden tendrils of hair curling from under her festive hat. "Perhaps the trouble is that you're too tall."

She looked so alluring that he couldn't resist bending to give her a kiss. She responded with enthusiasm, which provoked a chorus of cheers and hoots from the viewers. There was nothing like a wedding to put people in a jolly mood.

She emerged from the kiss flushed and laughing. "Time to return to the castle. I couldn't swallow anything more than tea this morning, and now I'm ravenous."

"I suspect that the wedding feast the Ashtons have organized has enough food to provide for the whole of Somerset. Shall we find out?"

She took his arm and they climbed into the open, lavishly decorated carriage waiting to carry them up to the castle. By prearrangement, inside the carriage was a sizable bag of shiny new sixpences. Rob stayed on his feet and called, "Thank you for joining our celebration!"

Then he tossed handfuls of glittering coins high in the air to shower down into eagerly waiting hands. Tomorrow he'd feel poor again, but at least this wedding was happening in proper style, thanks to their friends.

He settled beside Sarah and gave orders to the driver to head up to the castle, then handed her the last bright sixpence. "For luck, my lady."

She smiled and flirtatiously tucked the coin into her bodice. His gaze followed, riveted, as the sixpence slipped into the shadowed area between her breasts. "I shall have to locate that coin later," he said, his mouth going dry.

"It's interesting that after a lifetime of being told to behave modestly, I now have license to be bold with my husband." She pulled up the ivory silk skirt of her gown to reveal a shapely leg and a beribboned garter holding up her silk stocking. As she fiddled with the garter, she gave him a slanting, mischievous glance.

The carriage was high enough that only Rob could see her—but what he saw made him want to forget the feast and go direct to their bedroom. He swallowed hard. "That's more than bold," he said. "It's downright provocative."

She smoothed the skirt down demurely. "Then I shall resume maidenly modesty."

"Everything you do is provocative. Even that perfume you're wearing. It's delicate and floral, but with a hint of spice. One of Lady Kiri's concoctions?"

Sarah nodded. "She gave me two versions. One to wear in the day." She gave a slow, sultry smile. "The other for the night."

He laughed, caught between frustration and

amusement. More than either of those things, he was intensely glad they were back on their usual friendly footing. "I do believe you're trying to drive me mad. I'm considering kidnapping and ravishment."

"No ravishing till after I eat," she said pragmatically. "Think how unromantic it would be if I fainted from hunger!"

Their teasing took them all the way to the castle grounds, where they alighted in the middle of canvas pavilions and music and roasting food. Barrels of ale and tables covered with platters were everywhere. There was already dancing in the courtyard.

"Ashton doesn't stint when he sponsors a feast," Sarah observed.

"It's very convenient to have a generous duke as a friend," Rob agreed. "Which do you prefer first, eating or dancing?"

"Eating," she said firmly. "So I'll have more energy to dance."

He escorted her to the pavilion closest to the castle, which was designated for family and gentry guests. After they'd rebuilt their strength with some of the excellent food, they danced one country reel together. Rob wasn't much of a dancer, but reels were simple and Sarah was skilled enough for both of them.

Then they turned to their duty as hosts and took other partners. Rob danced with Mariah, Anna, and Bree, who was bursting with pride at being his partner. He even tried to coax his grandmother out. She refused, but couldn't seem to stop herself from smiling. He hardly recognized her.

Sarah was dancing with laughter and an endurance that would have surprised anyone who hadn't ridden across Ireland with her. He moved to the side of the crowd to observe. He couldn't take his eyes off her. Sarah was becoming the heart and soul of Kellington, he realized. Rob had the title and the bloodlines, but her warm charm and optimism were giving people hope for the future.

He was a lucky, lucky man.

After several dances in succession, Sarah stopped to catch her breath. Her slippers would never be the same, not after all this dancing. She'd retire the slippers to the back of her wardrobe and take them out sometimes to sigh over happily.

She was looking around for Rob when an attractive dark-haired woman in her early thirties approached. "We weren't properly introduced, Lady Kellington. I'm Helen Broome, wife of the vicar of St. Dunstan's in Bendan. Thanks so much for inviting us."

Sarah smiled. "Thanks should go to the dowager countess, since she told us who to invite from the local area. It included all the vicars for miles around."

"It's the advantage of marrying a vicar," Helen said drolly. "We may live modestly in drafty vicarages, but we do get invited to all the best local parties."

"I'm glad you could come." Sarah's brow furrowed. "Isn't Bendan where Bree, my husband's daughter, used to live?" It was the first time she'd said "my husband," and it was a strange sensation. She had a *husband!*

"Yes, Bree was born and raised in the village. She and my younger daughter were great friends." Helen gestured toward a group of men standing by the stables. "My husband is over there. The tall fellow in clerical black and wearing spectacles."

Mr. Broome looked very nice. "When we're settled, I hope you'll dine with us."

Helen smiled and said they'd be delighted. She was someone who could become a friend, and she could also provide useful information. "Bree's birthday will be in several weeks," Sarah said. "I thought we could hold a birthday party for her that would include her friends from Bendan. Does that make sense, or do you think two years at her age is so long that the girls in your village will have forgotten her?"

"Alice would love to see her, and several other girls were particular friends. Bree was very popular. What did you have in mind? It's a bit of a distance."

"I'd like to hold the party here. We'd send a coach to collect the girls, of course."

Helen's eyes brightened. "That would be splendid! I volunteer to travel along as a chaperone. I'd love to see more of Kellington Castle."

Bree skipped up, her hat missing and her dark hair spilling down her back. "Mrs. Broome! It's me, Bree! Is Alice here?"

"No, but I'm so happy to see you!" Helen gave her a swift hug. "I'll tell Alice that I saw you, and you're looking very fine. Your stepmother was just telling me about your birthday party."

Bree looked surprised but interested. "I'm having a birthday party?"

"We haven't had time to talk about it with the wedding," Sarah explained. "But I thought we could invite some of your old friends from Bendan and some of your new friends from here. Would you like that?"

Bree's eyes widened like saucers. "Can Alice come?"

"Of course," Sarah said.

Bree bounced, looking less like a young lady and more like a happy urchin. "Can we have the party in the ruins of the old castle? It's bloody picturesque!"

Sarah blinked. "Language, Bree. But yes, if the weather permits, we could have a picnic there."

Bree looked ready to burst with excitement.

"Thank you!" Then she spotted one of the Holt girls and buzzed off to tell her the news.

"She's looking very well," Helen observed as both women watched the girl dart across the courtyard. "I was worried for her after her mother died."

"Her grandfather was a dreadful old man," Sarah said. "He just dumped her here and left. Rob had no idea Bree existed. But he was delighted, of course." Sarah didn't feel she could ask outright about Bryony, but she was curious. "She seems a happy, healthy girl. That speaks well for her mother."

From the twinkle in Helen's eyes, she understood the curiosity. "Bryony was a very devoted mother. I presume Lord Kellington gave her money to stay away. Probably not a huge amount, but she managed it well enough to give herself and her daughter a comfortable life. She was beautiful—Bree looks just like her. She could have married, but she liked her independence."

"How did she die?"

"A fever of some sort." Helen sighed. "It was very quick. One day she was striding over the cliffs with her hair blowing straight out in the wind, and three days later she was gone."

Sarah bit her lip. "Poor Bree. So horrible for her."

"Yes, but she survived two years with her grandfather, apart from some damage to her language, and now she's here. She's fortunate."

Many children weren't. But Bree was happy now. Sarah vowed to do her best to see that she stayed that way.

Rob began working his way through the crowd, greeting acquaintances and introducing himself to guests he didn't know. He was thinking of finding Sarah for another dance when an unexpected old friend found him. Dark and enigmatic, Lord Kirkland was a former Westerfield classmate, wealthy shipping merchant, and spymaster.

Delighted, Rob offered his hand. "Kirkland! I thought I saw you in the distance, but decided I imagined it."

Kirkland shook his hand. "Congratulations, Rob. She'll make you an admirable countess."

Rob's instincts went on full alert. "Why do I think this visit is nothing as simple as coming to the wedding?"

"It was a surprise to arrive just as the wedding was beginning," Kirkland admitted. "Despite my reputation, I don't always know everything."

Rob's exhilaration vanished in a finger snap. This was Kirkland, the stormy petrel whose arrival signaled trouble. "Shall we retire to my ugly but private study?"

"Yes, but I'd like to collect Ashton. He'll want to hear this, too."

Which meant Kirkland's visit had something to do with Ireland and attempted abductions of duchesses. As Rob scanned the crowd for the duke, Kirkland asked, "Is the Catholic priest from this area?"

"No, he's one of my Irish cousins. We played together as boys." Rob glanced at his friend. "Do you want to interrogate him?"

"Later, perhaps," Kirkland said imperturbably. "Look, there's Ashton."

Rob signaled for the duke to join them, then guided his guests to the house. When Kirkland entered the study, he remarked, "I wouldn't call this ugly."

Rob stopped, surprised, on the threshold. The study had been transformed. The walls were whitewashed and attractive draperies replaced the dismal ones that blocked the light. Pleasant landscape paintings graced the walls, and a set of bookcases had been arranged behind the desk and stocked with books and interesting curios. Comfortable chairs had replaced the old ones, too.

"Sarah." Rob smiled as he turned, taking in all the changes. "She must have done this as a surprise." He gestured for the other men to sit. "What's the bad news?"

"The fact that you won't be working with me anymore is bad from my point of view, but probably good from yours." Kirkland frowned.

"I'm sure you've considered that the attempted abduction of the Duchess of Ashton was political."

Ashton nodded. "I've not heard of the group Free Eire, but I gather they're radicals who want England out of Ireland. Kidnapping a duchess could be considered a blow against the aristocracy, though I'm not sure why they'd go after Mariah. I don't own a square inch of land in Ireland."

"They'd not be averse to a large ransom," Rob said dryly. "The fact that your estate is in Wiltshire and easier to reach than other duchies might be why you were targeted. Do you have more information, Kirkland?"

Kirkland answered his question with another question. "Did you learn anything else about them that you didn't tell me when you sent your report?"

Rob frowned, trying to remember. He'd been tired when he wrote those first essential letters, and he'd kept them brief. "Did I mention that they may have a female leader? Though I can't swear to that since it was part of a conversation that took place over open water as we were sailing away from Kinsale. Does that matter?"

"Not unless she's French. I've evidence that France has been quietly funding some of the more radical Irish independence groups with the aim of creating problems in England's backyard."

Rob whistled softly. "That makes perfect sense. Some of the Irish would take aid from the devil himself if it would help them drive the British out of Ireland."

"They might have trouble getting the French out again," Adam observed. "But that wouldn't stop an angry rebel."

"Did you hear anything to suggest French support?" Kirkland asked.

Rob frowned as he thought. "They had to be well funded to mount their raid on Ralston Abbey and get away again. But I saw no real evidence. The person to talk to is my cousin Patrick Cassidy, the priest who's here at the wedding."

"Why did he come to Kellington?"

"To persuade me to improve conditions at Kilvarra, the Kellington estate in Ireland," Rob explained. "Since I'm cooperating on that, he's in charity with me and will probably talk willingly. Up to a point, anyhow."

Kirkland studied him narrowly. "Is he a radical?"

"He wants the English out of Ireland and no mistake," Rob said. "But he doesn't support violence. He's a member of the United Irishmen, which is a moderate group, but I suspect he hears about a good deal more that's going on."

"Will you introduce us?" Kirkland smiled wearily and got to his feet. "Here's hoping your cousin has had enough ale to loosen his tongue."

"He wouldn't tell you anything that might be considered a betrayal," Rob warned. "But he was appalled when I told him about the intended abduction of a young woman on the verge of childbirth. It's worth questioning him. I want to be there, though."

Kirkland's brows arched. "I'm not going to use thumbscrews, Rob."

"I know. But he'll talk more easily if I'm present."

Kirkland nodded acceptance of that as he started for the door. "Let's find the good father. I'm sure he'll have some interesting things to say."

And Kirkland would know exactly how to use anything he learned.

Chapter 34

The sun had almost set but the festivities were going strong when Rob sought Sarah out. She couldn't read his expression, other than the fact that he didn't look as relaxed and happy as he had earlier.

He bowed over her hand. "Time to escape, my lady."

"I'm ready," she said. "Being the bride is rather grand, but it's tiring to have to be charming for so many hours."

He smiled a little at that. "You charm as naturally as you breathe." He set his hand on her lower back and guided her toward the house. The warmth of his open palm was very . . . intimate.

It took time to reach the house because of people who wanted to chat and offer best wishes, but eventually they made it inside. As they climbed the stairs, he asked, "Your room or mine?"

"The master suite," she said. "The rooms are quite pleasant, and I thought the symbolism was appropriate."

"Starting a new phase of life in a new place? You're right, the bedrooms we've been using are nothing special." As they turned down the corridor, he added, "Thank you for your efforts in the study. You improved it out of all recognition."

"Good. Since you seem to end up there often, it needs to be welcoming." The passage ended with a series of doors leading to the various rooms that made up the suite. The large door in the center led to the sitting room while the others opened into dressing rooms so servants could come and go unobtrusively.

Rob was reaching for the middle door when Sarah said, "The doors are locked. I didn't want anyone planting bridal surprises inside."

"Good precaution," he said with approval. "Most such surprises are amusing to the pranksters, but not for the bride and groom."

She retrieved the key from under a vase on a hall table and unlocked the door. It didn't escape her notice that Rob seemed to gird himself mentally before entering. That was the trouble with family homes where generations had lived and died. There were always layers of memories, and not always good ones.

They stepped into a short passage leading to the sitting room that lay between the bedrooms. He took the key, locked the door, then turned to envelop her in a hug.

The embrace wasn't one of passion, but affection and comfort. She leaned into him with a small hum of pleasure as she wrapped her arms round his waist and rested her head on his shoulder. Mariah was right, she and Rob hadn't spent enough time together in the last few days. Being in his arms felt very right.

"I'm glad we're no longer on public display," he murmured. "Being the genial lord of the manor is tiring."

She chuckled. "You prefer lurking quietly in the background, don't you?"

"Lurking is much more my style," he agreed. "But you, my countess, make a superb lady of the manor."

"Thank you." She burrowed closer. "Credit goes to the duchess gown Mariah gave me. Wearing it would make any woman feel like a grand lady."

"I did wonder where you found a garment so magnificent on short notice. I should have guessed. You're fortunate in your family."

"It's your family now also," she pointed out.

"True," he said thoughtfully. "I'm having some trouble with the idea that the Duke of Ashton is now my brother-in-law."

She tilted her head back to gaze up at him. "But you've known Adam forever."

"Yes, but he was always a duke while I was a younger son, a younger student, and more recently his employee for various investigations. Being family is different. My life feels like a reshuffled hand of cards."

"Because it is," she agreed. "Are you still dubious about being an earl?"

"Yes." He grinned. "But I like that now there's room in my life for a wife."

He released her and took the last two steps into the sitting room as he peeled off his coat and cravat. As he tossed them over the back of a chair, he noticed his surroundings. The last rays of the setting sun poured in the windows like liquid gold, gilding the elegant furnishings and the vases of bright flowers set around the room.

"Are we in the right house?" he asked, startled. "This looks completely different from what I remember. And better. Much, much better. How did you manage such a swift transformation?"

"Mariah and I invaded the attics and found older furnishings," she explained. "Then it was just a matter of moving and cleaning."

"That must have been a substantial job! But the results are worth it. This no longer feels like it belongs to my father." Rob sat to tug off his boots, then took Sarah's hand and began to explore the suite. After admiring the earl's bedroom, he looked into his dressing room, where his own clothing was neatly stored.

"Harvey has been busy, I see. My wardrobe looks paltry in here. As I recall, the countess's dressing room is twice as large, so I hope you have a very large wardrobe."

"My dressing room is more than adequate." She smiled, anticipating his surprise. "Take that door next."

He did as she suggested, then stopped dead in his tracks. "Good God, a Roman bathhouse! This certainly wasn't here before."

"Space was taken from the countess's dressing room for this bath and a water closet through that door," Sarah explained. "According to Hector, several years after your mother died, your father had a mistress with extravagant tastes. She persuaded him to put in Egyptian style furniture and this bathroom before he tired of her."

"If she liked carved crocodiles, I'm not surprised she didn't last long." A tank was suspended above one end of the tub. He held his hand up near it. "Hot water?"

"There's a boiler in a little closet between the bathroom and the corridor, so servants can keep the water warm without disturbing us," she said.

Rob slanted a glance at her. "This could be . . . enjoyable. Shall we move on to your rooms?"

When she nodded, he opened the door to her dressing room and crossed through into her bedroom, his warm hand still clasping hers. He looked intensely—and provocatively—masculine against the serene, very feminine ivory and rose tones. "Well done, Sarah!" He smiled down at her. "The colors and furnishings suit you. A perfect English rose in her bower."

The warmth of his gaze made her pulse accelerate. "If you're hungry, there's food and drink on the table by the window," she said a little nervously. "The servants didn't want us to have to emerge for a day or two."

Laughing, he pulled her closer. "I like that idea." He bent his head and kissed her, his mouth warm and firm.

She melted into his kiss, tongues touching as they breathed each other's air. Finally the wedding ceremony and formalities were behind them and they were alone as husband and wife.

She was so absorbed in their kissing that she was scarcely aware of what he was doing with his hands until her hair tumbled loose. He slid his fingers into the falling locks and kneaded her head and neck with strong, sure fingertips. "Let's not summon your maid," he murmured as he deftly unfastened the back of her gown.

As he moved behind her and began unlacing her stays, she said rather breathlessly, "You're really good at this. Should I be concerned at your skill?"

He bent to kiss her throat through the golden fall of her hair. "If you're wondering if I'm a seasoned rake, the answer is no," he replied. "But I've wanted to do this since I first saw you."

"Really? You didn't show any sign of that," she said with interest.

"I was supposed to be rescuing you, not

ravishing you. Even with my best intentions, you'll notice that desire didn't stay entirely under control." He finished unlacing the stays and lifted them away, leaving her in her shift and slippers.

"I noticed." She kicked off the dainty slippers and was immediately two inches shorter. "Give me a few minutes to change and I'll meet you back here."

"I can help remove your shift," he offered, his eyes glinting as he ran his hands down her arms from shoulder to elbow.

She laughed. "Behave! I'll be back in a few minutes." She scooped up the duchess gown and her stays, then skipped into her dressing room. Leaving the gown on the floor would have seemed disrespectful.

She swiftly hung the gown, then stripped and donned the beautiful rose-colored muslin night-gown Mariah had given her. It was extremely helpful to have a sister who was a generous and well-dressed duchess.

The nightgown was full, long sleeved, and modest, but the color was flattering and the fabric flowed beautifully when she moved. She brushed her tangled hair down over her shoulders and dabbed on the night version of Kiri's perfume. It had a sweet floral innocence, but underneath was rich, sultry promise.

A quick look in the mirror confirmed that she

looked as a bride should look on her wedding night. Nervous, of course, but that was natural.

She took a deep breath, then returned to her bedroom. Rob stood gazing out the window, his hands clasped behind his back.

He'd changed into a magnificent banyan made of burgundy silk and embroidered with Oriental motifs in shades of blue and black. The garment was exotic and beautiful, and made Rob seem an intriguing and possibly dangerous stranger. Rather like the man she'd described to her friend Lady Kiri one day when they talked about ideal mates.

Then he turned with a smile and was her friend again. "I acquired this rather spectacular robe when I lived in India. They are experts in luxury. And you, my exquisite bride, look like the most luxurious female on the planet."

Before she recognized his intent, he swept her up in his arms and laid her in the middle of her canopied bed as gently as if she were porcelain. "Ah, Sarah, Sarah. Princess." He came down beside her, his arm around her waist as he leaned in. "You are so beautiful," he said huskily. "So exquisitely beautiful . . ."

This time his mouth was hot and hungry. Searing. She could feel the heat rising in her body, pooling with liquid intensity in unnamed places.

At first she enjoyed the intoxication of his

kiss, the heat and desire that called forth the same in her. Then he shifted to kiss her ear so that his torso was over hers. Even though he kept most of his weight off her, she had a sudden, frantic feeling of being trapped. She gasped and shoved instinctively on his shoulders.

He instantly rolled away onto his back, breathing hard and fists clenched. After a few moments, he said, "I'm sorry. I . . . seem to frighten you, and it's not the first time today that's happened. Do you . . . not want to be married to me?"

"No!" She scrambled up to a sitting position against the pillow-piled backboard. "If anyone should be apologizing, Rob, it's me. I have no reason at all to fear you—you've been unbelievably kind and patient. But . . . you're so *large!* Large and strong. And—I'm not."

He sat up and leaned back against one of the massive posts at the foot of the bed, facing her. His breathing was quick, but his face was controlled as he stretched his legs out beside her. His feet were large, in proportion to the rest of him. What had she once overheard about the size of feet reflecting the size of . . . ? Blushing, she looked away.

"I can't do much about my height," he said wryly. "I'm very aware of how petite you are. Not weak. Your strength and endurance are admirable. But you're so small and lovely that you look like you should be on a pedestal with a sign saying 'Look but don't touch.' Unfortunately, I have a powerful desire to touch."

"I'm not at all fragile. Remember that I was the very devil of a tomboy with my cousins." She frowned as she tried to analyze her reaction. "For a moment I felt trapped, but I'm not afraid of you, Rob."

"That's something," he murmured. "Was I moving too fast for you?"

"A little." She made a face. "But I must admit that I keep thinking that every one of our guests knows what we're doing in here. It's *embarrassing*."

"At least this isn't a royal marriage of the past when half the court crowded into the marital bedroom. It would take a strong man to perform under those circumstances!" he said feelingly. "But you're right that assumptions are made about wedding nights."

She grimaced at his mention of public consummations in the past. "Maybe I was meant to be a spinster," she said gloomily.

Rob became very still. "If you truly don't want to be my wife, the marriage could be annulled. It would be messy and complicated, but I'm sure it could be done as long as the marriage hasn't been consummated."

She shuddered as she thought of all the people who'd come to celebrate their wedding. Virtually everyone on the large Kellington estate and a goodly number of friends and family as well. An annulment would be a devastatingly public slap in the face for Rob, who had done nothing, *nothing,* to deserve that from her.

On the contrary, he'd given her—everything. "I most certainly do not want an annulment! It's time I married, and you're the only man I can imagine being married to." She shoved her hair back out of her face with an impatient hand. "I didn't expect to feel this skittish, though. I'm generally fairly sensible."

"I like that about you." He drew up one leg and casually rested his arm on it, a picture of sumptuously garbed relaxation. "If you were in love with me, you'd be less skittish. Though we've shared some interesting adventures, we haven't really known each other that long."

In a flash of intuition, she recognized that he wasn't relaxed at all, just very good at masking his tension. Her heart twisted when she remembered the shining certainty on Mariah's face when she went to Adam as his bride.

There had been equal certainty in Adam's eyes, and a kind of awe at his good fortune. So very different from Sarah and Rob.

Her jaw hardened. She'd taken vows before God and man just hours earlier. She couldn't walk away. She didn't *want* to walk away. Choosing her words carefully, she said, "Many couples marry without being in love and the marriage works out very well. We—or rather I—just need a bit of time to sort this out."

"Every marriage is unique," he said thoughtfully. "We can deal with each other any way we wish. The consummation needn't be tonight. We can wait until we don't have two hundred people outside speculating about what we're doing."

"And until my nerves are in better order," she said gratefully. "I'm so tired and frayed. It's not late now, but it has been a very long day." She covered a yawn. "I truly appreciate how tolerant you're being, Rob. You're a saint."

"Not even close to sainthood, princess," he said, a glint in his eyes. "But I'm tired, also. Too many hours of being on my best behavior. It's good to relax with you. Would you like something to eat or drink?"

"I'm not hungry, but a glass of white wine would be pleasant."

He swung from the bed, lit a pair of lamps against the encroaching darkness, then poured them both wine. She loved watching his smooth, efficient movements. He was like a sleek thoroughbred.

He returned to the bed and handed her one of the goblets, then clinked his glass to hers. "To my very beautiful bride."

She smiled and returned the clink. "And to my very handsome and amazingly patient new husband."

He sat against the bedpost again, one foot on the floor and the other leg bent underneath him. His aquamarine eyes were clear as water and his brown hair was tousled. She had a desire to tousle it further, but for the moment he was out of reach.

No, he wasn't the one out of reach. She was the one putting distance between them. And the sooner she closed that distance, the better.

Chapter 35

Rob gazed at Sarah as she absently sipped her wine. He loved watching her like this, with her marvelous blond hair falling free and the demure rose-colored nightgown, which was not as opaque as she probably thought it was.

"You said you wanted to kiss me from the first time you saw me," she remarked. "I thought you considered me fluffy and helpless."

"Yes," he admitted. "But that didn't mean you weren't powerfully attractive. Though I couldn't allow myself such thoughts." Only now did he realize just how much he'd been suppressing his desire. Now he didn't have to, which was good, because he no longer could. He wanted her in the most primitive male way, a fever in the blood that cried, *"MINE, MINE, MINE, MINE!!!"*

"Do you have the same reaction to Mariah?" she asked, irresistibly curious though she looked as if she wasn't sure she wanted to hear the answer.

"No." He hesitated. "It's hard to explain. Since she looks like you, she's very beautiful. But her essence is different. She lacks your Sarah-ness."

She laughed and looked even more enchanting. "A very diplomatic answer."

"It has the virtue of being true. I expect that Ashton would say something similar. That you're beautiful, but you lack Mariah-ness."

"What is the essence of a man or woman?" she mused. "The soul?"

"Perhaps. I just knew that you were very special as soon as I saw you." He smiled a little. "Since I'm a lurker by training and preference, you wouldn't have noticed me if I hadn't come to rescue you."

"Actually, that's not true," she said shyly. "The first time I saw you was at the wedding of Lady Kiri and Damian Mackenzie. You were lurking, but I thought you looked . . . interesting. I wanted to know you better."

He felt absurdly pleased. "Really? I've never had a beautiful woman single me out in a crowd."

"That you know of!" She grinned. "I wasn't the only female noticing you, but I couldn't just walk up and introduce myself."

He wished that she had, but the time was all wrong then. He'd have been flattered, and amazed, and then walked away.

But now there was time, and she was his wife. *Mine, mine, mine!* He should have known that marriage wouldn't be easy. Nothing in his life ever had been. They didn't have the love match that made everything seem right, nor did they have one of those pragmatic unions where both parties knew it was their duty to copulate so they got on with it in a businesslike manner.

Instead, he and Sarah were caught somewhere in the middle between a love match and a practical marriage. Call it a marriage of friendship. He wasn't quite sure what shape that should take, and neither was Sarah. He didn't doubt that they'd work it out, but for the moment, the situation was awkward.

Sleep would help. "Shall I turn down the lamps so we can get some rest?"

She gave him a luminous smile. "That would be lovely."

As he collected the wineglasses and set them aside, she said wistfully, "It's rather sad to sleep alone on my wedding night."

His brows arched. "It's sensible to delay the consummation, but I do want to sleep with you tonight even if we don't have a convenient haystack."

"Oh, good!" While he turned off one lamp and dimmed the other, she swiftly braided her hair into a long blond rope. Then she slid under the covers and patted the space beside her invitingly.

He removed his banyan and folded it neatly over a chair. Since he didn't want to unnerve Sarah more by adding male nakedness to male size, he didn't remove the loose linen shirt and drawers underneath.

Then he climbed into bed beside his bride,

who greeted him with a warm, sleepily trusting smile. She had a sweet and spicy female scent, enhanced by the exotic blend of her perfume. When he put an arm around her and she cuddled close, he wondered just how saintly he could manage to be.

Lying along Rob's strong body, Sarah felt her tension and nerves dissolve away. Surely the delicious animal warmth of sharing a bed was one powerful reason to marry.

Without the pressure to consummate the marriage, the attraction she always felt for Rob began glowing through her. So when he murmured, "There are many pleasant things that can be done well short of consummation," she made an agreeable sound.

He began gently caressing her, his fingers light and tantalizing. In the dimly lit night, with no spoken words, this was pure, uncomplicated pleasure. Her nightgown covered her from chin to ankles, so she felt quite decent. But the slow burn wherever he touched reminded her that muslin was very thin.

When his hand drifted down to cup her breast, she pressed closer. He began strumming her nipple with his thumb. Her eyes shot wide open as sensation flared through her. In the dim light, his strong features were caring and focused on her.

Hearing the change in her breathing, he murmured something wordless and soothing and transferred his attentions to her other breast. This time he bent to suck on her nipple. She gasped and her pelvis began moving involuntarily.

He recognized her body's craving more clearly than she did, for his hand stroked down between her thighs. His touch was feather light, yet it invoked heat and moisture and greater cravings. Her breath roughened as her world narrowed down to his skillful ministrations and her increasingly intense reaction.

She didn't even realize that his hand had moved under her nightgown until she recognized that his wickedly skilled fingers were touching intimate flesh, slickly sliding deeper, deeper. When he began stroking a tiny nub that seemed to concentrate her whole being in one spot, she moaned and gripped him with biting nails. Fierce need twisted tighter and tighter . . .

. . . until she shattered into blazing fulfillment. She cried out as her world fragmented. Dimly she recognized an irrevocable change.

Physical pleasure vanished as a torrent of grief and fear and despair swept through her. She broke into wrenching sobs without knowing why.

Rob's arms came around her and she clung to him as the one sure anchor in a broken world. He wrapped her close, stroking her head and back as she pressed against him, her tears saturating his shirt.

Gradually her sobs diminished. Softly Rob said, "I have absolutely no idea why that happened. Do you?"

She hiccupped and wiped her eyes with the sleeve of her nightgown. "Now I *really* owe you an apology! I'm sorry, Rob. I don't know why I fell to pieces."

"If that was what lay beneath your skittishness, it's powerful." He slid his fingers into her hair, soothing her like a kitten. "Do you have any idea at all? I'd like to think that heartbroken tears won't be a regular feature of our married life."

She bit her lip, forcing herself to think about the terrible grief that had torn her heart. How could she feel so miserable when the kindest, most attractive man she'd ever known had given her such intense pleasure?

The answer flared with blistering clarity. "It's because men *leave!*" she said raggedly. "They can't be trusted to stay, and it hurts so much. The pain never, ever goes away."

After a startled pause, Rob said, "This is about your father, isn't it? He just up and left and didn't return for over twenty years even though he loved your mother and you."

She nodded. "I always knew that he'd walked out and that somewhere out there, he was alive and enjoying life and cared nothing for me. He had Mariah, after all. He says that he went to the nursery and picked her out at random, but he's lying, I'm sure of it. She was always brighter and more attractive. So he took her and . . ." Her voice cracked. "He took her and left me."

"There's an odd contrast between you and your sister," Rob said thoughtfully. "Mariah had a rather volatile life with Charles, but she always knew that he loved her. Since she believed your mother was dead, she never felt abandoned. In most ways, you had a much more stable and secure upbringing, but deep inside, there was the grief of knowing your father had abandoned you. I imagine it wasn't helped when Gerald died."

"You're right. It sounds so foolish when said aloud, doesn't it? So trivial. I love my mother. I can't imagine growing up without her, as Mariah did." She sighed. "But you're right. My father's leaving left a hole nothing could fill."

"All of us have dark truths engraved so deeply on our souls that it really doesn't matter what the facts are. Being abandoned by your father was your truth no matter how much you now realize that your father was young and foolish and did something so stupid that it took him decades to sort it out."

She nodded. "Shedding some light on this particular dark truth will diminish it, I think. At least, I hope so." She wiped her eyes again, thinking she must look a fright.

Rob caught her gaze with mesmerizing intensity. "Sarah, I will never leave you. I am yours and you are mine for richer and poorer, in sickness and in health, forsaking all others. I can't guarantee that I won't die, but if that happens, my spirit will surely stay close and try to protect you. It will take time to overcome your old dark truth, but this is a new truth. *I will never leave you.* Believe me."

She almost began weeping again, but she managed to block the tears. Rob had surely had enough of her being a watering pot. "I do believe you," she said huskily. "In my head, at least. Belief will take time to reach my heart and soul."

Rob smiled warmly. "We have time. Take as much as you need."

She caught his hand and held it to her cheek, thinking how lucky she was to find a man with a deliciously dangerous edge who was also utterly reliable. Then it struck her that Rob's insights were not the kind of thing anyone came up with casually. He'd spoken with the voice of experience.

Raising her gaze to his, she asked quietly, "What is your dark truth, Robin? What pain is engraved on *your* soul?"

Sarah's words were a hammer blow that resonated through Rob's whole body. He knew that dark truths were buried deep inside him, shaping his life every day, but he did his damnedest not to look too closely.

Sarah caught his face in her hands and studied him worriedly. "Rob?"

He took a deep breath. "No one has called me Robin since my mother died."

"Would you rather I didn't?"

He rolled onto his back and stared at the brocade canopy, the ivory and rose colors ones his mother would have loved, and which suited Sarah so well. "I don't mind you calling me Robin, but hearing the nickname along with your question was . . . jarring."

She took his hand. "Because you looked into your own darkness?"

He nodded. "I realized that . . . I've felt second best, even with my mother. That no one would ever want me if they had any other choice." The darkness of that was a wave of bleakness and despair.

Sarah squeezed his hand hard, her biting nails pulling him from the darkness. "*I* want you, Rob."

Chapter 36

"I want you, Rob."

Sarah's words were followed by a devouring kiss as she pressed her body into his. Passion flared through him like red-hot lava. He managed to say hoarsely, "If you don't want to complete this, I must leave this bed."

"I find I no longer care what two hundred wedding guests are thinking," she breathed. Her hand slid under his drawers, gliding tentatively down his belly. When her fingers brushed his erection, he turned rigid, feeling that if he didn't make love to her *right now,* he'd die.

He barely realized what he was doing as he stripped off his shirt and drawers and threw them on the floor. He did, barely, remember that she was still a virgin and he must take care to hurt her as little as possible.

Luckily, she was simmering like a sensual teakettle from what they'd done already. She gasped when he worshipped her perfect breasts. Moaned as he trailed kisses down the soft, silken skin of her belly. Squeaked endearingly when his fingers trailed up her inner thighs and into the sweet hidden heat.

She was warm and pliant and willing and he

couldn't bear to wait an instant longer. Fighting to go slowly, he positioned himself between her legs and pushed forward. Her eyes shot open.

"Am I hurting you?" he asked raggedly.

"Not . . . not really," she said. "More . . . surprise."

Giving thanks, he moved against her tightness a fraction of an inch at a time until they were fully joined. The pleasure was exquisite, too intense to last. His body no longer under control, he thrust once, twice, thrice, then spilled into her with such intoxicating release that he lost awareness of himself and his surroundings and everything but his beautiful, welcoming wife.

Gasping as if he'd run a marathon, he collapsed on his side and folded her into his arms. "I'm sorry, Sarah," he panted. "I didn't mean to be so quick and heedless. I hope I didn't hurt you too much."

"That wasn't as bad as I expected," she said as she burrowed against him. "All the riding I've done might have made it easier."

"If so, I'm grateful." He groped for the towel that he'd tossed at the head of the bed earlier, then released her so he could clean them both.

There was very little blood, another sign of their relatively easy joining. The only other virgin he'd ever lain with was Bryony, and they were both so young and inexperienced that they didn't understand much of what they were doing. But if he recalled correctly, it had been more difficult for both of them.

That was the past. Sarah was his present and future. He settled back in the pillows and drew her close against his side, feeling pensive.

Sarah said hesitantly, "I'm surprised that you felt second best with your mother. From what you said, she sounded kind and loving."

"She was, but she always wanted a little girl." His throat tightened. "She died in childbirth. She'd been so excited to be with child again. She told me I was going to have a little sister and how much I'd like that. And then . . . she bled to death. The baby, the daughter she wanted, lived only a few hours and was buried in my mother's arms."

"Oh, Rob." Sarah pushed herself up on one elbow. The faint lamplight limned her flawless features and shining hair as if she were an angel. She bent into a kiss whose compassionate warmth flowed into him, through him, warming the never forgotten chill of his mother's death.

Knowing there was more to be said, when the kiss ended he pulled her down under his arm so that her head rested on his shoulder. "As you pointed out, such things sound trivial when they're said aloud. I know my mother loved me even if she wanted a daughter, too. But for all these years, on some level I've thought I wasn't a good enough son to satisfy her. She needed more than I could give."

"She adored you," Sarah said firmly. "What mother wouldn't? If we have a son, I hope he's just like you. Including tall."

He laughed, but under his amusement was wonder. Sarah spoke of children—*their* children —as a natural and welcome part of their future. Creating a family was an everyday miracle, but the knowledge was suddenly, breathtakingly new. "In that case, I'd want to register my desire for an exquisite little blond daughter to dote on."

"You might get twins," she warned. "They run in my mother's family."

"That would be a double blessing."

She stroked her hand down his chest, her fingers brushing through the brown hair. "There's more to your dark truths, isn't there? Reinforcement of the original feeling of not being good enough?"

"My too perceptive princess," he said wryly. "Once a dark and possibly wrong truth is in place, there are so many reinforcements. Certainly my father considered me second best and unworthy of the Carmichael name. My brother was sent to Eton, I wasn't. I wanted to be a noble officer fighting for my country, and instead I descended to the grubby ranks of thief takers. I cared about a woman with whom I wanted a future, and she left me for another man."

"Is this why you've been so uncomfortable with inheriting the title?" Sarah asked. "Because it seemed impossible and wrong that you could become Earl of Kellington?"

He frowned. "You may be right. I could reel off any number of reasons why I didn't want to inherit, but perhaps feeling second best lies under all of them."

"It's strange how dark truths persist even when the events turned out well," she mused. "The Westerfield Academy was surely much better for you than Eton would have been. And while boys may dream of military glory—have you ever talked to a soldier like Alex Randall about what war is like?"

"Enough to know that doing justice as a Bow Street Runner was a better choice for me," he admitted. "But army uniforms look much more dashing."

She laughed. "You would have looked splendid in scarlet regimentals. But you look splendid without them, too." Her fingertip circled his navel. "As for the woman who left you for another man—she had very poor taste."

This time Rob laughed. "No, she was wiser than I. She and I were too much alike and are better off with different mates." He gently massaged the back of her neck with his fingertips. "I know I am, and I hear she is, too."

"Then everyone lives happily ever after. I approve of that." Sarah exhaled softly, her breath a gentle warmth on his chest. "I'm tired, but not ready to go to sleep yet. I don't want this night to end."

His massaging hand moved down her back. "Neither do I. Tomorrow we'll need to settle down to the serious work of the estate. We have this one night without cares."

"Which is why I don't want to waste it." Her head popped up from his chest. "I have an idea! Let's try the bath. That tub is large enough for two."

The images of Sarah naked and wet were irresistible. He disentangled her and sat up in the bed. "I hope you know how to operate it. I found the mechanism intimidating."

Sarah laughed and swung from the bed. "I doubt that anything intimidates you! It's fairly simple, actually. I've been itching to try it ever since Mariah and I discovered the bathing room."

He donned his banyan again. "Do you have a robe? The night air is chilly."

"All the more reason to sink into a giant tub of hot water!" Sarah wrapped a flannel robe around her, slid her feet into slippers, then led the way to the bathing room.

Rob lit another lamp and followed. He hadn't looked closely earlier, being more interested in beds than baths, so he studied everything with interest. The deep oval tub was easily five feet long, and it was set in a polished mahogany box with a wide rim around the tub proper. Steps ran the width of the box to aid bathers climbing in and out. It looked fit for royalty.

"There are beautiful large towels in that cabinet." Sarah pointed, then climbed onto the lowest step of the tub and turned two taps. Water began gushing in.

"Hot and cold running water?" he asked with amazement as he pulled several towels out. "That must have cost a fortune to install! What a waste of money that could have been better spent elsewhere."

"Your father would have spent the money in unworthy ways anyhow, and at least this went for something we can enjoy," Sarah said practically. "I wouldn't have spent thousands of pounds on something so unnecessary, but if the house has to be let to a nabob, these luxury features will make a higher rent possible."

"Silver linings," Rob murmured as he lit the candles in the sconces. They produced a soft, romantic light. "I can't help thinking that for the cost of this bathing room, every tenant house on the estate could have had a new roof."

"Think about that tomorrow." Sarah smiled as she removed a bottle from the cabinet and poured several drops of oil into the rapidly rising water. The scent of herbs floated deliciously through the small room.

Rob sniffed. "Rosemary and lavender?"

"Among other things. This is a bath blend that

Kiri mixed for me. I love her experiments."
Sarah inhaled deeply. "One night of mad luxury
before we return to work. Shall I pour us more
wine?"

"Please do. Drinking wine in the bath is the
ultimate luxury."

Sarah headed to the bedroom and returned with
her hair clipped on top of her head and a small
tray holding wineglasses and tidbits of food.
"Look at these delightful nibbles!" Sarah popped
a cube of cheese into his mouth. "I think that
everyone at Kellington has worked to make today
special."

"We're their hope for the future, princess." Rob
fed her a morsel that combined biscuit, ham, and
cheese. She took it neatly from his fingers, along
with a deliberately provocative lick that made
his toes curl.

Judging that there was enough water, Rob
turned off the taps and set the tray on a broad
corner well suited to hold food or books. "Now,
my lady, we sample the bath. May I help you
remove your nightgown? I've been looking
forward to seeing all of you."

At his words, Sarah froze, her expression
appalled.

Rob frowned. "Sarah, what's wrong?"

"I . . . I don't want to take my nightgown off. I
can bathe in it."

His brows arched. "I could understand shyness,

but you don't look shy. You look worried. Do you have a birthmark? I assure you I will always think you're beautiful." Since she was still shrinking back against the wall, he added, "I hope we will be married for a very long time, princess. I suppose you can stay covered for the next fifty years. But I'd rather you didn't."

She took a deep breath, which made the light fabric of her nightgown shimmer delightfully. "It's not a birthmark I'm trying to hide. It's . . . it's a tattoo!"

"A tattoo?" he repeated, startled. "Where on earth did you acquire such a thing?"

She made a face. "I attended a boarding school for several years to acquire polish and meet more girls of my rank. One of the girls was quite wild and different. Her parents were Irish, but she'd grown up in India. I thought she was wonderful and daring and adventurous. She'd ridden elephants!"

"For a girl who craved adventures, I can see where she'd be irresistible as a friend," he said, amused. "Was she also a tattoo artist?"

"No, but she was interested in tattoos and was mad keen to create one. But it would have been almost impossible for her to tattoo herself, and I was the only girl in the school willing to allow her to experiment on me."

Rob couldn't help it. He began to laugh. "Sarah, you are an unending source of delight.

May I see this tattoo? Please? Or will you make me wait for fifty years?"

She sighed. "I suppose I might as well get this over with." She pulled her nightgown straight up over her head and stood revealed in all her satin-skinned, hourglass perfection before she crumpled the fabric and held it over her most private parts.

Rob temporarily stopped breathing. As beautiful as she was clothed, she was even more beautiful naked. "You are the most exquisite creature I have ever seen in my life." His body, which he'd thought satisfied, began stirring with interest.

Her smile was shy, but also pleased at his reaction. "The tattoo is back here, on the right side." She turned and revealed the small, roughly circular black design on the perfect curve of her derriere, which needed no decoration. "I liked the idea of a scandalous tattoo, but was too much of a coward to put it anywhere likely to be seen."

"A nice balance between rebellion and practicality. At least it's now possible to tell you and Mariah apart."

As Sarah snorted at his comment, he knelt for a better look at the twisting pattern. The tattoo was about an inch in diameter and a bit lopsided, but pretty. "It's a Celtic knot. Your mad friend did a good job for an amateur. I had no idea what mischief schoolgirls might get up to." He kissed the tattoo and stood up. "Didn't it hurt?"

Sarah made a face. "Dreadfully, but there was brandy involved, which helped."

He chuckled. "Without the brandy, there probably would have been no tattoo."

"You're right." She cocked her head quizzically. "What about you? You were a sailor. Do you have any tattoos?"

"No, I dislike being obvious. Shall we have that bath now?" He scooped her up and slid her into the water with a swirl of rosemary and lavender scents.

"Ahhh . . ." She breathed as the deliciously warm liquid rose to her shoulders. *"Wonderful! It's like visiting a hot spring spa, but it smells much nicer."*

"I think many people believe a hot spring has to smell dreadful in order to have medicinal properties." He opened a cabinet and found bars of soap. He handed her one. It had a spicy scent he couldn't name, but liked.

Setting the soap aside, she folded her arms on the rim of the tub and regarded him with bright-eyed interest. "And now, my newly acquired lord, it's my turn to see you in your bare skin!"

Chapter 37

"I'm much less beautiful than you," Rob warned. "No tattoos, but I have some scars. Also—my apologies for this—I'm showing clear indications of a desire to consummate our marriage again a time or two before morning. Not that I will. You need time to recover."

"I'll take those indications as a compliment," she said. She loved the sense of play between them. When she first met Rob, he was all sternness and business.

He untied the sash of his banyan and pulled off the robe, turning to hang it on one of the hooks on the door. She'd never seen a completely naked grown man before, and the sight was intimidating, fascinating—and rather arousing.

As she'd guessed, Rob was all lean muscle, his torso a triangle from broad shoulders to narrow hips. She kept her gaze away from his erection; that was the intimidating part. Hard to imagine that such a large object had been inside her.

Reminding herself that after the first shock, she'd liked it, she studied the rest of him. He hadn't been joking about the scars. She frowned. "Are those faint lines on your back lash marks?"

He nodded. "Acquired early in my days as a reluctant sailor. I fought and complained and tried to convince the captain that I was a kidnapped gentleman. He might have believed me since I spoke like a gentleman, but he wasn't interested in how I came to be on his ship. He just wanted me to work. A flogging by the bo'sun got the point across."

She gasped with horror. "How dreadful!"

"Floggings are common on ships. A wise man doesn't court them," he said tersely as he climbed the steps of the tub. He slid in at the opposite end, moving slowly so she wouldn't be engulfed by a tidal wave, but the water rose to her chin.

They settled carefully, her drawn up knees tucked next to his. The tub did hold two people, but there wasn't a lot of extra room when one of them was as tall as Rob.

She leaned forward and touched a gouged line on his upper left arm. "Is this a remnant of your Runner days?"

"I was grazed by a pistol ball. Luckily the man with the pistol was a terrible shot."

"Your history is written on your skin," she said. "Rather alarmingly so."

"This is nothing compared to the scarring an infantry officer might have," he assured her. He handed her one of the glasses of wine and took the other himself.

She tasted her wine. Red this time, since it

wouldn't stain if it spilled into the water. "This is life at its most splendidly decadent."

"Splendid, yes." He sipped his own wine. "Decadent, no. Having a watery wedding night with my exquisite new bride counts as an amazing gift, not decadence."

She felt her face pinkening. "This is probably not a story to tell our grandchildren, though."

"Definitely not." He offered her the tray of tidbits.

She took another of the small ham and cheese biscuits. "Eating and drinking in a magnificent bathing tub suits my admittedly modest notions of decadence." She took a cube of cheddar cheese with a dab of chutney on top. "By the way, I saw you and Adam and Kirkland heading into the house in midafternoon, and I didn't see you or Kirkland again for quite some time. Is there anything I should know about?"

"Sorry," he said apologetically. "I forgot to thank you for redecorating the study. It looks so much better that I almost didn't recognize the room."

"I'm glad you like it, since you keep ending up there. Later I'll make it even more like the library." She cocked her head to one side. "What about Kirkland?"

Rob sighed, losing some of his lightheartedness. "He thinks there might be French money behind the more dangerous Irish radical groups, including Free Eire. You spent days with them. Did you hear or see anything to support that possibility?"

Sarah frowned, trying to remember. Not easy when floating on a cloud of really fine claret. "I can't think of anything, except that once I heard Flannery telling one of his men that by the time they arrived back home, the payment from Claude should have come. Since Claude is a French name, that might mean something."

"It's certainly possible," Rob said with interest. "I'll pass that on to Kirkland before he leaves tomorrow. Even tiny scraps of information can add up."

Sarah yawned delicately and set her empty wineglass on the wide edge of the tub. "I'm finally getting sleepy, and you're the most comfortable-looking thing in sight."

It took some acrobatic ability, but she turned around so her head was at the same end as Rob's. His arm came around her so that she lay along his body, half floating. "Bliss," she murmured.

"You're quite comfortable, too. So much softness." He gently squeezed her breast.

She began idly stroking his chest, her fingers skimming the light texture of hair. Then she gave an experimental tweak to one of his nipples. It hardened immediately and he inhaled sharply.

"How interesting," she said. "A similar reaction to mine." She tweaked the other.

"You have a talent for this," he said in a slightly choked voice.

"Do I? Then I should develop it." She slid her hand down and gently clasped his "clear indication of desire." It stiffened to rock hardness and he gasped.

She explored further, learning the shape by touch and discovering what he seemed to like best. Difficult, since he apparently liked everything. Rob's eyes were closed and his breathing ragged as his arm clamped around her.

Knowing that she was creating such a powerful response made her feel intensely, wickedly female. It was also remarkably arousing. The heat growing in the hidden places she'd just discovered tonight made her hips start to pulse.

It occurred to her that if she wrapped her leg over him, they'd fit together very nicely. No sooner thought than done. She slid her leg to his other side and straddled him, half floating, her most intimate parts resting on his.

He gasped, "Dear God, Sarah!"

She slowly rocked, sliding up and down on that silken-hard shaft. He caught her hips and aligned them so he could bury himself inside her. They locked together so tightly that that spot of exquisite sensation rubbed hard against him with shattering results. She cried out, thrashing in the water as she lost control of her body.

He made a hoarse groaning sound in her ear,

his body surging as mindlessly as hers. She might have drowned if he hadn't held her head above water.

All strength dissolved and she lay limply on top of him, his arms locked around her waist. When she could breathe again, she said, "I really hope that we can keep this house and this bath."

Rob gave a choke of laughter and kissed her cheek. "Sarah," he said huskily. "My princess. You're the best thing that ever happened to me."

She'd had a lot more good things happen to her than Rob had. But he was moving rapidly toward the top of her list.

After the water cooled, they emerged from the tub. Rob used one of the large towels to give Sarah a brisk rubdown that left her skin tingling. After drying himself, he carried her into her bedroom. Though it wasn't actually necessary, she did love feeling his effortless strength.

She discovered that sleeping without night-clothes was another delicious decadence. In the future, nightgowns would be wiser since maids would enter early with chocolate or tea, but this night was theirs. She loved lying skin to skin with Rob within the protective circle of his arms.

One dim lamp had been left on as a night-light. As Sarah drifted toward sleep, she moved her left hand outside the covers and light glinted softly from her wedding band. Through the whole of her Irish adventure, she'd worn Mariah's wedding ring, first as evidence that she was the duchess, and later to keep it safe.

Mariah had received her ring back gratefully even though Adam could have bought her a new one studded with diamonds if she'd wanted it. That simple gold band was priceless for what it represented.

Sarah closed her hand, instinctively protecting her ring and what it stood for. Priceless because it was a token of the vows she and Rob had made to each other.

She fell asleep smiling. It would be a while before she believed on all levels that he'd never leave her. But she already knew that someday she would.

Chapter 38

Rob woke the next morning with reluctance because the night without cares was over. He gazed at the brocade canopy above and thought of all that had to be done. The money he'd retrieved from Buckley was disappearing fast. If he didn't hear from the family lawyer by tomorrow, he'd have to go up to London in person to find out what was going on with the Kellington finances.

The mere thought of all that made him tense. Then Sarah shifted in his arms and he moved his gaze from the canopy to her. She was soft and golden and utterly adorable. His tension disappeared. His new life might be demanding—but with Sarah beside him, it was all worth it.

Most of the houseguests were leaving. Some, like the Ashtons, had stayed longer than planned for the wedding. Patrick Cassidy was heading back to Ireland with Rob's man Harvey to see what could be done at Kilvarra.

Patrick shook Rob's hand in farewell, saying genially that Kirkland wasn't a bad fellow, doubtless because he was more Scottish than English and hence kin to an Irishman. Rob suspected that in the future, his cousin would be sending information to Kirkland if he thought it would benefit both Ireland and England.

Rob also asked Harvey to see if he could find a pony named Boru that had been given to a yawl captain in Kinsale in partial payment for a boat. And if he found another good pony suitable for a little girl, by all means buy it.

After the last of the guests had been sent on their way, Bree approached Rob, her expression belligerent, as if she didn't expect a good result. "Since there are no classes at the vicarage today, will you give me another riding lesson?"

Rob hesitated, thinking of all the other things he should be doing. Then he caught a look from Sarah that he interpreted as meaning that he should jolly well say yes. She was right. Estate work was endless, but his daughter needed attention now. "I'll meet you at the stables as soon as you can change."

She nodded, looking happier, and darted off to change. When she was out of earshot, Rob said to Sarah, "Bree seemed upset. Has something happened?"

"Not that I know of," Sarah said, her brow furrowed. "But she's gone through a lot of changes in a short period of time. At first, she was just grateful to be rescued from her horrid grandfather. Then there was the excitement of the wedding. My guess is that now life is settling into a new pattern and she's uncertain how she fits in to Kellington. Particularly now that you're married." Sarah smiled a little. "Being your daughter, she's facing it head-on rather than cowering."

"In a similar situation, what would you do?" Rob asked. "Fight or cower?"

Sarah laughed. "I'd look small and harmless and charm my way through."

"And you'd be very successful with that, too." He couldn't imagine anyone resisting her. Even his grandmother liked Sarah, though she tried to hide it.

He gave her a swift kiss on the cheek since anything more would get serious immediately. "I'll see you later."

"Smelling of horse," she said amiably. "Until later!"

Bree reached the stables just after Rob. In a riding habit that fit, she looked like a proper young lady, though her language could still be hair-raising. He and Bryony had created this child, but Bree was her own self. "You've been doing well with paddock practice. Shall we take a ride out onto the estate today?"

"That would be bloody marvelous!" Then she winced apologetically.

When they were mounted, Bree on a placid, elderly mare, Rob headed them north along the cliffs, past the old ruined castle. His daughter looked a little nervous to be riding without a leading rein, but she had good balance and riding instincts. She'd be ready for a livelier mount soon.

As they walked sedately by the castle, he remarked, "Have you spent much time exploring the ruins? They're really interesting, but they can be dangerous. Some of the old tunnels and walls are ready to fall. Don't go there without letting someone know where you are. Better yet, go with a friend."

She gave him a nod that he recognized as meaning, "I have no intention of doing what you say, but I won't bother to argue." He'd seen that expression on his own face when he was a boy. He hoped that if she wasn't obedient, at least she'd be careful. "Did you enjoy being a bridesmaid?"

Since she shrugged without answering, he asked bluntly, "You seem upset. Why? I can't help if I don't know what is wrong."

She glanced at him, her ice blue eyes unnervingly like his. "I s'ppose you and Sarah are going to have a bunch of bloody babies now."

So that was the problem. "We hope to in time," he said. "But you'll always be my oldest child."

"If you have daughters, they'll be Lady Sarah and Lady Mariah," she spat out. "Not 'that bastard Bree.' "

He winced. "Have you been called that?"

"A boy from the village said that. But I punched him in the nose!"

Sarah was right that Bree was a fighter. "Fighting isn't usually a very good solution," he said. "People who throw insults want a reaction. If you smile and act as if you don't care, they'll probably go away and find someone else to insult."

She frowned as she considered. "Mebbe, but I lose my temper when people are mean. 'Specially if someone calls me mum a whore."

"I'd have trouble with that one, too," he admitted. "Like most things, controlling one's temper takes practice. If someone calls you a bastard, remember that a much prettier term is love child. You're a child born of love. A lot of people can't say that."

She nodded glumly. "Mebbe, but I wish you'd married me mum."

"I wanted to," he said, wondering how many times he'd have to say that before she believed him. "I know you'd rather still have your mother, but you do have a father and a step-mother who will care for you."

"Bloody Sarah," she muttered under her breath.

Contrary to the good advice he'd just given, Rob's temper flared. "Bryony!" he snapped. He caught the reins of her mare and swung around to face his daughter, his eyes blazing. "You will not speak of my wife in such a way. Sarah deserves respect and courtesy at the least, and a good deal more."

Instead of cowering, Bree spat back, "What if I call you a bloody bugger?"

Rob released the reins. "Behaving badly does get attention. But behaving well will give you much more freedom to quietly do what you want." Remembering Sarah's words, he continued, "You've had many changes in a short time. That's upsetting. But don't lash out at people who don't deserve it. If you have problems, bring them to me."

Eyes narrowed, she asked, "What will you do to me if I don't behave?"

How the devil should he handle a belligerent girl child? A thought struck. "Riding a horse requires calm and good sense. A rider who is angry or out of control shouldn't be on a horse. Do I make myself clear?"

She looked appalled. "No pony?"

Hating that he had to say this, he said firmly, "Not if I feel you're being a bad horsewoman. So work on your temper and your language, please. It's one thing to use bad words by accident, but I recommend you cure yourself of the habit. Deliberately using bad language to insult is just crude."

After a long pause, she nodded. "But you really are a bloody bugger!" Then she turned the mare and headed back to the castle at the fastest pace her mount would go, which wasn't very fast.

Rob was torn between laughing and wanting to spank her. Neither would be a good idea. He followed, glad to see how easily she remained on the mare's broad back.

Was parenting easier if one started with an infant so parent and child grew up together? He made a mental note to consult Sarah. She might not have raised a daughter, but she'd been a little girl herself.

One who drank brandy and got tattooed. At that, he really did laugh. Family life might be complicated, but it certainly was interesting.

He arrived back at the stables to find Bree grooming the old mare. She had to stand on a wooden box to do it. She eyed him warily as he brought his own mount in.

He said peaceably, "I need experience at being a father. You need experience at having a father. Shall we work on this together?"

Her small face dissolved into a smile. "Yes, sir!"

Rather hesitantly, he said, "I've been meaning to ask you if you'd be willing to take the name Carmichael. I don't mean that you'd give up your mother's name. You'd be Bryony Owens Carmichael."

Bree bit her lip, looking ready to cry. "Too bloody right I'd like that!"

"Thank you, Miss Carmichael." As Rob unsaddled his horse, he decided that they were making progress. At least, he hoped so.

Chapter 39

Rob mentally listed his duties for the rest of the day as he entered the front hall of the house. He was intercepted by Sarah, who carried a bulging leather folio.

"The absent Nicholas Booth, third-generation solicitor of the firm handling Kellington's affairs, has arrived," she informed Rob. "I left him drinking tea in the small salon while I went for the financial plans you and Adam and I developed." She brandished the folio. "I was about to send someone for you."

Rob came to full alertness. The financial news was surely bad, but knowing was better than the limbo he'd been in. "Finally! I really was beginning to believe that he'd decamped with the family assets, except that there probably aren't any. What do you think of him?"

She considered. "Sober, earnest, and intelligent."

"That's encouraging." He offered his arm. "Shall we see what he has to say?"

She took his arm with an expression of rueful resolve. "For better and for worse, my lord! I put him in the small salon since it's one of the rooms that I haven't done anything with. He might as well know we're poor if he hasn't figured that out already."

They were walking across the hall when the dowager countess marched down the stairs, cane in hand. "I hear Booth has arrived. I wish to see him."

Rob hesitated. "Later, perhaps? Sarah and I are joining him for what is likely to be a rather grim discussion of family finances."

"Which is precisely why I want to be present," she said waspishly. "Kellington has been my home for almost fifty years, and I have a right to know what's going on."

Hard to deny that. "As you wish, ma'am. After you."

She nodded and led the way to the small salon, cane tapping brusquely. As they entered the room, the lawyer rose quickly and bowed. He was around forty, Rob estimated, of middling height and build. Booth and Rob studied each other in a mutual summing up.

After a few moments, the lawyer turned his attention to the dowager. "Lady Kellington. It's a pleasure to see you looking so well."

Her mouth quirked. "You lie as badly as your father did." She chose a chair and sat, her cane ready in case she wanted to wallop someone.

Rob said, "I'm glad to see you, Mr. Booth. I was on the verge of traveling to London to hunt you down." He offered his hand.

Booth looked as if he wasn't sure that such a comment from a Bow Street Runner was a joke. "I'm sorry, Lord Kellington. I intended to write you directly after receiving your letter, but the situation is complex. It took longer than I expected to assemble all relevant information, and I soon realized I'd best meet with you in person." Releasing Rob's hand, he glanced at Sarah. "Excuse me, miss, I don't know who you are."

"Another Lady Kellington," she said cheerfully.

He bowed. "I'm sorry, my lady. I didn't realize that Lord Kellington had a wife."

"We just married yesterday so it's not surprising you didn't know." Her eyes glinted. "And before you look too hopeful, I do not have a dowry that will make a difference to Kellington's finances. Shall we take seats and begin?"

Expression uncertain, Mr. Booth said, "This will be a tedious business discussion. Perhaps the ladies would like to be excused?"

"My wife knows more of estate management than I do," Rob said as he escorted Sarah to the sofa opposite Booth. "It's likely that my grandmother does also. Since they have vested interests in the situation, they're entitled to participate."

He sat down next to Sarah. A low table stood between their sofa and the lawyer's chair and a neat stack of papers lay in front of Booth.

Sarah set her leather folio down beside the lawyer's documents in a silent challenge. "Put us out of our misery, Mr. Booth. Will we have to lease Kellington Castle to a nabob while we retrench in a cottage somewhere?"

"I see you've been thinking about this, my lady," the lawyer said with approval. "No, the situation is very difficult, but not quite that bad."

Sarah caught Rob's hand and squeezed it. He squeezed back, feeling a stunning rush of relief. Apparently he was more attached to this blasted faux castle than he'd realized. Collecting himself, he asked, "Do you have a list of all the Kellington properties? I imagine anything unentailed is mortgaged."

"Sadly true. Here is a listing of real property and the mortgages." The lawyer lifted the top document from his pile and passed it over the table. "As you can see, every single mortgage is in arrears. With the death of your father and then your brother, mortgage holders might be waiting to see who the new earl is before they foreclose."

"On the off chance that the newest earl is wealthy? They're doomed to disappointment." Rob scanned the list. Besides Kellington Castle, which was entailed and couldn't be mortgaged, there were half a dozen smaller estates, including Kilvarra in Ireland. There were also several London properties and three businesses in the

Midlands: a foundry, a pottery, and some sort of mill.

He felt sick when he mentally added up the outstanding debts. Well over a hundred thousand pounds. What the devil had his father and brother done with all that money? He handed the sheet to Sarah. "I didn't see a mortgage for Kellington House. Is that entailed?"

Booth nodded. "Your grandfather added it to the entail. He was also the one who acquired most of the unentailed properties." He gave the dowager a respectful nod. "Your husband was an excellent financial manager, my lady."

The dowager was studying the sheet of properties and debts that Sarah had passed on. "A trait that doesn't seem to have been inherited. My husband put Kellington House into the entail so the family would have decent quarters in London."

Sarah said to Booth, "A madly extravagant bathing room has been added to the master suite upstairs. Do you know if the same was done at Kellington House?"

Booth grimaced. "Yes, I saw the bills as they came through. Extortionate."

"A great waste of money," Sarah said primly, but Rob saw the gleam in her eyes.

"What income is the combined estate producing?" Rob asked. "Or perhaps I should ask what it produced under my grandfather compared to what it does now."

"At its best, when your grandfather worked with mine, the annual income was in excess of sixty thousand pounds a year."

Rob gave a soft whistle. "What is the income now?"

"Between twenty and thirty thousand pounds," Booth replied. "Since your brother died before receiving the first quarter income, that payment is available to you. I've brought a bank draft for about six thousand pounds."

Combined with the money recovered from Buckley, that was enough to pay the running costs of the estate for several months. "Then we can make a start here at Kellington Castle. Sarah and my friend Ashton and I have sketched out plans for what needs to be done." Rob removed an outline from Sarah's folio and handed it to Booth.

"Do you mean the Duke of Ashton?" At Rob's nod, Booth said, impressed, "He's considered one of the best and most progressive landlords in Britain. You were fortunate that he was able to work with you."

"He's my sister's husband," Sarah explained.

The lawyer looked even more impressed as he studied the plans, brow furrowing.

Rob said, "We'll have to work in stages, of course. The first would include critical repairs as well as buying better breeding stock to improve the income in future years. The outline is very rough, of course, since we didn't have exact numbers."

Booth flipped to the next page. "Your assumptions and goals are good, though."

"Now that we've talked to you, we can firm up the plans," Rob said. "I assume I'll have to let properties that are in arrears go into foreclosure. Since Kellington House is well located, it can be leased to provide some revenue. Since you're far more familiar with the family properties, I welcome your opinions."

"Lord Kellington, you talk like your grandfather," Booth said with approval. "I do have thoughts about guiding the future of the estate."

"What about personal debts? I won't pay my father's or brother's gambling losses, but I'll try to settle tradesmen's bills. I don't want families put out on the streets because of my predecessors' profligacy."

"I can provide you with a listing of those debts." Booth grimaced. "Tradesmen have been besieging my office since your brother's death."

"Most such debts can be negotiated down," the dowager said. "A tailor who fears he won't be paid at all will be glad to recover half." She snorted. "Probably doubled his prices in the first place because he knew they would be hard to collect."

Feeling some relief, Rob said, "Mr. Booth, you have my permission to negotiate settlements wherever possible."

The lawyer nodded and made a note. "I've covered the estate's assets and liabilities, Lord Kellington. Do you have any significant personal assets?"

Rob paid all his bills promptly and had enough savings to carry him easily through the ebb and flow of his work, but it wasn't the kind of money Booth was asking about. "Sorry, no. I'll have to work with what the estate produces."

Sarah said hesitantly, "You once mentioned that when you left India, you gave some of your savings to your former employer to invest. How has that done?"

"I don't really know," he said, surprised. "I never think about the money I gave Fraser." That was money for emergencies or old age, if he survived that long. "But in his last letter, he said my investment was doing well. I'll write Fraser's London office to find out just how well."

"Wouldn't Rob have been entitled to a younger son's portion?" Sarah asked. "Marriage settlements always designate portions for daughters and younger sons."

"He would have been entitled to ten thousand pounds," the lawyer admitted. "But the money is long since gone."

The dowager rapped her cane on the floor. "Booth, you must be tired from your travels. Sarah, ring for the butler to escort Mr. Booth to a room." The words were courteous, but it was plainly a dismissal.

"Thank you, my lady." Booth tucked away his papers and got to his feet. "I shall see you later, my lord. You'll have more questions after you have time to absorb this."

After the lawyer left and closed the door behind him, the dowager fixed Rob with a gimlet eye. "Don't let go of any of the Kellington properties."

"I might be able to save one or two, but certainly not all of them. Not when they're all mortgaged to the hilt and in arrears."

"All are sound properties and good long-term investments. Your grandfather and I chose them most carefully."

"You and your husband worked closely together?" Sarah asked with interest.

"My father was a wealthy merchant so I cut my eyeteeth on business. My husband appreciated my knowledge." The dowager frowned. "Your father was not inclined to listen to females."

"Then he was a fool," Sarah said firmly. "I suspect that if he'd listened to you, the estates would be in far better condition."

"They would. But his first wife, Edmund's mother, was interested only in extravagance and a fashionable life," the dowager said waspishly. "Your mother wasn't extravagant, Kellington, but she lacked an understanding of financial matters and left such things to her husband, which was a grave error."

Her words gave Rob a better understanding of his grandmother's bitter tongue. Her opinion of him must be improving because this was the first time she'd called him by his title. Up till now, she hadn't really called him anything. "A man would have to be a fool to dismiss intelligent advice when offered."

"You have much better sense than your father and brother," his grandmother said tartly. "Give me the outline of repairs and investments you're considering."

Sarah handed the pages over. His grandmother skimmed the neat handwriting, nodding approval. "Quite intelligent, though you need to invest more in drainage for the southern fields. The crop yield will increase considerably if you do."

"I don't doubt it, but I don't know where the money would come from. What projects would you suggest I delay in order to pay for more drainage?" he asked, an edge in his voice.

"You both seem quite sensible for young people," the dowager said as she studied them with narrowed eyes. "I must say that I'm agreeably surprised."

Amused, Rob said, "The feeling is mutual."

"If you two aren't careful, you'll find yourselves in charity with each other," Sarah contributed, equally amused.

The faintest of smiles flickered over the dowager's face. "What would you do if there were no mortgages to pay on the unentailed property?"

"I'd evaluate each property," Rob said slowly. "I suspect they haven't been maintained as well as they should be, so the initial income would go to repairs and improvements. When properties become profitable, I'd put some of the income into savings and would consider new investments. But I'd want to know a good bit more about the subject before doing that."

"Then start studying," she said dryly. "I hold the mortgages for most of the unentailed properties."

Sarah gasped and Rob stared at his grandmother. Trying to make sense of that, he asked, "Did you loan the money to my father in the first place?"

"Of course not. I always knew he was a bad risk." She snorted. "I thoroughly disapproved of the mortgages and your father knew it so he borrowed elsewhere. I have my information sources so I kept track. When he died and the estate fell into Edmund's hands, most of the bankers decided to cut their losses. I was able to acquire all the mortgages but for the manor in Derbyshire."

"So you negotiated with them the way you advised Rob to do with the tradesmen?" Sarah asked with fascination.

"I bought them for about half the face value."

"Madam, I bow to your superior business skills," Rob said sincerely. "What do you plan to do with the mortgages? I doubt you trust me enough to just hand them over."

"Quite right," his grandmother said crisply. "You and your wife show promising attitudes and skills, but it's far too early to assume that you won't slip into the same bad habits your father and brother succumbed to. I shall continue to hold the mortgages, but I won't require payment if you follow the course of action you described today. Also, don't lease Kellington House. I wish to stay there when I'm in London."

It was almost too large to comprehend. He exchanged a glance with Sarah, who seemed as stunned as he. "I don't know how to thank you, ma'am."

"I'm not doing this for you, but for Kellington. I sincerely hope you'll be a better earl than your father and brother." She got to her feet and glared at Sarah. "And you, missy! Make sure you produce an heir promptly, and raise him to have good sense."

"I'll do my best," Sarah said meekly.

The dowager marched from the room. When she was gone, Rob scooped Sarah from the sofa and arranged her on his lap, then hugged her hard. He was close to shaking with shock. "We're going to survive, Sarah! We'll have some lean years ahead, but we'll be able to rebuild the estate as we hoped."

"When your grandmother was poking her cane into your almost-drowned body, I never, ever expected that she would do anything like this." Sarah laughed. "It turns out that you didn't need an heiress after all!"

He joined her laughter. "This makes me very glad that I followed my fancy rather than being logical and starting an heiress hunt." He kissed his wife's graceful neck. "Now that we've taken care of business, shall we go upstairs and celebrate?"

Sarah batted her golden eyelashes innocently while wiggling her sweet backside very uninnocently on his lap. "What do you have in mind?"

"I'll think of something." Holding her in his arms, he stood, no mean feat even with a woman as petite as Sarah. "You're my lucky charm, princess. My life has improved dramatically since I met you."

She linked her arms behind his neck. "So has mine, Robin. So has mine."

Chapter 40

Sarah awoke with a long, lazy yawn. She'd had no idea just how much she would like being married. Before she'd had rather fuzzy, mystical ideas about not marrying unless she was "in love." She'd learned that it was enough that she enjoyed Rob's company, trusted and respected him—and truly loved sharing a bed with him.

Rob was lying on his side with his back to her, so she rolled over to fit behind him, her body pressed along his and her arm around his waist. He made a soft, half asleep sound and clasped her hand, resting it over his heart. Sarah murmured, "Now that your grandmother has gone back to Bath, this finally feels like our house."

He chuckled. "She did take up rather a lot of mental space. I'm flattered that she's now willing to entrust Kellington to us."

"I give her credit for recognizing that if she stayed here, she'd be constantly interfering." Sarah breathed on the back of Rob's neck. "I invited her back for Bree's birthday party and she might come. Bath isn't that far."

"Between now and then, I'm going to have to take some trips. I need to visit the Kellington properties to evaluate what each needs. I'll start with the ones in this part of the country." He rolled on his back and looped his arm around her neck. "I hate leaving you, though. Could you come with me?"

She sighed. "I'd love to, but there's so much going on. For now, at least, one of us needs to be here."

"I'll take Crowell then. He's an excellent steward. Now that I've offered him a permanent position and some money for improvements, he's working even harder. It will be useful to get his opinion of the other estates." Rob's chuckle reverberated under her ear. "But I won't want to share a bed with him at night."

"I should hope not!"

He stroked her hair. "I love the way our lives are taking form, Sarah."

"So do I, but at the moment, I'm more interested in here and now." Her hand slid down his torso. She was unsurprised to find that he was already somewhat aroused. When she grasped him, he caught his breath and hardened instantly. "I think I'll climb Mount Robert," she said happily.

"Do with me as you will, princess," he said huskily. "I'm at your mercy."

She pulled the covers down and climbed onto him in a dry land version of what she'd done in the tub. This was a new position for her, but she thought it would work.

Theory rapidly became fact. She loved lying along his lean body, her hair spilling around his face as they kissed and caressed. The world narrowed down to hot blood and escalating desire. Not only was it easy to join together in this position, but also shockingly, deliciously stimulating.

Their union was swift but fiercely satisfying. As she lay panting on top of him in the aftermath, she breathed, "I never realized just how powerful marital intimacy is. I can't imagine doing this with another man."

"God willing, you won't have to." Rob pulled the covers up over their cooling bodies. "This is the 'cleaving unto one another' part, and I like it."

She rested her head on his shoulder, unable to forget that other women had been in his bed before her, even if they weren't wives. "Rob," she said in a small voice. "Does the fact that you've had other lovers make what we do . . . less special?"

His muscles tensed. "You don't believe in avoiding difficult questions, princess."

"I'm sorry," she said, her voice even smaller.

"Don't be," he said firmly. "The simplest answer is that each relationship is different. Unique. Impossible to compare. Bryony and I were very young, with all the passionate discovery of youth. My . . . companion during my

Runner years was my friend and professional equal. We were two lonely people who found comfort in each other's company, and occasionally warmth in each other's arms."

Sarah frowned thoughtfully. "We have a good deal of the passion, and also the companionship, I think."

"Yes, not to mention the fact that you're my wife." He laughed a little. "I still have trouble believing that! But it means that everything between us is shaped by the knowledge that we have made lifetime vows to each other with all the joys and responsibilities that go with those vows." He kissed her chin. "I refuse to get drawn into a discussion of beauty, charm, and allure! That wouldn't be fair to anyone."

"Wise man," she said, smiling as they relaxed together. She suspected that he'd been with other women as well. A mistress in India, perhaps. More casual encounters that hadn't left much of a mark on his life.

Now there was Miss Sarah Clarke-Townsend, who by luck and circumstance had become his wife. If he'd rescued a different woman and returned to England to find himself a lord, might he have married that woman? Perhaps, if they liked each other and were both in the mood to marry. It was a rather unromantic view of marriage.

Yet the fact of marrying *did* change the situation. She and Rob had pledged fidelity and responsibility. He was right that doing so affected the intimate side of their marriage, though she wasn't knowledgeable enough to define how.

Rob said with regret, "I hate to move, but the duties of the day are calling."

Equally regretful, she rolled off him. "Tonight is another night."

He sat up and kissed her. "And tomorrow will be another morning."

She made the kiss more than casual, amazed at the thought that she'd been skittish about marrying. If marriage was a gamble, she'd won her bet.

Rob was able to join Sarah for lunch that day. He enjoyed sharing the details of their days. This was another of the bonds of marriage, he was learning. Day by day they were becoming closer. Building a life as a couple.

It was a pleasant spring day and windows were open, which is why they heard the sounds of livestock as they lingered over tea. A bellowing bull, the baaing of sheep, and cackling roosters, followed by the quacks and honks of waterfowl.

"What on earth?" Rob rose and looked out the window, Sarah joining him.

Outside the castle was a convoy that included

two men on horseback and two wagons, each with a bull tethered behind it. The first wagon contained sheep, goats, and pigs in separate pens. The second carried caged poultry and rabbits. At least two roosters were included because they were crowing at each other.

"They seem to be all males," Sarah observed. "And very fine beasts they are! Did you order breeding stock and forget to mention it?"

"No." Rob broke into a smile. "But I think I know where they came from. See that man riding at the end of this parade?"

"Murphy!" she exclaimed with delight. "Adam's head groom. I think that other man might be one of the Ashton cowmen."

Rob caught her hand and headed for the door. "Let's see if this is what I suspect."

They reached the drive in front of the house as wagons, bulls, and horses rumbled to a stop. Murphy swung off his mount and approached, a letter in his hand. "Good day, my lord," he said formally.

"I believe you were calling me Carmichael when last we met. Why not go with Rob?" Rob offered his hand and a smile. "This lot must be a nuisance for a man who works with horses!"

Murphy grinned back. "It was an interesting trip. Took three days. The bulls are not fast walkers." He handed over the letter.

Rob broke the seal and read:

Rob and Sarah—

As I said before, the service you performed is beyond price and deserves a payment in kind. Your estate needs first-class breeding stock, and these are some of the best beasts in Britain. I'd never sell them, so I suppose that makes them beyond price. Please accept this breeding stock as a token of my undying gratitude.

Ashton

Rob handed the letter to Sarah. "Wonderful!" she exclaimed. "Much of Adam's original stock came from Coke of Norfolk, and he's been improving it ever since."

"Aye, my lady." The cowman joined them. He bobbed his head. "You won't find finer breeders anywhere in Britain. Where shall we put the stock? I want to get them settled properly. A journey like this 'tis hard on the poor beasts."

This was a man who obviously loved his work and his animals. "I'll show you to the barns," Rob said. "I assume you'll stay the night, maybe another day or two? I'm sure my stockmen can learn from you."

"Aye, his grace said we were at your disposal for as long as you want."

Seeing the conversation sliding toward the agricultural, Sarah said, "Mr. Murphy, I'm glad to see you again. I owe you thanks for what you did for me and my sister. Rob, I'll see you later." She gave a dazzling smile to all the men, including the drivers, and returned to the house.

As they walked toward the barns, Murphy fell in beside Rob. "His grace said you could also have this stallion I'm leading if you'd like it. Rojo is a first-class stud."

Rob took a closer look at the stallion, a handsome red chestnut. "He's magnificent! Why would Ashton think I might not want him?"

"Some men might feel insulted at the idea they need help with their horseflesh," the groom explained.

"Anyone who wants to insult me with a horse like this is more than welcome," Rob said with a grin. "This old estate is well on its way to getting on its feet again."

"Onto a lot of sets of four feet, and some two footers as well," Murphy said, a twinkle in his eyes. "You'll have a fine lot of new stock next year."

"And better yet a year later." Rob cast an admiring glance over all his new stud animals. Sheep and cattle were impressive, but rabbits and pigeons were a good source of meat, just as good roosters and ganders could improve the quality of eggs and poultry.

He stroked the silken neck of his new stallion. Trust Ashton to come up with a unique and perfect payment for the mission Rob had accomplished.

Chapter 41

The varied breeding stock animals were not the only beasts to arrive. A week later, when Rob was off acquainting himself with other Kellington properties, Sarah headed for the stables to go riding.

She was looking for Jonas when she saw that Rob's man Harvey had returned from Ireland and was grooming a tall pony in a stall. Sarah barely knew him, so this seemed like a good opportunity to remedy that. "Good afternoon, Mr. Harvey."

Then she recognized the pony he was grooming. "Boru!" she exclaimed with delight. "Is that really you?" Cooing, she offered the pony part of the apple she'd brought for the gelding she'd planned to ride.

Harvey touched his cap respectfully. "Rob asked me to see if I could find your pony after I finished at Kilvarra." He nodded toward the next stall. "He also said I should look for another pony that would do for Miss Bree."

"What a beauty!" Sarah leaned against the stall door, admiring the placid dappled gray pony. "Bree will love her."

Harvey patted the pony's neck. "She's a patient girl. Good for a new rider."

"How did things go at Kilvarra?" Sarah asked. "Are any tenants interested in emigration?"

Harvey nodded. "Aye, some are eager to try their luck in a new land. That was a good thought. I also discharged the old steward and hired on Father Patrick's brother. Much remains to be done, but the tenants' lot is improving."

As with Kellington Castle, it was a start. Sarah studied Harvey from the corner of her eye. He was a few years older than Rob, wiry and weathered. There was intelligence in his face, and a weary sense of experience. "How did you and Rob meet?" she asked. "If you don't mind my asking."

Harvey shrugged. "Don't mind. It was in India. I was a sergeant in the East India Company army. One night when I had too much to drink, I walked down an alley where there were some locals who didn't like foreigners. They attacked and would have killed me if I hadn't been yelling. Rob heard and came to investigate. Drove them off and did considerable damage. 'Course, they messed me up pretty bad first."

"So badly you had to leave the army?" she asked quietly.

"Aye." Harvey stamped his wooden peg leg on the floor. "Lost my leg below the knee. I almost died when the wound turned putrid. Rob saw that I was taken care of, then offered me work when it was obvious I wasn't much more use to the army."

"You might not have been much use to the army, but I gather you're good for other things," she remarked. "Rob values you as both associate and friend."

" 'Tis mutual." Harvey glanced at her askance. "Are you good enough for him, my lady?"

She smiled. "Probably not. But I'm working on it."

He laughed softly, and she knew that in the future, they'd be friends.

Rob had planned to return from Devonshire the next day, but instead he pushed on, anxious to see Sarah. It was near midnight when he and Crowell returned. A tolerant gleam in his eyes, the steward said he'd take care of the horses and sent Rob off to join his bride. Rob found it wryly amusing that he was the cliché of a besotted bridegroom, but there was no denying the reality.

When he entered the master suite, he went direct to Sarah's room. The earl's room had yet to be slept in. He entered the chamber quietly, not wanting to startle her awake. A dimly lit lantern gave enough light to show his wife sleeping innocently on her right side, her right hand under her cheek. She looked like a sleeping angel, her exquisite features serene and her blond braid falling over her shoulder.

"Sarah?" he said softly.

There was a flash of movement and suddenly

his wife was sitting up in bed, a cocked pistol held steady in both hands, the barrel aimed at his chest.

Rob froze, his hands in the air. Startling a barely awake woman with a gun aimed at him would not be wise.

"I thought I'd receive a warmer welcome," he said in his most soothing voice.

She recognized him in an instant and uncocked the pistol. As she set it on her end table, she exclaimed, "Rob, I'm so sorry! With you away, I've been having nightmares of the abductors coming after me again."

She slipped from the bed to wrap herself around him. He enveloped her in his arms. She was trembling.

He felt like the greatest fool on earth. "I'm the one who needs to apologize. I shouldn't have gone away, and I certainly shouldn't have startled you awake! I missed you too much to stay away for a minute longer than was absolutely necessary."

She tilted her face up and he kissed her. Passion seared, swift and shocking. He swept her onto the bed and tumbled down beside her. As he frenziedly unbuttoned his breeches, her hands and mouth and teeth were all over him, as urgent with need as he was.

She was ready, more than ready, her body hot and slick and demanding when he thrust into her.

She was his home, not this great pile of rocks. In Sarah he found peace and joy and shattering fulfillment.

Culmination was as swift and uncontrolled as their joining. Guessing that he'd have nail marks on his back, Rob rolled to his side and drew her close, gasping for breath, his cheek pressed to hers.

Sarah said with unsteady amusement, "Well, *that* was a fine way to wake up!"

He gave a choke of laughter. "I'm sorry. I really didn't intend to ravish you."

"I think the ravishing was mutual." Her arms tightened around him. "I kept myself very busy, but I still missed you dreadfully."

"As I missed you. I never really understood the madness of the newly married. I feel like an idiot—but I wouldn't have it any other way." He kissed her temple.

"Nor would I." She made the soft humming sound that reminded him of a contented cat.

"I hate to think I'll have to go off on another manor visit in a few days, but I need to do what I can while it's early enough in the year to implement changes." He sighed. "And I should go to London for a few days, too. I may need to kidnap you myself."

"Tempting, but not sensible." Sarah thought for a moment. "How about after Bree's birthday, the three of us go to London together? You can take care of business while I can show her the sights and take her to a modiste. I'd also like to engage a governess who could teach Bree and the Holt children. Mrs. Holt is a good teacher, but she has so many other duties that she'd be happy to give up that one."

"I like that idea," he agreed. "Have you found local teachers for the estate schools you want to start?"

"I've hired two infant teachers, but I still need a master and mistress for the older children. I'd prefer local people." She grinned. "I'm thinking of calling these the Kellington Hedge Schools with the motto 'education for all.'"

He laughed. "I like the name, but we don't want parents refusing to send their children because they fear lung fever from studying under the hedges."

"I expect you're right." She sighed happily. "So many of the things we can do to improve the tenants' lives cost so little. A year of education for all the children on the estate for less than the cost of a grand lady's court dress or a good hunting horse for a sporting gentleman."

As Rob rubbed her back, he said slowly, "I've begun to be grateful for the difficulties of my younger years because I lived life as very few aristocrats ever do. I've learned that people of all ranks of society have hopes and fears and dreams. They feel happiness and despair. Now I'm in a position to help some of them."

"I wonder what you'd be like if you'd been raised as a typical aristocratic younger son," Sarah said. "Much less interesting, I'm sure. I like you very well as you are."

"That's fortunate, since you're stuck with me," he said, his gaze tender.

They were amiably silent for a few minutes until Sarah asked, "How did you find your manor of Buckthorne?"

"Rather neglected, but not desperately so. The tenant is a good one who took care of a lot of the smaller problems himself. He was very glad to hear that improvements will be made. Since I needn't pay the mortgage, I can plow Buckthorne's revenues back into the manor. In two or three years, it should be profitable again."

"If that's true of the other properties, in a few years you will be very, very rich," Sarah observed.

"*We* will be very, very rich. Remember me saying 'with my worldly goods I thee endow'?" He frowned. "That reminds me that we need to have marriage settlements drawn up since we didn't do them before the wedding. Portions for daughters and younger sons, pin money and jointure for you. Whatever else is advisable."

"An advantage of all these unentailed estates is that they can be left to those daughters and younger sons," she observed. "That way they'll be comfortably established as gentry in their own right."

He ran a caressing hand down her side and over her hip. Since she hadn't been expecting him, she wore a plain, sturdy flannel nightgown. She still looked incredibly fetching. "As a younger son, I would have welcomed land of my own instead of money."

"Which you didn't receive anyhow. If you'd had the deed to a manor, you would have had something your family couldn't take away." She nuzzled closer. "We'll be much better parents than your father."

"I certainly hope so. I'll need to study how to do it right, though, since I've had no experience of what a good father is like."

"If you need a model, there's my uncle Peter, who was a wonderful father to his sons as well as me," she suggested. "Or Adam's stepfather, General Stillwell. His children and stepchildren are devoted to him." She snuggled closer. "But I think you'll manage on your own. You're doing a good job with Bree."

"I'm glad you think so." He looked at himself ruefully. "I may need aid in being a proper, respectful husband, though. I'm covered with travel dust, which I've inflicted on you and your bed."

"There's a cure for that." She smiled at him mischievously. "Let's take a bath!"

Laughing, he swung out of the bed and lifted her in his arms to carry her off to their magnificent tub. He truly was blessed.

Chapter 42

"It's a beautiful day for a picnic," Helen Broome said as she surveyed the castle ruins. She closed her eyes to listen to the boom of waves at the bottom of the nearby cliffs, accented by the piercing cries of gulls. "And a beautiful place for it."

Sarah agreed. The ancient stones were set in a lush carpet of green spring grass brightened by wildflowers. They'd chosen a quiet site protected from the wind by stone walls on three sides and a hill rising behind them.

On the fourth side, directly in front of them, a small headland thrust into the sea. Half of the brew house perched precariously on the lip, with remnants of walls and small outbuildings scattered artistically across the grass.

The dowager countess had come from Bath for the occasion, and she was ensconced in a Windsor chair brought from the house for her comfort. The old woman said querulously, "I thought the boy was supposed to be here today. His own daughter's birthday, after all!"

Sarah wondered if Rob realized that his grandmother called him "the boy." Compared to the dowager's initial reaction to her only surviving grandson, the words sounded almost affectionate. "Kellington has a lengthy ride home today, but he said he'd try to be here by mid-afternoon so he could join us."

Like Helen Broome and Ruth Holt, the other chaperones, Sarah was perched on a fallen stone. The eight children preferred the informality of sprawling on blankets.

Picnic baskets contained elegant little sand-wiches and delicious pastries accompanied by hot tea or bottles of tangy West Country cider. It was a feast fit for a birthday girl who was also celebrating a new life.

Bree had been ecstatic to see Alice Broome and her other two friends from Bendan. The girls had been entranced by Bree's romantic tale of being swept away to wealth and luxury by her lordly father. Her friends were nice girls, genuinely happy for Bree, and only a little envious. Meeting Bree's father would be the perfect crown for the tale, so Sarah hoped Rob returned in time for the party.

Having eaten well, most of the guests were content to bask in the sun and chat. The youngest Holt was asleep in his mother's lap. But as usual, Bree was full of energy. She bounced up from her blanket. "Sarah, would you like to see more of the ruins?"

Sarah would have preferred to bask in the

sunshine, but it was true she hadn't seen much of the site. "I'd love to. If you'll excuse me?"

The others waved her off good-naturedly. As Sarah followed Bree, she said, "I trust you don't go out onto the headland that's crumbling away. The other half of the brew house looks ready to fall off at any moment." She studied the land that thrust out into the sea just in front of the castle, wondering how much farther it had extended when the castle was built.

Bree looked a little guilty. "I did go out there once, just to see, but only once."

Sarah rolled her eyes. "I'm glad the headland didn't choose that day to collapse under your feet. Please be careful. Ruins are dangerous."

"That's what Papa told me. He said I should have another person with me when I explore." Bree grinned mischievously. "That's why I asked you to join me."

Sarah laughed. "Fair enough. I've only been here twice and haven't explored much at all." They climbed a grassy mound and she shaded her eyes to study the area beyond, which looked more like a village than a castle. "The ruins are really large, aren't they? I'm surprised that more of the stone wasn't carried away to build elsewhere."

"Mrs. Holt said the village was abandoned after practically everyone was killed by the plague," Bree explained. "People don't use the stone because it's seen as an unlucky place."

The path ran near the cliff edge. Sarah looked down to see a boat moored between the headland that supported the broken brew house and a wider headland to the north. The large yawl looked vaguely familiar, but Sarah was no expert on boats despite Rob's best efforts to educate her. She shaded her eyes with one hand and tried to see more detail. Several men were on the deck, but she was too far away to see much.

She frowned with a vague sense of unease. "Do boats moor here often?"

"Sometimes." Bree studied the yawl. "Usually smaller boats. Fishermen. I've not seen that one before."

"Is there a path up the cliff along here?"

Bree nodded. "It comes up the other side of that headland. It's quite the climb, but safe enough." Her voice quickened with excitement. "Do you think those are pirates down there? Or smugglers?"

"I don't know, but I don't have a good feeling about them. Can we get a closer look? I'd like to see if they've climbed the cliff."

Eyes sparkling, Bree led Sarah to a sunken lane that ran between old, collapsed buildings. "There's an old barn that's usable at the other end of the village. It would be bloody perfect for smugglers!"

Perhaps, but most smugglers were on the east

and south coasts, not on the west coast of Britain. They continued along the lane. At the end stood a broad, shambling stone building. Bree pointed. "There's the barn."

Two men came from the direction of the cliff path carrying a long, heavy box between them. Sarah grabbed Bree's arm and pulled her into the shelter of a fallen house in case the men looked their way.

She waited a few moments before peering around the old building that concealed them. No one in sight. She whispered, "Bree, I want to get closer to determine if these men are a danger, but I don't want you to come with me."

Bree looked mulish. "I'm coming, too. I know these ruins better than you!"

Seeing that her stepdaughter was determined, Sarah said, "Very well. But we must be very quiet and careful. This is not a game."

"I'll be careful," Bree promised. "If we move behind the houses on the other side of the lane, we're less likely to be seen."

"Lead the way." Sarah looked out again. No one in sight. As she darted across the lane after Bree, she wished she had the freedom of the trousers she'd worn in Ireland.

As Bree had said, their new route was better concealed from the barn. The old building had stone walls with empty windows and a crude thatched roof that was fairly recent. Sarah guessed that some of Rob's tenants used it for storage.

As they drew near, she heard the sound of voices. Familiar Irish voices. She froze in her tracks, heart pounding, and clutched Bree's arm to halt her forward progress. Very clearly, they both heard, "Now that we're here, how long till we go after that damned Runner and his bitch?"

It was the voice of Flannery, leader of the group that had abducted Sarah. Her stomach knotted with fear.

"Show some respect," a woman's ironic voice replied. She spoke like an educated English-woman with only a light Irish accent. "That damned Runner is now Lord Kellington, and I hear the bitch is now his countess." Her voice turned malicious. "All the more pleasure in killing them before we go after Ashton."

Bree stared at Sarah with shock, no longer thinking this a game. She opened her mouth to speak, but Sarah put a hand over it.

"I've never killed a bloody English lord before." This time the voice was O'Dwyer's. "I look forward to it."

"You'll wait your turn, boyo," a gruff Irish voice said. "I have a score to settle with that Runner. Then we can get on with the first Free Eire raid on England. Get people frightened of us."

Another voice spoke, this with a strong French

accent. "You Irish are so bloodthirsty," a man said with amusement. "That is what my master and I like about you. Free Eire is a finely crafted weapon to use against our mutual enemy."

The woman spoke again. "The Runner will be easier to get than Ashton. That damned duke has guards all around his estate."

"Kellington doesn't," the gruff voice said. "The locals talk mighty freely in the pubs here. 'Twill be easy to get into the house tonight." His voice changed. "Then we can wipe out the village. We'll put the fear of the Irish into these bloody English!"

" 'Tis a fine thing to start with people we already know and hate," the woman said with purring malice in her voice.

Sarah wanted to throw up. These brutes thought that slaughtering innocent, unarmed villagers would make them brave Irish heroes? They were just cowards who liked to kill so they picked easy targets. And the French were behind it, providing money and guns to sow terror. A perfect devil's bargain: the Free Eire beasts got to kill, and the French got to cause trouble for England.

Thumping of feet and a new voice said, "Where should we put these rifles?"

"In the back room, with the ammunition," the gruff voice said.

Heart pounding, Sarah was about to signal Bree for them to move away when she saw a dark, ferret-like man with an air of menace stalking toward the barn along the lane they'd used earlier. Sarah flattened herself to the ground and pulled Bree down with her, praying the man hadn't seen them listening under the window.

He might have seen movement because he glanced their way, but by this time Sarah and Bree were hidden by the tall grasses growing around the barn's foundation.

He entered and announced, "Sir, you told me to scout the ruins to be sure that no one was around. Turns out there's a bloody damned picnic at the castle! Three women and half a dozen little girls. Shall we silence 'em? Wouldn't want to fire a gun and alert the locals, but a little knife work will take care of them." He gave an ugly laugh. "I can do it all meself if no one wants to join me."

Sarah gasped, unable to imagine such viciousness. Then, horribly, she could.

The man's suggestion was met with silence, until the Frenchman said queasily, "You know that the empire supports the Irish quest for justice and freedom from English oppression. But do you really want your first strike to be the murder of helpless women and children? Surely that honor should go to more worthy opponents."

The gruff voice said, "You make a good point,

Claude. But what if they discover that we've landed here?"

Claude! He must be the man Sarah had heard mentioned when she was a captive in Ireland. Here was proof of the French involvement that Kirkland suspected.

"Why not wait to see if we are discovered?" the Frenchman said. "We are some distance from the castle and little girls are not likely to wander this far."

The woman snarled, "We can't let our raid fail because of squeamishness!"

As an argument started, Sarah whispered to Bree, "Go back to the picnic and get everyone away! Then go to the house for help. Be sure to say there are a number of armed men. The militia might have to be called." She prayed that there was a local militia, and it could be summoned quickly.

Bree frowned. "Aren't you coming too, Sarah?"

"I want to listen a little longer. If they decide to come after us, perhaps . . . perhaps I can do something to slow them down." Seeing Bree start to reply, she said sharply, "Don't argue! I'll be careful."

Bree bit her lip fearfully but nodded and slipped away. Sarah lay in the grass listening to the argument and wondering how her life had become so dangerous.

The woman in the barn walked outside, still

arguing what to do with the picnickers. The Irish rebel was middle aged, attractive—and Sarah recognized her. It was Georgiana Lawford, whom Adam had called Aunt Georgiana when he was young.

Just last year, the widowed Georgiana had tried to have Adam murdered so that her own son, Hal, could inherit the dukedom. She'd almost succeeded, too. More than once. When her vicious plotting had been revealed, Ashton had exiled her to her Irish childhood home, Ballinagh, instead of turning her over to the authorities, which would have created a humiliating scandal for the whole Lawford family.

As far as Sarah knew, there'd been no word from Georgiana since her return to Ireland. It looked like she'd found a rebel group to become an instrument of her revenge. This explained everything, including the attempted kidnapping of Mariah, who had been carrying Adam's child. By thwarting that, Sarah and Rob had become targets as well.

Georgiana's companions had also emerged from the barn into the sunshine. The oldest man put a possessive arm around her shoulders in a way that said they were lovers.

Coldly furious, Sarah considered what to do. Dear God, what if Rob was even now approaching the castle ruins for his daughter's party? Even if he was armed, he'd be no match for the number of armed men in Georgiana's party.

She frowned as she considered the possibilities. Barns usually had doors on both sides. If the weapons were in a back room and not guarded . . .

She worked her way around the barn on her stomach until she was out of sight of the people in front of the building. Then she stood and hastened to the back. Yes, there was a set of double doors on this end.

She considered cracking open a door to look inside, but old barn doors always squeaked, which would alert anyone inside. The window was too high for her to look in, but the old stonework provided plenty of footholds for climbing high enough to look inside. A good thing Sarah had been a tree-climbing tomboy.

Praying to go unseen, she peered through the corner of the empty window and saw no one. Cautiously she lifted her head higher, then sighed with relief to see that no one was inside. The room contained a few bundles of musty old straw from the year before, rusty tools leaning in a corner—and two long wooden boxes that looked as if they might contain rifles. Beside them were squarer boxes. Powder? Shot?

Palms damp with perspiration, she eased herself up through the window and made the short drop to the floor. Silently she moved to the boxes.

French words were stenciled on each. She opened the first and found a dozen shiny new rifles packed inside.

She lifted one out and examined it. This was a much sleeker and more deadly weapon than she'd used when she learned to shoot on her uncle's estate, but the principles were the same. She could handle it.

As expected, the other boxes held powder and balls. She wished she could take them away so the cursed invaders would have no ammunition, but they were too heavy. From habit she'd brought her reticule, so she emptied it of comb and handkerchief. Then she scooped a large handful of powder into the bottom and piled as many balls on top as she could fit into the little pouch.

Would she have the courage to ignite the powder if she'd been carrying a tinderbox in her reticule instead of a handkerchief? She'd be blown to kingdom come, but so would the barbarians of Free Eire. She was glad she didn't have the tinderbox so she didn't have to make such a decision. She loved her new life too much to want to lose it.

Should she load this rifle now, or run and load it when she was away? The instinct to flight was strong, so she took off for the back door, carrying the rifle in both hands. She was almost to there when the door to the front room opened and in stepped O'Dwyer, the vilest of her captors.

His expression blazed with vicious delight when he saw her. "Well, well, well, if it isn't the prissy little fake duchess!" He set down the box he carried and closed the door behind him. "I'll have a wee bit of fun with you before I call the others for their turn."

She backed slowly away from him toward the door, wishing she'd taken the time to load the rifle. But she'd wanted so much to get away!

"So what's the little girl going to do with her great big gun?" he jeered. "Even if you knew how to load it, it's damned hard to point a gun at a man and shoot, at least the first time. All you're good for is one thing, and I'm going to bloody well take that."

As he closed the distance between them, she made swift calculations. She could try to club him with the unloaded rifle, but it was so heavy that she wouldn't be able to move it quickly enough for a solid hit. He'd just take it away from her.

So let him.

"Aren't you going to scream, little girl?" he said nastily. "I'd like it if you screamed, 'cept it would bring the others before I'm done."

He made a grab for her and she swung the rifle hard at his head. But not so hard as to unbalance herself.

Laughing, he plucked the weapon out of the air with one hand. Sarah let him have it while she continued moving, spinning to her right. Half a dozen old tools were stacked in the corner and she grabbed the closest.

A rusty pitchfork. Terrified by O'Dwyer's ugly laughter, she stabbed the pitchfork at him with every iota of speed and strength she possessed.

Unprepared for her second attack, he cursed and tried to raise the rifle to block the blow, but it was too heavy and he was too slow. The rusty tines of the pitchfork tore into his neck. Eyes wide with shock, O'Dwyer staggered and fell onto his back, gouts of blood gushing from his wounds as his cry was strangled in his ruined throat.

Fighting off hysterics, Sarah held the pitchfork ready, but O'Dwyer didn't get up again. He moved once with a choked sound. Then . . . nothing. His eyes dulled and the blood slowed to a sluggish trickle. He wasn't breathing.

Sarah stared at him, shaking violently. *I've killed a man!*

This time she did throw up, folding to the ground and losing her delicate tea sandwiches and pastries into the musty straw. *Pull yourself together, Sarah! Go!*

Grimly she lurched to her feet and wiped her mouth with the back of her hand. Then she grabbed the rifle and bolted from the barn.

The outside air cleared her head a little. O'Dwyer was right, striking another person with intent to injure was hard, but if someone had to die in that barn, she was glad it wasn't her. She headed back to the castle ruins, wishing she'd worn stronger shoes.

She was at the far end of the village when she heard furious shouts behind. They'd found O'Dwyer's body.

She kicked off her slippers and began to run.

Chapter 43

Bree was gasping for breath when she reached the picnic area. The peacefulness of dozing children and adults seemed unreal. She stumbled over to the three adult women, her great-grandmother and the two vicar's wives.

Mrs. Broome saw her first. "Bree, is something wrong? Where is Sarah?"

"The kidnappers who took Sarah from Ralston Abbey are back!" Bree gulped for air before she could continue. "Irish rebels. They want to kill everyone in the village as a way of frightening the English. Mostly they want to kill Sarah and my father for causing them trouble before. Sarah sent me back to get everyone to safety."

The women stared at her. Mrs. Holt hugged her baby, Stephen, closer. "Surely you're joking! This . . . this isn't a good joke, Bree!"

"It's no joke," the dowager said grimly. "She's dead serious. Where is Sarah?"

Bree was better able to breathe now. "She wanted to listen to hear more of their plans, and maybe find a way to slow them down."

"What could she possibly do?" Mrs. Broome said, aghast. "How many men are in the group?"

"I don't know. We heard half a dozen or so."

Bree shrugged helplessly. "We saw their boat down in the cove. It wasn't huge, but there could be half a dozen more men on board." Above the constant sound of the surf crashing below the cliffs, she heard shouting from the direction of the raiders. "Bloody hell, the buggers are coming for us!"

"If they are, we'll never get to safety before they reach us," Mrs. Broome said, her voice calm but her eyes terrified as she looked at her daughter and the other children, who were now awake and staring.

"The tunnel." Bree ran her tongue over her dry lips. "There's a tunnel back in the ruins that runs toward the house. I've been through it often and it's muddy but clear. Once we're inside it, they won't find us." She bit her lip as she stared at the dowager. "It won't be an easy trip, though."

"I know that tunnel from my younger days," the dowager said, eyes narrowed. "I can make my way through, but I'd best go last so as not to slow anyone else down." She stood. "Come on, children. We're going to have an adventure."

Mrs. Holt carried her youngest and Mrs. Broome picked up the next smallest Holt child as Bree led the way into the ruins. The tunnel was hidden behind a partially collapsed wall in the old castle basement. When they reached the small entrance, she said, "Because I use it often, I keep candles and a tinderbox at both ends."

"How very practical!" the dowager said approvingly. "Strike a light."

Bree got to her hands and knees and reached inside the opening for her candles and tinderbox. Her hands were shaking so badly that it took half a dozen attempts to ignite the damp wick of one of the candles. She lit another candle from that so they'd have light at both ends of the procession.

Mrs. Broome said, "Alice, take one of the candles. Bree, you know the tunnel best so light another candle and run through fast as you can to summon help. Now *go!*"

Bree didn't have to be told twice. Protecting the candle with one hand, she crawled through the entrance and straightened, grateful the tunnel was high enough for her to stand. Then she took off into the damp and dark, praying she'd find help in time.

If something happened to Sarah because Bree had been too slow, she'd never, ever forgive herself.

Rob had resigned himself to being a besotted bridegroom. A mere three days away and he missed Sarah like sin. But he did look forward to their reunions. Even more, he was looking forward to taking her and Bree to London in a few days. He wanted to show his daughter the sights, and to meet his old friends as an equal.

By starting very early, he reached home with enough time to join the end of the birthday picnic. On his way, he stopped by the stables, where Bree's pony was waiting after spending the last few days in a tenant farmer's stables. Jonas had groomed and saddled Riona and put a bow in the mare's mane. Rob couldn't wait to see Bree's reaction when he led the pony to the picnic and presented her to his daughter.

Riona had a sweet face and an intelligent expression. Ponies could be wickedly clever, and he was sure that Bree would learn about horsemanship with this one.

Rob was halfway to the castle ruins when he saw movement by the old ice house, which was half buried in a hill. A small, muddy figure emerged and began running in his direction. He stared, astonished. Bree? Yes, it was his daughter, and she looked frantic.

Oblivious to the pony, she hurled herself into Rob's arms, sobbing. "Papa, Papa!"

Would she be this upset from a fight with another child? Surely not. Wrapping his free arm around her, he asked, "Bree, what's wrong?"

"The men who abducted Sarah have come back and they want to kill you and Sarah and everyone in the village!" she said, her words tumbling out. "They have a yawl in the cove and guns and they're horrible!"

Dear God, who could have predicted such a

thing? "Where is Sarah? And your grandmother and friends?"

"Sarah and I overheard the buggers talking— they're in that barn at the far end of the old village. She stayed to listen more and sent me back to the others. They're following in the tunnel." She waved toward the ice house as she gulped for breath. Though her face was smudged with dirt and there were tearstains on her cheeks, she had a hold of herself again. "I was sent ahead to get help."

"Good girl! Here's your birthday pony." He caught her around her waist and lifted her into the saddle. "Ride home and tell Jonas what's happening so he can summon the local militia. He's a sergeant in the troop and he'll know who else to call out. Tell him to be fast and make sure everyone is armed. Do you have that?"

She nodded. For a brief moment, she registered the pony. "For *me?*"

"Yes, her name is Riona. Now *go!*"

Heart pounding, he set off for the castle ruins at his fastest run. *Please God, don't let anything happen to Sarah! If someone has to die let it be me!*

But if he had any choice in the matter, no one from Kellington would be harmed today.

By the time Sarah reached the picnic area, all the guests had vanished, leaving a scatter of blankets and picnic baskets and the dowager's Windsor chair. She scanned the area but saw no one. Could they be escaping through the tunnel Rob had mentioned once? She hoped so.

She had no idea how to find it, but no matter since she wasn't going to run away. She might not have the courage to blow herself up, but she could damn well establish herself on high ground and slow those murderous devils if they came this way.

She scrambled up the high, very steep mound of fallen earth and stone that backed up the tall wall behind their picnic area. The ground on the far side of the wall was fairly level and a wooden bench had been placed there so visitors could sit and enjoy the magnificent view of the sea.

Two empty windows gave Sarah a commanding view of the small headland in front of the ruins. Perfect for shooting and ducking. A skilled marksman could control the whole area below, including a good section of the cliff path—and Sarah was a very skilled marksman.

Panting from the climb, she opened her reticule and emptied balls and powder in neat piles on the bench. Then she studied the ground below. The villains would almost certainly follow the cliff path since it led right to the picnic area.

Though she'd never hunted game as a girl because she didn't want to kill, she'd been able to best all her cousins at target shooting. Today was different. She felt a fierce, primitive fury. She was the Lady of Kellington, and she would use her skills to defend her friends, family, and land.

When the rebels reached the abandoned picnic area, they'd be within easy range, no more than fifty or so yards away. With a few well-placed shots, she could drive them onto the headland and corner them there for a while. Given the steepness of the slope, no one would be able to charge up fast enough to attack her without getting shot.

Tight-lipped, she practiced loading the rifle several times. She'd always been fast at reloading, and she'd need that skill today.

Should she fire to attract attention? No, anyone who came to investigate would be an unarmed villager walking into a death trap. Nor did she want to tip off Free Eire that she was here, she had a rifle, and she knew how to use it.

She loaded the rifle one last time. Then she waited.

It was only a few minutes till five men and a woman appeared. They walked with arrogance, sure there were no threats in this peaceful place. The men all carried rifles.

Georgiana Lawford strode beside the burly older man who was her lover and co-leader. When Sarah had met the woman socially the year before, she'd thought Georgiana rather tense and bad tempered, but she'd not seen hidden madness.

Now madness had emerged as a wild, dangerous kind of beauty. Georgiana was dressed all in black except for a blazing, blood red scarf that whipped behind her in the wind. She looked like the Morrigan, the Irish crow goddess of war, blood, and death.

Sarah waited until they were directly in front of her. Taking her time, she aimed the rifle at the weaselly man who'd wanted to slit the throats of the children.

O'Dwyer was right, it was hard to point a gun at another human being. But he'd also been right that the first killing was the hardest. She'd killed one man today, and if she was to try to kill another, she couldn't think of a better target than someone eager to murder little girls.

Taking her time, she lined up the shot, resting the barrel of the rifle on the stone sill of the window. Allowing for gusty winds from the sea . . .

She squeezed the trigger.

Ka-boooooooom! The gunshot echoed across the water as the rifle kicked into her shoulder with bruising force.

The baby killer crumpled to the ground. As his comrades shouted and looked around for the source of the shot, Sarah swiftly reloaded.

Ferociously she tamped down her horror at

this violence. All of the people below her were committed to killing innocents and they deserved to be shot.

She aimed at the man nearest to her. He moved as she squeezed the trigger so the shot only grazed him, but he cried out and dropped his rifle.

Grimly pleased with herself, Sarah reloaded and shot again. Another wounding.

Yes! As she'd hoped, the five still standing retreated onto the headland to take shelter behind the walls of ruined outbuildings. One of the men, Flannery, she thought, figured out her location and returned fire. His ball ricocheted off the wall above her.

She ducked and reloaded. There was another window a dozen feet down the wall. She shifted to it and shot again, once more ducking immediately.

More shots smashed into the wall in front of her. A stone on the upper edge of the wall toppled back and almost hit her. She dodged, snapped off another shot, ducked below the edge of the window. How long could she keep them pinned down?

As she finished reloading, she heard a sound behind her. Panicking at the knowledge that one of the rebels must have already crept up behind her, she swung around, rifle at the ready.

"You really should stop pointing firearms at me," Rob said mildly, standing absolutely still. "It makes a man feel unwanted."

"Rob!" Seeing him behind her, tall, calm, and utterly competent, made her dissolve into frantic relief that she was no longer alone. She dropped the rifle and tumbled into his arms. "Oh, Robin, I was afraid I'd never see you again!"

He gave her one hard kiss, then held her away from him, his gaze steadying. "I heard shooting and came in the back way. What's the situation?"

She pulled herself together, wiping a grimy wrist across her eyes to stem incipient tears. "Adam's Aunt Georgiana is behind this. She and her lover are the leaders of Free Eire. There's a Frenchman with them who probably supplied the rifles and ammunition. It sounds like they want to spread terror in England by slaughtering innocent villagers, and Georgiana persuaded them to start here because of us."

Rob swore under his breath. "I understood why Ashton didn't want to turn her over to the law, but I wondered then if mercy might backfire on him."

"I don't think anyone could have predicted that she'd take such monstrous revenge," Sarah said with a shudder.

He gave a sharp nod and peered out the window. A rifle ball struck the wall and Rob stepped back. "It looks like you've cornered them on the headland. Well done! How many?"

"Four armed men and Georgiana, I think. There must be men on their yawl below. I don't know if others came up from the boat. My guess is no." Suppressed panic spiked again. "I . . . I didn't know how long I could hold them off."

"You are truly amazing, princess." He caught her hand, lending some of his warmth. "But you're not alone now. Since there's only one rifle, shall I take over?"

"Please!" Now that Rob was here, she was shaking with reaction and probably couldn't even reload her weapon, much less shoot accurately. "Here, it's loaded."

He accepted the rifle and peered out a window. It took him only an instant to aim, shoot, and pull back to safety as several rifles fired back.

"Nice, accurate weapon the French produced." As he reloaded, he raised his voice and shouted, "Surrender! You're trapped and a militia troop is on the way!"

Georgiana Lawford shouted back, "Carmichael? I don't see any militia coming!"

"I'll be damned if I trust myself to English justice!" the gruff voice added in a bellow. "Show your head, boyo, so I can blast it off!"

"It's a standoff," Sarah said, her voice shaking. "It will take time for any militia men to arrive, and when they do, charging out onto the headland would be suicide."

"Rifles may not be the answer." Rob took a quick look out the window to survey the slope below that led out into the headland.

Then he stepped back to evaluate the wall, shoving at several of the irregular stone blocks. "This wall is on the verge of collapsing as other walls have in the past. If we push on the right side, which seems less stable, we might be able to create a little avalanche to give Georgiana and company something else to think about. Shall we try?"

Sarah smiled crookedly. "Show me where to push. But don't expect much."

"Every bit will help." He swept the remaining powder and shot back into her reticule and set it on the ground. Then he lifted the wooden bench and pressed it horizontally along the wall about four feet above the ground to broaden the area affected. "Push at the left end and we'll see what happens. Ready? One, two, *three!*"

They shoved together hard. She could feel the focused power in him as he dug his heels into the turf and pushed. She did the same, and felt some movement in the wall. They pushed again, and yes, the wall was wobbly. A third time.

With the fourth shove, the right half of the wall gave way abruptly and stones began to tumble down the steep slope. Rob yanked Sarah back to safety so she didn't follow them down the hill, keeping low in case anyone seized the opportunity to shoot.

Wanting to see what happened, Sarah looked warily out the other window, which remained in a much diminished section of wall. "Good heavens!"

Rob joined her and together they watched the stones they'd knocked over smash into other walls below, freeing still more stones to create a crushing avalanche. Sarah hadn't realized just how steep the slope was, or how much speed falling stones could acquire going down it.

Panicked shouts rose from the Free Eire rebels as they saw the avalanche of stone hurtling down at them. A man stood only to be knocked over by rolling rocks that pounded into the low walls that no longer offered the rebels protection.

The earth itself shook. Then, with a sound like rolling thunder, the headland crumbled, sending ruined buildings and murderers plunging into the sea.

Chapter 44

Rob wrapped one arm around Sarah as they stared down at the boiling sea. A tower of water blasted into the air, followed by foam and massive waves as the heaving sea swallowed a vast chunk of earth, the remnants of castle out-buildings, and the monsters who'd come to slaughter his family and friends.

Sarah asked in a choked voice, "Do you think anyone survived?"

He gazed into the chaos of water and stone. "No."

He'd known the headland was undercut from years of waves and weather, but he hadn't expected to trigger its complete collapse. Shoving the wall over had been merely an attempt to complicate the situation. He'd never imagined . . . this.

But he wasn't sorry.

Sarah pointed. "See the yawl that brought them? I think it's the one they used to take me to Ireland. They're raising their sails to leave."

The yawl was pitching in the waves created by the fallen cliff. "Wise of them. With their leaders dead, retreat is the only sane thing to do. My guess is that the remains of Free Eire will disband and members will join other groups that don't have a personal vendetta against Ashton or us." He studied Sarah's pale face. "If you want to have strong hysterics, feel free. You've earned the right."

"I'm all right now that you're here, but oh, lord, Rob! I don't ever want to have another adventure as long as I live!" Like a marionette whose strings had been cut, Sarah folded jerkily onto the grass. Her pretty pale summer gown was stained with grass and dirt and her hair had fallen loose. She looked like a tomboy who'd been playing with her cousins and fallen out of a tree rather than a woman who had single-handedly held off a gang of murderers.

His indomitable golden chick. He felt unbearable tenderness along with other emotions he couldn't name. He wanted to wrap her in his arms and protect her from the world. He wanted to lie down and make mad, passionate love to her. He wanted . . .

He locked down his churning emotions and settled on the turf beside her, drawing her under his arm. "I am reminded that princesses are descended from warrior kings and can become warrior princesses. How did you acquire the rifle and ammunition?"

"I stole it from where it was stored in the back room of the old barn." She gestured toward the ruined village. "I was about to leave when . . ."

She swallowed hard, barely able to speak. "O'Dwyer, the vilest of the kidnappers, came in. He planned to rape me, then hand me over to the other men to do the same. When he grabbed for the rifle, which wasn't loaded, I let him have it while I reached for the rusty tools in the corner."

"You knocked him out with a spade?" Rob suggested when her voice failed.

Her muscles tensed. "The tool I grabbed was a pitchfork. When I struck him with it, he . . . he died."

"Oh, Sarah!" He turned to embrace her completely. She burrowed into his shoulder, sobs shaking her small frame.

"That's not all," she said as she struggled for composure. "I also shot the man who wanted to slit the throats of all the children and the other women. I—I've killed two men today."

He swore under his breath. "I should have been here! You shouldn't have had to face a gang of murderers alone." He hugged her hard. "Though you did an amazingly good job of dealing with them."

She looked up and gave him a twisted smile. "Women are good at doing what needs to be done."

"True. But few are called on to defend their people against such violence. Fewer still could have done it as effectively as you." He realized that he was shaking inside. The idea of losing her was so horrendous that he could barely wrap his mind around it.

Sarah was . . . everything. She inspired the kind of intoxicating passion he'd found with Bryony when passion was a miraculous new discovery. She had the wit and companionability of Cassie, and the tough mindedness as well. All wrapped in that ineffable, heart-shattering Sarah-ness.

Fumbling for words, he said, "When my former companion left me, she said that we were both too self-sufficient, too incapable of needing anyone or anything, to ever fall in love. She was right then."

He skimmed his fingertips down the side of Sarah's face. "I was so used to living that way that I didn't even recognize how I came to need you more powerfully than the air in my lungs. I need your laughter and your kindness and your competence. I need to be with you or the world is only half alive. I love you, Sarah. Now and forever, amen."

He raised her hand and kissed it. "You don't have to say anything in return. Just . . . stay with me and be my wife for always."

Sarah bit her lip and tears started in her eyes. "I didn't realize the power of marriage, Robin. I didn't know the bonds created by the physical intimacy, and even the simple fact of sharing a bed. Nor did I realize how day by day, building a life together turns two people from 'you and me' to 'us' as we face the world as one."

She lifted his hand and pressed it against her cheek. "True love is placing one's soul in another's keeping. You have my soul, Rob. I love you, always and forever."

She raised her face and he kissed her, awed by her honesty and sweetness. She was his beloved, his mate, his friend, his life.

His *wife*.

Epilogue

Kellington House, London, May 1813

As Sarah entered Rob's dressing room, she said, "Are you ready for the dowager's 'my grandson the new earl is nowhere as dreadful as the family claimed' ball?"

He laughed as he studied himself in the long mirror, making a minute adjustment to his cuffs. "For the sake of her own pride, she has to show very public support for me. She can't admit that the new earl is a disgrace to the family name."

"True, but she's also getting rather fond of you." Sarah chuckled. "I've counted at least half a dozen times when she has mentioned your resemblance to your grandfather, which is a major sign of approval."

"Having seen portraits of him, I must assume the resemblance is more mental than physical. But it's good that the Carmichaels are presenting a united front to society." Satisfied with his appearance, he turned from the mirror.

Sarah's eyes widened as she got a clear view of her husband in his perfectly tailored evening clothes. The dark blue coat showed his broad shoulders to maximum advantage while bringing out the blue in his eyes, and the breeches accented his powerful thighs. He looked like a lord. A man of authority and consequence who was handsome and exactly fashionable enough without being too fashionable. "Dear heavens, is this the disreputable rogue who carried me across half of Ireland?"

His eyes glinted with amusement. "You see before you the results of letting Ashton march me off to his own tailor."

"Since Adam is universally acknowledged to be one of the best-dressed gentlemen in London, one can't fault the results." Sarah circled her husband admiringly. "Your felonious new valet seems to be working out well. You look splendid and he hasn't yet stolen the Carmichael silver."

"When Smythe came for the interview and recognized me, he almost bolted, but he was the best-dressed thief I ever caught and he's acquired legitimate valet experience since then," Rob remarked. "Since he swears he's now on the side of the angels, I thought he'd make a good valet and he'd understand me better than most."

"There is a certain logic to a reformed thief serving a retired Runner," Sarah agreed. "And if he strays, you'll personally hunt him down?"

"Exactly." Rob caught her hand to stop her circling. "You haven't given me a chance to say how amazingly beautiful you look."

"You saw this gown when we married," she

pointed out as she dropped an elegant curtsy with a swish of her ivory and gold silk skirts.

"Yes, but then you looked ready to flee the church. Since you decided to stay, you look more beautiful every day." Rob leaned forward for a careful kiss that wouldn't wrinkle Sarah's dress.

"Flattery will get you just about anything." She leaned into his kiss. "Mmm . . . Can we skip the ball and lock ourselves in the bedroom?"

"Not tonight, princess," he said as his clock struck the hour. "Time to collect Bree and make our grand entrance."

Ordinarily a girl as young as Bree wouldn't attend a ball, but Rob had been adamant that she be presented to society with the new earl and countess to prove that she was a beloved daughter of the house. The dowager had made only token protests about the impropriety of it; she was in a fair way to doting on her great-granddaughter.

When Rob opened the door to the corridor, sounds of music and talk and laughter drifted up from the ground floor. Bree joined them, her face blazing with excitement. Sarah would swear the girl had grown an inch and added years of maturity since her birthday. She was well on her way to being a diamond of the first water. "You look lovely, Bree! But please don't grow up too fast."

Rob nodded agreement. "I'm already thinking

how much I'll hate it when suitors start begging for your hand. I won't want to let you go."

Bree giggled, looking twelve again. "I won't marry until I'm very old. At least twenty-five."

"I shall hold you to that." He held out his right arm. "Lady Kellington?" After Sarah took it, he offered his left arm to his daughter. "Miss Carmichael?" Bree took his arm proudly. "Then come, my ladies! We shall face London society together."

They moved to the head of the sweeping staircase, which was wide enough for all three of them. At the foot of the stairs stood the dowager, her face lighting up as she saw her family. She glittered with diamonds, looking every inch the society grande dame.

The dowager had orchestrated their entrance well. As Sarah descended on Rob's arm, she saw friends smiling up from the crowd of upturned faces. Mariah and Lady Kiri, and yes, there was Lady Agnes Westerfield, Rob's cherished headmistress.

Sarah was struck by two insights. Tonight, finally and fully, Rob had accepted his role as the Earl of Kellington, head of his family and influential man of affairs. Being Rob, he'd never waver from doing his duty.

As for herself, she realized how for many years she'd drifted, adapting comfortably rather than striving for the dreams she'd thought she'd never achieve: a happy home, a loving husband, and God willing, children.

She glanced at Rob's strong, calm profile. Catching her glance, he smiled back with deep intimacy.

Her return smile was radiant. No wonder she had spent so many years without finding a man she wanted to marry.

She'd been waiting for the perfect rogue.

Center Point Large Print
600 Brooks Road / PO Box 1
Thorndike ME 04986-0001 USA

(207) 568-3717

US & Canada:
1 800 929-9108
www.centerpointlargeprint.com